Brenna Lyons

RENEGADE'S RUN

RENEGADES #2

BLURB

When the DoPT's Alpha-One agent is sent to infiltrate the Randall family, the last thing Jonas expects is to fall for Sarah Randall. Sarah knows Jonas is keeping secrets from her, but she has no idea how deadly those secrets might be.

The Randalls and Thompsons are back in the follow-up to *TYGERS*. In a world where the type of power Katie and Kyle possessed is now commonplace, psi-gifted are urged to serve the government. The Supreme Court has ruled that forcing compliance is unconstitutional. Thus, major powers like our old friends are free to live in peace as long as they don't use their powers for illegal gain.

Jonas Paige was sent into service at ten, when his family decided they didn't want a freak in the house. Now, he is given what sounds like a simple assignment. He has to get close to Sarah Randall, the untalented member of the great free family, to get the others to come into service. No one has managed to do that so far, but Jonas is the best. But, is Jonas willing to accept that his bosses are using a threat to Sarah to ease his way in?

BONUS READS:

"Renegade"- Set twelve years after *TYGERS* and fourteen years before *RENEGADE'S RUN*, we see Jonas Paige at the beginning of his DoPT contract. He's a seventeen-year-old powerhouse under the thumb of Andrew Baker. Even then, Baker is plotting to use Jonas's weaknesses against him, if a renegade doesn't get to him first.

"Max-Sec"- Once, Ginny was the only human contact Alex had. Now, she's the only chance he has to be free of his past. Ginny only wants to help...and to find out where their relationship might have gone. Alex is the most powerful talent she knows. He's deadly, unstable—and sexy.

PUBLISHER

DEDICATED TO...

Sean, whose love of sequels keeps me exploring my worlds, over and over... Yes, Sean, number four is being written...ALPHA HOUSE is already in planning.

Advantage Child Care, where I learned how surprising kids can be...

Dad and Rob, who are always there rooting in my corner.

NOTE:

The products listed as *Trojan 2020*, *Kevlar silk*, *ice gel*, *skin bands*, *Plastilyte*, and *Hypoglide 30* do not actually exist and were created for this book. Appreciation to the *Trojan, Analog, NEXTEL* and *Kevlar* companies for their fine products and names that everyone will recognize as the best of the best. Appreciation to *Lynnhaven Mall* and Sandbridge in VA Beach and *DeSalle's* in Pittsburgh for many good times over the years.

PROLOGUE—RENEGADE

October 10th, 2014

Jonas Paige ate his entire meal in record time, Markham shooting him a knowing look. The Double Quarter Pounder with Cheese meal, super-sized, with a Coke, large chocolate shake and a half-dozen fresh-baked cookies were gone in three minutes flat—a minute and thirty faster than Jonas's fastest, so far.

He overdid it on the fireworks this time. Jonas was depleted, and he'd need more fuel when the meeting was over, but he resisted the urge to pull out his stash of candy bars. There was no need to advertise how much he'd used.

Sometimes, he wished he could read Markham, but Evan—*Markham*, he reminded himself—wasn't the model for the E-series shields without good reason. He was unreadable and beyond even Jonas's control, which made him the perfect keeper for a talent like Jonas.

At seventeen, Jonas had already been a field operative for a year. He was the youngest agent the DoPT, a joint subdivision of the DoD and NSA, had ever put into service. The agency had to petition the courts to have him emancipated so Jonas could sign his release from the Clinton Training Academy and his contract with the Department of Psi Talent.

Jonas glanced around the room at the assembled dignitaries. The president was there, of course. Meredith Jordan was flanked by her security chiefs, Andrew Baker— head of the DoPT, Childress from the DoD, Bryant from the NSA, Cullen from the FBI and the guards designated to protect them all from one seventeen-year-old boy drinking a milkshake. At five thousand dollars a pop, Jonas calculated that the E-series shields purchased for these people to watch him do his stuff added up to a hundred and twenty thousand dollars.

He smirked behind his cup as he drank the last of his shake. That was a fine example of tax dollars at work. They spent that much money to protect themselves from a government employee who earned forty-five thousand a year, plus a room in one of the converted apartment buildings outside Boston, where keepers watched him twenty-four/seven. The brass wanted DoPT far from the capitol, unless they were on assignment—but not too far. They wouldn't even be staying in D.C. tonight, but rather flying back on the ten o'clock flight.

Jonas sobered. After the show he just put on, they'd never remove those shields again.

Ostensibly, this was an education seminar for the brass. *Come one! Come all! See what our number two rated agent can do to those three-thousand-series and five-thousand-series shields.*

Realistically, Jonas realized he had just been used as a sales gimmick. Anyone with the money to do so would upgrade. Except for politicians, no one who mattered would have one, and the truth of what he had just done would never be revealed. If it was, there would be a panic.

The military, police, and security companies wouldn't or couldn't make the outlay for all but the highest brass and the employees placed in the most sensitive of posts. The rest would be stuck with 3000- or 5000-series shields. If a renegade learned to do what Jonas and Paul Griffin could do, and that was sure to happen eventually, those shields meant nothing.

Jonas scowled as he felt the touch on his shield. He recalibrated into an E-shield, mimicking Markham's usual style. He saw Baker grit his teeth and bit back a laugh. Only Baker could be that careless.

Markham leaned across to him. "Knock it off, Paige. Don't piss him off."

Jonas sobered. "He's trying to pierce my shield. You know the rules against that."

"And, you really believe the head of DoPT plays by the same rules set for us?"

Jonas shook his head, and Markham sat back, satisfied that he had fulfilled his duty. No, Baker had his own agenda and his own rules.

* * * *

December 21st

Jonas cruised the length of the bar a second time, scratching at the sensor glued behind his ear and trying to ignore the keeper in the corner. He knew the man was there for his protection, though he wished it was Markham instead of Willet.

Willet wasn't there for his physical safety. Even without his talents, Jonas was deadly—not that he'd ever had to use it. If someone raised a hand to him, he had no doubts that as many as half a dozen guns or talents would lay the perp flat.

No, Willet was there to ensure that Jonas didn't get himself arrested on a violation of the Renegade Act. Hence, the sensor that recorded his activity. Right now, Willet's readout would show his personal shield and thought scans— class one talents. As long as no higher classes registered,

Jonas was safe from the Renegade Act. No class two emotional touches, no class three illusions and thought plants, no class four coercion, and certainly no higher-class controls.

The agency allowed that Jonas had the need to blow off sexual frustration like any other man, and they fully endorsed it, as long as he used his condoms like a good DoPT operative. But they couldn't take the chance that some woman would accuse him of coercion or control. Tempers were high, and a jury just might believe the accusation, without concrete proof otherwise.

A woman smiled at him, and Jonas scanned before laughing and moving on. *Jailbait. Big time.* She may be stacked and experienced, but she was also fifteen, flashing a fake ID and drunk. No jury in the world would buy that Jonas didn't know with his scan documented.

He locked gazes with another woman, and his smile spread. *That's more like it.* This one was thirty-one, tipsy but not drunk yet and very interested. She had broken up with her boyfriend and was trolling for a catch.

At six foot two and two-fifteen, with loose black curls and smoldering — *oh, how I love it when women think that about me* — brown eyes, Jonas was everything she was lusting after.

Lucky me. Jonas slid up to the bar next to her. "Buy you a drink?" he offered.

The bartender wouldn't serve Jonas alcohol. Baker would have his balls for that, but he would serve Jonas great mocks that would fool a cop, unless a Breathalyzer or blood test was taken, and he'd serve anyone Jonas bought for whatever they could legally have.

"Sure." She assessed him blatantly, and Jonas could hear her plans for the evening clearly.

He motioned Joe behind the bar to keep it flowing for the lady, her visions of the sex ahead sparking more than a general interest.

* * * *

Jonas groaned, as the pounding on the door started. He recognized Markham's shield from three rooms away. He'd recognize it from a mile away if called to. He dragged himself from the bed and started pulling his clothes on with a series of curses.

Valerie rolled over in bed, wincing at the sound.

Ouch! Her hangover was severe.

"What the hell is that?" she grumbled.

"I'd guess it's my brother rolling me out for work." Jonas glanced at his watch as he buttoned his jeans. *Three hours early? Markham better have a damn good excuse.*

"How would he know you're here?"

"He saw us leave together last night. You go to that bar often?" He knew she did.

"Yeah."

"So does he."

"What does that have to do with anything?"

Jonas shrugged. "Maybe, he knows you or knows someone who knows you."

She nodded sleepily, as he pulled his running shoes on without untying them and dragged his T- shirt over his shoulders.

Jonas leaned down and kissed her forehead. "Gotta go."

He sprinted to the door, as Markham pounded again, then dragged it open, glaring at his keeper. Jonas pulled the door shut and walked down the hall without greeting the other man.

Markham fell in beside him — not smiling, not frowning.

Just Markham, as unreadable as always. "I wasn't scheduled, and it's five-thirty. This better be good."

"Did you use protection?"

"What do you think?" It was in the contract—no unprotected sex, unless it was with a spouse. The DoPT wasn't worried about HIV. Okay, maybe they were, but they were more worried about tracking his children all over creation.

"It's my job to ask, Paige."

"Yeah. I used it. No little talents from me, just like a good operative."

"All four times?"

"Christ, Markham! Where's the mic?"

"No mic. You emit a spike over your sensor when you come. Every time?"

"Yes, every time. No visible leaks or tears. That's the next question, right?"

Jonas wondered at the fact that he wasn't required to take the used condoms with him. Other women had inseminated themselves that way in the past. He figured it was one of three things. Either the DoPT secretly wanted a few little screw-ups created by their best, or they figured any woman stupid enough to take that chance with unknown sperm these days deserved what she got. Or maybe it would just look suspicious.

Markham sighed. "It's my job."

Jonas grumbled a curse as he pushed open the security door and headed for Markham's SUV. The lock popped as he reached the door, and he opened it and dropped into the passenger seat. Markham sat in the driver's seat and eyed him.

Jonas nodded and pulled his seatbelt on. "I fight renegades and terrorists, and you're worried about my seatbelt." He put up his hand before Markham could say it. "I *know*. It's your job."

Markham nodded then started driving. At the first red light, he grabbed a bag from behind the seat and tossed it to Jonas. "Get suited up."

Jonas glanced over his shoulder and noted the two suitcases. "Where are we going?"

Markham motioned for him to dress and waited for Jonas to open the bag before answering. "Lauderdale. Al Qaeda terrorists have a cell gearing up for something big there."

Jonas dropped his shirt on the floor and pulled on his Navy blue DoPT T-shirt with the Kevlar silk lining. It was required travel gear when they might be needed for a terrorist in the air or in an airport. "Why me? There are other agencies that handle this stuff." He pulled on his gray sweat jacket and zipped it to high on his chest to cover the white DoPT logo on the front and back of the T.

"They've hired a talent."

"Ah. Renegade. That makes more sense." Jonas did terrorists when necessary, but it wasn't his first duty.

"This comes at a bad time, Paige. With the new recruiting measures—"

Jonas nodded. "You're preaching to the choir. I had this briefing days ago."

Recruiting? Why didn't they just call it what it was? People were being forcibly relocated to the training academies. After his demonstration in October, certain factions had decided that talents without keepers and registration were too great a danger. A charter of emergency powers had been created.

It had been a week since the forced round-up began. Norms were up in arms and screaming at their congressmen and senators. Half of them seemed to fear an uprising of angry talents, and the other half were debating talent rights and the constitution.

Talents were understandably irate. Taken from their homes, jobs and families to be indoc-ed like prisoners, tested and drafted into service; there were already petitions to the Supreme Court on the constitutionality of the entire thing. Jonas secretly hoped that the talents would win.

He rubbed his chest distractedly. They'd be restrained when necessary. That was the part Jonas had hated worst when he was sent to Clinton.

Jonas hadn't wanted to be sent to the training center, but he hadn't been drafted. Before the original draft of the Renegade Act in 2010, people hadn't batted an eye at anything done to talents. They barely did now, but the Act did give some guidelines, though not much.

When Jonas was a child, parents routinely sold talented children as property to people who would use them illegally or abandoned them when they learned the child was talent. Or, like Jonas, they simply signed away their parental rights and made their children wards of the government at Clinton or one of the other nine academies.

It was still common practice to make a child a ward, and no questions were asked as long as the child passed the tests that proved he or she was a talent. The government rationalized that the children were better cared for in the training academies than with parents who would abuse or abandon them. Jonas wasn't so sure about that.

He had been ten when his parents decided they didn't want a 'mind-crushing freak' in the family. That was what his father had called him just before he called the Child Talent Authority to take Jonas away. The CTA hadn't questioned his father's decision. The note from school, as always, was enough proof for them.

Jonas had been understandably upset. He'd played around with his talents a little, but he had never done anything hurtful or cruel with it. In fact, in the incident in question, Jonas had been protecting a smaller child from a known bully; a three-time loser in the reform system named Brian Miller.

He hadn't hidden his anger well, and the staff at Clinton had restrained Jonas more times than he cared to remember, the steel bands almost crushing his ribcage while the web bands held his extremities. Worse, the backboard was placed in an isolation chamber, with an electronic psi wave signature humming in the walls to keep the prisoner from using his talents.

Markham's hand closed on his shoulder. "It's over."

Jonas nodded and fought to draw a deep breath, still feeling the pressure of the bands. "You always know."

"Your hand and your breathing are dead giveaways. You know you're auto-stimulating the illusion of pressure."

"I know." He did know, but it was something the psychologists couldn't break him of.

"You're worried about the talents they're rounding up, aren't you?"

Jonas nodded. "All those broken families, split up...not allowed to see each other. At least mine chose to dump me."

"But, you didn't choose it. That's why you empathize."

Jonas nodded and forced his hand into his lap. *Don't get involved. Don't appear involved.*

"You know, they say they have a family they brought in who blow you and Griffin away."

"A family? A whole family?"

"Not quite. Mom, two sons and a nephew. The rest of the family got left behind."

"Thought so."

Seventy-five percent of children born to a talent parent tested as talents. To his knowledge, there were no cases where two talents had produced children together yet, but the first generation were just starting to have children. With the academies, it would happen. Two talents could theoretically produce talented children at or near one hundred percent.

"They're light years ahead of anything else we've seen. Mom is in her mid-forties, now."

Jonas stared at him. "Forties? That has to be wrong."

There were no major talents older than thirty. Everyone knew that. It was an unexplained evolutionary step.

"Wrong, and she may not be the first. It was a family secret of sorts."

"How far back does this go?"

"We think the first in their line was born in 1928— Tiberius Monroe Matthews, but it could go back further than that. There are newspaper reports of strange occurrences back to 1870 involving them."

Jonas whistled a long, low note. "Flashpoint."

Markham nodded. "They lack some of your skills, but what they do have... Let's just say, I'll pray they never go renegade."

"How good are they?"

"Shields I'd kill for, control of the highest levels ever encountered, the ability to inflict true physical damage by thought not related to telekinesis, psi link within their little clan, true telepathy—"

"Christ! How do you live untrained for forty-some years like that?"

"They don't. They train their own, act as their own keepers...and do it well."

"Train for what?"

"To stay sane, I guess. They don't use it, unless they feel they have to."

"Never?"

Markham stared at the dark road and didn't answer.

"Markham? Never?"

He shrugged. "There are questions."

"What kind of questions?"

"Unanswered questions. The kind of questions we don't like to see."

"They're renegades?"

"Not now."

"When? How?" He had to know.

"It's unproven."

"Dammit, Markham!"

"Mom and the nephew might have killed. We aren't sure."

"There's more, isn't there?"

Markham nodded. "She was five, and he was four."

Jonas found breathing difficult. "Lethal toddlers?"

"So, they believe."

* * * *

February 14th, 2015

Jonas glanced around the hotel room and scowled. It was Valentine's Day, and there was no hope of either love or lust for him. Even if he wasn't dead on his feet from almost two months of tracking, Markham had him on his leash.

He closed his eyes and daydreamed of when he turned twenty-five. According to his contract, his keeper would be more a formality and less a babysitter, then. He could go on trail with as much or little backup as he deemed necessary; and though Markham would show up to debrief and keep his logs, he wouldn't interfere along the way.

Even then, the keepers would keep track of his sexual exploits, often to embarrassing extremes. Jonas had learned after his night with Valerie that the keepers were placing bets on his conquests by radio now. How long to contact, how long 'til consummation, how many times— Jonas forced himself to shake it off. At least he was getting laid. It was the price he paid for what he had going for him.

Markham came in and tossed a bag of food on the bed next to him. "Eat before you drop."

Jonas's mouth watered, and he grabbed it up. It was *Boston Market*—half a roast chicken, a double order of mashed, a large side of herbed corn, cornbread, two slices of cherry pie and the largest cup they had of Barqs. Jonas had to admit one thing about the DoPT, DoD and the training academies. When you were on their dime and doing things their way, they fed you well.

Of course, they didn't have much of a choice. The only alternative was having their operatives and trainees dropping like flies, falling into a near-comatose state or dying. That extreme hadn't happened yet, but that didn't mean it couldn't.

The use of talent required varying levels of energy from the operatives. When the drain was too high, the available sugar was leeched from the bloodstream, and the operative entered shock-state. Carbs were life. Few agents traveled anywhere without emergency carbs, even around town while they were off duty. You never knew when you might have to stop a renegade, and having no means of recharging could literally mean death.

Jonas looked at his plate in surprise. Eating had become automatic over the years. The entire meal was gone in five minutes. Still, his blood screamed for more. He reached for his belt pouch and pulled out a Three Musketeers Bar and a snack pack of Oreos.

Markham raised an eyebrow at the move. "You did too much."

"I did my job."

"What did you get?"

"Whoever he is, he's good. I get ghosts, and then he fades away. It's almost like he realizes people might be looking for the release of talent. They're somewhere near the cruise docks. I'm getting closer."

"Good. I hate February in Florida. Forty degrees and raining just *isn't* my style."

Jonas stifled a laugh with a mouthful of cookie. Raised on the waves of San Diego, it was about as far from Markham's style as you could get. "So, what's the news?"

"There is a TV, Paige."

"You know I hate watching the bullshit parts. You give me the highlights."

Markham nodded, swallowing a mouthful of chicken. "The Supreme Court has accepted the case. They want briefs submitted within thirty days."

"That fast?"

He shrugged. "There are a lot of American lives at stake here, and there's a lot of pressure for a decision on both sides. Guess who the benchmarks are?"

"The Randalls and Thompson?"

"You got it. They're all at Carver now."

Jonas looked up in surprise. "They put them together?"

Markham shrugged again. "Doesn't seem to matter. The psi link and telepathy are unlimited anyway. If they want to organize, there's no stopping them. So, when Marcus Randall and his team of lawyers for talent rights filed the injunction and demanded they be roomed together, what was the point in fighting it?"

"How old are the kids?"

"Kyle Thompson is no kid. He's your age."

"He's the nephew?"

Markham nodded. "Steven is twelve, and Alexander is ten."

Jonas looked at the last bite of his candy bar in rising distaste. He set it on the nightstand and curled away onto his side on his bed, rubbing his fingertips over his chest. "How are they handling the unanswered questions?"

"Amazingly enough, they have a ton of evidence indicating that they have never gone renegade. They have journals and depositions from everything from police officers to doctors, stating that they were, in fact, fighting renegades. Isn't that a kick in the pants?"

"Yeah. That's great."

"Paige, you okay? I've never seen you walk away from food."

"Fine. Just worn out."

"Okay. Well, unless civil liberties have died, they'll win. There's no way the constitution will support this."

Jonas pressed the heel of his hand into his solar plexus. "What about the damage that's already been done, Markham?"

"The stigma? Yeah, that sucks, and it can't be undone easily. Those people have been marked now. Jobs, neighbors— It's going to be a mess. There'll be lawsuits and reparations, but there's no way they can ever make things right."

Jonas forced his body to take a deep breath, despite the mounting pressure from the phantom bands over his chest. "No. They never can."

* * * *

April 1st, 2015

Jonas ambled down the avenue and away from the docks. He was close. He knew he was.

He ducked into the bar just outside the Port Authority. He could do that now. Markham had arranged for bartenders in a few of the local bars, trusted government employees who could breeze into town with fake papers and get hired on to serve a certain adult-looking teenage powerhouse some mock drinks and report back when he seemed to be onto something. If Jonas needed to find perps, and wandering around wasn't helping, he could always trust that someone would show up at a bar eventually...especially one that served food.

The agents weren't talents. The presence of talents besides Markham, who was white noise to Jonas, would only be counterproductive to what he was trying to accomplish.

Jonas let his mind wander, drinking in the thoughts and feelings of people around him without using an active class that would ping on his adversary's radar. His adversary was good...too good. Jonas had never spent more than two months on a trail before. He'd almost doubled that already on this one.

There were three sailors in the corner.

He smiled. They called the area Liquordale.

Too bad it isn't P-Can this trip. I have family there. Or Puerto Rico. Not much to do there but pick up some Bacardi 1863, and the Captain will always give up a torpedo tube to 1863.

The last trip they made to Puerto Rico, one of the firemen on board had made a weapons sign so the tube read 'Booze loaded.' Jonas chuckled at that.

"Can I get you something?" the bartender asked.

It was Peterson, he noted. Jonas had worked with Peterson before. He was a good man in a fight.

"Sure. Rum and Coke."

He sighed as he realized Peterson wasn't paying attention. The agent was making a real rum and Coke.

"Hey, make that a special," Jonas added.

Peterson's head snapped up, and he bumped the glass into the sink. It would look like an accident to anyone else, but Jonas knew he did it on purpose. "Yes, sir." His eyes reflected his fear. If he'd've handed Jonas that glass, it would have meant his job—after Markham finished with him.

Jonas nodded as he took the glass from Peterson. He knew the drill. It would be a Coke with a synthetic rum extract that would mimic the real thing, right down to the smell on his breath, but wouldn't dull his senses or break any laws.

He sipped at the offered drink. It had a bitter aftertaste, but he imagined real alcohol would taste worse. When Jonas was twenty-one, he'd be allowed to drink moderately off duty, but he'd never be allowed to take even a sip on duty.

The woman in the corner was sizing him up.

Bigger and with a lot more stamina than you're counting on, honey.

He sighed. She wouldn't be here much past dinner. He might have talked Markham into letting him blow off some steam tonight, just a few hours at her place. Jonas glanced at her out of the corner of his eye. Damn! She was built.

The last man in the room was strangely silent. Jonas couldn't send a spike to check for a shield, so he used a passive class that wouldn't ping, something only he could do, unless the great Randall family could. He read the man's shield and mimicked his own to it to examine its layout.

Jonas switched back to his personal shield in a mixture of excitement and disgust. It was mechanical, a 3000-series. It wasn't the renegade, but it might be one of his men. Even the least talent had a personal shield, and with the way the renegade was fading out, he had a good one. Such a smooth fade wasn't mechanical in nature.

The only reason to use a mechanical shield if you had your own was if yours was weak, and you were facing a talent you knew could crush your shield. Baker was never without a neuro-mechanical shield around Jonas and Griffin.

It never failed to slay Jonas that the brass lived in fear of their top two operatives.

He drank a mouthful of his rum and Coke and ordered food. The guy had just settled in and ordered a meal of his own, so Jonas had time to build up his blood sugar. Peterson lowered his face to hide his wide eyes as he took the order— an order of cheese fries, a platter of fried mushrooms, cheese sticks, onion rings, a basket of tortilla chips with a spinach and cheese dip, a basket of calamari and a slice of apple pie a la mode. Peterson knew Jonas had a target in mind if he was carbing up like this.

The food came out one dish at a time to minimize the impact of how much he was eating, and Jonas drank another mock rum and Coke with every offering. No one seemed to register the fact that he kept eating, and he forced himself to eat slowly to avoid drawing attention to himself.

Jonas watched the news while he ate. There was coverage of the Supreme Court trial, though not inside the courtroom. The Randalls were brought in, unrestrained but surrounded by a ring of federal agents.

Katheryn was an intense-looking woman with long black curls that were only lightly grayed. She had one arm around a blonde boy who looked ashen and wide-eyed. That was Alexander, he realized.

The blonde man beside her was obviously Kyle Thompson. He held her other arm hooked through his own. Even though his face showed no sign of it, Thompson was scanning. Jonas could tell.

Over Katheryn's shoulder, Jonas spied Steven. The boy's hair was only slightly lighter than his mother's was. He scanned his vibrant blue gaze over the crowd angrily, and Jonas closed his eyes. If one of them renegaded, it would be

Steven. He was twelve, and he was lethal. He was in Jonas's class, and either Jonas or Griffin would be set on his trail.

Two more men joined the first suspect, both wearing 3000s.

Paydirt. Jonas just had to wait for them to move and hope they led him where he needed to go. In the meantime, he had a second slice of pie.

He had three more mock rum and Cokes while he waited for them to leave. When they rose to go, Jonas kept his position for the first block and a half while he handed Peterson two hundred to cover the bill and tip.

When Jonas made his way out into the night air, he walked at a leisurely pace, as if he had nowhere to be. Now that he'd locked on their shields, he had only to keep them within a few blocks to keep from losing them.

He hesitated at the edge of a motel parking lot.

Now what? He could have Markham call in eyes for the night, but those hotdogs were known to want the glory of the terrorist bust without taking the renegade into account. The renegade was Jonas's primary concern. The terrorists came second, though Jonas would handle as many of them as he could. Overall, the renegade could do far more damage in the long run.

Jonas could take a room for the night and call Markham from a pay phone on his way in. Strictly speaking, that wasn't protocol. There was no cover story, and it could raise suspicion.

He sucked in his breath, as a warm body sidled up to him.

"Waiting for someone?" The voice was low and inviting, and the female hand on his arm reminded him that it had been more than three months.

Jonas looked at the woman from the bar with a wide smile. "I was, but I think I got stood up."

She adopted a pout that he found less appealing than her inner hopes. "Wife or girlfriend?"

He laughed. "An older brother who probably got lucky and forgot all about me."

She pressed her body to his. She was drunk but more than a little interested. "Living well is the best revenge, you know."

Jonas wrapped his arms around her and kissed her. It wasn't protocol. From having sex with a woman without his sensor and keeper to ditching Markham, he was breaking a lot of rules, but it gave Jonas cover when he needed it and some much-needed down time while he got the job done. "Do you have a room here?" he asked.

"Are you interested?"

She does. "Absolutely."

* * * *

April 2nd, 2015

Jonas kissed Ronnie goodbye and pulled his jacket over the plain, Kevlar silk-lined T-shirt Markham insisted on for tracking. The jacket was Jonas's idea, a windbreaker with Kevlar silk backing the soft lining. With cop-killer rounds out there, two layers of protection couldn't hurt.

He let himself out of her room and strolled away with a smile on his face. Ronnie only lasted twice, but it was an enjoyable two, and with one part of his mind always occupied with keeping tabs on his prey upstairs, Jonas got a good bit of information while he enjoyed himself.

Jonas had a name for their renegade now. From the sleepy musings of the men in the other room, he knew the renegade was a man named Martin Dillon. He was twenty-six, blond, brown-eyed, roughly one point eight meters tall and ninety kilos. Jonas did the conversion smoothly. That placed Dillon at a cool five foot ten and two hundred pounds.

He'd stop by the room later and have Markham run a check. *Much later.* Jonas grimaced. Markham was gonna be pissed that he hadn't checked in last night, but telling Ronnie he had to call his babysitter would have definitely been a bad move.

Jonas caught a movement out of the corner of his eye and noted Peterson hurrying toward him. He motioned a finger to draw the other agent's attention as he stepped onto the sidewalk, then shook his head.

Peterson halted and looked away, but Jonas could feel his confusion. Knowing a thought scan would be a permissible way to pass information when he couldn't stop to talk to the other agent, Jonas sought out the situation in the only way he could...and grimaced at what he saw.

Markham had the entire team of agents under him searching for Jonas. When Peterson reported that Jonas left the bar about five minutes after three men and had carbed up, Markham had called him names Peterson hadn't ever heard before for not reporting in sooner. Then Jonas didn't show up back at the hotel, and Markham had the men out for half the night trying to find him in fear that someone got the drop on him.

If Peterson saw him and let him go, he'd have to answer to Markham. On the other hand, if he screwed up this detail, he'd have to answer to both men—and Baker. *Better Markham alone,* Peterson decided.

"Right answer," Jonas whispered as he rounded the man and kept walking.

Peterson's relief was instantaneous. Then he started dialing Markham. He couldn't follow Jonas now that he'd been warned off, but he could get Markham on his trail before they lost Jonas entirely again.

Jonas filtered out Peterson, as the agent recoiled from the force of Markham's outburst. Jonas would have to face Markham later. The renegade was his highest priority. Markham wouldn't fault him that. That was his job.

His stomach grumbled. What Markham would fault him for would be waltzing into a ring of terrorists and a renegade low steam. Jonas fished in his belt pouch and started eating all the candy and cookies he had on hand. It was a lousy way to carb up his bloodstream, but it would have to do, unless they passed a place to grab some complex carbs and a protein stabilizer.

When the candy was gone, Jonas dumped the empties in the top of an open trashcan. Markham wouldn't like to see it, but it was better that his keeper knew Jonas was doing his best to prepare, even if it meant depleting his stash for later.

He used the Porta-meter tube from his pouch to check his blood sugar. It was standard equipment for both trainees and field operatives. Jonas kept in mind that his blood sugar would rise a little from the candy he just ate, but it was still too low for his comfort.

Jonas sighed as he pulled out his emergency stash. As a rule, he hated the cane cubes—the sandy sugar they carried for emergencies—but he was stuck. It was better to force down cane than get caught short. He ate ten of the twelve cubes he had and ditched the gold wraps in the next open trashcan he passed. Like it or not, Jonas was charged as he could be.

His prey was up ahead, and they had to be getting close. It had been a mile and a half, and they were nearing the piers. *Most people wouldn't walk much further than this, anyway.*

Jonas stopped. His shielded leaders stopped, then started to move again after a few moments.

Damn! There is a checkpoint. Jonas had expected as much, but it did cause certain problems. If he used active talent to get past the guards, he'd never make it to his renegade.

He cursed his luck. If Markham were with him, Jonas would have stun-spray and Markham's gun. As it was, he had hand-to-hand. No, not even that. He had hand-to-their-weapons and talent he couldn't touch without lighting up the entire sector.

Jonas read the direction and distance to the shielded men. They had turned left down the pier beyond the warehouse he was standing in the shadow of. Jonas smiled and turned back. He'd be a little soggy, but he had an idea.

No one gave Jonas a second look as he walked down the neighboring pier. After all, there wasn't a band of terrorists and a renegade on that pier.

Jonas climbed down one of the maintenance ladders on the far side of the pier, grimacing at the smell of harbor water. If this got complicated, they'd *smell* him coming before he used talent.

He winced at the cold water. If Jonas had any other options, he'd take one of them, but from what he'd garnered from his friends last night, he was running out of time. They'd be moving out of their little nest soon. Jonas either chanced losing his renegade or took the plunge.

The sun was barely above the horizon, and the day was darkly overcast. *Storm coming in soon.* Even so, Jonas stayed underwater as much as he could, following his sense of the shielded men to their vessel.

It wasn't impressive. It was a simple barge, but a big one with machine shops and tons of cargo room.

Jonas hauled himself up the ladder on the side and rested atop one of the pier cushions designed to keep the vessel from hitting the pilings. His hands were shaking, and he considered backing out. He'd worked too much in getting here, used too many of his precious store of carbs in conventional means. He shouldn't be considering this. Every ounce of Jonas's training said he shouldn't engage a renegade in this state, but it was now or never. He wished Markham was here to save the day.

Small bursts of talent caught his attention. His renegade was inside, and if Dillon was inside and using talent, he had to have a source of carbs that Jonas could tap if he needed to. If he could make it to Dillon without incident, Jonas had a chance of completing his mission and living to tell about it.

As he suspected, there were no guards topside. He had bypassed at least one and probably two checkpoints by swimming across. Jonas padded down the deserted corridors inside, following his shielded buddies and the continuing bursts of talent.

Jonas scowled as he examined those bursts. Something was wrong, but he couldn't put his finger on it. The bursts...weren't *right*. He pushed the thought away as he came out on a catwalk two stories above the floor of the cargo area.

He sank into the deep shadows and performed a head count. *Fourteen.* Markham's intel from the mission brief said there were only eight plus the renegade. Without accurate numbers, Jonas couldn't be sure he had them all. Markham —

Jonas froze. Markham's shield was closing, not a neuro-mechanical E-series but Evan himself, and four neuro-mechanical E-shields. Christ! Markham didn't know where the checkpoints were, though he would be expecting them.

All hell broke loose on the floor below. The checkpoint guards had raised the alarm before Markham barreled through them with his backup.

The talent below started charging up for an assault. Jonas identified his focus — class eight telekinesis. He was after Markham.

Jonas held his breath and stepped forward, firing up. He had never tried what he was doing now. No one ever had. This was desperation at work. Jonas fired off one class seven hold after another, feeling the 3000-series shields splintering under the force of his mind, until six of the men below were under his control.

The renegade's concentration faltered, and his head raised in slow motion, searching for Jonas.

Jonas fired off commands to his human puppets. *Kill the renegade. Kill the other men. Don't stop shooting.*

The sound of gunfire echoing in the enclosed space was deafening. The renegade found Jonas with — *her* eyes. It wasn't Dillon. It was a woman in sweats and a jacket, her hair tucked under a ballcap. Jonas felt his heart start pounding, as she flew backward in a spray of blood. He backed away.

His mind worked overtime, as Jonas reviewed what he knew. That was what was wrong with the bursts. They were a different flavor of talent than he'd been reading while he'd been tracking.

Not Dillon? Christ! There were two, and Jonas didn't know it. The intel said one renegade. *Was Dillon one of the men in the crossfire below?*

No. They were all dark-haired. Where the hell is he?

The answer to that question came in the form of the tearing pain in his chest. Jonas hit the metal grating that had been under his feet moments before, the air rushing from his lungs. If he could have pulled air in again, Jonas would have screamed.

He locked his hand to the source of the blood flowing down his chest. *Cop-killers,* his mind supplied numbly. The Kevlar silk helped some, but he still had shrapnel wounds.

For a single moment, Jonas felt as if the metal bands of the restraints were cutting into his ribs again. He couldn't breathe; the hum of the psi wave cut his consciousness away from the calming interaction with those around him. Only shields worked inside a psi wave, but Jonas felt even that flickering.

The sensation eased, and Jonas found that he could manage a shallow breath. His mind dimly registered a class two calming being used on him. Jonas furrowed his brow. Markham couldn't do that. He opened his eyes to the sight of Dillon squatting over him.

"DoPT?" the renegade asked in a ragged voice.

Jonas nodded, still trying to regulate his breathing.

"Who are you?"

He tried to answer, but Jonas found that he couldn't maintain his breathing yet. Worse, he'd over-extended. The shaking set in, and he groaned as it jarred his wound.

Every operative reacted to the shock-state differently. Some went catatonic. Some fell into a deep sleep that was impossible or near impossible to rouse them from. For Jonas, there was the shaking. Sleep would come next, if he didn't recarb first, but the shaking would continue until he recarbed or died.

Dillon muttered something then pulled out the vial holding the remaining two cane cubes. "Two? Only two? You deserve to die."

He popped both of them into Jonas's mouth. It wouldn't stop the shaking, but it would keep Jonas from passing out for a few minutes.

Dillon dragged Jonas's wallet out of his front pocket and flipped it open to his driver's license. Jonas would have to tell Markham so his quarters could be moved.

If I survive that long.

The sound of gunfire echoing down the open passageways let Jonas know that Markham had reached the second checkpoint. He hoped Evan made it through all right. Jonas was in no shape to help him.

Dillon uttered a string of curses that made Markham's outburst from that morning seem like a walk in the park. "Alpha-Two? I couldn't just shoot any old DoPT operative. I had to shoot the boy wonder."

Jonas stared at him in surprise. *How could he know that without a DoPT shield to reference?*

Dillon started to pace, keeping a wary eye on the downed man and issuing his speech. "You're on the wrong side, boy. Don't trust Baker as far as you can throw him. If you ever catch him without that damn shield of his, take a peek for yourself."

He stopped abruptly and tossed the wallet back on Jonas's chest. "They've broken through. You'll be fine. Trust me." Dillon sprinted away, leaving Jonas gasping for breath under the force of the pressure on his chest.

Trust a renegade? Oh, what fun today is turning out to be!

Markham thundered over the metal flooring and out of the darkness. He dropped to his knees beside Jonas, peeling back his jacket and shirt to survey the damage. Over his shoulder, Jonas could hear Peterson calling in a life flight for him, while Goulden pulled a telescoping backboard from his medical kit and readied it.

"No," Jonas protested weakly, eyeing the device.

"Pressure bandage." Markham met Jonas's gaze as he caught the bandage Goulden threw him. "Only until we get you to the hospital. You have my word."

Jonas whimpered, as Markham applied enough pressure to make it feel as if he'd been shot again. His shaking intensified, and Goulden grabbed one blood-soaked hand to get a reading on his Porta-meter.

The older man's face hardened. "Jeez! We need to recarb, but we don't want to fill his stomach. Any suggestions?"

Markham glanced up at him. "Cane. Most punch for the least amount of pukable material."

Jonas managed a strangled laugh.

Goulden crouched over him. "We saw the evidence of your carb-up on the way in. Are you completely empty?"

Jonas raised the vial with its payload of two crumpled gold wrappers for his inspection.

Goulden nodded then turned to Markham. "You carrying?"

"My pouch."

Peterson took over feeding Jonas the cane cubes, while Goulden and another agent Jonas didn't recognize strapped him to the backboard. They moved him to the deck to wait for the helo.

Jonas sucked down all twelve of Markham's cubes, and the shaking receded to a mild shivering.

Markham nodded. "Glucose IV in the helo. Call that in, Peterson." He jerked his head to one side, and the other agents backed off. "Want to explain this?" he demanded of Jonas.

"Two renegades. Got one. Dillon got me—got away."

Markham grumbled a curse. "Damn intel. Full name?"

"Martin Dillon." Jonas managed a weak smile. "Prints on my stuff—wallet and cane." He sobered. "Need to move."

"I'll take care of that." With four buildings available, hiding Jonas out somewhere else wouldn't be too hard to arrange. "Any other pressing details I should be aware of?"

"Used a woman for cover last night while I was picking thoughts of the terrorists in another room. Used protection. No vis—" He grimaced, as Markham increased pressure on his wound.

"Enough of that."

Jonas managed a weak laugh. "Two times."

* * * *

April 3rd, 2015

Jonas yawned, then grimaced as pain ripped through his chest. He panted off the spasm and scanned the room until he found Markham. He knew Markham would wait for him to wake before leaving him in the care of other agents. Jonas wouldn't be surprised to learn that Markham gowned up and stood guard over him in the OR.

"Feeling okay?" Markham asked.

"Okay is a subjective term. I'm not dead. I suppose, I'll heal."

Markham nodded. "Yeah. Those two layers of Kevlar silk minimized the damage."

"Good. How bad will the scar be?"

"Not bad. They had the plastic surgeons in there."

There was a long, awkward silence. Jonas tried to read Markham's expression, but he kept it as guarded as his mind.

Finally, Jonas looked away. "I wouldn't have gone in if I'd known. You know that."

"I know it. Even with this screw-up, the brass is impressed. One of the renegades skipped, but the rest was beyond anything they've ever seen before." He sighed. "Our intel was at fault. If we were right—"

Jonas nodded. "I realized that when I counted heads. I was trying to hatch a better plan when the renegade I took down fired up to take you out. I should have realized the rest could be wrong, too. I reacted. When I realized the renegade I took down was a woman—"

"You knew you were looking for a man?"

"Yeah. My brain picking the night before gave me a name and description to work from. And, I was running out of time. All I needed was a place, so I tailed them."

"Well, Baker will be here later to do the debrief on you."

"Baker?" Baker didn't do debriefs. Markham was his detail boss, as well as his keeper. "Why Baker?"

"This is big news. We kept the renegade out of it, but the whole world knows that an unnamed DoPT operative took out a terrorist enclave."

"And?"

Markham shrugged. "You know Baker. He wants his face in the news. He's a politician at heart. If the talent rights groups keep gaining momentum, he may have a shot at the presidency in another twenty-five years or so...when he's a respectable age to hold it."

Jonas swallowed a sour lump at the thought.

Dillon's words danced in his mind. *"Don't trust Baker as far as you can throw him. If you ever catch him without that damn shield of his, take a peek for yourself."*

He furrowed his brow. *Dillon knows Baker?* "Markham, was Dillon ever DoPT?"

"Not according to the file on him. Why would you ask that?"

Jonas grasped at any excuse. It wouldn't do to admit that he didn't trust Baker. He never had, but that was beside the point. "If he's not DoPT, he has a friend on the inside. He knew I was Alpha-Two, by my name. I wasn't carrying my ID and badge—just my driver's license. How did he know I was Alpha-Two?"

Markham's face darkened, and Jonas sucked in his breath in surprise. His keeper was scared shitless. Jonas could see it in his expression. More surprising, Jonas could feel it from him.

"Why didn't you tell me that?" he demanded.

Jonas rubbed the bandage while he considered it. "I was injured, Markham. It slipped my mind until now."

"That was damned important, Paige."

"Look, Ev—" He met his keeper's heated glare and felt his cheeks darken. *No first names. Don't get involved.* That was the first rule of an operative.

Don't get involved with renegades for the obvious reasons. Don't get involved with co-workers. It's a dangerous business, and people die. Don't get involved with victims. That makes a lost one harder to deal with. Don't get attached to your family. They can be used against you.

Well, Jonas didn't have to worry about that one.

Markham raised an eyebrow. "If you slip like that in front of Baker, he'll have your head. Worse, it will all be over. I'll be reassigned, and they'll find a keeper you can't ever hope to get attached to."

"Sorry." It was his weakness. People were his weakness. Jonas hid it as best as he could, and Markham didn't turn him over to Baker, like he should.

"All right. We'll tighten up while we try to trace his source."

Another awkward silence descended on them. Jonas wondered at that. They didn't spend a lot of time talking. Considering the circumstances, that made sense. Still, Jonas had never found the silence between them awkward before. Well, he hadn't since he was still at Clinton, and he was first introduced to his future keeper.

Jonas panned his gaze over Markham. The man was tense, and he kept his eyes averted. "What's going on with you?"

Markham sighed. "The Supreme Court ruled for the talents. They've been ordered set free immediately. They put out the bare bones of the decision today with the full draft to follow later."

"That's good news, Markham." *It is, isn't it?*

"Since the case dealt with talent rights in general, they've made several rulings about past practices."

"Please, tell me they made the restraints illegal."

"No. They were deemed a necessary step in avoiding harm to self or others, though the chest bands will be web or leather now."

Jonas nodded. "Figures," he grumbled.

"They ruled that selling talent children is illegal, though people will just bypass that with private adoptions. Abandonment was always illegal. They ruled signing your child away like..." His gaze flicked to Jonas and away again. "It's illegal now. Parents have to go through a legal process. There will be case studies and keepers to help children stay with their families. There will be social workers and psych tests. Only when there is no workable solution will children be remanded to the training academies. You can seek reparations under the ruling."

"I don't want it. I don't want anything from them." Markham would know the 'them' he meant. Jonas wanted nothing from his former family. "The ruling is enough."

Markham nodded and stood. Jonas thought he'd leave, but he set up a debrief recorder.

Jonas felt that tightening in his chest again. "I thought you said Baker was doing the debrief."

"He is."

"Then, what is this?"

Markham sighed. "You'll see." He stepped back to Jonas's side to get them both in the frame. "Markham, Evan. DoPT, Kappa-Two. Date April third, twenty-fifteen. As required by the Supreme Court ruling of same date, I am informing DoPT operative Jonas Paige of his legal standing."

He motioned for Jonas to sign in officially on the recorder. "Paige, Jonas. DoPT, Alpha-Two. Date April third, twenty-fifteen."

Markham nodded. "By ruling of the Supreme Court, I am required by law to inform you that the ruling assumes some training academy students have been coerced into entering service when they would not have chosen to serve in the

DoPT otherwise. By the ruling, if you so choose, you may dissolve your DoPT contract immediately with no penalty and no loss of benefits or bonus. Do you wish to exercise that option at this time, defer decision to a later date or refuse?"

Jonas felt his head spin. *Free from my contract with benefits and no thirty-day notice? But, where would I go? What would I do?*

I could make good money in security — if anyone would hire me in the current uproar and at my age.

No keeper, but no one at my back either? A stab of fear shot through him.

"Paige?"

He rubbed his hand over his chest, trying to calm the mad pounding of his heart and head. "Refuse. I'll keep my contract."

"You have the right to defer. If you refuse outright, you have to give notice, and your benefits will be based on the twenty-year chart, as agreed in contract."

"I understand. I refuse. I'll keep my contract."

"Understood."

* * * *

April 6th, 2015

Drew Baker sat behind his desk, rolling a glass of scotch back and forth between his fingertips and looking at the files on his desk. Quinn Bryant of the NSA and Roger Childress of the DoD sat across from him. Of the two, Baker knew to fear Bryant. He was a dangerous man, and he was talent, something Childress didn't know and didn't need to know.

"What do we do, now?" Childress demanded. "Dillon is still out there, and now he knows we're onto him."

Baker sipped his drink. "We keep him away from Paige. Dillon on the loose is infinitely preferable to him convincing Paige to join him."

Bryant's icy blue eyes seemed to glow in the gloom of the dimmed office. "You think Paige isn't telling us the whole truth?"

Baker shrugged. "There may have been more said than a threat that he was on the wrong side, but whatever it was, he's not buying. Paige refused giving up his contract outright. If he had doubts, he wouldn't have done that. He'd've deferred."

Childress scowled. "Damn Supreme Court is screwing up everything. With the Randalls and Thompson on our side—"

"Can it," Bryant barked. "You can't force talent to comply. All we could do would be to hold them. We might have convinced Thompson and the younger boy eventually, but Katheryn and Steven were a lost cause. Of all of them, Steven is the one we want most."

Baker nodded. "Very true. But, I may have a long-range plan for them. There are ways to convince people."

Childress leaned forward across the desk. "For instance?"

Baker watched the news coverage of the Randall family reunion at Greater Pittsburgh International Airport over the other two men's shoulders. Steven Randall swung a girl in his arms. She was laughing and crying at the same time. She was a beautiful young woman. She was also the key that unlocked Steven Randall and any other Randall he cared to reel in. She was Steven's only weak spot.

"Oh, there are ways."

Bryant turned to look at the screen, but the image had moved on to a reporter talking about the court decision. He leveled a suspicious look at Baker but made no comment.

Baker kicked back in his chair. Childress and Bryant didn't need to know about Sarah. She was too important to let these two idiots screw up a good thing.

Childress shook his head and changed the subject. "I don't get it. If you don't want Dillon turning your Alpha-Two, why are you sending Griffin after him? Wouldn't turning your Alpha-One be worse?"

Bryant rolled his eyes. "Griffin is eight years older than Paige, and he's met plenty of paranoids in his time. Dillon only has a shot at Paige, because he's young and idealistic. He's not jaded yet."

Baker drained his drink and looked into the glass. That was more information he wasn't sharing. Paige wasn't Alpha-Two. He was Alpha-One, and his raid on the terrorists proved the test results, beyond a shadow of a doubt.

He had to figure out a way to keep Paige under his thumb, but young Jonas had no real weaknesses. Oh, he got involved, and Baker knew that, despite Markham's effort to hide the fact from him, but it just didn't affect him enough to be useful. How do you get someone involved?

CHAPTER ONE

January 10th, 2028

Jonas Paige stretched his shoulders, wincing as the handcuffs cut into his wrists. *Markham is gonna be pissed about this one.* At least, Markham couldn't blame this screw up on Jonas. This one was indisputably the guardsmen's fault.

He smirked at the National Guardsmen left to watch his movements, two men too young to realize what they were facing. They wore mechanical shields, so they thought they were safe. Jonas wondered how they would handle it if he proved that the old 3000-series shields were useless against a talent like himself. Their boss would come strolling in to find his men playing cards with their prisoner, Jonas's hands uncuffed, their rifles at his feet, and their side arms tucked into his belt.

Jonas could do that. Even the 5000-series was no match for him. He had proven that to a panel in D.C. back in 2014. His bosses, those less powerful than Jonas was, wore E-series shields when he or Griffin was in the building. The E-series was the best shield available, a true neuro-mechanical that every president since his demonstration had worn when a talent might be close by—in other words, they wore them constantly.

It might do the military good to find out what a real talent could do, before one of these poor saps died because he trusted a 3000-series against a renegade with even half of Jonas's talent.

He sobered. Markham wouldn't want him to prove it that way. It flirted with the Renegade Act.

Jonas enjoyed the relative freedom of having Markham as his detail boss. If he broke the laws governing him, Markham would be his keeper again.

The few freedoms he had would be lost. Markham hadn't been his keeper in six years. It was a small distinction, but it meant the world to Jonas.

Of course, if Markham was still my keeper, I wouldn't be sitting here in cuffs.

Jonas shifted against the wall, earning him a suspicious look from the younger guard. He couldn't affect his own release that way, though heads would roll for his treatment. Maybe Markham would make a rather personal demonstration of their shields' ineffectiveness part of that punishment. Jonas would be first in line to volunteer his expert proving.

Who am I kidding? The DoPT would never allow that. Still, it was an amusing thought.

He would suggest a military proving to Markham. These poor saps didn't deserve to die that way, just because their bosses were clueless of the danger. Of course, even if he proved it to the military as he had to the panel, they wouldn't upgrade all the grunts to E- shields. It wasn't cost effective. Not when there were only a dozen known talents who could crush mechanical shields.

Jonas looked to one of his guards. "Can I get a drink?"

It was the least they could do. They'd taken his stash of replacement carbs, so he couldn't recarb. The shaking was severe, and it would only get worse until he carbed up or died.

Oh, is Markham gonna be pissed.

The guardsmen, like police and other military, had been briefed on how to treat both renegades and DoPT operatives. Even a renegade wasn't treated like this.

"You'll get one soon enough." The guardsman sneered at him.

"Come on, man. I've been here for two hours with nothing to eat or drink. I haven't even had a head break. Even POWs have better treatment than this." Jonas shifted, trying to find a comfortable position on the floor.

"Most POWs aren't mind crushers."

Jonas grumbled several harsh curses under his breath. His body complained loudly at this treatment. Jonas had expended considerable energy. He needed carbs, and he was thirsty. His bladder was beginning to ache. Worse, the cold, tile floor had sucked much of his body heat away in the first half hour.

He looked at the clock on the wall wearily. It had been two hours since he had been imprisoned for doing his job.

Where is Markham?

A chilling thought occurred to him. What if they hadn't called Markham? What if they hadn't even called the DoPT to report a renegade yet? If all they did was call the police, the call might have been lost in the shuffle. Jonas swallowed a lump of fear. He needed to recarb soon, and only the DoPT would force that on the guardsmen.

Jonas closed his eyes and laid his head back against the wall behind him, too tired to fight shock-state.

Markham is really gonna be pissed when he finds out about this.

"What're you doing?" The guard's voice was tinged in panic.

Jonas sighed. "Don't sweat it, junior. I'm too damn tired to hurt anyone. I can't eat. I have to sleep."

Sleep came next in Jonas's personal shock-state. He fought to normalize his breathing as his natural sensors shut down. There were no chest restraints and no psi wave. It was just sleep and his shock-state shutting him down.

* * * *

Jonas forced his eyes open. He was vaguely aware that he was lying curled up on his left side on the cold tile. Someone took off the cuffs, and he groaned as he moved his stiff, bruised arms. Jonas was rolled to his back. He smiled weakly as Markham's face loomed over him.

"Christ!" Markham ran his fingers over Jonas's cheek and settled on his pulse.

There was a pinprick of pain on Jonas's middle finger that announced Markham measuring his blood sugar with the Porta-meter.

"Christ! Didn't you give him anything?"

Another voice came from far away. "Dealing with your renegades isn't in my training."

Jonas recognized the cold voice. It was Davis, the guardsman who'd slapped him in cuffs. He mouthed the man's name with a grimace.

Markham nodded in understanding. "You've had memos, and you know he's not a renegade."

"He killed that man. That guy's brains splattered over five rows of people."

"Paige did his job. Dillon was both a renegade and a terrorist. The laws are pretty damned specific. Dillon would have killed everyone in his way. Paige was duty bound to stop him, any way it took."

Jonas scrunched up his nose at the sugar Markham pushed into his mouth. The reading must have been really low, if he started with cane cubes instead of the candy bars in Jonas's pack. Or, maybe they hadn't given Markham his pouch yet. He could be working from Markham's own stash.

Jonas sucked on the cane without comment, though he hated eating it. Beggars couldn't be choosers. Cane would keep him alive and draw him out of shock-state.

Markham nodded as Jonas's pulse started to normalize. "Send someone to the *McDonald's* on the concourse. One of mine. He'll know what to get."

Jonas sucked down another cube, his mouth watering for the food that was coming. It would be his usual: a Double Quarter Pounder with Cheese meal, super sized, with a Coke, a large chocolate shake and—*they know I'm hurting*—a half dozen of those fresh-baked cookies. Jonas shuddered at the thought. It sounded like Heaven to his starved body.

Markham would start him with the Coke, until the shaking subsided. Then he'd be allowed to eat the rest. If the whole meal lasted more than five minutes, Jonas would be amazed.

He had a more pressing problem than food. Jonas touched Markham's arm with trembling fingers. "Head," he rasped out.

"They didn't take you?"

His groan was answer enough for Markham. His boss's face darkened, and he nodded stiffly. Markham shouldered Jonas to his feet and half-dragged him to the men's room in the hall.

Jonas kicked it into gear. He needed Markham to steady him, but damned if he'd disgrace himself by not managing his own bathroom routine. Jonas drank several handfuls of water after he washed his hands, and Markham growled his displeasure again.

Back in the room, Markham lowered Jonas into a chair and popped another cane cube in his mouth. "Okay, Paige. I've seen the tapes. Let's get your statement recorded."

Jonas nodded, grimacing at the bruises that ringed his wrists from the handcuffs he'd worn for God knows how long. "What time is it?" he grumbled, too tired to look for the clock and mindful that his watch had been confiscated, along with everything else he owned.

"Seven-thirty."

"Six and a half hours." *It's a miracle I'm not in the hospital.*

Even though mind reading was one of Markham's weaker skills, he nodded his agreement. "No care in all that time?" he whispered.

Jonas shook his head.

They'd had this discussion before. Despite the Department of Psi Talent's charter of powers from Congress and proven history, prejudice still ran rampant in the ranks of the guardsmen and police officers they dealt with. No matter how many renegades and terrorists Jonas took down, to the National Guardsmen on airport duty, the distinction between a DoPT talent and a mind-crushing renegade was little to none.

"Why did you put up with it?" Markham asked.

"You know why."

Markham nodded. He knew why.

The Renegade Act was touchy business. Jonas would have been controlling someone for his own gain, though he would have only been protecting his rights under the 2015 ruling of talent rights by the Supreme Court. He'd accepted their treatment rather than risk reprisals under the very law he upheld every day of his life.

At full power, Jonas might have fought it out and apologized later. He might have, but probably not. As it was, they would have killed him...with full support of the law. The guardsmen may have kept him weak on purpose, in fear or in hopes of making him try something that would give them the right to destroy another mind-crusher. Or, maybe they'd hoped the shock-state would destroy him for them. Any fool with the slightest training could spot the signs of shock-state in a talent.

Markham sighed. "There will be hearings," he promised.

Jonas nodded. There were always hearings. "I know." *But nothing will change.*

"Tell me what happened, Paige."

This part was easy. Jonas had been through hundreds of debriefs in the last fifteen years. He had been signed into the academies at ten, before the Supreme Court rulings. His family hadn't wanted a mind-crusher in the family, so Jonas had been enrolled in the Clinton Training Academy. He'd taken his first mission at sixteen.

Since his parents had signed away all rights to him, it had been a simple matter for the DoPT to get emancipation for Jonas, so he could hit the field two years early. Baker had convinced the guardians at Clinton that keeping a talent like Jonas in the training academy was a joke. It had been. The courts had no problem emancipating Jonas, so he could sign his contract and collect his keeper. Markham had been with him ever since.

Jonas stared into the recorder. "Paige, Jonas. DoPT, Alpha-Two. Date January tenth, twenty twenty-eight. Mission unscheduled. Logan International Airport, Concourse Charlie."

He accepted his food from Grant, setting it on the chair Markham slid to him and taking a long drag on the Coke. "I was waiting for boarding on flight forty-nine seventy-two as ordered when I felt a psi release, class four coercion. I tracked to the source and discovered renegade terrorist Martin Dillon leaving the security checkpoint.

"A passive scan showed Dillon was carrying two weapons and had one norm counterpart with one weapon and a five thousand series shield." He drank down half of his Coke in several gulps.

"Dillon recognized me from the incident in Fort Lauderdale in twenty fifteen. He nabbed an airline employee, used a class seven hold on her, and pointed one of his weapons to her head."

Jonas's stomach grumbled, and he glanced at his food in longing. *Debrief first.* He gulped down the rest of the Coke and reached for the milkshake.

"By statute one twenty-nine of the Renegade Act and two fifty-seven of the twenty twelve terrorist fact sheet, I was duty bound to use any means necessary to subdue Dillon and his counterpart and affect the release of the hostage, Janice Pearson."

Jonas sucked down a quarter of his milkshake, glad to note that the shaking was finally subsiding. "I exerted a class seven break and hold on Dillon's counterpart, ordering him to turn his weapon on Dillon. Once he had nullified Dillon for me, I ordered him to put down his weapon and wait for his arrest, while I exerted a class two calming on the hostage."

Markham nodded, and Jonas sucked down another quarter of his milkshake.

"Arrest phase," Markham informed the recorder.

Jonas's jaw tightened. "The guardsmen took Dillon's counterpart into custody and took statements of fact from the airline security who had been coerced. Guardsmen Davis and Simmons approached me. I showed my badge and ID, but I was cuffed and detained as a renegade."

"Detention phase."

"I was placed in a detention room with no furnishings and armed, shielded guards for six and a half hours, until DoPT detail boss Markham arrived. In direct violation of DoPT directives, I was allowed no food or water to replenish my stores lost in the line of duty. Nor was I permitted basic prisoner comforts as allowed by both criminal law and the Renegade Protection Act."

"Show your wrists to the recorder, Paige."

Jonas pushed up his sleeves and rotated his arms to show the bruising.

"Eat your food before you collapse on me again."

He nodded and dug in. The entire meal disappeared in two minutes flat, while Markham recorded his observations of Jonas's condition and filed formal charges on Davis, Simmons and their crew chief.

When the recorder switched off, Markham pocketed it. "You ready to travel?" he asked.

"I'll grab something on the way out. Where's my pouch?"

Markham laughed heartily. "Bottomless pit. You always were. Peterson has it."

"You use a lot, you replace a lot." Jonas followed Markham to the concourse.

"You used too much," Markham chided him. Even as detail boss, he was responsible for Jonas.

"Janice would have died, and it wouldn't have been too much if they'd've let me recharge right away."

"Janice?" Markham shot him a stern look.

Jonas blushed.

"You gotta stop getting personal with them. When you lose one—"

Jonas nodded as he stopped at a snack shop and started grabbing pretzels, chocolate, and Coke that Markham would put on the expense account. He made a mental note to ask for his wallet, watch and pouch in the SUV.

"Yeah, I know. Don't get close." He always screwed that one up. Jonas closed his mind tighter, so Markham couldn't penetrate.

I want to get close, close to someone.

* * * *

February 10th, 2028

Jonas groaned at the sound his cell phone ringing. He fumbled it off of his nightstand and hooked the headset over his ear. He scowled, bleary-eyed, at the caller ID, noting that it was Markham. "Dammit, Markham! I just got back from the Capitol job two hours ago. At least give me six or seven before you drag me back out again."

"Unavoidable. Brush those pretty black curls of yours and put on a clean shirt. I'll pick you up in ten."

Jonas uttered a long string of curses as he dragged himself out of bed and shoved the phone in his rear pocket. Any other time, he might have wondered if Markham had them turn on the visual sensors again. After all, how else would he know that Jonas had tumbled into bed in his jeans and running shoes instead of nude, as usual?

"Put on a clean shirt," he grumbled. "Not get dressed. Put on a clean shirt. Cute, Markham."

He used the bathroom and splashed cold water on his face to jolt himself awake. There was no time for coffee, unless Markham let him grab some on the way. Jonas dragged a DoPT sweatshirt over his shoulders, then ran a comb through his hair.

He looked at his reflection critically. At six foot two and two-thirty, he was a formidable force to deal with, even without his psi talents, and talents he had in spades. Mind reading and the basic shields aside, he had mind log and control abilities, EM burst and a bit of telekinesis. Add his infamous shield identification and mime abilities, and Jonas was a talent no one wanted to cross.

But he never stopped. His dark eyes had a permanent set of bags, and he already had a few gray hairs showing above his ears. Jonas rarely got laid anymore. When did he have the time for it between the assignments he was handed?

Jonas headed to the door, as he sensed Markham coming, and met him at the elevator as the doors opened. His keeper—*what else would I call Markham, if the visuals have been turned back on?*—didn't comment on the move. Markham had his observation tactics, and Jonas had his. There was seldom need for small talk between them. Why would there be?

Jonas would always be watched. It was part of his contract. It amazed him that they still kept such close tabs on him, but he supposed when you were the second most powerful talent in service, people were afraid you'd renegade.

Twenty minutes later, they stepped off the elevator and onto the DoPT secure level. Jonas went through the usual checks: fingerprint, DNA imaging, and a psi scan. He gave the pup doing the scan a tweak for his grating touch.

Jonas strode into the conference room with Markham at his heels. Baker was there, decked out in his E-series shield. Flanking him were Childress from the DoD and Bryant from the NSA. Both had their shields on.

That wasn't a surprise. This face-to-face meeting, however, was something of a surprise. Baker didn't want anything to do with Jonas. The head of DoPT had worn an E-series from his first meeting with the fourteen-year-old trainee, until the E-series prototype had been developed and tested. He never took a chance with Jonas. The first production model of the E-series was still used by Baker today.

Markham didn't bother with a shield. The E-series shields were modeled after his mind. E for Evan Markham; how much safer could you get? Markham's other talents might be weaker than most talented children, but his shields were nearly unequalled. That made him the perfect keeper for a talent like Jonas.

Baker waved them in. "Sit down, Paige. We have a lot to discuss."

He took his seat across the table from them, lounging as if this meeting meant nothing to him. His senses were on high alert. Jonas had never trusted any of these men, Baker least of all. "What are you dragging me back in for?"

"Griffin went renegade."

Jonas whistled a long, low note. Paul Griffin was Alpha-One. Until he went renegade, he was the proven top talent with the DoPT. His renegade run meant two things. Jonas would be issued a new badge proclaiming him Alpha-One on the way out of the building, and it would be his assignment to stop Paul Griffin before he did irreparable damage. Read that to mean...before he kills someone.

Jonas raised an eyebrow. "Why?"

Baker steepled his fingers in front of his face. "We don't know. Maybe you can ask him."

"Maybe this is Griffin's way of going into retirement. He never did like red tape."

Jonas reminded himself to say Griffin and not Paul. *Don't get involved: not with a victim you could lose, not with co-workers who might go renegade and not with free agents you might have to hunt. If you can help it, don't get involved personally with anyone. They can be used against you.*

Bryant shook his head. "He did damage on the way out. He can break an E-series."

Jonas rubbed his forehead and glanced at Markham out of the corner of his eye. As usual, his keeper looked unruffled. Only Markham could seem unruffled by the news that he was finally taking the same risks as everyone else.

"Where am I going?" Jonas asked.

Childress cleared his throat. "Pittsburgh."

"Why the hell has he gone there?"

Baker scowled at the DoD agent. "He hasn't, but you are."

"Shouldn't I be after Griffin before—"

Baker shook his head. "The DoD has decided we can't afford to lose you to this fight. You're the last Alpha. We have Betas, but there are Alpha renegades to take down. We need to stack the deck, especially in a case like this one."

Jonas modulated his shield to an E-series, as Baker touched it. It was an old game between them. Jonas had no doubts that his own shield was sufficient, but he didn't like to give Baker a lot of time examining his personal shield. Jonas's ability to mimic other talents' shields was what made the jump from mechanical to neuro-mechanical shields possible. If Jonas could do it, someone else could. The last thing Jonas wanted was Baker being able to mimic his shield.

He considered what Baker had just said. He was the last Alpha on the rolls, the last true powerhouse. There was a certain pride that went along with being an Alpha. "I don't use gimmicks."

"No gimmicks. We need you to recruit some reinforcements," Baker assured him.

A nervous tremor started in his stomach. Jonas didn't like the sound of that any better. He rankled at the idea of backup and keepers, but recruitment was a sticky thing. The 2015 Talent Rights Act wasn't something Jonas wanted to mess with any more than the laws for conduct were.

"Who?" There were plenty of Alpha-class free agents on the streets, but if they weren't in service, why try to convince them?

Childress slid a set of files across to him. "The first two are our target recruits. The other two would be a bonus, but we're not counting on them."

Jonas forced his hand to steady as he took the files from the table. He groaned aloud as he thumbed through the tabs. "You're insane. They're free agents. They were a Supreme Court case, the definitive case that wrote the rest of the Act. They'll never come in on this."

Childress darkened, fury written on his slim face. "It's true we've failed in the past—"

"This one is hopeless." Jonas tossed the files back. "It's been tried at least a half dozen times."

Baker shrugged. "Seventeen, to be exact."

Jonas laughed harshly. "What's changed?"

Bryant trained his cold, blue laser-edged gaze on him. "You."

"I may be the best, but even I'm not that good."

"You have special attributes the others didn't have."

"For instance?"

"You get involved. Your instincts make you reach out to people."

Jonas felt the heat rising in his cheeks. They weren't supposed to know that. He thought Markham was keeping that under wraps, but maybe it leaked through.

"The others were too practiced at being detached."

"Who am I supposed to get close to?" Jonas shifted nervously. Operatives didn't get close. They weren't given assignments where they had to get close.

A new file slid to him. Jonas broke out in a cold sweat as he took it. He flipped it open to the stats page. His gaze riveted on a candid shot of a woman with long, dark hair flying around her face in a strong wind. Her blue eyes were compelling, wary even in the picture. He scanned the fact sheet. Sarah Angelique Randall was born January fifth, 2003.

Jonas furrowed his brow and pulled Steven's file from the stack Childress pushed back to him. Steven Christopher Randall was born January fifth, 2003. Steven had an official photo from before the courts ruled the drafting of psi talents was unconstitutional. He glared at the camera. At twelve, Steven had lived with enough hate of his captors that he had to be restrained for a simple photograph.

Jonas rubbed his chest. He remembered the restraints.

He looked at Baker over the files. "His twin? She saw him dragged off at twelve. They took her brothers, her cousin and her mother from her. You think she's going to help you? You're nuts."

Bryant laughed. The sound was strangely chilling. "She doesn't have to help us." He shot Jonas a speculative look. "Of course, if you could convince her to allow us to fashion a new series of shield on her, there would be a substantial bonus in it for you."

Jonas startled and looked at her file again. "She can shield?"

Baker cleared his throat. "It's her only talent—we think. She's good, Paige. She puts Markham to shame. Every time we tried to get a deeper reading, she hid behind her shield."

A smile touched Jonas's lips. "In a family like that, a good shield would be her only defense." He sobered. "If she has a shield that good, I don't understand what you want me to do."

Bryant's smile sent a chill down his spine. "The only reason you'll be using talent is if you're forced into it. As far as Sarah Randall is concerned, you're going to be a normal, untalented man."

* * * *

Jonas pulled one of his DoPT T-shirts out of his suitcase and threw it across the room. There'd be no need of those. They might blow his cover. A selection of his DoPT clothes, his badge and ID would be in Markham's hands, for the duration. Jonas growled in frustration as he pulled nondescript clothing from the drawers. Some were Kevlar silk-lined but unmarked by the DoPT logo. He would wear a DoPT T-shirt under a jacket on the plane, but that would be turned over to Markham before they left the Greater Pittsburgh International Airport.

Get close? They don't want me to get close. Why don't they use the right word for it? They want me to seduce her. Jonas ground his teeth at the assignment he'd been given.

He closed his eyes and visualized the picture of Sarah in her file. Jonas couldn't imagine any man not wanting to get her into bed. Still, he wasn't in the habit of getting laid for any cause but his libido.

Jonas glanced at Markham. Ten years his senior, Evan already looked like an old man. His face was heavily lined, and his light brown hair had gone mostly gray in the last fifteen years.

Markham crossed his arms over his chest. "It sucks. I know." He sighed. "Look at it this way. You've picked up women in bars before. You've picked up women to get a room close to a subject before. It's sex. Can you honestly say you wouldn't like to tag that?"

Jonas groaned. "I never lied about my reasons for getting them there. It was sex. I wasn't sleeping with them to get something from them. Even when I needed a reason to be where I was, I still wanted laid."

"You're not this time, either. Forget getting her to agree to the shield model. They want you to get her in bed with you. After that, you're off the hook. So, you draw your paycheck to get laid." Markham shrugged.

Jonas stared into the suitcase as he placed the stack of clothes in. "What if I want more, Markham? We're not supposed to get this close. They're putting me in a bad place. What if I can't do what they order me to do this time?"

"I don't know. Maybe we'll have to resign and learn to live as free agents."

Jonas smiled. "We?" This was the Evan he'd known for the last six years, not the agent who had cameras on him but the one who knew him better than anyone, without the cameras.

"You've seen me slip often enough. You know my mind. Where you go, I go. You know that."

"You want out of this mess, don't you?"

"Don't you?"

Jonas sighed. That was a dangerous question, especially when he was so tired. He decided a change of subject was in order.

"Do you have any idea how long it's been since I've tried to pick up a woman?"

Markham laughed heartily. "Seven months, eighteen days, and two hours. I checked in the SUV. Her name was Susie, and you got laid twice that night. Slow night for you."

Jonas stifled a laugh and threw another of his DoPT T-shirts at him. "I'll take your word for it. Hope I'm not rusty."

"You're good at what you do. You always have been."

Jonas turned back to the dresser to hide his expression. He wasn't sure that was what he wanted anymore.

CHAPTER TWO

February 15th

Sarah Randall locked the door to the store and pocketed the keys. It had been a long day, and she was more than ready for bed. Home was only fourteen blocks away, and the evening was cold but clear. She straightened the collar of her peacoat against her neck and started walking.

Steven would have a fit if he knew she was walking. He'd demand that she wait for the bus at the corner.

Sarah smiled and added a little extra power to her shield. *Steven isn't here.*

For the first three blocks, she reveled in the air on her face. Sarah shivered as she felt the first probe against her shield. She slowed and looked around. Someone was hidden in the darkness, a talent—possibly a renegade.

She considered her options. There was deserted street for one block ahead and two blocks back. She sped up. There were people as you got further onto the main strip and homes a few blocks further up.

She sucked in her breath as a man stepped out in front of her. He was about six feet tall, but she couldn't tell much more about him between his oversized coat, knit hat, and the dim light that seemed to disappear into the blackness of the trees beside them.

Sarah felt the spike of pain as he tried to punch through her shield. She pushed away her panic long enough to slam her shields up fully.

Usually, she didn't bother, but this renegade was stronger than the usual ones. He knew what he was doing.

Most of them didn't. Most of them let a little talent go to their heads and discovered what they were dealing with quickly enough. This one was different. He was no two-bit hood.

The man furrowed his brow, then smiled and pulled out a knife. "Fine with me, sweetheart. You want to do this the hard way. I can do it the hard way."

Sarah pulled out her wallet and tossed it to him. Renegades were easy to handle, and unarmed muggers weren't much harder, but she didn't tangle with weapons. Mac had taught her better than that. "Take it. It's all yours."

He pocketed the wallet and took a step toward her. He shot her a blatant once-over, head to toes and back. "Thanks, but that wasn't really what I had in mind."

She took a step back reflexively. *Why the hell didn't I wait for that bus?* If she survived this, Mac and her brothers, Steven and Alex, were going to kill her. As he closed on her, Sarah considered her options.

He was a renegade. That meant he had nothing left to lose. She was fighting for her life now. It was time to pull out the tricks Mac and the guys had taught her and hope for the best. If this renegade knew how to defend himself physically, she was in a world of hurt. Her hand-to-hand had always been weak.

Sarah took him head on. He was surprised, but only for a moment. He blocked her blow and knocked her into the light pole behind her. Flashes of light exploded before her, as Sarah hit the ground. For one agonizing moment, she locked on the moonlight glinting off the knife blade. Something blocked her field of vision, and everything went black.

* * * *

Sarah groaned as she moved her head against the pillow.

"Are you okay?"

She held her breath, and her heart took up a frantic rhythm. She didn't know that voice. Sarah searched her memories for some explanation and grasped at the memory of the man with the knife. It wasn't his voice either, the man who'd attacked her. This voice was deeper, warmer.

Sarah snapped her shield up and curled into a ball on the bed. From the sheets against her cheek, she knew it wasn't her bed she was in. She had jersey cotton knit. As much as she wanted to know who he was and where she was, she was afraid to open her eyes.

She could contact Steven, if she never wanted to hear the end of this. No, that definitely wasn't an option. Wherever she was and whatever was going on, Sarah had to get herself out of it.

"Sarah, are you okay?" His hand touched her shoulder.

Sarah scrambled away from him, pushing her back against the headboard and striking out blindly as her pupils adjusted to the light in the room. She blinked several times, taking in the man standing next to the bed.

He was tall and broad-shouldered. His black hair curled over his forehead, nearly reaching his deep brown eyes. His hands were up in a calming gesture.

"It's all right, Sarah. I won't hurt you."

She shook her head. "How —"

A blush came up on his cheeks. He pulled her wallet from his back pocket and reached his hand out to her with it. "I took the liberty of getting your wallet back for you. Check it. Everything's there."

Sarah took it from him slowly. "Why did you help me?"

He shrugged. "You needed help."

"Where are we?"

"My apartment."

She moved further away on the bed, automatically searching for an exit.

"It was close. We weren't exactly inconspicuous, and I didn't think you'd want to have your name tacked to that renegade. Things should be calmed down now. I'll take you home or call someone for you."

Sarah got to her feet and pulled her coat on, shoving her wallet in the deep pocket. Steven would be worried sick. "I have to go."

"I'll take you."

"No." *If Steven sees me with —* "Who are you?"

"Jonas Paige. Look, either I'm walking you the last six blocks home, calling you a cab or calling someone for you. Which is it?"

"Thank you, Jonas, but—"

He stepped in front of Sarah, as she moved toward the door. "Which one? You're not leaving here alone."

Sarah looked up at him, swallowing the lump in her throat. She didn't have time to wait for a cab. Steven would have half the force out looking for her soon. She had no choice. She nodded. "Okay. Come on." She glanced at her watch and groaned. "Steven is going to kill me." He would have felt the assault on her shield. There was no doubt about that.

Jonas fell into step beside her, pulling on a coat from the hook beside the door. He wrapped his arm around Sarah when she weaved on the stairs and pulled her to his side as they reached the street.

"So, who is Steven?"

"One of my brothers. He...uh...expected me home over an hour ago."

Jonas laughed, and Sarah moved further into the warmth of his body.

"He's protective of you?"

"Extremely." *And it's about to get worse.* "How did you take on that renegade?"

"E-shield. Without his psi talents, he wasn't much of a fighter."

Sarah glanced up at the skin-tone disk behind his ear. She read his shield, scanning it for continuity. It was an E-series. As she expected, Jonas didn't notice her check. She was glad neuro-mechanicals didn't alert the owner to checks like that. Then again, only Steven could tell when she was doing it. Maybe no one else could.

"Is he..." she hedged.

"Yes. Does that bother you? It was him or us." Jonas looked away, but she saw the blush spread down his neck.

"No. I guess you didn't have a choice, and it's not illegal if you kill a renegade in defense, is it?"

He shook his head.

Sarah liked that he wasn't happy about what he had done. Some people would be boasting about killing a talent. Jonas seemed upset about it.

"Sarah?" Jonas glanced at her. "This is going to sound really tacky."

"You want to take me out?" The idea warmed her.

"I sure wouldn't mind. Guess you hear that a lot."

She sobered. "No. No, I don't."

He tried to wipe the look of surprise from his face. "I wouldn't ask now, but what if I don't, and I never see you again?"

She laughed lightly. "Can I think about it?"

"Does that mean I'll get to see you again?"

"I know how to find you." He'd see her again. Considering the jerks she'd met in her time, Sarah was more than willing to give Jonas Paige a chance.

"What if I look you up? After all, I'll know how to find you, too."

Sarah spied him trying to bite back a smile, and she smiled in return. "All right. Since you put it that way, look me up for dinner on Friday. Six o'clock at my place."

"Can I bring anything?"

"Just yourself."

"I can handle that."

He moved his arm slightly to invite her closer to him, and Sarah took the hint. They walked the last two blocks in silence.

Sarah thought that Steven might have skipped the opportunity to stick his nose in or not felt the assault before she reinforced her shields. She realized she was wrong when he stepped out of the shadows at the corner of her building, just as she and Jonas reached the door.

Steven was livid. Sarah could read his mood clearly, though he was trying to hide behind his shield. She was glad he didn't try to talk to her telepathically. It would have the effect of shouting on her battered mind.

She patted Jonas's hand. "You should go. This won't be pretty."

Jonas hesitated, eyeing Steven. "If you're sure."

"I'll be fine. I'll see you again?"

He smiled then leaned to press his lips to her cheek. His voice rumbled against her ear. "Put ice on your head when he leaves. Promise me."

Sarah moved her face to kiss him in return. "Thank you, Jonas. I'll see you Friday."

"Or sooner." He backed away, nodded to Steven and turned to go.

Sarah smiled at his retreating back. Jonas wanted to see her sooner.

Steven stepped up next to her. Sarah saw the look of concentration on his face and felt the probe he leveled at Jonas. She elbowed him roughly. Steven knew better than that. Even she'd only scanned Jonas's shield.

"Don't. Don't do it, Steven."

"Who is he, Sarah?"

She sighed. "Come in. The least you can do is get warm."

Steven nodded and followed her through the security door and up the stairs. The moment her apartment door swung shut, he started in again. "Who is he, Sarah?"

Sarah pulled off her coat and hung it on the hook, not turning to look at him. "His name is Jonas. I like him. Leave it alone."

"Where'd you meet him?"

"Around." She felt Steven's mind like a caress against her shield and fortified it. "Don't. It's my life, Steven."

Sarah turned to face him, and the color drained from his face. When Steven surged toward her, she stepped back in shock. His fingers touched the edge of her lower lip, and she winced.

"What happened? I felt it before your shield blocked me out, but I hoped I was over reacting." Steven half-dragged her to the kitchen and started making an ice pack.

Sarah sank into one of the chairs. "Make it two."

He glanced at her over his shoulder, and his entire face lit in fury. "Show me." Steven slammed the freezer with a thump that made her head ache.

She took his hand and guided it to the goose egg on her scalp.

"Hold this." He pushed the ice pack to the lump and headed for the phone.

"What're you doing?"

"Calling Dad."

"Put the phone down."

Steven gaped at her in obvious disbelief. "Don't do this, Sarah."

"It's over. The damage is minor. All you'll do is get the whole family upset for no good reason."

"No good — "

"No good reason," she repeated.

He hung up the phone and sat across from her. "Spill it, and make it good."

Sarah took a deep breath. "It was a renegade." She put up a hand to stop him before Steven could start in. "Jonas saw it happening and — took care of the situation for me. We hid out at his place, until things died down."

"Where is the renegade? Why didn't you call me?"

"Call you? Are you nuts? Do you really want the DoPT and the DoD connecting you to a renegade? I wouldn't have called you if I was in the worst hellhole in the city."

"Where's the renegade?"

Her cheeks started to burn. "Let's just say that Jonas doesn't need to be connected to the renegade right now either."

Steven took a couple of deep breaths before he answered. "He's talent?"

"No. He has an E-shield." She put her hand up to stop his protest again. "You know I can tell. It reads as an E-shield. Without talent to back him, the renegade was nothing but a two-bit punk with a—" Sarah winced in the realization that she'd said too much. She'd let down her guard, because it was Steven she was talking to.

"With a what, Sarah?"

"A knife."

Steven buried his face in his hands. When he met her gaze again, he looked tortured. "Why do you insist on living here? Why won't you move home?"

"Because it's the only way I get any peace. At least this way, you're the only one in range of me."

Steven sighed and ran a hand through his dark hair. "Be careful. Something just doesn't feel right here."

"Look, I'll admit that Jonas saved my butt—"

"I *mean* Jonas. I'm not stupid enough to think ordering you not to see him won't send you straight to him. Just be careful."

Sarah nodded. "I'll do my best."

* * * *

Jonas stormed into his apartment, knowing Markham would be there. "Tell me. Tell me that renegade wasn't a set up or kiss me goodbye," he promised.

Markham grimaced. "They didn't tell me until after the fact."

"Dammit, Markham. He could have killed her. I had to kill him. Not a clean psi kill, either. I had to dust off the hand-to-hand we learned in training. I had blood on my hands. I've never had blood on my hands before."

He paced the floor while he ranted at Markham.

There was no chance of anyone but DoPT hearing them. The building was owned by the DoPT. The agents who typically lived in the two apartments, presumably to monitor the Randalls and Thompson, had been temporarily reassigned, leaving the apartments open for Jonas and Markham. The décor was tasteful, if understated, and not at all Jonas's style. He'd already planned to tell Sarah that it came decorated this way.

"I know. It wasn't my idea."

"Where'd they get him?" Jonas glanced at Markham as he turned to make tracks the opposite direction.

Markham sighed and rubbed his forehead. "He was busted by DoPT three days ago. They made him a deal, kill someone they wanted killed and walk away...until he gets caught the next time."

Jonas stopped pacing. His head spun, and it was hard to breathe. "They ordered him to *kill* Sarah?" The list of laws they'd broken was staggering.

"They knew you'd kill him first. They didn't want any slip-ups. You had to get close to her. The psych guys said inducing a trauma—"

"I'm done. I quit. Tell them."

"I don't think it's that simple."

"What do you mean?"

"Whatever the plan is now, it's clean. No innocents get hurt."

"She got hurt tonight."

"Beyond that, no one gets hurt. If you pull, it's going to get ugly. You're almost an even match for Griffin. No one else comes close. If you pull, they'll get the Randalls and Thompson any way they have to."

"Then have them put me on Griffin. Get these people out of the line of fire."

"I tried that. They lose you without backup, and they're screwed."

"They won't lose me," Jonas argued. He'd promise another five years in writing to get their paws off Sarah and her family.

Markham raised an eyebrow."You're guaranteeing that?"

Jonas nodded.

"You're *guaranteeing* Griffin won't kill you?"

"You know I can't. Dammit. I don't want her in the middle of this."

"Neither do I." Markham sighed. "When do you see her again?"

"Friday. Maybe sooner."

"The sooner, the better. These guys are antsy."

"This sucks. Quote me, *on* the record, that this sucks."

"Yeah, I know it."

CHAPTER THREE

February 17th

Sarah smiled as Jonas stepped into the shop. It was a quiet night, so there were long periods of inactivity where she found her mind wandering, mainly to him.

"You're early," she teased him.

"I'm impatient. I lasted two days." Jonas leaned across the counter, balancing his weight on his folded arms. "Make you a deal."

"What kind of deal?"

"I'll meet you here after work and buy us dinner. What are you in the mood for?"

Sarah frowned. "What about the dinner I was planning for you?"

"Are you saying I have to choose?"

Sarah's breathing hitched at the hungry look in his eyes, hungry for more than food. "No. You don't have to choose."

"What are you in the mood for?" His voice was low and full of erotic invitation for anything she was in the mood for.

She blushed. *Food. He means food, Sarah.* " Um— Anything really. Pizza or burgers. I'm easy." Her blush deepened. *Why did I say that?*

His smile widened. "I doubt that. What time should I pick you up?"

"Eight."

"Eight it is." He hesitated for a minute and glanced at her lips. "I'll see you then."

Sarah watched him to the door. Jonas turned and waved as he disappeared onto the street. She sighed. Why did he affect her this way? She'd never been tongue tied and scattered until she met Jonas.

* * * *

Jonas was there right at eight. He forced his hands to still as Sarah locked the door to the store. He had faced down renegades and stayed calmer than this. *Damn the DoPT!* He wanted her. Jonas had done little more than dream about her and study the files in Markham's apartment for the last two days.

He made a decision, a deal with himself. He'd take out Griffin and retire. Even if Sarah wouldn't give him the time of day, Jonas couldn't get into a mess like this again. For better or worse, this was the last thing he did for the DoPT. He hadn't broken the news to Markham yet.

Jonas smiled as Sarah glided toward him, his body making demands already. *Dinner,* he reminded himself. *Sarah agreed to dinner. She wants more, but she agreed to dinner.*

For a single, terrifying moment, he couldn't decide how to proceed. Jonas hadn't been this lost around a woman since he was sixteen. He laughed. "I'm not usually this hopeless."

"Good. At least, I'm not the only one."

Jonas wrapped his arm around her shoulders. "What do you want for dinner?" If he asked Sarah what she was in the mood for and saw that breathless reaction again, he wouldn't make it to dinner.

"Do you have a car?"

"Sure. I brought it with me since I didn't know where we were headed."

"Good. We'll get take-out from *DeSalle's*. It's only a few blocks past my place, but it's cold out tonight."

"Your place?"

"We could go to yours." She blushed lightly.

Jonas swallowed a sour lump. He was watched too closely. If he took her there, there was every possibility that they'd be recorded somehow.

He'd already refused the sensor he was required to wear when he picked up women, the one that recorded his use of talent to keep him from being arrested for accusations of coercion or control that would violate the Renegade Act.

"This is an assignment," he had insisted before he left, shoving the disk back into Markham's hands. "I don't wear sensors on assignment."

It was a lie. Jonas wasn't wearing the sensor, because this was Sarah. He'd be damned if he'd let them record the telltale spike that announced his climaxes. Sarah wasn't like that, and he wouldn't do it to her. There'd be no bets placed on her.

Jonas smiled. "I just didn't want to impose. I'd like to see your place."

She nodded. "Okay. Let's go."

DeSalle's was a little hole in the wall restaurant, but their subs were great. Sarah's apartment was in the neat little red brick apartment house on Warrington that he'd walked her to the first night. It was bigger than he'd expected from the outside view, two big bedrooms with a walk-in closet in the larger, a full bath, a large living room and eat-in kitchen.

Sarah's touch was everywhere. The colors were soft peach in the living room and master bedroom, green and tan in the bath, blue and white in the guestroom and kitchen. There were paintings depicting knights, ladies and mythical creatures on the walls and lace and eyelet falls hung over the windows.

Dinner was over far too soon, and Jonas found himself torn. Every instinct told him to make his move. It wasn't the job pushing him. That was what was holding him back. He hated that the job was involved.

Jonas wiped his hands on his jeans. He couldn't do it. As long as the job was part of it, he'd have this argument with himself. It would never feel right.

Jonas stretched his arms over his head and smiled at her. "Well, you've probably had a long day." He stopped, as her smile disappeared. "What's wrong?"

"I just—" A pained expression clouded her features. "Never mind."

"No. Tell me."

Sarah laughed. "I guess I've come to expect something different from men."

He touched her cheek. "I'm not just some guy, and I don't want to treat you like some woman I just picked up in a bar."

"You do that often?"

Jonas shrugged. "Not often, but I have."

She nodded. "What do you want?"

"That's not easy to answer. Part of me wants to be someone you can trust and care about."

"And the rest?"

He took a deep breath. "The rest of me wants to be like every other guy who's ever laid eyes on you."

Sarah shook her head. "What does that mean?" she asked uncertainly.

Jonas fought back his shock. She confused him on so many levels. Didn't she know how beautiful she was? What had she come to expect from men? "I want you. I can't imagine any man *not* wanting you."

She blushed. "Which side is winning?"

"I want more than just taking you to bed." It was true. Jonas almost winced at the truth of it. He wasn't letting anyone lay bets on Sarah, and he wasn't screwing her for the damn assignment and walking away. However Jonas worked this out, he wasn't doing that.

"How much more?" she whispered.

"I don't know." He didn't. Did Jonas really want to get into something that would last a lifetime and make her a target, in a new and frightening way? Even if he quit the DoPT, Jonas had enemies. By quitting, he'd make more enemies. If Sarah was with him, she could and probably *would* be used against him.

Sarah walked across the room to the hall.

Jonas followed her, praying that he hadn't blown it the whole way.

But she'll be safe.

From Baker? Maybe not.

She turned back to him, biting on her lower lip as she considered something. "Do I at least get a goodnight kiss?" Sarah asked.

Jonas nodded, dumbstruck that she wasn't showing him the door. He cupped her cheek and touched his lips to hers. *God, I want this.*

She opened for him. Jonas groaned as he swept his tongue into her, exploring her.

The door was at her back. Was he forcing her back, or was she leading him to it? Jonas pressed his hand to the smooth wood next to her head, claiming Sarah's mouth more urgently. Had he ever been this crazy to have a woman? Somehow, Jonas didn't think he had.

Sarah's hands wrapped around his waist, drawing him the last inches to full contact. His half-erect cock snapped to full attention, and she tilted her hips to brush her warmth to his erection.

Jonas broke off the kiss, running his lips up her cheek to nip at her ear. "If I don't leave—"

"Do you want to leave?"

He sighed. "No. I don't."

"Then don't."

"But—"

"We both want more, Jonas. I'll take more of what you are sure of, until we both know what the more consists of. Is that okay with you?"

"More than okay." He scooped her up and headed to her bedroom.

Sarah pulled his shirt up as Jonas followed her down onto the bed. "Do you—" she began. She broke off on a groan as he kissed her.

"Yes," he breathed against her lips.

All DoPT agents had protection. Part of their contract was no unplanned pregnancies. Jonas was never sure if the precaution was to ease the public's fears of purposely breeding talents or to keep the DoPT from having to track too many potential rising talents.

Either way, condoms had come a long way in twenty years. The new ones were nearly one hundred percent STD resistant and pregnancy protection, between the new Plastilyte material and the increased technology in spermicide.

The new Trojan 2020s supposedly felt like not wearing any protection at all. Jonas couldn't comment on that. He'd never had unprotected sex. He could say for sure that the 2020s were better than anything he had ever used before their introduction. They were all he'd used for the last seven years.

Jonas pulled his shirt off for her and went to work on Sarah's. He wasn't sure what he expected to find beneath the work T-shirt, but the silk bodysuit wasn't it. He smiled as he ran his tongue over the nipple straining against the fabric.

"Kevlar silk?" Jonas didn't need to ask. Most of his work clothes had Kevlar silk linings. Two layers of it had saved his life in Lauderdale.

Sarah blushed. "Steven insisted. He had four of them delivered, after my little run-in the other night."

"I see." His smile widened. Jonas unbuttoned her jeans and leaned to capture the zipper between his teeth. "Let's see how far this extends."

"Jonas, I—"

"Do you want me to stop?" Jonas played the zipper tab on the tip of his tongue.

"Are you crazy?"

He laughed. "Then let me play."

She nodded, her eyes wide, as he pulled the zipper down and planted a kiss low on her abdomen...at the top of the curls that he could barely make out beneath the silk. Sarah arched to him, her breathing ragged.

Jonas pulled her jeans off her legs and surveyed the length of her. *She isn't just a job. I won't let her be.*

She ran her hand down his chest. "Jonas?"

He cursed his inability to read her directly and used her expression as a guide. The confusion he saw broke his indecision. Jonas pulled her body to his, seeking her mouth with his own as he found the snaps at the crotch of the bodysuit. Sarah's hands closed at the waistline of his jeans. She smiled against his lips as she pushed them over his hips.

Jonas nipped at her lower lip. "What is it?"

"No underwear."

"That bothers you?"

"Not in the least."

She ran a hand over him, and Jonas stilled, gulping in breaths as his mind fought to function.

Sarah kissed his throat and chest as she continued to play with him. "I like how accessible you are."

Jonas pulled away abruptly and dragged his jeans off. He stripped her bodysuit off and settled over Sarah, shuddering at the skin-to-skin contact.

"I'll show you accessible," he promised.

"Jonas?" She was trying to rein in her fear, but he could see it clearly in her eyes.

"I won't. You have my word." But, he'd never wondered before. He'd never wanted to know if the Trojan 2020 ads were accurate...until now.

Jonas captured her mouth. Wanting or not, he wouldn't have sex with her without protection. His contract could be damned. Even if they ordered it, he wouldn't do anything she wasn't comfortable with.

He locked gazes with her and sank to capture a rosy nipple in his mouth. He savored her body, the faint taste of musk and soft skin teasing at his senses. Her reactions were sweet music, from her mewling cries to her hands gripping lightly in his hair.

Sarah pushed Jonas to his back and took his length in her mouth. Jonas felt his control slipping. That didn't happen to him. The E-shield went first, and he locked down on the rest to avoid a mishap, slamming his personal shield into place, as he felt Sarah's mind touch his. He hardly had the presence of mind to worry that she might see the change, before the pleasure and his rational assurances that less than one percent of talents could differentiate shields tore the worry from his mind.

Her thoughts and feelings flooded him. When had Sarah dropped her shield? Her need hit him, prompting a groan. She wanted more than his body, and no woman had ever wanted that. Jonas had always been turned on by how much women wanted his body. He was more than turned on by a woman who whose wants went beyond it.

His body tensed in response. "Sarah, unless this is all you want, I need to do something else quick."

She smiled sweetly as she released him. "Where are your condoms?"

"Front pocket of my jeans."

Sarah leaned down and came up with a handful of little red packets. She raised a questioning brow. "Jonas?"

"Would you rather learn that you share my stamina without being prepared?"

Sarah shot him a heated look as she dropped all but one condom on the nightstand. "Is that a promise, Jonas?"

"Give me half a chance to prove it, and it will be." He sucked in his breath as she started rolling the Plastilyte down his length. Her expert fingers sliding over him were driving him crazy.

"Now, now. I thought you wanted to prove your stamina?"

Jonas was never one to pass on a challenge. His smile widened. "Up for a bet on who breaks first?"

"What bet?"

"Whoever breaks first is at the complete mercy of the other for the next round." He'd played this game before. With his attributes, Jonas had never lost.

"What kind of mercy?"

"I won't do anything you're uncomfortable with."

Sarah seemed to be considering the possibilities.

"Do you have any toys?" he pressed.

She nodded. "How many rounds?"

"Until you ask me to stop." Usually, that was an exaggeration, but one look at the interest in Sarah's eyes made him believe it wouldn't be tonight.

She smiled. "You're awfully sure of yourself."

"Hmm. Are you so sure of yourself?" It was a taunt, but something told him that would do the trick.

"It's a deal."

Bingo. "Are you sure?" He gave that an edge of challenge.

"I'm game. Hope you enjoy being tied up."

Oh, yeah. A little bondage sounds good. But— "You first," he promised.

Jonas flipped her beneath him and slid deep inside her in one smooth motion. Sarah gripped his shoulders, and he could feel her fight to control her body's rise. He smiled as he took her hard and fast, matching each movement to what her body craved of him.

"Jonas, please."

He kissed her, possessing her utterly. Jonas released her mouth as Sarah cried out, her body contracting around him. He made her next rise slower, savoring the wicked thoughts coursing through her mind until he pushed her over again. He'd have to let himself lose one of the rounds. Sarah's ideas for tying him up had Jonas looking forward to losing, something he'd never contemplated before. Unable to hold off, he followed her over.

Sarah cradled his head to her shoulder. "You've convinced me. I'm at your mercy."

Jonas glanced at the painting above her bed, not trusting himself to look at her yet. He didn't want her at his mercy. He didn't want Sarah at anyone's mercy, but he'd just set her up for it. Jonas had no idea how Baker intended to use this against her, but the bastard would somehow.

He scrutinized the painting, pushing away his gloomy thoughts. Jonas recognized it. It was called *The Accolade*. Jonas had thought he was the knight in shining armor once, but had he ever had that much honor? He felt the familiar ache settle in his chest.

* * * *

February 18th

Sarah smiled at the sight of Jonas. She had provided breakfast in bed, and he was returning the favor by washing the dishes. He wore only his jeans. She had pulled on his shirt as a lark, earning her a heated look from him and an offer for her to keep it, if he could see her in it again.

The man hadn't lied about his sexual appetite. He had lain with her for a long time after their first time, but at her first sign of renewed interest, he had been ready and willing again. Actually, he was more than that. Jonas was attentive, skilled and tireless.

As he'd foretold, he outlasted her. After their fifth time together, Sarah had laughingly asked for a reprieve.

Jonas had chuckled. "Only a reprieve?"

"If you think I'm letting you go that easily — "

Sarah smiled wider. She had been exhausted when she'd asked for that reprieve, but she had another reason for asking. Irked by picking up his sister's emotions when she dropped her shields again and again, Steven had threatened to come over at three in the morning. To keep the peace, Sarah arranged for Steven to pass the rest of the night in peaceful, undisturbed sleep.

She glanced at the clock on the wall. It was nine thirty. Any normal person was up by nine, and Steven was typically up by seven or earlier. Sarah wasn't letting Jonas go easily at all.

It was time for the next round. Jonas had lost two rounds the previous night, and she'd lost three. She was at his mercy for the next round. Sarah snuggled to his back and reached her hand around to stroke him.

Jonas groaned and hardened under her fingers. "Sarah?"

"I think my reprieve is over."

"It is, if you keep that up."

"Good."

She kissed the back of his shoulder and unbuttoned his jeans, feeling his length straining against her hand. Jonas's breathing hitched, as she reached her other hand into his front pocket and pulled out one of the condoms still stuffed in it. Sarah stroked him as she tucked the condom into his hand. Jonas hesitated then ripped the pack open and started rolling it down his length. Sarah eased her hand away as the material covered him. Jonas turned, then scooped her onto the edge of the countertop.

He kissed her, running his hands under the shirt. Sarah gasped as his fingertips caressed her, making delicious little circles up her inner thigh until he reached the moisture gathering for him. Jonas didn't speak; his actions said it all for him. He possessed her, his mouth relentless as he buried two fingers in her, driving her to the edge.

Sarah wrapped her legs around his waist, urging him closer. Jonas eased his hand out and shuddered as his length slid home in her. Sarah leaned back, accepting the last of him as he lowered his forehead to hers with a groan.

Jonas rocked deep inside her for a moment. "The table or the wall, Sarah? Tell me, please."

She smiled. "You choose. Which would feel better for you?" She wanted him to enjoy himself this time. Not that Jonas wasn't enjoying himself. He most certainly was, but even Sarah could tell he was a talent using what he read from her unshielded mind to please her.

The first time she dropped her shield for him, it had been unplanned. Sarah had lost concentration on a level she had never encountered before when Jonas touched her. Once she realized what he was doing and how miserable it made him to do it, she couldn't help but drop her shield for him to show him how much she enjoyed what he was doing.

Sarah wasn't sure if Jonas could tell she had a shield, that she was talent. Not every talent was capable of identifying other talents. Alex didn't have that skill. If Jonas was a weak talent or unskilled, he might not realize that she had a shield, and he wasn't simply receiving sporadic thoughts from her. Many talents were limited in their range and receptiveness.

The only thing she knew for sure was that Jonas didn't want her to know he was talent. He was always careful to keep a shield up. But did Jonas do that because he knew she was talent, or because he didn't know and couldn't take the chance of her realizing his shield was down?

Sarah dropped her shield, filling her mind with the thought of him taking control and doing whatever he wanted. Jonas lifted her and moved to the wall, his movements suddenly fierce and driven. Sarah shattered as he surged into her again and again, only raising her shield when the contractions were easing and Steven was promising to be there within an hour. She didn't answer him.

Jonas's E-shield disappeared in favor of the one that was always in place. He was never fully open to her.

Not that having him unshielded would have done her much good. Mind reading wasn't one of her talents. Sarah was a minor empath, and she found that she could read Jonas slightly, even through his shield, as she could with Steven. She was also an expert at reading any use of talent in her range, not just the active classes that her mother and brothers could sense, but even the passive classes like identifying shields and feeling thought scans against unshielded norms.

The shift in his shield was what had tipped Sarah off that Jonas was talent and not a norm with an E-shield in the first place. When his shield shifted from the E-series to his personal shield that first time, she'd considered calling him on it for a split second, until she felt the emotions coursing from him. Whatever his reason for lying to her, emotions never lie, and Jonas wasn't trying to hurt her.

Sarah was what the DoPT would look for in a keeper, so the emergency charter hadn't allowed them to seize her with the rest of her family. She was psi-linked to Steven, and her whole family—except Dad— could communicate telepathically with each other, but all of her powers were non-combatant. That meant she wasn't deemed a danger to the general public under the witch-hunts of 2014 and 2015.

Jonas climaxed, roaring as he tensed inside her. She felt his regret washing over her. He was like this every time. Jonas wanted her desperately, but he always felt guilty afterward.

Sarah bit her lip as she considered the strange phenomenon. Either Jonas didn't know she was talent and feared she'd leave him when she found out he was, or he knew she was and feared the same thing for a different reason.

If she was a norm, she might refuse him out of prejudice or ignorance. Since Sarah was talent, he would fear she'd leave him because of the problem of children. In the few cases where two talents reproduced together, there had been no norms born yet. Researchers were tentatively placing the odds at or near one hundred percent talented offspring.

Sarah kissed him, drawing her shield more firmly around her. If either of them had something to fear, it was her. She was part of the infamous Randall family. Chances were higher than average that all her children would be powerful talents, even if she married a norm. Worse, very few talents would willingly risk censure by appearing to ally with the great house.

* * * *

Jonas walked into the apartment and past Markham to the bed. He curled on his left side with his hand pressed to his chest. The whole way back, he had considered his options.

If Baker made him leave now, he'd resign. He'd tell Sarah he had to leave on business, but Jonas would be back—in thirty days, when his time after notice of end of contract had been served.

Markham walked into the room and leaned against the doorframe. "I take it you did it?"

"Go to hell, Markham."

"Paige—"

"Is this a debrief?"

There was a moment of tense silence. "No."

"Then I'm taking the fifth."

"An update, then."

"They better not have booked me on a flight yet. Whether they order me to leave now or not, I promised I'd have dinner with her, and I will."

"They're not ordering you back. They want you here."

"Why?"

"Getting close to Sarah is only the first step in getting close to the others."

"I want to quit, Markham. This isn't what I trained for."

Jonas closed his eyes, remembering how Sarah felt in his arms that morning. He hadn't wanted to leave, but Sarah said she had family matters to attend to for part of the day. Jonas had been afraid to leave her, afraid that he'd be dragged back to Boston...or worse, that the DoPT would swoop in with their grand plan and make her hate him.

"No one gets hurt this way," Markham reminded him quietly.

"She gets hurt this way. You don't think she's going to feel betrayed?" *I'm going to get hurt.*

Markham groaned. "Ah shit. What do you want?"

Jonas turned away, too tired to keep Markham out of his mind. On some level, it made it easier to have Markham know where he stood.

"You're serious, aren't you? You'd ditch your contract and blow this job for her."

"Are you going to turn me in?" Jonas knew he should. As a keeper, Markham was required to inform Baker when his charge was out of their control.

Markham didn't take time to consider it. "No."

"Why?"

"What would you do if they sent Hall or Pendle to try for her?"

Jonas shot off the bed to Markham, stopping short of hurting him, but by a narrow margin. "They can't," he growled, wondering if that was the plan if he flaked.

Markham sighed and motioned to Jonas. "That's why I won't turn you in."

Jonas darkened and took a step back. "Because I'd renegade?" The thought shook him. He'd never considered renegading before. Quitting, yes, but never that. Jonas ran a nervous hand through his hair and turned away.

"No. Because you might be in love with her."

"I can't live like this, but I have to do what they want to keep her safe. Which is worse, Evan?"

Markham set up the recorder silently, then pulled Jonas to the bed.

"I'm not debriefing this one on the recorder," Jonas insisted; the thought of reciting times and positions and pillow talk made him ill.

"You're right."

"Then what the hell am I doing?"

"Recording our notice for end of contracts."

"You said—"

"We're recording them. I won't file them until it comes to a head. When they push too far, or when you know for certain you have to tell her and risk her life that way to keep her from something worse... You just tell me when that happens."

Jonas managed a weak smile. "Guess you're Evan now."

* * * *

Sarah hit the buzzer for the downstairs door without asking who it was. It had been fifty-six minutes since Steven's threat. Who else would it be? She pulled the apartment door open and waved him in theatrically.

Steven paused for a moment to scowl at the oversized shirt she wore under her terry cloth robe, Jonas's shirt. He stormed into the living room and dropped down on the couch. "I take it he's gone?"

"Jonas? Yes, he's gone home, but he's having dinner with me again tonight."

Steven raised an eyebrow. "Dinner?"

Sarah chuckled. "Well, we did eat last night."

"Please tell me you protected yourself, at least. I know you bared your mind and soul to him every— Oh, God, I hope that was every time."

"It was, and I did. Mom and Dad drilled that into me. If I ever do decide to have children, it won't be an accident."

"Why? Did it ever occur to you that he might be talent? That dropping your shields could have consequences?"

Sarah fortified her shield as the guilt settled in. She forced the smile on her face to stay steady. She didn't typically keep important things from Steven, but he'd take the news that Jonas was talent in the worst possible light. Then her entire family would descend on her.

"Yes. I considered it."

His eyes narrowed. "And?"

"And it's my life, Steven. I need this, maybe forever. Please don't mess it up for me." She dropped her gaze, hoping he wouldn't press her on this one.

Steven groaned. "He means that much to you?"

Sarah nodded, pulling back tears. "I'll have enough problems when he figures out who I am. If this has any chance of—"

"You didn't tell him?" Steven's voice was edged with panic.

"Oh, that's worked well before," she bit out sarcastically.

Steven cringed, probably remembering her broken heart when she learned that David, the guy she'd liked in high school, had only taken her virginity on a bet to fuck one of the famous family of talents. It had taken the entire family to keep Steven from renegading. Uncle Bruce and Mac had arranged a discussion with David that shut him up and kept him away.

Or maybe, he was remembering Tim and how Sarah had spent the night they broke up crying in Steven's arms. She had dated Tim for a year in college, had been sharing his bed for more than six months. Sarah had been confident of Tim's feelings for her, so confident that she told him about her family.

He had walked out on her that same night. His love for her wasn't nearly as strong as his love of a future political career. While the daughter of a writer and a doctor and granddaughter of a cop and a lawyer would make a fine political wife, he couldn't afford to be compromised by people believing him controlled by the Randalls.

Steven came to sit beside her, wrapping her in his arms as he had after each of those disastrous break-ups. "You'll have to tell him eventually."

"I know." *Not soon. Please, not soon.* "Don't sic Mac on me. Please, Steven."

"You know me better than that."

* * * *

Jonas shifted nervously and pushed the buzzer for Sarah's apartment. There was something liberating in knowing he'd recorded his resignation. It was meaningless. He hadn't even filed it, but he knew that Griffin would be his last job. Only the threat to Sarah kept him from filing now.

What can they do?

He wouldn't put hurting her past them. Not after the scam with the renegade, but how would hurting Sarah benefit them?

They can't take her.

Well, they could, but where could they possibly hide her? Her prints or picture would pull up her file. Even the DoPT had laws governing them. Jonas was that law. If Baker did something illegal against her—something more than already had with the renegade, Jonas was the only legal protection Sarah had.

Markham was making discreet inquiries into the master plan, but either no one knew or no one was talking. In the meantime, Jonas resolved to strengthen what he had with Sarah. In the end, he hoped that would be the one thing he had left.

The door buzzed for him, and Jonas wondered at the fact that Sarah didn't ask who it was. A chilling thought occurred to him as he pulled the door open. What if a shield wasn't all she had?

He knew for a fact that Sarah could test his shield, that she could at least see if he had one. Baker said that they weren't really sure what her talents were. All they knew for certain was that she'd never used an active class around them, but what about passive classes? If she read his mind, it was over.

Jonas forced himself up the stairs. He'd never worried about a renegade seeing through him, even when he was an adult-looking seventeen-year-old being served mock alcohol in dockside bars. He didn't want to examine his reasons for being afraid she'd see through him too closely. If Markham was right, and Jonas was in love with her—

She could be used against me. They wanted to use Sarah against her family. One hint of a serious involvement on his part, and Baker could use her against him too. He pushed the apartment door open, still lost in thought.

"In here," Sarah called.

Jonas turned from the kitchen and went back to the living room. His confusion melted into a raging need. The room was lit by a dozen candles. Dinner plates and covered platters were laid on the coffee table, and cushions were spread on the floor for them to sit on.

Sarah's arms wrapped around him and her breasts pressed to his back. Jonas groaned as she started peeling his shirt up his torso, his back wonderfully alive to the feeling of lace and velvet.

"Sarah, if you do this, dinner will be cold before we eat."

She nipped his shoulder as she dropped his T-shirt to the floor. "It's meant to be cold. I knew hot food would be a mistake."

"Why?" He ran his hands behind him to investigate the outfit she wore, learning the teddy by Braille.

Sarah unsnapped his jeans. "I knew it would just get cold before we got to it."

Jonas turned in her arms, sweeping her to the cushions. He ran his palms up the velvet over her stomach to the lace covering her breasts. "Will we ever have a hot dinner again?"

Her laugh was husky and inviting. "Only if you show up early while it cooks."

Jonas smiled. "I'd have to make love to you in the kitchen, so we can make sure it doesn't burn," he warned.

Sarah's eyes darkened. "Any time."

CHAPTER FOUR

April 5th

Sarah wound her fingers in the curls on Jonas's chest. He groaned in response, and she felt him harden against her thigh. The last five weeks had done nothing but intensify his reaction to her touch.

Jonas spent most nights with her now. She saw him every evening after work and most mornings until he left for work. In fact, there hadn't been a single day she hadn't seen him since Jonas showed up at the store with the offer of dinner.

He had a key now. Sarah had never trusted a man enough to give him a key to her apartment, but the payoff was worth it. Coming home to a meal and Jonas was well worth the risk of that key.

Sarah pulled Jonas toward her in invitation. He kissed her, his mouth and hands urgent this time. Sometimes, Jonas was a slow, tender lover, but even when his actions were demanding, he was thorough, single-minded in his approach to making love to her.

She dreaded what she had to do. Steven had become demanding in the last week, and her family was picking up on the tension between them over family dinners. Sarah had to ask Jonas to dinner with them soon. That meant telling him who her family was. She had to do it now, before he made love to her again and captured more of her heart.

"Jonas?"

He continued his exploration of the spot behind her ear, his voice rumbling against her. "Yes?"

"I have to talk to you."

He moved his attention to her breast. "Talk," he invited her.

Sarah sighed and ran her hand over his shoulder. "No, I need to talk to you. For a few minutes."

Jonas looked up at her with questioning eyes. He nodded and distanced himself on the bed. "I'm sorry. Please." He motioned for her to continue.

She took a deep breath to steel her resolve. She had to do this. "Would you have dinner with my family this Sunday?"

He smiled. "Of course. Why wouldn't I?"

"Well, that's what I need to talk to you about." Sarah hesitated, hoping he was really as different from every other guy she'd ever met as he seemed. "Do you know who Katie... Who Katheryn, Steven and Alex Randall are? Who Kyle Thompson is?"

"Yes. Doesn't everyone? How could you live in this city and be older than fifteen and not know?"

Sarah blushed. *This is going badly.* "Jonas, I—"

He ran his knuckles over her cheek. "Sarah, I met Steven the first night, remember?"

She buried her forehead in her hand. "Oh, no." How could she be so stupid? Most people would recognize Steven on sight.

"Did you honestly think I didn't know who he was? Why do you think I was afraid to leave you with him in his state of mind?"

Sarah pulled away, suddenly unsure. "You knew all this time?" *Is he another David?*

"Of course. If I cared about that, would I have come back? If it bothered me, I could have walked away."

She wished she could read him better. Jonas seemed sincere. He definitely wasn't a Tim, but he could still be pulling a David on her.

"Why did you come back?"

"Because I couldn't stop thinking about you." He pulled Sarah into his lap, nestling her to the proof of his arousal. "I've wanted you since the first time I saw you. Why would your family make any difference to that?"

Sarah blushed and looked away, unwilling to voice all the ways it could make a difference.

Jonas cupped her face back to his, searching out her expression. "Oh, God. Please tell me some idiot wasn't that stupid."

She shrugged, trying to adopt an indifferent look. Her mother made that expression look so easy, but it wasn't as simple as Sarah thought it would be. "Some men are stupid."

"Did he have sex with you because of who your family is or leave you because of it?"

Sarah bit back tears. *So much for indifferent.* "They —" She shook her head.

Jonas's face went crimson. She could feel his outrage clearly through his shield.

"Men? They? Sarah, please tell me."

"I haven't had much luck with men, Jonas. I'd about given up hope that there was an honest man in the world who wasn't related to me."

He stroked her face. "Which extreme am I fighting?"

"Both. I think you've proven one wrong." She managed a weak smile. "After all, you came back."

"Would you let me prove the other one wrong?"

"How?"

Jonas laid her back, lifting her hips. Determination burning in his eyes, he took her clit in his mouth, trapping it between his tongue and teeth, nipping and soothing it.

Sarah reached for his head, but Jonas swept her hands to her stomach, clamped in his free hand. She whimpered as he laid a kiss on the sensitive bundle of nerves and traced the seam of her labia with his tongue.

He groaned into her as Sarah wrapped her ankles over his shoulders and her personal lubricant flowed over his questing tongue. Jonas raised his head, raining hot panting breaths on the engorged area between her thighs.

His hand tightened around her wrists, just the slightest increase in pressure. "Don't move." He issued the order then moved his hand away, keeping her pinned in his sights. Jonas pulled the two pillows from his side of the bed under her and eased her down onto them.

"Jonas?"

"Comfortable?" he asked, drawing his finger along the same line his tongue had explored moments before.

Sarah nodded, unable to form words as his arm and back muscles rippled beneath her legs. She shivered at the feeling of his lips on the inside of her thigh. He kissed and blew little puffs of air over her sensitive flesh up the few inches back to her core.

His tongue returned to the seam, darting just inside before teasing her again. Sarah tightened her legs around him, needing more, but Jonas tortured her with the promise of what she wanted most. She reached for him, and he returned one hand to holding her still for his intimate ambush.

Jonas laid a kiss on her thigh. "You want more?"

"Jonas." She pleaded with him, pulling herself closer to his mouth.

He braced her hips. "More?"

"Yes."

"Good. Tell me when you're convinced."

"What? Jonas, what do you—"

"Why am I here, Sarah? Tell me that, and I'll prove it."

"I don't—" She sucked in her breath as he returned to his teasing. Sarah squirmed beneath the assault, trying to think clearly. "Me."

Jonas stilled, raising his head until they were face-to-face again. "Tell me."

"You want me. Not my family. Me."

He shook his head. "Not good enough."

"You're not in bed with me for my family, one way or the other."

"Not good enough." Jonas lowered his mouth.

Sarah cried out in frustration. *Why isn't it good enough?*

He kept her on the edges of orgasm, pulling back just enough to keep her from completion. It was maddening, but still she felt—

"Love."

In the silence after her whisper, she heard his breathing hitch. "Say it."

"You're here because you love me?" Jonas hadn't said it, but had there ever been any doubt? She hadn't said it either.

"Do I?"

Sarah floundered. "Don't you?"

"Let me know when you're sure." Jonas released her hands and buried his tongue in her, driving her body up to the edge and sending her into a shattering free fall of pleasure.

When she screamed his name, Jonas pulled the pillows away, cushioning her as she fell and unwinding her legs to push her knees up and out as he rose up over her. The tip of him, already covered in Plastilyte, pressed to her. Sarah pressed back, trying to force the heat of him into her.

"Are you sure, Sarah?"

"You love me."

He waited for more from her, his expression intense.

"I love you, Jonas."

"You're sure?"

"Yes."

His face erupted in a wide smile, which morphed into an exquisite expression of pleasure and pain as he eased into her little by little, each thrust taking more of her. His pace was agonizingly slow, drawing out to the barest possession of her and sliding back to claim her again. Sarah dug her fingers into his shoulders, searching for an anchor in the storm raging through her body.

Jonas nipped at her ear. "That's right. Show me, Sarah. Show me what I do to you."

Her entire body was alive and aware of him. Sarah felt each individual hair that rasped past her aching nipples. She felt each play of muscles beneath her fingertips and against her stomach and legs. Jonas braced her knees up further, pushing deeper with the movement. Sarah felt her nails bite skin. She started to pull back, but Jonas groaned in pleasure.

"Yes. Show me, Sarah."

His deeper thrusts had Sarah thrashing her head back and forth and urging him on with helpless little sounds of pleasure that she didn't seem able to control. None of her reactions were under her control.

"What are you doing to me?" she asked weakly.

Jonas stared at her, hopelessly lost in his own enjoyment. "I'm making love to you. No one's ever done this for you before. Please tell me."

Sarah swallowed a whimper as he changed position slightly. She'd never felt anything like this before. "No. Only you." She had no doubts that no one else would touch her like this again.

"Forever."

He pushed fully inside her, freezing at the pinnacle and roaring out his release. His come scalded her through the Plastilyte between them. She loved the feeling of his heat inside her. Sarah wondered how it would feel to have all of him, his uncovered length and that searing release touching her, finding places he couldn't reach, even as deep in her as he was now.

Jonas pulled Sarah to him, cradling her head to his chest. "I'm sorry," he breathed.

Sarah tensed in his embrace, spasming as she joined him. Her mind wouldn't seem to work. Everything was feeling. His hands, him inside her, and his weight on her were Sarah's only anchors, and the endless waves of sensation sought to drag her from those anchors. She gulped in air between waves, her mind struggling to piece together his final words. *Sorry for what?* There was absolutely nothing Sarah could see that he did wrong.

He kissed her. "I'm sorry I couldn't wait for you."

She bit her lip. *He's hiding something. Why is he hiding something?* "No. There's more."

Jonas blushed. "I'm sorry that no one's ever made love to you before."

Sarah felt a twisting knot in her stomach. "Has anyone made love to you before?" She didn't ask him if he'd made love to anyone else. She knew from experience that you could pour your soul into a relationship and have it shortchanged on the other end.

"No."

She nodded. Sarah had expected that answer. "Then I'm sorry."

Jonas shook his head. "Don't be. It wasn't the same. Those men—" He sighed. "You thought there could be more than there was, didn't you?"

Sarah nodded.

His expression softened as he touched her cheek. "With me, there were no lies. It was just sex, and everyone knew it was just sex."

"Sounds lonely."

"It was, but no one got hurt."

Sarah nodded. "So, you'll come to dinner?"

Jonas chuckled. "I said I would."

"You're not worried about meeting the Randalls?"

"I'll wear my E-shield."

"Do you have a gun?"

Jonas made two aborted attempts at speech before he forced something forth. "Do I need one?"

Sarah shrugged. "Maybe. If I'm bringing a man to dinner, my uncles will show up for sure. They're a little protective, and they tend to carry guns." She bit back a smile, intending to tell Jonas that it was an exaggeration—in a minute.

He swallowed hard then nodded. "Thanks for the warning, but I think you're joking." Jonas hoped she was joking. That much was written in his mind.

She nodded to put him at ease.

* * * *

Jonas pounded on Markham's door, ready to break it down if Evan wasn't quick enough about answering. Evan raised an eyebrow at his state of mind as he swung the door open and motioned him in.

Jonas pushed past him. "Were they DoPT? Were they set up?"

"Who?"

"The men in her past. I'd guess the one who left her wasn't. What about the ones who screwed her because—"

Jonas rubbed a hand over his face in frustration. It was easier to face the rage. It was easier, because his alternative was facing the fact that he was sleeping with Sarah as part of a plot to set her up somehow. Jonas was no better. He was sleeping with her because of who her family was, despite the fact that his feelings went deeper and his motives had seemed purer in the beginning.

How could Jonas ever have believed that he was doing this only to keep her safe? He wanted Sarah, he loved her and he'd compromised her to get her. He should have run the other way rather than sleep with her. How was this showing her love?

Evan flipped open his pocket PC and loaded up Sarah's file. "According to this, you're the first DoPT agent who's been allowed anywhere near her."

Jonas sank into the couch, sighing in relief. "Thank God." The thought of Pendle or Peterson touching her was like a knife in his gut.

Evan shook his head. "Can I sign off, or do you need something else?"

"Yes. No. Why do I need a gun to meet her uncles? I was so shocked, I forgot to ask. I mean, I know they're protective, but who are these guys? Are they trained professionals or just well-meaning uncles?"

"Sarah doesn't have uncles. Even Katheryn and Keith have no uncles. Only child syndrome or, in Katheryn's case, one of two sisters and the husband died a long time ago. Damned if I know what she's talking about."

"Great. What else can go wrong?"

"When are you meeting these delightful souls?"

"Sunday. Family dinner. My cover better be foolproof by then. If these guys are trained, they'll be checking soon."

"No one has checked yet."

"That's good news," Jonas grumbled.

"Your cover is tight. It's been tight since day one. You can start showing up to work any time you want to. The sooner the better, if someone is going to start checking."

"Tomorrow. Anything special added to the usual that I need to know about?"

"*Analog*? What's new there? You took some online audits at Pitt before reporting in to the North Side plant from the one north of Boston. I'll have a printout of what was placed in the Pitt computers for you tonight."

Jonas nodded. The *Analog* headquarters north of Boston, with its three plants in that area, allowed Jonas to use his knowledge of the area and claim he had been moved elsewhere in their infrastructure. *Analog* was more than willing to play along for two reasons. The first was that they had the exclusive government contract for producing shields. The second was that they got Jonas or one of his counterparts as free expert labor whenever they needed cover in an area where *Analog* had a plant.

"Guess I better beef up on my semi-conductor knowledge." Jonas sighed.

Evan scowled at him. "Like you ever forget anything."

* * * *

April 9th

Jonas willed his heart rate to slow as he stepped through the doorway into the two-story house on Primrose. Sarah squeezed his hand in reassurance as the mob of people turned their way.

"Oh, man," he breathed around his smile. "You have a lot of family. They don't bite, right?"

"Four are missing. Looks like the Thompsons didn't make it tonight." Sarah was biting back panic, though she was good at hiding it.

Katheryn moved first, smiling as she crossed the room. Jonas waited for the brush against his shield but none came. Either she knew he was shielded, or she really didn't believe in using what she had, just as they stated before the Supreme Court.

Sarah released his hand to hug her mother. The two chatted while Jonas shut the door, feeling his skin prickle at the eyes assessing him. Those were confident, professional eyes.

He turned back and clasped Katheryn's offered hand. "It's a pleasure to meet you, Mrs. Randall."

She laughed heartily. "Lesson one. I'm Katie. My husband is Keith. No one is formal here. Come meet the bodyguards."

Jonas cracked a smile. "Bodyguards?" His senses were never wrong.

"Humor them. We're two of only three women in a family of men. It makes them feel important."

He nodded, trying to decipher the situation. They were trained, and they weren't family. He wasn't sure what the game was, but it was making him distinctly nervous. Jonas wound his left arm around Sarah as they made their way into the center of the room.

Keith came first, taking Jonas's hand and welcoming him. At least Sarah's parents were reasonable people.

Alex came next. The young man had a firm handshake but a wary expression. Jonas resisted the urge to rub his ribs. He'd seen boys broken like that before.

Steven wasn't broken. Despite his psych profile at exit, he wasn't broken.

Katie waved Steven over. "This is my oldest, Steven. Come meet Jonas."

"I've met him. Hello, Jonas."

Jonas nodded to him. "Steven."

Steven's stance was relaxed, but Jonas could read the aggression in him. This was what the academies did to Steven. He wasn't broken. He was untrusting and angry. He was also protective of his twin.

Without exception, each of the family members examined Steven and Jonas carefully, trying to make sense of this new piece of information.

Katie looked to her older son. "You have? When? Why didn't you mention it?"

Jonas willed his reaction away, as Sarah and her twin exchanged a flurry of discussion via telepathy. *So much for shields being all she has.*

Sarah blushed deeply.

Steven shrugged. "When they started dating. I figured Sarah'd subject him to the firing squad when she was good and ready."

Katie's look was all warning. "Spill it. Don't make me find out on my own."

Steven shoved his hands in his pockets and gave his sister a bland look, as if inviting her to get herself out of the mess she was in. Katie looked from one to the other with an assessing eye. She turned her attention to Jonas fully, and Sarah snapped.

"Oh, all right." She scowled. "I got mugged, and Jonas happened along at the right time."

Steven looked unimpressed with her quick thinking. Jonas, on the other hand, was amazed. Sarah had told the absolute truth without telling them the things that would cause them the most concern.

Katie's eyes widened in shock. "Any particular reason you didn't tell us this?" she demanded of her daughter. She offered Steven a venomous look. "Or you?"

Sarah rolled her eyes. "Look at the reaction I'm getting and ask me that again with a straight face."

One of the men on the couch stood, and Jonas gasped. He was a bear. He was at least six foot five and three hundred some odd pounds, almost all muscle despite the gray hair and lined face that marked him in his late sixties or seventies. Jonas found himself wishing that he had liberated some stun-spray from Evan's stash. This man surely had some training in hand-to-hand combat, if not more than Jonas had. There was a fury rising in him as he stood, though his face remained impassive.

Sarah backed off a step, and Jonas wondered if she felt his rage with psi talent or knew him well enough to know what he was doing.

The man's voice was calm despite what he was feeling. "I didn't see a police report on that, young lady."

Sarah hesitated, at a loss for answering that accusation. Steven raised an eyebrow at her discomfort. That annoyed Jonas, Steven's taunting even more than her discomfort.

Jonas stepped in, taking his life in his hands as he tightened his hold on Sarah in comfort. "She didn't want to worry anyone, and since we saw on the news that he got picked up that night on another charge—" He swallowed hard as the larger man turned on him. Jonas put his hand out, willing it not to shake. "Jonas Paige."

The man folded Jonas's hand inside his giant mitt. "You chased this mugger off?"

"I couldn't just leave Sarah at his mercy, could I?"

He nodded. "Tentatively, you're okay with me."

Jonas cracked a smile. "Until my background check comes up clear?"

Keith laughed heartily. "Don't put it past them. They did one on me, and I work for the city offices."

Jonas swallowed the sour wave burning his throat. He'd have to warn Evan about this development, though his cover was secure. He found his ability to think on his feet taking a vacation, so he nodded quietly.

Sarah stepped in. "Oh, back off, Uncle Bugsy." She turned to the next man on the couch, a thin, pasty man with a spray of freckles and angry green eyes. "And you, can it," she warned him. "I can see you firing up. There will be no interrogation tonight. Got it, Prentice?" She didn't wait for his agreement before moving on.

Sarah simply stared at the final man. Jonas waited for a flurry of telepathy that never came. Whatever passed between them was an understanding beyond words and without need of pleasantries or tricks. The man nodded his agreement.

Sarah sighed. "Thanks, Mac. Now that we've settled that, let's get dinner on the table. I'm starving."

Dinner passed enjoyably enough. Jonas learned that the blue-shirt uncles were police officers who'd worked with Katie's father. He got a good feel for the three men during dinner. Bugsy was quietly protective, Prentice was noisy about it and Mac was watchful.

Jonas held his breath at two light, questing touches on his simulated E-shield. The first touch was Steven, and the second was Alex.

Their examination didn't bother him. His E-shield would be the perfect imitation. What did bother him was the discussion they had by telepathy afterward. Worse, at the touches on his shield, Sarah gave her brothers dirty looks and sent a flurry of telepathy out that had Steven raising his eyebrow and Alex blushing deeply.

Jonas feigned confusion at their reactions, his heart pounding. He pretended not to feel the touches on his shield, because he wouldn't feel them if it was a neuro-mechanical shield. He acted the part he needed to play, all the time worrying about her reactions.

Sarah felt what they were doing. What else can she do?

The interrogation took place despite Sarah's warning. Jonas answered countless questions about his job with *Analog*, his education, his family and his life growing up. His cover kept much of the information factual. It was always easier to bend the truth than to lie outright.

Of course, his cover story made Jonas the only child of dead parents. It listed his move to Clinton as moving in with his Aunt Rose after his father was killed in the Iraqi bombings of 2007.

It also listed schools he'd studied at, schools that, in reality, Jonas had only been permitted a short visit to in order to gain personal experience of the campus. He'd audited courses at the schools, so he showed on the rolls as a student, but Jonas had never been permitted to attend any of the high schools and colleges he listed in his cover story. He'd used this cover many times, and sometimes Jonas wished it were true.

All the uncles took mental notes while he talked, but Mac was the loudest about it. He was the one Jonas had to watch. He was also the only one who dared broach the subject of the mugger again.

"Tell us about the mugger, Sarah."

She nodded as if he'd commented on the weather. "Not much to tell. He was just some punk after my wallet."

"And?" He missed nothing. Mac could be a formidable enemy.

"What, Mac? What are you asking?"

One brow arched. "You know what I'm asking."

Jonas pretended to ignore that. Was she a mind reader?

Sarah sighed. "I had a split lip and a bump on the head."

Katie shot Steven a sharp look that had Jonas wondering if he was considered his sister's keeper. Maybe he was. After all, Sarah knew he'd be waiting for her at home, though she didn't use telepathy the night she was attacked. The Randalls could link. Was Steven her closest link?

Steven shrugged. "She told me to put the phone down."

His mother rolled her eyes. "Since when do you listen to your sister?"

"Since when does she listen to any of us?"

"What else isn't she telling us?"

Jonas noticed that she didn't ask Sarah. Was Sarah superior to her stronger siblings in her shield? Baker had insinuated that she was.

Steven eyed Sarah and sighed. "He had a knife."

Sarah shot him a look of dismay. "Steven, how could you?"

"She can tell," he answered uncomfortably.

Sarah blushed and nodded. "Yeah, I know." She smiled at Jonas. "See why I live away from home?"

Jonas nodded, wondering what the reaction would be to their usual nightly activities or to the fact that Steven withheld the fact that her mugger was a now-dead renegade. Despite the show the twins put on, Jonas knew Steven was still covering for her.

* * * *

April 12th

Jonas pulled his *Nextel* radio up to the hood of his clean-room blues. "Yeah, Mike?"

"Someone downstairs to see you. Julian MacRey."

"Be right down." He cycled out of the room, stripping off his suit and smoothing his hair before leaving the area. Jonas hit a head on the way downstairs. Stripping and resuiting unnecessarily was something Jonas avoided, so it was a definite need by the time he came out of the fab.

He checked his watch on the way down the stairs. It was lunchtime. He would have had to strip down anyway.

Jonas nodded to Mac as he passed the security desk and swiped out. "Can we talk over lunch? I only have thirty."

"Sure."

The coffee shop was two blocks away. Mac turned down Jonas's offer of food, though he did get a coffee. Jonas kept it light: a hoagie, chips, triple espresso, and an oversized cookie.

"What's up, Mac?" He took a bite of his sandwich.

"What's up with you and Sarah?"

Jonas surveyed Mac as he chewed and swallowed the bite in his mouth. "That's a little personal, don't you think?" He took another bite before he could say something self-righteous.

Mac sipped his coffee. "Maybe, but considering you've spent five of the last six nights at her place, Grandpa Mac asks the question."

Jonas choked, biting back pure rage as he forced the mouthful of sandwich down. "You're watching us?"

Mac had been watching them for three days before Jonas went to dinner, if the six days was accurate. He'd escaped the DoPT only to have new keepers making their bets on him and Sarah?

Mac shrugged. "Old habits die hard. Carol and Katie. Now Sarah—"

"What did your background check show, Mac?"

"Except for that little case of assault when you were sixteen, I think you know you came up clean."

Jonas blushed. They'd used that touch in his file before, but Evan forgot to tell him about it this time.

"It was necessary, justified." The actual incident happened at Clinton. Jonas had been eleven. The girl he had been protecting had been fifteen. She'd given him his first kiss.

"Yeah. I heard that."

"What's the problem, Mac?"

"No problem. Just grandfatherly concern."

"Having me spied on goes a little beyond grandfatherly concern."

"Not in this family. Keith used to complain that APBs on their vehicles were commonplace."

"So, you've always done this. That makes it right?"

"Maybe not. Why is it so hard for you? Keith could look me in the eye and tell me what he wanted."

"It's private, Mac. It's between Sarah and me." If Jonas wasn't debriefing to the DoPT, he wasn't doing it for Mac.

"You'll stick by that?"

"Absolutely."

To his surprise, Mac smiled. "Perfect. If you did any less, I'd wonder what Sarah saw in you."

Jonas tried to work his mind around that. "Did you wonder what Katie saw in Keith?"

"No. Keith was what I would expect for Katie. You are what I'd expect for Sarah."

CHAPTER FIVE

May 10th

Sarah kept her shield firmly in place, as she had all day. Steven would wonder at it, but better that than have him pick up her distress and come here where he could actively pick her thoughts...after he goaded her into dropping her shields.

She glanced at her watch and groaned. She had put this off long enough. Sarah sat on the couch and shut her eyes as her hand closed on the wand on the table. Her hands were shaking. She couldn't seem to stop them from shaking. Sarah took a deep breath and opened her eyes. She stifled a sob and dropped the test back on the table.

Sarah curled up in the corner of the couch and wrapped her arms around her stomach. "Oh, Christ. What do I do now?"

Pregnant? But they were always careful. The condoms were near one hundred percent effective. They never forgot or passed on them. They never had a break, and the condoms only failed with a break.

Okay, we've never noticed a break.

She groaned again, putting her face in her hands and feeling incredibly sick. "He won't even believe it's his," she decided miserably. *Even if Jonas does, what will his reaction be?* It wasn't like either of them were aching for this.

Sarah scooped up the test and box, making sure she had all the inserts, wrapping them up in the CVS bag and tossing them in the trash. She shifted her weight from foot to foot then pulled out the garbage bag and jogged out to the dumpster. Sarah didn't know what she was going to do yet, and having Jonas find that in the trash would be a colossal blunder. She stared at the dumpster with a lump in her throat before she went back in.

She heard the phone ringing as she locked her door again. Sarah answered, though her heart screamed at her to let it ring. "Hello?"

Steven didn't beat around the bush. "What's wrong, Sarah?"

"Nothing. I'm just tired. I'm fine." *Liar. What am I doing?*

"Bullshit. Hiding behind that damn shield doesn't do you much good when you let it flicker because you're so upset. Do I need to come over there?"

"No. I'll be at dinner tonight." She would be, but she'd have to tell Jonas before then. Either Sarah would show up with Jonas, announcing that they were having a baby, or she'd show up alone, announcing that she was an unwed mother deciding between moving home and having an abortion. Sarah couldn't hide this from Steven in close quarters, even if she tried.

"You better, and the explanation better be good."

"It will, Steven. I promise."

He hesitated. "Let down your shield, Sarah."

She groaned. He wanted to gauge her state of mind, since he couldn't read her at this range.

"No." Sarah rolled her forehead against the tile next to the phone.

"Drop your shield, or I'm coming over there."

"Steven—"

"I mean it."

Sarah sighed. She did her best to calm her emotions and offered him a lighter version of her shield.

Steven sucked in his breath. "I'll be there in thirty minutes."

"No. I'll see you at Mom and Dad's in two hours, but I have to get ready now. There's really nothing you can do, Steven. I have to figure this one out on my own."

"Is this about Jonas?"

"No. This is about *me*."

Steven sighed. "Don't be late." He paused. "Will Jonas be with you?"

Sarah took a ragged breath. "I don't know. Maybe."

"This is a story I have to hear."

Sarah held the phone long after Steven hung up. She retreated to the shower and let the water work on her tense muscles. She willed her heart to slow.

She had an hour to figure out how to tell Jonas he was a father. No. That was the wrong approach. That assumed he *wanted* to be a father. Sarah was the one who was pregnant. His place was optional, whether she kept the baby or not. She had to remember that.

* * * *

Jonas stilled with his hand on the door. Something in Evan's face scared him. "What is it?"

"Close the door." Evan's voice held a cold edge.

Jonas swung the door shut. He hesitated for just a moment before he crossed the room and sank to the couch. "Hit me."

"Baker called me."

Jonas closed his eyes. "I'm not leaving. I'll resign."

"He doesn't want you to leave."

"What *does* he want?" *Whatever it is, it's sure to suck.*

Evan didn't answer. Something hit Jonas's leg and thumped to the couch beside him. Jonas opened his eyes and picked up a hundred-count box of condoms. They were Trojan Specials, a textured version of the 2020 in a blue wrapper. It wasn't a style he typically went for.

"And?" he asked in confusion.

Evan winced. "They want you to use these for a while."

"How long? Why? Evan, I don't get it."

"They're doctored to fail. They want her pregnant."

Jonas fumbled the box and watched its spiral to the floor. "Why?" Spitting that single word out took all the brain power he currently had.

Evan pushed off the chair and moved to the bedroom doorway, bracing his fist on the frame, his shoulders bunching. "The psych guys said they'll all be easier to control that way. She'll feel... Sarah will be apprehensive, and her family will do anything to protect her."

"She'd abort." It hurt to consider it. Jonas wanted Sarah. He wanted children with her, but he'd rather see her abort than have them use her that way. *If I repeat it to myself a few hundred times, I might start to believe it.*

Evan sighed. "The psych guys say there's an eighty percent chance that she wouldn't."

Jonas kicked the box of condoms across the room. "It's time, Evan. They've gone too far."

"You'll probably lose her."

"I know, but she's too important to me to do this to her."

"They won't like this. It will be all-out war, when I send that file."

Jonas sighed. "Her family will protect her if she won't let me."

"You're sure?"

"I have to do this for her."

Evan nodded and pulled the recorder out of his jacket pocket. "Last chance to back out, Jonas."

Jonas walked to him and pulled the recorder from his hands. His fingers shook as he punched up the saved file. "Your last chance, Evan. I'll record a new one without you, if you want. You'll be out of the line of fire."

"No. Send it."

Jonas hit the send button and pushed the recorder into Evan's hands. "I have to— I'm getting ready now. Sarah is expecting me."

"Good luck."

"Thanks." He paused in the bedroom doorway. "I'll need my badge and ID, Evan."

"I'll leave them on the coffee table."

* * * *

Sarah was no closer to an answer when Jonas used his key on the downstairs door. She opened the upper door for him, managing a weak smile in response to the kiss he planted on her cheek. He met her gaze, and she was struck by how guarded he was.

Or is he simply reacting to my scattered state?

She decided she couldn't put this off. "I have to talk to you."

Jonas nodded and closed the door. "A lot of that going around, I think."

Sarah shook her head in confusion as he steered her to the couch. Sitting so he was facing her, he motioned for her to start in.

She felt her heart speed. "No. You first." Either Jonas came here to break it off, or he came here to tell her he wanted more. If it was the former, she wouldn't confuse the issue. If it was the latter, he might change his mind after she told him what she had to. Sarah promised herself to stick to that.

Jonas took a deep breath. "Okay." He took her hand. "Sarah, I told you I want more. I do. I want forever, but I haven't been very honest with you."

Sarah laughed in relief. "You're talent. I know that."

He blanched. "I'm more than a talent." Jonas rubbed his free hand over his mouth. "I quit my job today. I quit, because I can't keep doing the things they want me to do."

Her stomach rebelled. "Please tell me you're not a renegade."

Jonas shook his head. "No. I'm not a renegade, but they may make me out to be one before this is over."

"I don't—"

He squeezed his eyes shut. "Promise me you'll hear me out."

"Jonas?"

"Promise me you won't walk out on me. No matter what I say in the next few minutes, promise me you'll let me explain everything before you make a decision."

Sarah nodded, then realized he couldn't see her. "All right."

He opened his eyes, tortured eyes. Jonas changed his shield to a weak version of his inner shield, and Sarah felt the stark terror in him.

"I love you, Sarah. Please, never doubt that, but the people I— They won't take this lying down. You're only safe with me or your family, until this blows over. I hope you'll choose me, but that's not likely. I know that."

"These people would hurt *me*, because *you* quit?"

Jonas nodded.

"Can't you go to the police?"

"This is bigger than that. There are a lot of very important people involved in this." He closed his eyes. "Very important talent, I mean."

"Then call—" She swallowed a sour lump. *What a bit of irony this is!* She couldn't even say it. Sarah never thought she'd tell someone to go to *them* for help.

"DoPT?"

Sarah laughed weakly. "Stupid, huh? If you only knew—
"

He shook his head. "Oh, I know. I know better than you can imagine."

"Jonas, I'm getting really confused." If he wasn't a renegade, how would he know about the DoPT? Was he a refugee from the academy witch-hunts?

"I can't call the DoPT, because they *are* the DoPT."

Sarah wanted to say something, to ask something, but she couldn't seem to breathe. She couldn't think.

Jonas pulled a leather billfold from his pocket and flipped it open to reveal a badge and ID. Sarah locked on the DoPT insignia in disbelief, shaking her head in mute denial of what he was telling her.

"I was DoPT, Sarah. I quit. I can't—"

"I was just a job?"

"No. I would never—"

"Why are you here, Jonas? Why Pittsburgh?"

He hesitated. She could feel his guilt and misery.

The same reaction he had in the beginning every time we —

"Sarah, hear me out, please."

"They ordered you here, didn't they?"

He nodded. "Let me—"

"Did they order you to *fuck* me, too?"

Jonas paled. For a long moment, they simply stared at each other. "It wasn't like that, not for me."

Sarah stood and wandered across the room with her arms crossed under her breasts and her stomach twisting. "They did order it. Didn't they, Jonas?"

"Yes, but it was never about that. Not for me. If I hadn't, they were going to send someone who wouldn't give a damn and—" He stopped, burying his head in his hands. "I always cared. I wanted to find a way to keep you safe. Please believe me."

"Why? Why me? I'm no weapon."

"Your family is. I need to talk to them, Sarah. I need to explain what's going on, before this hits the fan."

She fought the urge to throw up. He'd used her to get to her family? As always, Sarah was the weak link.

"No. I'll explain it."

How can I explain this? It would take all of them, including Mac, to keep Steven from renegading this time.

Is that their plan? Make Steven an outlaw, so the rest of us will have to work a deal?

"Sarah, I need to—"

Sarah faced him, her fists on her hips and fighting back tears. "Why? So you can prove to them how reckless and stupid I've been? Don't you think I have enough proof of that already? Leave, Jonas. I'll handle my family my own way."

Jonas stood. He shook his head and edged toward her. "Please let me do this. It's my fault. Let me—" He reached out to touch her cheek.

Sarah felt the last of her patience fade away. She punched him in the solar plexus and was out the door before he dropped.

She sprinted up Arlington to Eighteenth then slowed to a walk, tears streaming down her face and her knees shaking. Sarah was glad it was already dark, though she hadn't grabbed her coat, and she'd be shivering by the time she reached her parents' place with only the light knit sweater to protect her against the chill wind on the hilltop.

She stuck to the shadows, hoping that Jonas wouldn't follow her. Still, she didn't start running again, even when she thought her legs could handle it. Sarah was in no hurry to explain to Steven that she fell for a DoPT operative and managed to get pregnant to him.

She stopped, her mind working at top speed. "Oh, no." Was that their plan? Was there a way to arrange it so the condoms would fail?

Sarah started walking again, much faster than before. She needed to talk to Mom and Dad. Mom would be calmer than Steven would, and Dad would have the technical knowledge she needed. She'd handle Steven later.

A man waiting at one of the PAT bus stops along Arlington smiled as she approached. "You have the time?" he asked.

Sarah shook her head. "Sorry. No wa—"

The spray hit her in the face, and Sarah sucked in her breath in shock at the icy sensation. The man caught Sarah, as her legs crumpled under her.

Her entire body tingled then went ice cold and leaden. She couldn't feel. She couldn't speak. She couldn't move. Panic settled in, and Sarah reached automatically for Steven. Her mind was trapped in the same shackles that had her body. She could think, but all conscious action had been shut down.

She watched helplessly as the man passed her into a dark panel van and closed the door behind them. There was a small lamp on, and Sarah could make out three faces hovering over hers.

The first man nudged one of the other two inside the van. "Move it before she contacts the others."

"Relax. We have five minutes until the stun-spray wears off. More than enough time." He raised a syringe and forced the air out of it.

The third man was huddled over her arm, probably preparing an injection site. Anything that worked that quickly was probably going into a vein and not a muscle.

Sarah wanted to scream. Failing that, she wanted to close her eyes, but she couldn't manage that, either. She watched as the second man leaned over her, knowing he was giving her the injection but blissfully unable to feel it.

The third man nodded, and something glinted in the lamplight but was gone before she could identify it. "Got the ring. I'll hand it off. Glad I'm not the one telling him."

An image of Steven going renegade when someone handed him her ring made her want to cry. If Sarah was crying, she couldn't feel it. She didn't think she was. Her vision wasn't blurred, as she would expect it would be.

"No shit," the first man agreed. "If there's any talent I want to face less than her family, it's Paige."

Jonas? Would Jonas renegade when they told him? They certainly seemed to think that telling him wasn't something they wanted saddled with. *Why didn't I listen to him? He wanted me to stay put and listen to him.* All she could come up with was that it had made sense at the time.

The third man reappeared, hovering over her and reaching a hand out toward her face or neck. Sarah couldn't feel his touch and she couldn't move her eyes to track the movement.

He pulled her eyelid further up. He seemed jumpy, worried. "This stuff won't hurt her, right? I mean, we hurt her, and Paige—"

"Stow it," the second man ordered. "We wouldn't do anything to hurt this lovely lady. She and that baby of hers are gonna keep Daddy in line. As long as they're healthy, Paige is gonna do exactly what we want him to do. That sucker's actually in *love* with her."

Sarah's vision blurred, but she didn't think it was with tears. Everything seemed disjointed, hazy. She managed a strangled groan as her eyes fluttered shut.

* * * *

Jonas sprinted to the street, still gasping for breath. There was no sign of Sarah, but he hadn't expected that there would be. Sarah had four minutes lead-time on him, and she ran the dash in high school.

He slid into his car and started up Arlington. She'd take the shortest route to her family. He cruised along, searching for her in every dark corner, until he reached the top of Sterling city steps. Jonas parked and sprinted down to

Primrose and across to the Randall house. He pounded on the door, his breath coming in sharp gasps.

Alex opened the door. His blue eyes narrowed in suspicion. "What are you doing?"

"I need to talk to your parents."

Katie's voice came from the other side of the living room, sounding calm. "Let him in, Alex."

Jonas bolted past him to where Katie sat curled under Keith's arm. Jonas looked at their confusion in growing unease. They should be upset, angry. "Where's Sarah? She's here, right?"

"No. Should she be?" Keith asked.

Jonas found forming a response nearly impossible. She should be. He couldn't have passed her. Her parting words filtered through his mind. Sarah ran from him, but she couldn't have ignored what he said and run blindly. "Where else would she go? Where would she feel safe?"

Steven stepped out of the dining room, looking murderous. "Why would she need to feel safe, Jonas? What have you done?"

"Later. This is important."

The younger man's face darkened in anger. "I knew whatever was upsetting her came back to you, but she denied it."

"You talked to her? When? Can you reach her now?"

"A couple of hours ago. No. I can't touch her when she's shielded."

Jonas shook his head. It wasn't him she was upset about two hours ago. He was wasting time. "Steven, where would she go?" he demanded.

"She only felt safe with us or you. You know that."

"Then she's running blind. We have to find her."

"Why?"

"Because the DoPT is going to crush her, if we don't."

The room was still and silent for several heartbeats.

Steven paled, and the fight seemed to go out of him. "Why, Jonas?" His voice shook, and his hand rubbed at the phantom restraints.

Jonas shook his head, tucking his hands in his back pockets. "I quit my job for her. I told them—" He sighed. "I told them to stuff my contract."

"You're DoPT?" Katie whispered.

Jonas didn't meet her eyes; he couldn't look her in the face after what he'd done. "I was."

Steven took two unsteady steps toward him. "What's your designation, operative?"

Jonas felt his face heat. "Alpha-One." He scowled as he said it, a foul taste flooding his mouth. "You see, they won't be very happy to lose me. If she walks away from me, I can— No. I *can't* deal with that, and I can't let them hurt her by walking away. But, I can't do what I'm ordered anymore, so I quit."

Steven launched at him. Jonas saw it coming and let him land the blow. It was the least he deserved for this.

"Can't you see what you've done?" Steven raged.

Jonas nodded, wiping the blood from his split lip on the back of his hand. "Help me find her. Once Sarah's safe, if she wants, I'll—" He rubbed his hand over his own set of phantom bands. His ribs seemed constricted, and he fought to take a deep breath. "Let's just find her."

Steven nodded and grabbed the coat Alex threw to him. Keith and Katie's coats were in his hand and ready to be tossed to them when a soft knock came at the door. Alex stopped in his tracks and turned toward it.

Jonas held his breath. Maybe he'd beaten her here. Maybe she took Eleanor or Eighteenth instead of Sterling. Maybe she sat down somewhere to cry or collect her thoughts. She could knock. If Sarah hadn't grabbed her keys, she might have to knock.

Alex pulled the door open then looked back at Jonas in confusion. Over his shoulder, Jonas could see Evan.

Jonas felt his knees start shaking. He knelt heavily and leaned on the coffee table, pressing the heel of his hand against his ribs and gasping for breath. Keith made a move as if to help him, but Evan was there first.

"Calm down, Paige. You're the only shot she's got. Don't make me stun-spray you to stop you."

Jonas nodded and forced a single decent breath in. He forced a second...then a third. "Baker, Bryant or Childress?" he panted out.

"Couple of Bryant's boys, herded by one of Baker's goons. Those idiots went unshielded against me." Evan cracked a half smile.

Jonas managed a weak laugh that ended on a sob. He tried unsuccessfully to bite it back. "Where is she?"

"En route to Clinton." He checked his watch. "By the time we reach county, they'll be in the air."

Jonas nodded and started to push to his feet, but Evan dragged him down.

He shook his head. "They're not screwing around, Paige."

Jonas threw his grip off. "Neither. Am I."

Evan pulled a small wooden pen box out of his coat pocket with shaking hands. He dragged Jonas's hand up and closed his fist around it. Then he backed off, pushing to his feet, making sure he was well out of reach.

Jonas stared at him. For a moment, words escaped him. Then they exploded into the stillness of the room. "What the hell is *this*, Markham?"

"A message. A warning. You know our assignment. I have the brief in the recorder. Came in just before I got here. You decide. You know what they're capable of."

"She has no offensive—"

"Can she prove that?"

Jonas winced. Proving you *didn't* have talents wasn't nearly as easy as proving you did.

"Open the box, Jonas. For the love of God, open the box." Evan was pale and jittery.

He thumbed open the little brass catch and forced himself to breathe. Her ring was inside, set on a thick band cut from her sweater. Jonas fingered the fabric then pulled it back in confusion.

His breathing became strangled again, and he fought back tears. *Sarah is pregnant? She needed to talk to me. Steven said she was upset; I knew she was upset. She wanted to tell me something, but I announced I had something to tell her. If I'd have let her talk—*

Jonas fisted the case in his hand, pressing it to his chest. He forced himself not to rock back and forth. He forced his lungs to work. He needed to think.

* * * *

Steven watched the play of emotions on Jonas's face. He couldn't see what was in the box, but whatever it was affected the DoPT operative deeply. The initial sadness dissolved into shock. Jonas closed the box and pressed it to his chest. A tear escaped down his cheek.

Steven cleared his throat. "What is it?"

Neither Jonas nor Markham answered him. Jonas didn't seem to realize that he had spoken. Markham looked at Jonas nervously, as if waiting for him to snap.

"How?" Jonas rasped out. "Tell me how, Evan."

The older man took a deep breath. "Let's call it sabotage and leave it at that. You know how they —"

"They set me up? They did this to keep me on the rolls?"

Markham shrugged and reached his hands behind him. "They needed something you cared about."

Jonas launched at him, bellowing out a scream of rage. Markham pulled a small spray can from behind his back and unloaded it in Jonas's face. He tossed the can away and caught Jonas smoothly as the larger man crumpled. Markham lowered him to the floor with a sigh.

"I'm not your enemy, Jonas, and I'm not your keeper anymore. You know who the enemy is, but to get to him, you have to play his game." He checked Jonas's pulse and glanced at his watch. "Four minutes fifty. I know what this is like for you."

Keith shook his head. "What did you do to him?"

"Stun-spray." Markham swore fluently and turned to Katie. "Mrs. Randall, I can't— I know you don't owe him anything, but you can do class seven controls, and I can't. Could you force his breathing for him?"

Her eyes widened. "I thought stun-spray was benign."

"It is. He...has a phobia."

"And you sprayed him?"

"It was that or the pistol. He'll recover from stun-spray a lot quicker than a bullet. He's not wearing Kevlar silk tonight."

Katie knelt at his head and started working on Jonas. "What phobia?"

Evan darkened and flicked a glance at Steven. "Restraints."

Steven rubbed his chest at the memory. He looked at Jonas, remembering his reactions when he saw Evan and when he tried to say he'd walk away from Sarah if she asked.

"He was in those damned training academies?" he demanded of Markham.

He nodded. "Six years. They offered him the chance to be emancipated at sixteen, if he signed his contract. Who wouldn't, in his place? A keeper instead of iso? For Jonas, it was the best offer he had."

Steven did some quick mental math. "He was already hunting when—"

"Yeah. Remember the cell of terrorists in Fort Lauderdale the day before the Supreme Court decision was announced?"

Steven nodded. "A single DoPT agent," he quoted. "Jonas? *Jonas* killed fourteen terrorists?"

"Thirteen, all with three-thousand-series shields, and a renegade. The other renegade shot him in the chest. Jonas was wearing Kevlar silk, but it was a cop-killer bullet. He was seventeen."

Steven rubbed his ribs with a grimace. "Why didn't he get out of his contract after the ruling?"

"He was a scared kid. His family turned him over at ten. He had no home to go to. He was an emancipated seventeen year old with nowhere to go, no prospects and an associate's degree from Clinton, in a society that *hated* talents. You figure it out."

"So, he stayed in."

Markham scooped the box up and threw it to him. "Fourteen years ago, Jonas had nothing to get out for. He was safer in than out. Now he does have something, if your sister gives him the chance to make this right."

Steven looked at the box in confusion.

Markham sighed. "Jonas loves her. He's *always* loved her. Take a look. Look inside and see what he's lost. See what the stakes are."

Steven opened the lid. He pulled out the ring and put it on his pinky finger. It was the ring he'd bought Sarah on their thirteenth birthday, a simulated emerald in a silver band. She'd worn it for half of her life. Steven had never seen Sarah without it, from the day he gave it to her...until now.

He moved the peach knitted band aside. That was no doubt a piece of her favorite peach sweater. Beneath it lay the test strip.

That was what set Jonas off.

"Shit. Oh hell," he whispered. Steven stumbled back until he collapsed in a chair.

"What is it?" his mother asked, calm in her concentration.

Steven looked to Markham for confirmation.

The older man nodded and answered for him. "She's pregnant. She found out this afternoon."

Keith groaned. "Sarah wouldn't—"

Markham rubbed his neck. "Do you need to know the technical side, Dr. Randall?"

"Yes. I think I do."

Markham flipped a red packet to him; his father examined it, his brow furrowed.

Keith shrugged. "So? It's a Trojan twenty-twenty. They're the best on the market, nearly foolproof. If Sarah and Jonas were using these, there should have been no problem."

"Unless they're tampered with. Put some water in it."

"What will I see?"

"Tiny droplets outside the reservoir tip. Not much, but if you spend more than a minute or two inside after climax, it's enough. They weakened the Plastilyte with citric acid and replaced the spermicide with Hypoglide thirty. I imagine they did years of testing, finding the perfect balance to make them useless without making it obvious that they were useless."

Keith's face paled. "Hypoglide? But that—"

Markham grimaced. "Yeah. They educated me in its clinical uses."

Steven shook his head. "Let me in on it."

His father nodded. "Hypoglide thirty is used in fertility clinics to supercharge sperm and keep it alive long enough to find an egg. It helps men with a low sperm count or poor motility manage natural pregnancy. If they fixed these to let a few sperm out, the Hypoglide would keep them alive and moving long enough to do the job."

Jonas made a sound halfway between a groan and a whimper.

Markham checked his watch. "Two minutes, Jonas. Hang on for me."

"Why do this? If he loved her anyway, why arrange *this*?" Steven asked.

Markham squatted next to Jonas and checked his pulse, nodding his thanks to Katie. "Two reasons. The psych guys decided that a baby would give them forty-five percent more control over Jonas than Sarah alone."

Keith ground his teeth in fury. "They said *what*?"

"Oh, yeah. You'll love these guys, Dr. Randall. They said there was an eighty percent chance that Sarah wouldn't abort before they nabbed her. They said there was a sixty percent higher probability that they would fall for each other if Jonas had to save her life, without any forewarning that it was coming, of course. Wanna know how they arranged that little treat?"

Steven's stomach lurched. "The renegade."

"What renegade?" Alex demanded.

Steven jumped. He had almost forgotten Alex was in the room. "The—the mugger. Oh hell. That was their doing?"

Markham nodded. "Oh, yeah. Once Jonas cleaned the blood off his hands, he almost went and replenished it with Baker's."

Keith shook his head at Steven. "The mugger was a renegade, and Jonas killed him. You knew all of this and decided not to share?"

Steven felt his face darken and looked away. Seeking safer ground, he changed the subject. "What was the other reason for the baby?"

"Take a guess. Jonas is Alpha-One, and Sarah is a Randall. You do the genetic number crunch on that one and see what it looks like to you."

"Bastards."

Steven startled at the sound of it coming from Katie's mouth. He nodded in agreement. "What's Jonas supposed to do?"

Markham cleared his throat. "Get you and your mother. Get as many of you as we can to help him take down a powerful renegade. We know Kyle will pass. Beyond that—"

Steven's head spun. "If it's a renegade, what's the problem? What are you so nervous about?"

"I don't think he's a renegade."

Alex spoke up again. "What is he?"

"A former operative who found out something he shouldn't have."

"I'm out. I can't do this."

Steven snapped a look of disbelief at him. "Alex, this is Sarah we're talking about. We don't have to kill this guy, right?"

"I won't turn an innocent man over to them."

Evan cracked a smile. "You're off the hook, Alex. The psych guys said you're the least suited to this, anyway. We weren't seriously looking to take you with us."

Alex sighed in relief. "You still can't hand an innocent man over to them."

"Jonas will work out the details. They're not going to let Sarah go, either way. She's the key to Jonas and to all of you. Our only chance is playing their game long enough to get to her."

* * * *

Jonas watched the briefing. Actually, he spent most of the time staring at his hands and listening to the sound of Baker's voice, promising Sarah justice under his breath.

The pertinent facts filtered in.

Griffin was a dead or alive assignment. Jonas wondered what Griffin knew to rate that.

They were headed for Virginia Beach. That wasn't a surprise. Griffin had worked renegade con there before he was convinced to sign his contract.

Evan turned off the player.

Jonas looked at him in confusion. "That wasn't the end. The marker didn't flash. Why did you turn it off, Evan?"

He blushed. Evan never blushed.

"It was private... For your eyes only. Baker's way of rubbing it in and reminding you what the stakes are."

"You watched it?"

"I had to know what I'm dealing with, if you decide to watch it."

His heart stuttered. "*If?*"

Evan looked ill. "Christ, Jonas. I wouldn't suggest it. Take it as read, in my opinion."

"Afraid you'll have to stun-spray me again?"

"Yeah. Actually...I am."

Jonas rubbed his temple, wincing at the dull ache settled in there. "I have to do this."

Steven leaned toward the player to switch it back on.

Evan seized his wrist. "No way. You're not seeing this one."

"She's my sister."

"Which is exactly why you're not watching it."

Katie rose and pulled her son up with her. She motioned to Keith to follow them. "I get the feeling that this one is too personal. Let's go."

Steven shook his head, and a flurry of telepathic messages flew back and forth between mother and son. He nodded to Evan, speaking through gritted teeth. "You get your way this time. Don't expect it every time."

Katie placed a hand on Jonas's shoulder on their way to the stairs. "You don't have to do this, Jonas."

"I do. Believe me, I do. I have to know his game."

She kissed his forehead, then nodded before she left. Jonas touched the spot in surprise. His own mother had never treated him like that, at least not that he could remember. They were upstairs before Evan reached for the play button.

"Last chance to back out, Jonas. Nothing will be the same after this."

"Show me."

Evan pressed the play button and turned his back on the screen with a pained look.

Baker's face appeared, gloating already. "Well Paige, it seems you've done your job perfectly." He steepled his fingers in front of his face. "According to section ten, subsection bravo of your contract, I'm afraid I'll have to insist that you complete your current assignment before discharge. At any time during that assignment, you may choose to withdraw your resignation with full reinstatement."

Jonas gnashed his teeth. "Dream on."

"I thought I'd leave you with some memories of this assignment. I hope you'll enjoy them as much as I have."

Jonas felt the bile rising in his throat.

Evan asked his question hurriedly. "Are you sure? You don't have to—"

"I have to know," Jonas snapped at him.

A montage of images assaulted his mind. Sarah was pressed to her door the first time he kissed her. Snips he recognized from the first time they made love, Sarah against the wall in her kitchen, in her shower, on the cushions in her living room, months of sexual encounters flipped by, making him dizzy.

"That bastard watched us. Every time, he had us taped."

Switch. Sarah stared into his face, her hands on his shoulders while Jonas was poised over her. "I love you, Jonas."

Switch. Sarah sat in her living room with Steven, Jonas's shirt clearly visible in the open neckline of her robe. "It's my life, Steven. I need this, maybe forever. Please don't mess this up for me."

"Oh, Sarah." A lump formed in his throat, and Jonas swallowed, trying to dislodge it.

Switch. Jonas brushed her hair back from her face. "I love you, Sarah. I'll always love you."

Switch. Sarah flopped on the couch, dropping her chin to her chest as she reached for something on the coffee table. Her hand shook. She sobbed, dropping the test back on the table and curling into a ball on the couch.

"Oh, Christ. What do I do now?" She paled and put her head in her hands, groaning. "He won't even believe it's his."

"I would have. Why didn't I let you tell me?" Tears pricked at his eyes, and he blinked them away.

Switch. Sarah rushed up Arlington Avenue.

A man stepped into her path, smiling. "You have the time?"

Sarah shook her head and ducked around him, mumbling the beginnings of an answer.

Jonas's gaze locked on the can of stun-spray. He gripped the arms of the chair hard.

The spray hit her full in the face, and she recoiled.

"No." He shook his head. "No. Not that."

Sarah crumpled into the man's arms, and he smiled in his victory. As he swung her to his chest, his face was outlined in the light. It was Pendle. He passed her into a panel van.

Baker filled the screen. "That's quite a woman, Paige. You got close. You got as close as I hoped you would. Getting close means someone can be used against you."

He moved, and the camera followed him, pulling back to reveal Sarah, unconscious on a stretcher. Baker touched her cheek, and Jonas fought the tightness in his chest.

"Don't worry. It's just something to help her sleep. It won't hurt her." Baker caressed her stomach. "It won't hurt the baby, either. You've naively given me everything I ever wanted, Paige."

Evan tackled him, as Jonas launched out of his seat with a scream of pure fury. "No. Don't destroy it," he shouted over him.

On the screen, Baker looked at Sarah and laughed. "Your girlfriend and baby are waiting for you, Paige. Make the right choice for them."

Jonas fisted his hands. The only right choice was getting her out of Baker's hands. Killing that bastard would be icing on the cake.

CHAPTER SIX

May 11th

Sarah felt the spike of pain in her head first, followed by the swirl of morning sickness. She swallowed the sour wave and tried to shift position but found she couldn't move. She snapped her eyes open in a panic and pulled against the web bands holding her nearly immobile.

She reached out to Steven, desperate to touch his mind. Sarah couldn't feel him or hear him. Even when his shield was fully up, she typically had a sense of his presence, no matter how far away he was.

She had nothing. She couldn't find anything...anyone, no emotions. Sarah was always surrounded by emotions. Even shielding didn't completely block them out.

She screamed, the sound echoing off the plain white walls and ceiling. Tears ran down her face, as she fought the bands holding her to the lightly padded surface beneath her. Where was she? How were they doing this to her?

They let her struggle for several minutes before a voice interrupted her. "Calm down."

She tried to find the man whose voice she'd heard, but she couldn't feel anyone or see anyone. She panted, examining the smooth walls. Was he on a speaker?

"That's better."

It was definitely a speaker. The voice came from above her and to the back right. Tracking that voice gave her some measure of purpose to calm her mind. Sarah sniffed back her tears. There were people. She simply couldn't feel them, for some reason.

"The silent treatment?" the man asked, trying to prompt some response from her.

Sarah fought to keep her hands from shaking. "What is there to say? You're not going to open the door and let me go home."

His laughter wafted back to her, ethereal in the misty white around her. Was the lack of sensation making her other senses play tricks on her, or was she still drugged? She couldn't seem to tell which.

"Not the outside door. No. We need to understand each other, Sarah. You know how the academy runs. Unless you force us to, we won't hurt you. You don't like being restrained in the iso chamber, do you?"

"No." That was it. She couldn't feel anyone because she was trapped inside the psi wave. She calmed her heart rate. All she had to do was get outside the isolation chamber, and she'd be able to talk to Steven.

"If you promise not to cause any trouble, we'll take the restraints off. Will you work with us?"

Sarah bit her lip. They thought she had offensive talents? Would it be better to admit that she didn't and put them at ease or let them fear what she was so they'd keep their distance?

"Sarah, I'm not like other headmasters. I will have your word, and I will hold you to that word. That's the way things run at Clinton. Do I have your word that you won't cause trouble if the restraints come off?"

"Yes. You have my word. I won't cause any trouble." *Let them worry.*

The voice didn't respond.

Sarah forced herself to take slow, even breaths. Her heart started pounding again. "Hello?" she called. "Hey, did you hear me? I said you had my word."

No answer.

She bit back a sob. *They're playing with me.*

She started humming a tune to help her keep track of the time. That would only work for the first few songs, but it might be enough.

It was five minutes before she heard the click of metal and felt a rush of fresh air. Two men moved into her field of vision, watching her warily. Sarah swallowed a laugh when the first one turned his head. A silver disk was settled behind his ear. They were wearing industrial E-shields against her. One man removed her restraints, while the other kept a can of the spray pointed at her.

Sarah rolled off of the padded table. She was stiff and shaky when she made it to her feet. The first man reached out to steady her.

She jerked away from his outstretched hand, flattening herself against the wall. "Don't. Don't touch me."

He put a hand up to keep his counterpart from using more of that spray on her.

Her mind whirled. Was it stun-spray they'd used on her? She vaguely remembered one of them saying it was. It would make sense. Sarah could appreciate why no one wanted to experience it twice.

The man took a slow, deep breath as if in relief. "There's a restroom in there. You can clean up and use the toilet. There are clothes for you to change into."

Sarah nodded and fled to the small room, closing the lockless door behind her. She tried to reach Steven again, but the psi wave extended here. She shut her eyes, fighting back her panic. They wouldn't give her much time in here. Sarah completed her bathroom routine as best as she could. There was no shower, but there was soap at the sink. There was also a toothbrush, toothpaste and a brush. She stopped short of changing into the Clinton coveralls.

The guard who'd tried to touch her raised an eyebrow as she came out. "You didn't change."

"Nor do I intend to. I don't belong here. I didn't do anything wrong, and I didn't ask to come here. I'm not required to wear that rag."

He nodded. "Okay. I won't force you to wear it." He motioned to an air mattress and a tray of food that had been placed on the floor while she was in the restroom. The table was gone. "Make yourself comfortable, Sarah."

She felt her mouth go dry. Sarah shook her head in disbelief; she inched toward the outer door. She couldn't stay in here. She didn't want to stay in here. "I can't— He promised."

No. He promised to let me out of the restraints, not out of iso.

Desperation sank in. "I promised. I haven't hurt anyone. I *won't* hurt anyone." Sarah stopped herself from admitting that she couldn't hurt anyone.

The other guard blocked her way. "We can't let you out of here yet. You know the rules. It's a minimum of two days for incoming prisoners."

"I'm not a danger," she pleaded. *I'm not a prisoner, but they won't believe that.* "Please..." Her breathing hitched. "You have my word. He said they'd take my word for it, the headmaster."

The first guard tried to take her arm, but Sarah dodged away from him toward the restroom.

He shook his head sadly. "In a day or two. You have my word on that. Behave, and they won't extend your time in here." His voice was pleading with her for understanding.

She slid to the floor in the corner, willing herself not to cry. They may see it on the camera, but they wouldn't see it in person. Sarah wouldn't give them the satisfaction. It was all she had left.

They left without any further comment, and she curled her bare feet under her and let the tears fall. She shook with the force of her sobs.

When she was cried out, Sarah staggered to the air mattress with its beige paper blanket. She laughed harshly. They'd left her with no belt, no shoestrings, and no linens she could use to harm or defend herself. The blanket would keep her warm, but was useless as a noose or garrote. Steven had told her about these blankets.

Sarah crawled onto the bed, sinking into the soft, velvety top. She looked at the food, but her stomach rebelled at the thought of actually eating it. There was no glass or stoneware and no silverware, not even plastic silverware. There were plastic cups of milk and juice, a sandwich, chips and sliced fruit.

She closed her eyes and rolled away, wrapping the blanket around her.

Is it lunchtime? It seemed like a lunch-style meal.

She had no way of knowing for sure. She had no real concept of day or night. Sarah hadn't been wearing a watch, but even if she had, it would be gone. Her ring and bracelet were gone.

Sarah considered her position. They were required by law to provide her with three meals a day. She'd use that as her clock. It was noon. When dinner came, it would be six.

Breakfast would be eight. It wasn't much, but it would keep her sane.

* * * *

Sarah kept her eyes closed, though she knew the door had opened. She recognized the guard's voice, the one who was pleading for her understanding.

"You have to eat, Sarah. Think of your baby."

"Why? So you can use us against Jonas or so you can take my baby from me? Where's the up side for my baby or for me?"

"It's not like that. They wouldn't—"

She snorted. "Sure, like they wouldn't kidnap me off a city street with stun-spray, when I haven't done anything wrong."

"The file says—"

"Shove it."

"Who's Jonas?"

"Like you don't know."

"I don't."

"You will," she promised.

She didn't know what to believe, but Sarah was much more inclined to believe Jonas since the conversation in that dark van. Those men seemed honestly frightened of Jonas, and they were using her against him. Sarah couldn't read them while she was stun-sprayed, but she was inclined to believe that they weren't acting. Fear isn't an easy emotion to fake that realistically.

The guard's hand closed on her shoulder, a gentle pressure that might be seen as support. Sarah tensed, but she didn't give in to the urge to hit him. Physical assault would extend her time in iso. Steven had tried it often enough to know.

"Is Jonas the baby's father?"

Sarah closed her eyes and turned further away, wrenching her shoulder out of his hand. She wasn't playing whatever game he was. The time for games had ended. This was war.

He sighed. "Sarah, please eat. If you don't, they'll force it down you. They'll restrain you again and use IVs if they have to."

When she didn't answer, he left the room quietly. Sarah pulled the blanket over her head, cutting out the smell of roast chicken.

* * * *

May 12th

The guard didn't ask her to eat the next morning. He stared at the tray for a long moment before taking it away. Of course, they would have seen the disastrous results of her attempt to stomach the milk and juice on the cameras. They weren't supposed to have cameras in the restrooms, but they could probably hear her vomiting in the main room with the door slightly ajar as it was.

Except for using the restroom, Sarah hadn't left the bed since she'd crawled in it. What was there to do?

She kept the mantra alive in her head. *Lunchtime tomorrow is two days since I woke. If I don't attack anyone, I'll be free then.*

She tried not to dwell on the comment the other guard made.

At least two days...

No. They can't keep me here longer than that. I haven't done anything wrong.

When the guard left, she looked at the tray and groaned. Her mouth watered. It seemed that someone was stacking the deck. This meal wasn't caf fare like the others. Her favorites were laid out before her, tempting Sarah and teasing her starved senses. That was all she had in here between her guard's visits, the sound of her own voice and the smell of food, soap and sweat.

Breakfast was Belgian waffles, precut for her, with maple and walnuts, sausage, peaches and cream, and hot chocolate. It was a mountain of food.

As if making her decision for her, her stomach voiced its complaint.

Sarah ate slowly, savoring every bite.

At least they feed their abductees.

She only ate half of the huge meal before her stomach gave her a warning that she was overdoing it and risking a repeat of the previous night. Sarah put down her plastic spork with a sigh of regret.

She headed to the restroom. Sarah looked at the coverall and winced. Her sweater was ripped, and her clothing smelled foul. She'd been in them for two nights and more than a day.

No. I may have to concede defeat when it comes to eating, but what I wear is another subject altogether.

Sarah brushed her teeth and hair, scowling at how greasy her hair was. She could wash her face and hands. She could wash her arms and chest if she didn't mind getting her jeans soaked in the process, but with only a small tea towel, there was little else she could manage unless she got really desperate and inventive.

She screwed up her face at her reflection and returned to the bed. Sarah stared at the ceiling until her eyes started playing tricks on her. Startling bursts of color danced on the surface of the white backdrop. She fell asleep to the hypnotic sight.

* * * *

Lunch was an egg salad sandwich, carrot sticks with Green Goddess dressing as a dip, cheese cubes, milk, apple juice and cherry pie ala mode. She managed to eat most of it.

When the guard came in with her dinner, he spoke the first words he had all day. "Considering changing your clothes yet?"

"Not seriously. I can't even shower in here. What's the point in changing clothes?"

"Your choice. I won't force you." It was too nonchalant, an almost practiced disinterest.

"Something I don't know?"

"Something you do know." He shrugged as he collected up her lunch plates. "Everyone wears the coveralls here."

Sarah shook her head. "Students and inmates wear the coveralls. I'm neither. I'm a prisoner of war."

"You sure eat better than a prisoner." He nodded toward the fried shrimp, calamari, stuffed mushrooms, steamed vegetables, garlic mashed potatoes and raspberry cobbler on her plate with a grimace.

"Only because your bosses know what Jonas will do if I'm not well cared for."

"Who is Jonas?"

She considered her answer for little more than a second. "Pray you don't ever find out."

Sarah wasn't released at lunchtime the next day. Her guard made it clear that she wouldn't be...until she wore the Clinton coveralls. Sarah steeled her nerves, believing nothing could change her mind. She could survive iso. She'd done it for more than two days. She could do it as long as she needed to.

* * * *

May 13th

Katie rubbed her forehead. Her entire body ached. She hadn't realized how draining the constant use of talent was. Even fighting Ty hadn't been this intense.

Jonas does this on a regular basis? She shook her head. *No wonder Evan looks like an old man at forty-one.*

"No, Keith. No news yet," she grumbled into the phone.

"It's been three days. Steven's never been out of contact with Sarah this long."

"I know."

"How is he?"

"Bad. He needs her. Knowing she's at Clinton makes it all the worse. You know how he feels about the academies." Katie sighed. "How's it going on the home front?"

"Dad got Steven a leave of absence."

"Good. How'd he manage that?"

"Family emergency." She could almost picture Keith's shrug. "Dad's a senior partner."

"He didn't tell them anything, did he?"

"No. He jokingly said he'd promise them another big talents' rights case without giving them details to buy Steven more time...if we need it."

Katie sighed. "I hope we'll have her back before then."

"I—" Keith groaned into the phone.

"What is it?"

"Mac and the guys."

"Oh, hell. How bad is it?"

Mac's voice came on the line. "You tell me, Katie. What is going on that Keith won't tell us? Where have you and Steven gone?"

"I can't tell you that, Mac."

"Katie—"

"There's too much riding on this. If we screw up—"

"Who? Tell me who has Sarah, and we'll end this."

"It's not that simple. I wish it was."

"You're a Randall, Katie. If they can pin you as a renegade—"

"It may already be too late for that, Mac." She ran her fingers over the DoPT badge in her back pocket that announced her as Alpha-Three. "Everything we're doing is in defense of our family, but that may not be enough to save us. I'll accept that, if Sarah is safe."

"Katie," he warned her.

"She's pregnant, Mac. They know it, and they made it clear that they'll exploit that or anything else they have to in order to get what they want."

"Christ. Where is Jonas? Does he know?"

"He's with us."

"Why?"

Katie rolled her forehead against the wall beside the phone. "He's talent, Mac. Sarah didn't tell us, because she didn't want us to worry about her."

"She wanted this?"

"She wants Jonas. She wants him enough that being talent ceased to matter to her."

"What can I do to help?"

"Keep the guys out of our way. If they investigate this one, they'll get hurt."

"By you or Jonas?"

"Neither. Leave it alone, Mac. If they don't hurt you, they might hurt Sarah as a warning."

"I don't like this, Katie."

"Neither do I, but we have to play their game."

For now.

"What assurances do we have that they won't hurt her?"

Katie grimaced. "They won't, unless we force their hand. She's a Randall, and she's pregnant."

"They're afraid of you and Steven?"

"No. They want a Randall baby."

Mac sucked in his breath.

"We'll do our best, Mac. She's safe for seven or eight months, if you keep the guys out of this."

"Will do."

* * * *

May 15th

It was two more days before Sarah broke down and put on the coverall. The lack of stimulation got to her. She could handle the absence of books and TV, but five days without conversation—worse, with no emotions touching her mind—pushed Sarah over the edge.

Her guard smiled as he led her from the iso tank to her room. Dinner was waiting, and the room had a full bath, but neither held appeal for her. Sarah curled on the bed and let the emotions wash over her. She shivered in the familiar input, dropping her shield to drink in as much sensation as she could bear.

Sarah started to cry.

* * * *

Steven stumbled, then stopped and sank to one of the benches along the boardwalk. She was there. After five days, Sarah was there.

He reached out to touch her unshielded mind. *"Sarah?"*

Steven felt the riot of emotions as they washed over her. She was crying so hard, she couldn't think. Sarah was happy, sad, lonely, sick... She was in hysterics.

He dropped his face into his hands and stifled a sob. *"God, Sarah. Please talk to me."*

"Steven? It's really you?" He could feel her disbelief.

"What did they do? Are you okay?" Who was he kidding? She wasn't okay.

Sarah started laughing hysterically, then she was crying again. *"Isolation. Please don't leave me, Steven. Please don't."*

"Iso?" He slid off the bench to the cement, rubbing the tight spot in his chest. *"Christ! Why?"*

She spent five days in iso? He had hoped she was drugged into unconsciousness. Steven remembered his own time in iso. He was a basket case after a few hours.

"They won, Steven. I have to play by their rules. I'm a prisoner. I can't go in there again."

He felt her guilt and exhaustion clearly. *Sarah feels guilty for caving after five days?*

"Five days, Sarah. I could never have lasted that long." He couldn't let her feel guilty for that. How could she survive five days?

"I wasn't in restraints, Steven. I still folded."

"You weren't?"

She hesitated, and he felt her fear, her panic. They'd used the restraints on Sarah. Nothing else would make her feel that terror.

He fisted his hand in his shirt and stared at the ocean through the tears gathering in his eyes. *"Sarah?"* If he knew for sure that they'd used restraints on her, there would be hell to pay when this was over.

"At first... They wanted to show me what would happen."

"You can't. They can't do this." How long was she in restraints? He wouldn't ask her that.

"They have a fake file, Steven. They don't believe me. They...wear E-shields. I don't know what they think I can do." She was desperate.

Evan was right. There was no way for her to prove she was telling the truth.

"Play along, Sarah. Leave the rest to us."

Her mind went dead still. *"No Steven. Don't do this for me. Don't let them use me against you."*

"We're doing only as much as we have to. You stay safe. Do whatever you have to do to stay out of iso." He hesitated. *"Take*

care of that baby." That was half of their hold. That was half of her protection. Without the baby, there were much worse things they could do to Sarah.

She started crying again, what he was sure were hard, wracking sobs. *"Does Jonas know?"*

"He's worried sick. Let me give him good news next time."

Sarah was fading, the exhaustion winning. Steven started to draw back, but Sarah's grip tightened on his mind like a vice. He stiffened in shock and fear combined.

When did she learn that trick? What is it? It was almost like a binding, but Sarah had no offensive talents.

"Please don't leave me, Steven."

"I won't leave you. I'll always be here." He brushed against her mind softly.

Sarah started to fade off again, her grip loosening as she gave in to her need for sleep.

"I'll never desert you, Sarah. I'll always be here."

Her mind was muddled. *"Tell Jonas I love him. Tell him... Sorry I hit him, Steven. Promise me."*

"I promise."

She sank into a troubled sleep. Steven stayed with her for almost an hour, stroking her mind in comfort whenever he felt her fear or upset.

When he finally pushed to his feet, walking to the hotel room was nearly impossible. He was stiff and sore. Worse, he found himself reaching to Sarah almost constantly, reassuring himself that they hadn't locked her away from him again. Steven pushed the door open and walked past the others without comment.

Evan checked his watch, then scowled at him. "Where the hell have you been? You should have checked in forty-five minutes ago."

Steven couldn't answer. He curled into one of the armchairs near the window with his knees as close to his chest as he could pull them. He stared at the barely-visible caps of waves, at a loss for words, his hand plucking at the front of his shirt where he had fisted it earlier.

The room was silent. No one moved. At last, his mother crossed the room to him and tried to touch his face, her mind brushing over his shield.

Steven grasped her wrist before she could connect with him. "Don't. Not now."

Katie nodded and took a step back. "Then tell me."

"Five days," he whispered.

"Steven, she'll contact you. When she can, she'll contact you."

"Those bastards kept her in the tank for *five days*."

Jonas paled. He punched the headboard beside him in frustration, then scrubbed his face with his hands. He didn't look at Steven. "How bad is she?"

Steven closed his eyes. "I told her to do whatever she has to do. She can't go back in. She's exhausted. She's terrified. She isn't even capable of being angry right now."

"Restraints?" he whispered. Jonas rubbed the bands that weren't there. "Steven, did they use the restraints?" he demanded.

He winced. "At first. You were right. There's a fake file somewhere. They think she's a prisoner, a renegade. The time in iso was the worst for her. She has to touch my mind. If they take that away from her again—"

Jonas groaned. Stephen opened his eyes to the sight of him curling to the bed.

"What did I do to her?" he whispered with what sounded like the beginnings of tears.

"She doesn't blame you."

"You can't know that. You said you can only read emotions from her at this distance, not thoughts."

"I didn't have to read it. Sarah wants me to pass a message to you. She loves you and she's sorry she hit you."

For a long moment, Jonas didn't reply. "Evan, I need you to make a call to Baker."

Evan nodded, as if Jonas had given him a full explanation. "It just might work."

Katie looked from one person to the next in confusion. "What are you going to do?"

Evan's smile was vicious. "Give Baker incentives to keep her happy. When I'm done with him, they won't dare put her in iso again."

* * * *

Jonas listened to the call, trying to find the humor in it he typically would. Evan played Baker well. Jonas closed his eyes and listened to Evan's side of it.

"Is the damn phone secure?" Evan barked.

"Well, it's your ass if it's not. So, I'd be sure if I were you.

"Lousy. You pull that shit with her, and you want to know how Paige is? Are you nuts or just plain stupid?

"What do *I* mean? Have you read the files? Sarah may be weaker than I am, but her family's not.

"Yeah, that's right. Unlimited range within their family, remember? That doesn't just mean the ones you can actively use. That means all of them. All of them can reach her, wherever you take her.

"Why don't you check with your monkeys at Clinton? You told them she was a renegade prisoner. You *idiot*. Five days in iso. What did you tell them? Did you tell them she murdered a dozen norms in cold blood? Five. *Days.* They were antsy enough when they couldn't reach her, thought she was drugged unconscious. You have three scattered talents now.

"How do you *think* she is after five days in the tank?" he bellowed. "Get this straight. You're screwing around with a shaky balance. Any time she's upset, your precious talent consortium will be useless. Now that they know what you've done to her, any time she's out of contact, they'll be useless. You want me to play keeper? I'm playing keeper to three neurotics, and you're making it worse. Do you want this to fail or what? Do you want psychotics...worse, psychopaths on the roam? That's what you're shooting for.

"Well, that would be a smart move." His voice went into deep sarcasm at that statement, as if Baker wasn't capable of finding a smart idea, if it bit him in the ass. "I'd suggest that everyone be damn careful with Sarah from here on out, if I were you.

"Yeah. You'll get your damn updates. Just muzzle those Clinton creeps, or there will be nothing happening to update you on."

Evan hung up the phone and sighed. "I hate that man."

Katie's voice bordered on exhaustion. "That makes— Oh, dozens at least."

"Hundreds. Thousands, maybe."

Jonas didn't bother to open his eyes. "Will it work?"

"For a little while," Evan speculated. "She's safe, until we get our hands on Griffin. After that, all the rules change."

"She better be. Otherwise, I can't promise anything. You know I'll renegade, if it comes to that."

"I know. I'm hoping to plan a real old-fashioned jailbreak, though."

"How? They'll have E-shields all around her."

"Yeah, but you have the real thing to train on. You've busted shields before."

"True mechanicals and weak biologicals. I've never breached a decent biological or a neuro-mechanical before."

Evan sat on the bed next to him. "We have time, and we have an edge."

"What edge?"

"Katie is a genius at dissecting the workings of any talent used. Steven can link outside his family, and you can neuro-model and crush shields. If it weren't for your mind, the E-shield would have been impossible to make. If you can make it, you can break it. By putting the three of you together, they made a *big* mistake. By the time we're done, you may all be crushing E-shields."

CHAPTER SEVEN

May 16th

Sarah wiped the sleep from her eyes as she wandered to the bathroom. She used the toilet, then moved to the shower, standing under the hot spray and washing off layer after layer of grime. The shampoo and soap weren't the type she'd typically use, but they were better than nothing. She pulled on a nightgown in the same Clinton navy blue and beige as the coveralls, brushed her teeth and curled back into bed.

A knock came at the door, and Sarah startled. *They're knocking, now?* She pulled the blanket up over her waist, a real blanket this time. "Come in."

She rolled her eyes at the sight of her usual guard. *So, he's my keeper?* Sarah could have laughed at that. If only he knew that he was probably more talented than she was, what a joke that would be.

He ignored her expression, though she had no doubts that he saw it. He placed a stack of clothes on the foot of the bed. "You're expected at breakfast. I'll be waiting outside, when you're ready. The cameras have been ordered turned off in your quarters, but the sound will be left on. You don't have to worry about getting dressed in this room. No one is watching." His features were tense, as if that speech was very hard for him to have to deliver.

Sarah stifled a smile. "What if I'm not hungry?"

He scowled at her. He was furious, and he wasn't shielding it well, though his face didn't show the depth of it.

She wondered why he'd stopped wearing the E-shield. Did he know she wasn't a threat? Had he been ordered to treat her like any other inmate and rely on his personal shield?

His voice was low and full of menace. "I don't give a damn if you're hungry or not. When the head of DoPT comes to see you, you see him."

Sarah swallowed a sour lump. "Andrew Baker is here?"

She had seen the oily, dark-haired man on the news for the last fifteen or so years. He was the original operative, the obvious choice for head of DoPT, when it became its own agency instead of a joint subdivision of the DoD and NSA. Word was that he had a shot at the presidency in ten or fifteen more years.

The guard's brow went up, and he offered a tense nod. "Who the hell are you, Sarah?"

Sarah shook her head, suddenly terrified.

His scowl demanded more of an answer than that.

"Sometimes it's not who you are but who you know."

"Jonas?"

She nodded.

"Who is Jonas?"

She shook her head.

The guard set his jaw and nodded, slamming the door behind him on the way out.

Sarah reached for the clothes with shaking hands. They were lacy and frilly, silk dresses, nothing like what she would choose to wear. These clothes weren't chosen to replace what was at her apartment. These were clothes chosen for Baker's enjoyment.

She pushed them away and headed for the closet, pulling out one of the Clinton coveralls obviously stocked for her in her size. Sarah didn't know what Baker's game was, but there were worse things than wearing the coverall.

* * * *

Andrew Baker stood as she entered the room; he motioned to a seat across the table from him. Sarah bit back a sarcastic response and took her seat.

There was a covered plate in front of her. She forced herself to remove the stainless steel lid and pick up her fork, the first real silverware Sarah had seen in six days. The plate was stoneware with the Clinton logo, and there were real glasses. They either believed that she wouldn't dare make a move against Baker or that he could stop her before she did.

At the moment, both are true.

Even though the thought of sharing a meal with him made her feel ill, Sarah refused to let Baker see it. She cut a corner of her omelet and started eating without acknowledging his presence.

Baker took his seat as she started chewing, obviously realizing that she wasn't going to offer any pleasantries. "Why are you wearing the coveralls? I sent clothes for you."

"I know many people admire you, Mr. Baker. I'm sure most of them do exactly what you want. I'm not going to *be* one of those people. If you want a woman to dress up in frilly smocks for you, get a girlfriend." She took another bite of her omelet and averted her gaze.

Baker had gone red in fury, a fury that had his shield flickering for a moment of tense silence. He cleared his throat and uncovered his own plate, feigning indifference. "You don't want to wear the academy coveralls, but you won't wear street clothes when I supply them. You confuse me."

Sarah coughed on a bit of egg that headed down the wrong pipe.

Street clothes? Who wears street clothes like those?

She didn't rise to the bait. Until she knew Baker's game, it wasn't a safe bet. "Why lock me up for five days to get your way, then change your mind? I don't play mind games, Mr. Baker."

"Drew... That wasn't my doing. I wasn't aware that there was a battle over your clothing or that you had been detained in the isolation tank."

Sarah raised an eyebrow at him. "Why don't you get to the point, Mr. Baker?"

His expression hardened. Calling him that after he'd asked her to call him Drew upset him. Did he want to play at being friends, or were those dresses a sign that he had other thoughts in mind? Sarah slammed her shield up fully, as Baker brushed over it.

He smiled. "It wasn't my doing. I assure you that things will be different now."

Sarah surveyed him for telltale signs that were not present. "How so?"

"What do you want?"

"Open the front door and let me leave."

Baker looked at her in shock.

"Thought so."

"Besides that."

"From you? Not a damn thing."

Baker sighed. "I thought your brother and Paige were tough. You're impossible."

She shrugged. "I'm female."

Sarah ate three more bites of her omelet, while Baker studied her. His look was inscrutable. His shield was firmly in place. Sarah had no idea what he was feeling, though she wished she did.

Emotions coupled with words and body language could usually allow her to read people very well. Baker didn't want her having any clue to his ultimate goals. He was good at hiding what he was after. He must have been good to get Jonas into this mess.

"One of the top Navy OBs has been assigned to you. He'll be transferred here in three weeks."

"Don't bother. Your hacks aren't laying a hand on me."

Baker rubbed at his temple. "That's got to change. There's never been a baby like this before."

Sarah laughed harshly. "One between a two-bit talent from an important family and an operative you want to blackmail? God willing, this is a first. I'm almost afraid to ask how you managed this. The Trojan boys will be pissed at you, Mr. Baker."

Baker cracked a smile that didn't reach his eyes. "Don't worry. We set up Paige nicely. Our guys have been working on the perfect sabotage for ten years."

She rolled her eyes. "Typical man. You set *me* up. I'm the one who's carrying this baby, and I'm the one being used as a hostage to keep Jonas under your thumb."

"You really don't understand, do you?"

"What is there to understand? You ordered Jonas to fuck me, hoping he'd fall for me. Even if he didn't, your psych tests probably indicated that a baby would be his weakness. I got the 'why me' part. You can kill a whole flock of birds with one stone.

"Why *Jonas*? Did the psych tests say he was the most likely sucker, or does he have something special you don't want to lose? Were you *already* losing him and needed someone to use against him?"

Baker laughed long and hard, his whole body shaking with the force of his mirth. His eyes twinkled. Sarah felt the omelet fight to come back up.

"Yes, he was. You really don't know who he is, do you?"

Sarah tried for nonchalant. "Jonas Paige. He's a talent born in Portsmouth, VA to a Navy Dad and a school teacher Mom in nineteen ninety-seven."

"Jonas Paige. He's Alpha-One. As far as we know, he is the number one rated talent in the world. He has been since he was fourteen. No one comes close to his numbers."

"He can't be."

"He doesn't know. You think we were stupid enough to tell him that?"

Sarah felt an icy knot forming in her stomach. She wanted to run back to her room, but she wouldn't give Baker the satisfaction of seeing her rattled.

"You want to own a super baby." She didn't make it a question. She didn't need to. Oh, Jonas was important to him, but their baby was much more important.

Baker smiled, looking more like a vampire than a politician. "The OB will be here in three weeks."

"He can take his tests and poke around, but he's not doing a full exam as long as I'm stuck here."

Baker shrugged, steepling his fingers in front of his face. "In time. Anything you want, you can have, Sarah. Ask for anything within reason, and it's yours within twenty-four hours. There will be no strings, no games. If it can't be provided by the staff here, I'll have it sent to you."

"Jonas threatened not to cooperate?"

"His keeper did it for him. He's not worth anything to me, if he can't do his job. You—" He narrowed his eyes. "You are worth quite a bit to me."

"For the baby or for Jonas?"

"On more levels than you can *possibly* comprehend."

Sarah nodded. Baker wasn't going to make his move now. He didn't dare, but it would come when he thought he was safe. Baker wanted a super baby from the Randall-Paige connection, but he didn't want it to stop there. She was sure of it.

"I'm not very hungry, Mr. Baker. I'd like to take a walk, if we're done here."

"Anything you want, Sarah. Anything."

She wasted no time. Sarah left the conference room without slowing down.

Her guard shot after her. "What are you doing?" he demanded.

"Where is the lawn?" She kept moving away from her room, sure that she had been placed far from doors.

"The what?"

"Courtyard? Garden? Outside area, presumably surrounded by a fence or wall and sporting green growing things and something that passes for fresh air."

"You haven't—"

"Check again, Rambo. I've been cleared for damn near anything but walking out the front door." Sarah came to a T and looked at him expectantly.

The guard looked around in confusion, then shook his head. "This way." He led her to a rec room full of tables of children and teens playing cards and board games, air hockey and ping-pong.

Sarah crossed her arms over her chest. "This is what you call a garden? No wonder the kids hate it here."

"No. This is what I call a place for you to relax, out of your room, while I check out your story. If I get the green light, I'll take you outside. Agreed?"

Sarah settled onto a woven couch and nodded, and he went to a locked phone on the wall. The guard kept Sarah in his sights at all times, as if he expected her to bolt for a door the moment his back was turned. Was that what they told him to expect? Well, if it weren't for the fact that she knew there was no way out, Sarah might have done just that, but why expend energy on a hopeless cause? If Steven couldn't escape, there was no way she could.

He returned and nodded stiffly. "Let's go."

She could feel his confusion and frustration, but she didn't comment on it. It was obvious that Sarah's carte blanche treatment was going to cause tension between them, but that was hardly her concern. As long as the guard stayed out of her way, Sarah didn't care about much else.

"Your story checks out. You're to be kept on Max-Sec lockdown wing. That is non-negotiable. So, don't ask. Other than that, everything is negotiable."

"I was told everything but walking out the front door was a given, not simply negotiable. Baker going back on his word already?"

"Everything will be based on your ultimate safety. Max-Sec is where you stay, for your safety. In lockdown, no one else will be able to get to you."

Like Jonas. "All right. I think I can live with that. Who decides?"

"What?"

"Who decides whether or not to grant a request?"

"Headmaster Fuller. Who else?"

"Yeah. About that... I should probably warn you that Baker has already told me he will override, if I ask. Maybe you should let Fuller know." It was a bluff, but it was a good one.

The guard looked at her in stunned disbelief. "Well, Baker agreed with Max-Sec placement, so I wouldn't try pulling rank on that one."

"Fine."

He grumbled under his breath as they walked.

Sarah looked at him out of the corner of her eye, wondering if she could get information from him that might be useful. "What did they tell you about me?"

The guard shrugged. "You're a reformed renegade who is the key to a renegade cell. Is Daddy a renegade?" His snide tone announced that he believed it of her.

She would have laughed if the thought of it didn't make her physically ill. "Hardly."

"Yeah. When you were brought in, the DoPT idiots only told us you were a renegade who had to be doped for transport. Hope they creamed those fools as badly as we got it."

"I'm sure they did," she lied.

"The newest word I just got is that you were taken into protective custody against your wishes. You have a death wish? I hear that Griffin is after you, and you want to stay on the streets?"

"Who's Griffin?"

"Yeah, right. Whatever, sweetheart. You're not afraid of Griffin. I get it."

She shook her head. "I don't know Griffin, and the only people I have to fear are the ones who dragged me here."

"Look, I know you think you're hot shit, but don't bite the hand that's keeping you alive."

Sarah gaped at him, then forced her mouth closed. "What gave you that idea?"

"I've seen your file, the parts of it that aren't classified that is."

"What does it say?"

"It's your file," he snapped at her.

"If it was *my* file, I'd have some clue what you were talking about. Since it's obviously *not* my file, you'll have to tell me."

He shot her a look of pure exasperation. "Your name is Sarah Anne Adams, right?"

"Adams? Anne?"

He nodded.

Sarah started laughing, her sides aching in moments. "Oh, that's rich. I can't believe they had the balls to pull this one off."

"I don't get it."

"Go on, please. This is the best laugh I've had in a week."

"What's to say? I wondered, though... What really happened with your grandfather? The study was inconclusive."

He pushed the door to the courtyard open, and Sarah brushed past him into the enclosed play area and garden. She didn't answer. Sarah couldn't stop laughing long enough to answer. She walked to the swing set and sank into one of the black, flexible swings.

The guard followed her. "You still claim it's not your file?"

"It's not, but now I know whose file it is."

"Really? Whose?"

"What's your name?"

"Boyonton."

"A first name go with that?"

He darkened in fury. "Why do you need to know that?"

"I don't. It's simple, Mr. Boyonton. A name for a name. I'm stuck here, anyway. You tell me yours, and I'll tell you what file to search for. The choice is yours. Oh, and even the woman whose file they sacked was never a renegade."

"If you're not a renegade— If you really don't know who Griffin is— Why are you here?"

"I told you that a long time ago. What you believe is your own choice."

She watched Boyonton wander away to one of the metal benches to study her. Sarah started the swing moving, drinking in the warm air and sunshine.

* * * *

Bill Boyonton sighed. He wished he had more to report, but Sarah Adams was the most closed-mouthed woman he'd ever met.

He'd started reporting on her the first night. Her initial report said that she was a renegade who could bring down Griffin. Every report since then stated the same. But, Sarah claimed she didn't know anything about Griffin.

She wasn't the typical detainee. *Who gets brought to Clinton as a prisoner but has everything but the keys to the front door after meeting with Baker?* Sarah came out with more freedom than she went in with, and Baker had a cow about her treatment before he was out of D.C. Why would Baker take an interest, and who was keeping him informed on her?

What kind of prisoner does Baker meet with personally, for that matter? It had never happened in the ten years that Bill had worked the floor. What did Sarah have on Baker? Whatever it was, it was powerful.

Bill wished he knew more about this Jonas guy. Whatever Sarah had on Baker seemed tied up in him somehow. Jonas was the reason she ate like she did. Bill had seen pregnant talent at Clinton, even prisoners, and they all ate the same caf fare as everyone else...except for Sarah Adams. Jonas was the reason Baker came to see her. Jonas was some badass Sarah seemed to feel Bill would regret meeting, but Jonas wasn't a renegade. At least, Sarah claimed he wasn't.

It was time to get to work. Bill used no talent. It would tip someone off, even if he only used passive talent. A few of the keepers could spot that. He pushed a string of thoughts into an unshielded portion of his mind. To any talent scanning him, it would look like Bill was simply considering everything he knew about Sarah Adams without drawing any conclusions about what he had seen and heard. To Paul Griffin, wherever he was hidden away, it would be a comprehensive report to be picked from his mind with no talent from Bill.

Bill knew it would be Griffin this time. After Sarah's outlay of talent when she was released from iso, Deb Tyler had told him she was calling in Griffin.

If Sarah was contacting someone, at least part of what he knew was true. Whether her conversation was personal correspondence or a report about Griffin remained to be seen, but Griffin would want to be in on anything that might compromise him personally.

Griffin's presence brushed over Bill's mind. Bill didn't balk at it. That was the way the system ran.

"Tell her your name, Boyonton. We have to know what Baker is up to. Play her game as long as it's safe." Griffin's mind didn't recede, but he seemed distracted. *"Ask her if Jonas is DoPT."* Griffin left his mind before Bill could give himself away with his surprise.

He pulled his shield tight. Bill knew Griffin was ex-DoPT, and he knew why Griffin left. Had this Jonas guy learned what Griffin had? If so, why use Sarah against him? Who was Sarah to him? Was she his sister? Maybe his wife? She was too old to be someone's daughter, if he was talent. No, Jonas had something else on Baker. If he had what Griffin had, Baker would kill him outright, not use a hostage against him.

Bill surveyed Sarah as she left the swing and ambled over the grounds. Either she was very important...or Jonas was. Sarah seemed to think Jonas was the important one, but Bill wasn't so sure about that. After all, he'd heard they were sending some hotshot doctor from Charette in Portsmouth to deliver her baby, rather than letting the doctor on staff handle her.

Sarah broke his train of thought by announcing that she wanted to return to her room. Bill waved her toward the door.

He considered the best way to approach the subject with her. In the end, he launched right in. "Tell me about Jonas."

She eyed him warily. "It's probably better if you don't know."

"I caught the fact that he's talent. You claim he's not a renegade. Is he DoPT?"

Sarah looked away without answering, and the blush didn't tell him anything definitive.

Bill sighed. She was hard to get information out of. "Is Jonas your husband?"

She looked back to him, and she visibly wavered. "Yes. He is."

Time to try and back her into an answer. "So, I'm wondering... How does a former renegade end up with a DoPT agent? How does a relationship like that make it past the keepers? Or were you on a tracking job with him that got...physical after hours?"

Sarah turned on him, exuding fury from every pore. "I am not, nor have I ever *been*, a renegade." She turned on her heel and stalked back to her room.

Bill caught the door, as Sarah tried to slam it in his face. He leaned so close to her that he could feel the heat of her breath on his cheek. Fear tainted the air around them, and Bill softened.

This is a hard-boiled powerhouse renegade? Highly unlikely.

"Bill," he whispered. "My name is Bill."

Sarah seemed to have trouble breathing. She nodded. "Look for the file on Katheryn Anne Randall," she whispered back.

Bill moved his hand in a daze, and Sarah closed the door between them.

Randall? She's probably a DoPT wife, but she knows Randalls? Of everything he'd heard so far, that made the least amount of sense.

* * * *

164

Bill stared at the computer screen, rubbing his aching neck. Much of Katheryn Randall's file was court-sealed under the 2015 decision, but the remaining portion was enough. From the stats sheet, he could tell Katheryn's file had been altered for Sarah.

He grumbled to himself. "Katheryn Anne Randall, born Katheryn Anne Adams, but maiden name is O'Hanlon? Skipped that on the changeover. Father was a Pittsburgh police officer and mother was an office worker for the City of Pittsburgh. Check and check. Same date of birth save the year. Same city of birth. Same list of talents? No way."

He closed the file and sat staring at the wall.

How did Sarah know what file to look for? How would she know Katheryn Randall at all?

On a hunch, he cross-referenced Katheryn Randall to Sarah as a wildcard in the DoPT database. There were no matches. He tried with Kyle Thompson. No matches were found. He punched in Randall and Thompson as line item searches. The family group files came up. He tried cross-referencing Sarah against Alexander and then against Steven Randall. None of them brought up a file for her. He tried cross-referencing Sarah Anne Adams to first Randall and then Thompson. Still, nothing matched up.

How did she escape the roundup? Well, she might not have, though the academy rules seemed to surprise her. Sarah might have met the Randalls in one of the academies. She'd be about Steven or Alexander's age.

If so, she had a file somewhere, but her fingerprint on intake brought up the Adams file. Even passive talents capable of being keepers had files with fact sheets, unless they were closet talents who managed to duck the witch-hunts.

Passive talents weren't seized in the roundups, but they had files.

Sarah has a file. I'm sure of it, but how can I find it?

He glanced at his watch, then shook his head. It was dinnertime, and he only got Patterson to cover for him that long. Bill pushed off of the chair and wound his way through the corridors that would take him to Sarah's room, stopping to get her tray from Fuller's personal cook.

From the smell of it, Sarah was having Italian tonight. Bill's mouth watered. The students and guards were having gorilla head, a crude military name used for decades to describe the piles of roast beef with gravy that barely qualified as food.

That should have been his first clue that Sarah had something big on Baker. Word was that when Fuller gave his daily update stating that Sarah wasn't eating the caf food, Baker's office ordered Fuller to have his staff provide for her and even submitted menus for her.

He furrowed his brow. From the shit that came down, he could only assume Fuller hadn't made a point of telling Baker that Sarah was being kept in iso.

He nodded to Patterson, and the young man knocked on the door. One of the safety precautions was that Sarah could never eat in the caf with the students or prisoners if she had special food. Somehow, Bill didn't think Sarah would balk at that.

Patterson opened the door for him when she called out, then disappeared to dinner without a word. Bill put her tray on the bedside table and headed for the door. He heard her sharp intake of breath when he closed it and sat in the chair across from her.

Sarah's expression was nothing short of panicked, and Bill was struck again by how unlikely it was that she was the woman her file attested. Even if Sarah feared restraint in the iso tank, she wouldn't fear Bill, not if she was what that file said she was.

"Who are you, Sarah? How did you know Katheryn Randall's file was the one they changed for you?"

"Katie. She prefers to be called Katie. And Alexander is Alex."

"How do you know them?"

"Did you research her like a good operative?" A strained smile pulled at her lips.

"Of course. I cross-referenced all the Randalls and Kyle Thompson for anyone named Sarah."

"And?"

"Unless it's in the court-sealed portions, there's no connection."

"What does that tell you?" she prodded.

"I don't know. You might have met them in the roundups, which would be impossible for me to trace. You might have met them in Pittsburgh, which would be even more impossible to trace."

Sarah looked crushed, as if his determination that tracing her was hopeless ended some chance for her.

"I should have found you," he guessed. "The cross-reference should have shown me a file that's not there."

"Did you read her fact sheet? Did you read it carefully?" Her eyes were raw and red from crying.

"I searched all of them with a fine tooth comb. History, family, talents, hobbies. What should I have found, Sarah?"

She didn't answer. She curled away from him on the bed.

"Who are you, Sarah?"

"I don't exist. He erased me."

"Jonas?" Why would a DoPT operative delete a file? How would he? The interlocks were supposed to prevent that.

"No. Not Jonas."

Bill could tell she was done answering questions for now. He headed for the door as Sarah wiped tears from her cheeks.

"Please eat, Sarah."

He heard an answer that sounded vaguely like an affirmative as he closed the door.

Bill hit the panel for full lockdown. Since Sarah was the only talent in Max-Sec, lockdown came after dinner, unless she decided to make a request for him to take her somewhere else in the building after that. Bill felt a pang of regret for her situation, but aside from her walk, it seemed Sarah never asked for anything.

He was halfway to the caf to collect his own dinner — unappetizing as it was — when a sick certainty sent him back to his quarters.

Jonas didn't erase her file. No DoPT operative has that kind of clearance, but Baker does. He wasn't supposed to have it, but he had it. That was part of what Griffin had on him. Did Baker erase her? If he had, how could Bill prove it?

DoPT files were out, but he could still access public records. Bill accessed the cross-reference for the Randalls and Thompson again and pulled up the family files. Alex and Steven were close to her age.

She mentioned Alex by name. She didn't mention Steven. Do people call him Steven, or doesn't she know him well enough to know?

He tried Alex first. There was no police record and the minimum of school records. He huffed as he clicked on the birth record. Sometimes the birth stats that states kept had useful information. Bill scrolled down the screen, scanning all of the junk information on the page.

"Mother maiden, Katheryn Anne O'Hanlon. Father, Keith Alexander Randall. Date, time, doctor, hospital, length, weight... General information. Who the hell cares that she had an epidural? Family stats."

Bill froze and read the line three times before he whispered it aloud. "Family placement, third. Alex was the third baby Katie had, not the second." He opened Katie's file in a separate frame and checked the stats sheet again. "Children, two. Steven and Alexander."

His heart started pounding. He pulled up Steven's birth record and scrolled down to the family placement block.

Was the missing child younger or older than Steven? Younger was unlikely. The boys were only twenty-one months apart. Katie would literally have had three belly-to-belly pregnancies. Still, Katie and Keith married while she was pregnant with Steven. But babies were tracked by their mothers on birth records, not fathers. There was no saying the missing child was Keith's.

Bill stared at the block in shock. "First." *When was she born? If the missing baby is Sarah, when was she born?*

Sometime between September and January would be Katie's only possible window to have another child and still be pregnant in time to have Alex.

How do I proceed from here? Without an exact date, it could take hours to find her.

He scanned Steven's birth record while he considered ways to minimize his search. He stopped and stared at the General Information section. "Premature, six weeks. Explanation, delta." Bill scrolled down to the key. "Delta, multiple birth." He forced his breathing to normalize as he scrolled back up to the General Information section again. There was an X in the box for multiple birth and a notation. "One of two. Twins. She had twins." *Steven and Sarah. It even sounds like a pair of twins.*

His hands shook as Bill ordered a search for a birth record in Allegheny County, Pennsylvania for Sarah Randall on January fifth, 2003. The certificate came up with little more than a minute of delay. Bill groaned as he pressed the print button.

There she is. "Sarah Angelique Randall. Mother maiden, Katheryn Anne O'Hanlon. Father, Keith Alexander Randall. Two of two in a multiple birth."

Bill closed down the files and folded the printout into the pants pocket of his beige uniform with the navy blue Clinton logo. He forced himself to walk back to Sarah's room. Running would draw attention.

He disengaged the lockdown panel with his card key, then knocked at her door. He heard her voice and let himself in. Bill crossed to the bed and picked up her tray. "Come on. It's a beautiful night. Let's eat in the garden." *Where no one can hear us.*

"I'm not very hungry, Bill."

Bill sighed and leaned his face down close to her ear. "Come with me, Ms. Randall. You are Sarah Angelique Randall, aren't you?" he whispered.

She turned her tear-stained face to him with wide, hopeful eyes. "Yes. Yes, I am."

He smiled in triumph. "Then come with me."

CHAPTER EIGHT

Sarah fought her terror back, keeping it carefully masked from Steven. She wasn't sure what she was doing. Getting Bill involved seemed like a good idea at the time, but she wasn't so sure anymore. Every ounce of her being told Sarah that she needed an ally. Her gut instincts told her she could trust Bill Boyonton. Still, she was scared to tell him anything else. Even if she did, what could he do but get himself in serious trouble with Baker?

She looked at him out of the corner of her eye. Bill was slightly taller than Steven but a few inches shorter than Jonas was. His hair was dishwater blond like Aunt Carol's, but his eyes were so dark they were almost black. Bill usually seemed serious, bordering on grim, but he occasionally broke into an engaging smile and irreverent wit that made him personable. When he showed concern, it seemed completely genuine.

Sarah sighed as Bill opened the door and preceded him out into the cool night. She took a seat on one of the benches, and Bill set the tray between them.

"Eat something, while we talk," he ordered.

"Tell me how you figured it out, first."

Bill handed her a folded sheet of paper, and Sarah took it with shaking fingers. She stifled a sob at the sight of her birth record.

He cracked a smile. "You're not erased. You're just erased from the DoPT database. Some talents would consider that a blessing."

"If there wasn't a fake file in its place. How did you do this?"

"When I looked up Alex's birth record, I realized there was a child missing from your mother's file. When I looked up Steven's, I knew you were twins. After that, it was easy. If you hadn't been twins, it might have taken me half the night to find that birth record."

Sarah nodded. "Well, I'm halfway there, I guess. You know who I really am."

"What else is left?" He seemed nervous.

"Don't worry. I don't want you to fight my battles. I just wanted to prove to one person that the whole file is bullshit. I barely pass as talent. That's why—" She bit off the rest.

Bill took a deep breath. "You're bait, aren't you? They're keeping you on the line to hook the bigger fish."

She nodded miserably. That described it perfectly.

"If it makes you feel better, I know the file is bullshit. If you were what that file said you were and had done what that file said you had, you wouldn't be afraid of a keeper at an academy. Would you?"

Sarah shrugged. Alex was afraid, and he blew her away.

"So, which big fish do they have hooked?"

She rubbed her forehead to hide her indecision. "I think I've lost count. At least four that I know of."

"Is your husband— Is Jonas one of them?"

Sarah pulled the lid off her plate and picked up the meatball sub, still barely warm. She took a bite, considering the question. Sarah wasn't comfortable discussing Jonas, though she wasn't sure why. Something in Bill was too intense when he asked.

He sighed and tried examine her facial expressions, but Sarah ducked him and looked down at the plate, at the sautéed sugar snap peas—wilted from the time they spent on the plate with no attention—and milk with apple brown betty for dessert.

"I don't get it. You tell me you're a Randall. I've heard the story of lethal toddlers. Believe me, I've got the picture of why the DoPT wants that baby. What I don't—"

He looked at her in shock, as Sarah choked. Her eyes started to water, but she managed to swallow the mouthful of meatball. She glanced at him and away again. What would Bill's reaction be if he knew how bad it really was? She decided not to find out. Sarah took another bite without answering his questions.

Bill motioned expansively. "Your twin brother is one of the most stunning talents alive. Assuming he's protective of you— I'm assuming he's protective of you." He let the statement hang between them.

Sarah nodded, not trusting herself to speak and using the mouthful of sandwich as her excuse. She swallowed and took a bite before he could ask another question.

Bill nodded. "Okay. You have a hyper-protective powerhouse who was lethal at four backing you."

Steven was lethal in infancy, but if he doesn't know it, he doesn't need to. She nodded again, chewing slowly and waiting for the other shoe to drop.

"Steven Randall and possibly the entire Randall-Thompson family are looking for blood, and you warn me, not about Steven and the others, but about Jonas. What does that say to me, Sarah?"

Sarah shrugged and forced herself to swallow. Bill blocked her mouth with his hand as she tried to take another bite. She blanched at the intensity of his expression.

"It tells me that, whoever Jonas is, he's more spectacular than Steven Randall."

She stared at the tray, her appetite gone as her stomach rebelled. Sarah dropped her sandwich back on the plate, then pulled her knees to her chest.

"It tells me that, of the two of them, you're confident Jonas is the one I would have to answer to, if it came to that."

He waited for an answer she wasn't ready to give him. Sarah closed her eyes.

"Is Jonas DoPT?"

Sarah groaned, replaying her last conversation with Jonas. "He was." She looked at Bill, feeling a cold sweat take hold of her. "He quit for me."

Bill tried to hide his shock. The realization of what she was saying seemed to sink in slowly. "Oh hell."

* * * *

Bill chewed two more Tums Ultra, bringing his total so far up to eight. It wasn't helping. He was running out of time. Griffin would be waiting for an update, and Bill had to decide what to tell him.

If Baker was going to this much trouble to keep Jonas, the guy was a hot ticket for whatever side held his cards. For the first time, Bill wasn't sure he should file his report. If Griffin decided the best course was to nullify the hold Baker had on Jonas, it was a death sentence for Sarah. Bill didn't doubt that Griffin was capable of making that call. A dead or alive was serious business, and Griffin wasn't the type to end up dead. There were rumors about the power Griffin had.

Only the Randalls put him to shame. The Randalls and some guy named Jonas, who was DoPT until he quit for his wife...who happened to *be* a Randall? What kind of a powerhouse was capable of infiltrating the Randall defenses? Even Griffin had failed to make it inside. Bill shuddered.

He pushed the thought away. Griffin wouldn't make such a stupid mistake. He'd rather deal with Jonas and the Randalls while they had a common enemy than make an enemy unnecessarily, especially that dangerous an enemy.

He let himself out into the garden and kicked back on the same bench he'd shared with Sarah earlier. Bill pushed the new information to the front of his mind, replaying conversations and discoveries without adding any of his own thoughts to the feed.

Griffin touched his mind. *"So, Baker finally managed to get something on Jonas."*

Bill remained passive. Asking anything would mean using telepathy.

"Keep her safe, Boyonton. That woman and her baby are the keys to bringing down Baker's whole scam." He hesitated, and a wash of amusement came over the connection. *"Yes. This will work out well. Paige will owe me one for keeping her safe, and that's a good way to start our association."* Then Griffin was gone.

Bill winced, trying to hide it by scrubbing a hand down his face. "Paige. Shit. It *had* to be Paige."

Paige was a legend, the youngest operative that ever hit the field. He was the talent who'd killed thirteen shielded terrorists and a renegade in less than five minutes in Lauderdale. He was second only to Griffin, but Griffin was getting old and Paige was in his prime.

In his prime and with good incentive to crush Griffin for Baker.

"Protect her," he muttered. "Let's just hand out impossible tasks." How much protection could he honestly be, if push came to shove?

Bill was a keeper, more or less. He had a shield weaker than Sarah's. *Well, whose isn't weaker than Sarah's? She's a powerhouse in that.*

He had weak telepathy and decent mind reading. Bill could only affect class two emotional touches and weak class three illusion. He couldn't get past even a 3000-series shield. In a pinch, his bare hands and stun-spray were all he had going for him. If anything substantial went down, Bill wasn't sure he would do Sarah any good.

He sighed and scrubbed his hands over his face. At least setting himself up as Sarah's bodyguard meant Steven Randall and Paige wouldn't be gunning for him, when they finally did make it this far. Someday soon, there would be a war over her, and Bill had no doubts he was on the right side.

* * * *

Steven smiled as he felt Sarah drop her shield for him. She hadn't dropped it all day, and she'd buffered it several times. Her distress was evident to him even through her shield at times, but Sarah wasn't being hurt and she didn't ask for his help, so Steven kept that to himself. The last thing he wanted to do was slow Jonas down on this manhunt.

"Steven, are you there?"

"I'm here. Are you better, now?"

"Yes." She said it too quickly for his comfort.

"What's wrong?"

"Long day, but ending on an up note."

He fisted his hand. *"Why a* long *day?"*

"Well, when you get dragged out of bed to have breakfast with Andrew Baker, things can only go uphill from there."

"Christ!" Steven rubbed his neck roughly.

"What?"

His head shot up at the note of panic in Jonas's voice. Steven waved him off, closing his eyes to the hotel room around them. "*Are you okay?*"

"*Peachy. I'm the damn belle of the ball, though he's pissed off that I won't dress up for him and call him Drew.*"

Steven groaned and swallowed a sour wave at the thought. "*He's coming on to you?*"

"*Not yet. We're going head to head a lot.*"

"*I thought I told you to stay out of iso.*"

"*Some things are non-negotiable.*"

"*Like?*" he asked.

"*I'm not letting his precious OB touch me. There is no way, Steven.*"

He sighed and scrubbed his hands over his face. "*It might come to that, Sarah.*"

"*I'll handle it when I feel it's necessary and not before.*"

"*Understood. What did he want?*"

"*To offer me anything in exchange for a smooth ride until he tries to take super baby from me. I have carte blanche. I've only used it to demand fresh air and sunshine so far.*"

"*He admitted that?*"

"*Why not? What does he have to fear from me? You and Jonas — That he has to worry about, but why would he worry about me?*"

"*What else?*"

"*We didn't make a mistake. We were sabotaged somehow.*"

"*We know. Baker rubbed it in when he told Jonas you were pregnant.*"

"*He's awfully damn proud of it.*"

Steven grimaced at her frustration. "*There was no way you would have known. It was pretty damned ingenious.*"

"*And effective.*"

"*Anything else?*"

"*Yeah. I owe Jonas a kick in the pants.*"

He opened his eyes and shot Jonas a startled look. "*For?*"

"*Alpha-One,*" she exploded in his mind. "*I will kill him for this.*"

"*He didn't tell you? He told me, when I asked.*"

She hesitated, and a wave of embarrassment washed over her. "*Maybe I didn't give him the chance. He showed me the damn badge. I—I guess I didn't look.*"

"*But you're still mad?*"

"*Yes! He has no idea—*" She seemed to be fighting something out with herself. "*Never mind. He doesn't need that stress right now.*"

"*What? If something's wrong, we need to know.*"

"*It's nothing. It's just something Baker has been lying to Jonas about, but it would only hurt him. I think it would. I don't know anymore.*"

Steven shook his head. Maybe a change of subject would help. "*What's the up note? After that, I think I could use some good news.*"

"*I proved to my guard that the file is a fake.*"

"*How?*"

"*I sent him to Mom's file. I figured out that they re-wrote hers for me. My file— It's been deleted from the DoPT database, but Bill tracked down my birth certificate. I don't know what good this will do me, but at least he knows I'm not a former renegade now.*"

Steven furrowed his brow. "*I thought you said they used Mom's file.*"

"*I said they changed Mom's file.*"

"Those bastards," he spat through gritted teeth.

He waved Jonas off again. "*Who is Bill?*"

"My keeper, Bill Boyonton. He — I trust him, but I don't know why."

"How much do you trust him?"

"Not as far as I can throw him, which is about a thousand times further than Baker. He hasn't gotten anything but proof of my innocence from me. That's all I need him to know."

"Maybe you should keep it that way."

"I plan to." He could feel her exhaustion beating at her.

"Go get some sleep. This has been too much."

"Good night, Steven." He felt the touch of her mind, then she faded away.

Steven glanced at Jonas. The larger man moved his hands nervously, his arm muscles bunching while he weighed every move Steven made.

"She's fine," Steven assured him before Jonas could ask.

"Don't give me that. What's wrong?"

"Baker came to visit her, and I'm sure he's less than impressed with her level of willingness to be a good little soldier."

"He didn't—"

"He doesn't dare. Besides, he's too busy trying to win her over to piss her off now."

Jonas tensed, and Evan moved away from him. Steven had seen that move before. Evan thought Jonas was about to blow.

"Win her over? In what way?" he demanded.

Steven scowled. "Does *anyone* call him Drew?"

Jonas uttered a long string of explicit curses.

"Don't worry. Sarah doesn't call him that, either. She also refuses to dress up pretty for him and accept his offers of any little bribe she wants. Color her less than impressed."

"If he touches her, I'll kill him, whether I have Griffin or not."

"If he touches her, we'll form a line." *Dibs on first.*

Steven glanced at him. *No. This is the wrong time to tell Jonas about Baker's plans for his baby.* "She says she owes you a kick in the pants for being Alpha-One."

"She didn't let me tell her," he groaned.

"She didn't say for not telling her. She said for *being* Alpha-One." He cracked a smile that Jonas didn't return.

"She's not going to forgive me."

"Sure she is. You two never got a chance to work this out."

"I need to talk to her, Steven."

"You want me to play go-between?"

"No. I want you to link to me and let me channel through you, so I can talk to her directly. I need this, Steven."

Steven shook his head. "There will be no secrets, Jonas. I'll see everything in your mind. You can't shield me out of anything, if I do this."

"I don't care. I'm not proud of my life, but Sarah means more to me than any of it. I have to touch her mind again."

He nodded. "Okay. We'll try it on Mom after we eat dinner. We have to get it down first. Sarah doesn't have time to waste when she links. It tires her too fast."

"Tell her to request a standard pouch. Extra carbs and a Porta-meter can't hurt."

"Next time I talk to her."

"I don't think they'll refuse her, unless they're worried she'll carb up to cause damage or injury."

"If it's up to her guard, she won't have to worry."

"Why?"

"She proved the file a fake."

* * * *

Steven took a deep breath. He was entirely certain that he didn't want to take a stroll in Jonas's mind, but he had agreed to try. Steven had agreed for Sarah. He owed her any measure of comfort he could provide. He had promised to keep her safe. Worse, he'd kept information from his family that might have kept her safe.

He linked to Jonas, carefully avoiding the operative's memories until after he'd shown him how to speak to Katie. Steven retreated further into Jonas's mind, registering the background conversation as he scanned memories.

Thousands of images surrounded him, stacked like building blocks in intersecting rows like city streets. Steven wandered through, touching on scenes from Jonas's life.

Steven only lingered on memories of Jonas's early days at Clinton for a moment. It was too painful to watch and too much like his own time in the academies...with one very big difference. Jonas had no loving family fighting to free him. He had no brother to room with, once the injunction passed. Jonas had nothing better to hope for than a DoPT contract.

Steven didn't linger much longer on his life as an operative. Jonas's life had been pressured and frightening. He was good at what he did, better than Steven would have been. Still, Jonas was worn and jaded. He couldn't trust his co-workers, and he lived under orders never to get close to anyone.

The few times a year Jonas managed the time and desire to find a woman, it was a shallow encounter, meaningless because he wasn't allowed to care as much as because it was recorded. How could a man ever care for a woman and allow bets like the ones placed on some of the women Jonas had picked up over the years?

Steven sped through the memories, praying he'd never allowed Sarah to be treated that way. If Jonas had, there was no way Steven would ever link Jonas to her. He touched the early interactions Jonas had with Sarah and about Sarah, marveling at Jonas's attempts to protect her from the DoPT.

Jonas had refused the monitoring sensor. He'd been terrified and sickened when they'd forced him to kill for her. He was furious that they put her in danger. Jonas had tried to pull out of his mission several times only to be blackmailed back in by his concern and growing love for Sarah.

He was well and truly trapped. Jonas loved her so much that he'd tried to walk away rather than do what they wanted. When she'd pursued, he caved, but Jonas hated what he was allowing to happen, even as he acknowledged that he couldn't live without her.

Steven tried to ignore the time Jonas spent with Sarah. It was too private, too personal. Still, he couldn't help but feel the passion mixed with the regret. Sarah was everything Jonas had lacked for twenty years. He desired her on a level Steven had yet to encounter.

Steven turned from the scenes of Sarah in Jonas's arms. Watching would make him no better than those DoPT freaks. Beyond that, one look at the expression on his sister's face told Steven that Jonas had become the center of her world.

He turned his attention to the moments when Jonas learned Sarah had been taken. Steven experienced his fear and remorse, his rage, his resolve to get her back — Jonas had been shocked to learn that she was pregnant, but discovering it only fed his guilt at playing into their hands and his determination to convince her to stay with him once he freed her. Jonas had planned to ask Sarah to marry him before she was taken.

"*Steven?*" Jonas's voice bordered on terror.

He released Jonas and opened his eyes to give him a sheepish nod.

Jonas looked away. "I'm not proud of my life, Steven."

"You should be."

* * * *

May 17th

Katie reached for the phone beside the bed with a grumbled complaint. Steven and Evan had gone to pick up food, while Katie recarbed and recharged. "What?" she barked into the receiver, grimacing at the thought that it might be Keith.

"Good afternoon. I take it government work doesn't agree with you, Katie?"

She sucked in her breath, her eyes flying open.

"Mac? What—"

"Which agency?"

"Dammit, Mac. They'll kill you."

"Don't sweat it. They didn't see me. Some government goons sacked Sarah's place and left with a bag of her stuff. Be straight with me. Who are we dealing with?"

"*We* aren't dealing with anyone, Mac. You can't get in the middle of this."

"Unless you give me a good goddamn reason to stay clear, I'll be a lot further involved very shortly. I have plate numbers, photographs—"

"Mac!"

"Answers," he ordered.

"It's a joint expedition. It's big."

"Spearheaded by?"

"Mac, they have Sarah."

"Spearheaded by? There is only one way to keep me out of this."

"You only need one guess."

Mac grumbled a series of curses. "That's what I figured."

"You have your answer, Mac. You need to back off."

"I'm covering your butt."

"How?"

"Sarah has officially been listed as a missing person. The information I got today will be filed but oddly passed over in the investigation...until it needs to be investigated. Am I understood?"

Katie stifled a sob. "Mac, I— Thank you."

"It's okay. If you need anything, you call me. How bad is it?"

"I hate it, but—"

"She's your baby girl. We'll get her back."

"Thanks, Mac."

"That's what grandpas are for. The DoPT took on the wrong family."

* * * *

Sarah relaxed her shield. It had been another long day, but Baker was still trying to put her at ease. A sea bag of her most comfortable clothes, loose-fitting clothes that would fit longer over the baby, had been delivered to her room that afternoon. Jonas's T-shirts had been brought, too. *At least shirts won't be a problem for this pregnancy.*

She had been so excited, she'd contacted Steven to celebrate freedom from the coveralls. Even as Sarah reached out to him, she had blushed at how childish she was being, but it turned out that Steven had been hoping to hear from her. He'd told Sarah to ask for a standard pouch and went back to his duties with a touch on her mind and a promise of a surprise to come that evening.

Bill had radioed her request out and did her one better. Her pouch had been delivered...along with a miniature fridge full of fruit, milk, juice, Baggies of cheese cubes and assorted snacks. He had smiled at her shock. His comment that no one wanted the Mom lacking in food had sobered her, but not for long.

Sarah curled in bed, wearing one of the long nightshirts she hadn't worn since Jonas came into her life more than two and a half months earlier. Had she spent an entire night alone in all that time? Not from the first night he'd made love to her until the DoPT kidnapped her, she realized. Sarah missed sleeping with Jonas, and she missed making love to him. She imagined his hands on her, his kiss—

A touch brushed over her mind, and Sarah startled. It wasn't Steven. She started to slam her shield up...and she heard him.

"It's me, Sarah. Please don't."

Sarah barely breathed. *"Jonas?"* How could he do this?

"It's me. Steven is linking for me."

She nodded then remembered that Jonas wasn't with her, as Steven wasn't with her. *"Why?"*

"I had to touch you again, even if it was like this."

Sarah felt his hesitation, his uncertainty. She brushed her mind over his, a light caress to let him know she needed it as much as he did. Sarah closed her eyes, as his groan rumbled through her consciousness.

"I'll get you out of this, Sarah. I'm so sorry."

"I know."

"I would have told you I was Alpha-One. I didn't want to admit it, but I would have told you."

She hesitated. Would it be better for him to know or not? *"I know."*

"What was that? Would it be better for me to know what?" An edge of something between panic and anger flavored the feed.

"I didn't say that."

"You didn't have to. Sarah, I'm not Steven. I'm —"

"Stronger. I know."

"Then tell me."

"You're top rated. You have been since you were fourteen, but Baker refused to tell you. I think he was afraid to tell you."

"I was Alpha-One all those years?"

"Yes. No! You're number one everywhere. You're top rated in the world."

His disbelief washed over her. She felt his struggle to make sense of what she'd told him.

"See what I meant?" she asked.

"I'll get you out of this. I promise I will."

"Jonas, Baker —"

His mind soothed hers. *"Shhh. I know. Please, don't say it. I won't let him take the baby."* Jonas struggled with himself silently.

"Jonas?"

"I want so much. This is the wrong time to ask, but I have to know if there's any hope for us."

Sarah found forming the words impossible. She touched his mind again. *"How much more do you want, Jonas? Have you decided yet?"*

"I told you, I want forever. I meant it. I want you and our baby." He hesitated. *"Please tell me you're willing to have the baby. I know what it means, Sarah. I'd do anything to make — "*

"Yes."

"Yes, what?" he asked.

"I'll have the baby. We'll work this out. Some things are non-negotiable."

"Like?"

"You tell the DoPT where to stuff it, and we live in Pittsburgh."

His laughter echoed in her mind. Sarah gasped at the touch on her abdomen, knowing it was psi induced. He caressed her body, heating her blood.

"Marry me, and you have your wish. I already quit the DoPT."

"They didn't accept it," she complained. Sarah groaned as his touch made delicious little circles on her body. She missed this.

"It's recorded. The receipt of file is recorded. The clock is ticking. Say you'll marry me."

"Get me out of here and to a JP."

His touch moved to her mouth, the sensation of fingers tracing her lips.

"Jonas..." If he could do this, he could —

"Not this time, Sarah. Steven is linked to me."

Sarah blushed. Steven could hear and feel everything. She felt her brother's amusement at her mortification in the background.

Jonas demanded her attention again, his touch on her cheek. *"I promise to learn to do this on my own. Now that I've seen how Steven does it, I think I can mimic it. Would you like that?"*

"Yes. I would."

The next touch on her lips felt like his lips. *"I'd like it, too. Take care. I love you."*

"I love you too, Jonas."

CHAPTER NINE

July 7th

Sarah smiled as she handed the ball back to the child who had lost it. The little girl smiled shyly and scampered away, and Sarah felt a pang for her. She couldn't be more than six. Sarah wondered how hard the counselors and social workers had tried to keep her with her family before they sent her to Clinton.

Most of the children out right now were under the age of ten. Only a few of the two dozen or so in the play area were teenagers. Sarah learned that most of the teens preferred the rec room, library or gym at lunchtime, taking their outside time before dinner, before the area was off-limits to everyone but staff and Sarah. Only the "malcontents" came out here with the little ones at lunch break.

Sarah sank onto one of the benches, laying her head back and closing her eyes to drink in the sunshine. A shadow fell over her, and she smiled. It would be Bill with her lunch tray. As long as she ate a generic-looking cold lunch, Sarah was permitted to eat outside. For the summer months, sandwiches, fruit, cheese cubes and veggies with dip were Sarah's preferred foods anyway.

"So what is it today?" she asked.

"Ask your servant, not me," a young male voice drawled.

Sarah opened her eyes, shading them against the sunlight and making a mental note to ask for sunglasses when Bill got back.

She took in the boy standing over her. His red hair half-covered stormy, gray eyes. Sarah guessed him to be about seventeen. If he was eighteen, he could sign himself out. If he were a prisoner, he wouldn't be allowed with the children. His face was set in a scowl, and his arms were locked over his navy-clad chest.

When Sarah didn't answer, he reached a hand down and flipped the edge of the cuff she'd made in one of Jonas's oversized shirts that came in the sea bag. "What makes you so special?" he demanded.

"I'm not student, staff or prisoner. I just got landed here, so I wear what I choose."

"What are you then? Some DoPT geek on R and R?"

Sarah cracked a smile. "Hardly."

She noted the two other teens edging up behind him. Where were all the keepers? There was always supposed to be one or two in the play area. *Maybe there's an emergency somewhere else?*

"Then what are you doing here?"

"The same thing you are. Waiting for the day they open the front door for me." She sobered. That day might come faster for the boy than it would for her.

"Then go. I hear you get everything you want."

"Not everything. Not nearly everything."

"Show me what you can do. Show me what makes you so special."

It was a challenge, and Sarah knew it. He was the leader of this little group, maybe even a hotshot on campus in talent. But, what was she supposed to do about it? Hide behind her shield?

Sarah smiled and fortified her shield. "What's your name?"

He hesitated, his head cocking as if in confusion. "Why do you want to know that?"

"What?" she taunted. "You let them turn you into one of them? Are you afraid to use people's names?" She put her hand out for him to shake. "I'm Sarah."

He hesitated. Sarah could feel his confusion as his shield faltered. On one hand, he didn't like her insinuating he was becoming a DoPT clone. On the other, he wasn't proving his place as the best on the block if she refused to fight him.

His anger spiked and his shield came up. He brushed her hand away and sent a spike at her shield. He was strong, but he wasn't as strong as Steven and Alex were. It didn't even take her full power to make him recoil a step in surprise.

"Now, was that nice?" she chided him gently. Sarah brought her hand back up. "I'm Sarah, and I'd like to keep this civil. Shake my hand and tell me your name. That way, we're friends, and no one gets hurt. Right?"

He looked at her hand warily, and his jaw tightened. Sarah stood and adopted a relaxed fight stance. It might come to that, and she wasn't going to meet him at a disadvantage.

His face darkened. The next spike was stronger. Sarah gasped as she snapped all her power into rebuffing him. Her hand fisted, as the exertion sent a ripple of pain coursing along her mind. Sarah wished she could bind him somehow, but that was offensive talent that she didn't have.

The boy reeled back as if she'd struck him, his eyes glazed and his mouth slightly agape. The two teens behind him backed off, one with her hands up in a calming gesture. The boy swung his head around as if looking for aid, and Sarah could feel his fury at their retreat.

"Tell me your name and end this. I don't have to be your enemy."

He pushed his hand through his hair, revealing a deep scar on his temple, studying her. "Why?" he asked quietly.

"It's the civilized thing to do."

"Are you always civilized?"

Sarah laughed. "Hardly, but I do try. I am when I can be."

He charged at her, and Sarah sucked in her breath. *Thank goodness for Grandpa Marcus and Mac. Thank goodness that all my blue-shirt uncles believed in a woman being prepared to defend herself.* Sarah planted the heel of her hand up into his jaw and swept his feet from under him.

He landed hard, and Sarah retreated to a spot closer to the building. He didn't stay down long, and when he came up, she could tell he was far from finished. Sarah prepared for his next run. She'd have to go for the solar plexus or the groin, and she'd have to hit it hard and solid. He started his run with a bellow of pure rage.

At the last moment, Sarah found herself swept to the side, wrapped in a man's arm. She looked over her shoulder at Bill as the stun-spray came up. Sarah shouted her protest and turned back to the boy as he crumpled. She elbowed Bill in the chest. He dropped her, huffing out his breath in surprise.

Sarah knelt next to the boy, wincing at the panic coursing from him in waves. She could feel it clearly now that he couldn't shield her out. She took his hand, raising it so he could see her holding it. "I know. They've done it to me, too. Just look at my eyes, and we'll count it down. Five minutes. Just five. I know it feels longer."

Bill tried to pull her back, then moved his arms to block her next blow. "Back off, Sarah. They have to take him to iso." There was no anger in his voice, just a plea for her compliance.

The boy's fear fueled her resolve.

"Or what? You'll put me in there, too? I have news for you, buddy. You'll have to do it."

"Sarah, it's not me. It's the rules."

"You make these kids hate you but want them not to rebel? Dream on."

"You want him to hurt you? We have to make the punishment harsh, or he will."

"You think I'd ever let him touch me? You think I haven't been trained well enough to take down an untrained teenager? Remember what company I keep. I have taken them all down, Bill. *All* of them," she growled meaningfully. "Bar none. I could have stopped this kid cold at half his age, and you know it. You think what I'd already done to him, coupled with the next move I had planned, wouldn't have been lesson enough for him?"

Bill leaned until he was nose to nose with her over the boy's body. "We *have* to enforce the rules."

"Try it, and all hell will break loose. You have my word on that."

They stared at each other without moving a muscle. Sarah lost track of time. She resisted the urge to glance at the other keepers standing behind Bill. This was between the two of them. The other keepers weren't her concern.

Bill dropped his voice to a whisper. "He'll try to hurt you again if you let him. He won't fear what will happen."

"And giving him triple time in iso will make him hate me worse. It won't teach him anything. Trust me. You think I'm afraid to go back in?" Sarah feigned indifference, though her heart was pounding at the bluff.

"Do you have any concept of what you're doing?"

"Yes. You know who I trained with and how I trained. With their worst years behind me, what can you possibly challenge me with that's worse?"

He kept his position, locked on her eyes, as if he was trying to talk her into letting the boy go. As the minutes passed, the color rose in Bill's cheeks.

Sarah gasped as the boy tightened his grip on her hand. She met his soft gray eyes and felt his internal struggle against the drug in his system.

"Jer-my," he groaned. "Jer-e-my Flynn."

She chuckled and squeezed back. "Glad to meet you, Jeremy. If you're civil, I think we can get these guys to back off. Are you ready to be civil? This is your chance, probably the only one I can win you."

Jeremy managed a shaky nod. A tear tracked down his cheek. "Thanks...Sarah."

She changed her grip and shook his hand, smiling at his participation in the move. "You are your own keeper, Jeremy. Never forget that...and never depend on someone else to do the job for you."

* * * *

Bill guided Sarah back to her room with a hand on the small of her back. She held herself stiff and straight as a queen. Bill had no doubts that she allowed him to touch her, that any time he'd touched her she'd allowed it. Sarah could have stopped him, at any time.

He pushed her door open, and she went to the bed, curling her legs under her as she sat. Sarah didn't look at him. She hadn't said a word to him since Flynn started coming out of it. After that, all of her attention was on making sure the boy was going to be all right.

Bill sighed, unsure of where to start. "I'll get you a new tray," he offered.

"Don't bother. I'll snag some fruit and cheese from the fridge."

He nodded. "I have to change. I'll get Patterson—"

"No. Just lock it down for a while. I'll be fine."

Bill hesitated. The milk and juice drying on his clothing was uncomfortable, but he couldn't leave it like this. "You scared the hell out of me."

"I know. I'm not that rusty."

"When I felt you strike— Damn, that tray flew."

Sarah looked at him in confusion. "Shield. I don't have offensive—"

"Bullshit! I don't know what that was. It was like nothing I've seen before, but it was high powered. It had to be an active class, or I wouldn't see it."

"Someone else must have—"

He scowled at her. "You think I'm incompetent? No one else in here has that kind of firepower."

"No. I'm sure you're not incompetent, but I think something short-circuited. I'm a keeper and barely that."

Bill sank into the chair and rubbed a hand over his mouth. She seemed sincere.

"You really don't know what you're doing, do you?"

"Seeing as how I'm biting back the urge to insist that I don't *do* anything, I'd say the answer to that question is no."

"Do yourself a favor and don't mention this to anyone."

"Everyone here except you thinks I'm a powerhouse renegade."

"Everyone but Baker and anyone reporting to him."

She bit her lip. "Good point."

"So, let's keep this one between us." *Completely between us. This one is too dangerous to leave unshielded for Griffin.* Though, Griffin would love it if Bill found a way to let him know.

"Might as well, since I'm clueless."

Bill nodded. He rose to leave. "Sarah, what you did for Flynn—"

"Jeremy."

"What you did for Jeremy was a good thing."

"Thanks, Bill."

* * * *

August 1st

Sarah smiled as Jonas's mind touched hers. She closed her eyes. *"Well, hello."*

"Are you okay?" he asked urgently.

Sarah swallowed hard, shielding her upset from him. She'd learned to compartmentalize herself where Jonas was concerned, but his urgency showed that she hadn't done an efficient job during the course of the day. She'd taken down her third student that morning, a young powerhouse named Danny.

"I'm fine," she assured him.

"Uh, uh. You know you can't pull that. You're hiding something from me. I may not be able to pierce that shield of yours, but I can tell when you're doing it."

Damn! Sarah had to tell him something, and it wasn't going to be that she was proving herself the king of the hill at Clinton for her own protection. Jonas would go ballistic if he knew that one. Snatching on the other annoyance in her life, she decided on her ruse.

"The OB is just trying to talk me into all sorts of stuff I am not going to agree to."

"Sarah?"

"He took his blood tests. The ultrasound shows a healthy baby. I feel fine."

"Sarah, you're — what — five months now or close to it?"

"I don't want them watching. I don't want Baker — "

"I know," he growled.

"You want me to."

He hesitated. *"I want you and the baby to have the best care. I want you both healthy."*

"I don't like it."

"Neither do I." A burst of amusement passed over the link.

"What is it?" she asked.

Sarah stifled a groan as she felt the psi-induced touch of Jonas's fingers on her thigh. *"Jonas, Steven — "* She didn't want him to stop. She missed this so much it hurt.

"Uh, uh. I'm soloing, sweetheart. Surprise." His fingers moved higher, under the line of her nightshirt.

She panted, her body reacting to what she knew rationally was just a phantom. It felt so real. Sarah closed her eyes and imagined Jonas leaning over her with his hand between her legs, slowly edging upward.

"It is real." His lips brushed over hers, as his fingers dipped into the depths of her, already wet for him.

Sarah clamped her legs together, adding her own friction to Jonas's sweet torture of her. She bit back another groan as she felt herself soaring toward a climax.

"Come for me, Sarah. I've missed feeling you come for me." His fingers hastened, driving her higher.

Sarah moved her hips restlessly, as if she could force him deeper. Jonas obliged her whim. She cried out softly as his thumb stroked her clit.

"Come with me, Jonas. Please, come with me."

"I will. Would you like to feel it?"

"Oh, yes."

Sarah tensed at the impressions he fed her, Jonas stroking himself to visions of her enjoyment. He was on his back in a bed, his hand pumping his length, squeezing lightly at the base and under the head. She licked her lips as a drop of his precome slid down the head. He was close, as close as she was to coming.

His voice rumbled through her mind, rough with the need she felt clearly through the link. *"I'm going to come in you, Sarah. Our first time when you're home, I'm going to know what you feel like without the Plastilyte."*

"Yes!" Sarah screamed the word to him over the link, gritting her teeth to keep silence in the room. Visions of his scalding heat inside her drove her over. Her body reacted fiercely, contracting around the psi-fingers within her as a wave of her cream washed down onto her thighs. She shook in the intensity of it.

Jonas's cry of release echoed through her. Still connected, Sarah felt that scalding wave on his hand, on his leg. He sent a swirl of psi-induced heat as a teaser to her, causing her to bow up at the feeling of it within her.

"Inside you, Sarah. All of me."

"God, yes. Promise me." Her body was wracked with the contractions coursing through her; her legs moved restlessly in her need for him.

His lips brushed over her ear, his hand still stroking deep inside her. *"Promise me you'll let the doctor do his job, and I promise to come in you every chance you give me, until the baby's born."*

"It's a deal." She groaned aloud as he slowed his movements. *"Don't stop."*

CHAPTER TEN

September 1st

Jonas gasped at the joy he felt from Sarah. He reached for her automatically. *"What is it?"*

"Another sonogram."

He felt the tightness in his chest. Another step he'd missed. Jonas had missed the moment when Sarah had to start wearing his shirts over the maternity jeans and sweats Baker provided for her, when her own clothes were too tight over their baby. He'd missed soothing her morning sickness, indulging her cravings and massaging away her aches. He'd missed the first butterfly stirrings of their baby inside her. Now this.

"Did it go well?" he asked, trying to mask his pain from her.

"Perfect." There was a smug satisfaction in Sarah's manner, and she was carefully shielding something from him.

"Tell me. Share everything with me."

"Do you really want to know?" She was teasing him.

"I do. I want to know everything."

"Do you want to know what our baby is?"

"What it is? I don't understand."

"A boy or a girl. Do you want to know?"

"They could – You know?"

She misinterpreted his flustered response, closing off another piece of herself from him. *"If you don't want to know, I'll keep it hidden."*

"No! Sarah, tell me please." His heart ached as he felt her pleasure at the request.

"It's a boy, Jonas."

"A boy." Jonas laughed heartily, earning him curious stares from the others. Jealously, he shielded her with his mind to keep her family away from this one private moment in their little family. *"Have you thought of a name?"*

"Jonas?"

"Yes?"

"No. I mean... You don't want me to name our son after you?"

"No. I don't. Maybe as a middle name. I want something better for him. Is there another name you'd like to use?"

Sarah hesitated. *"Mac."* It was the barest whisper in his mind.

He grimaced. *"Mac Paige?"* She didn't want to name him Mac Randall, did she?

"Julian. Mac's first name is Julian."

"Julian Paige. That sounds much better."

"Julian Jonas Paige. Do you like it?"

"Yes. I do. I love you, Sarah."

"I love you, too."

Sarah was suddenly weary. He didn't need to search her mind to know that she hadn't carbed up before she contacted him.

"Take a nap. Eat a snack." He sent a kiss to her forehead. *"We'll talk again tonight. I promise."*

Sarah's mind touched his as she fell asleep. Jonas stayed with her for several long moments, reveling in his newfound knowledge. He had a son.

"I'll be there soon, Sarah," he promised her.

The time was right. Katie and Steven didn't know what they were looking for, but Jonas did. He knew how to get to Griffin now. Griffin would be jumpy, but there was one chance. Jonas had to go alone and lay out his plan in person.

He had everything he needed. He had a plan. He had the drive to make Griffin listen. Best of all, he had several things to offer in exchange for Griffin's help. A way to Baker and the combined power to kill the SOB was just the tip of the iceberg.

The greatest treasure Jonas had to offer Griffin was the knowledge for breaking shields. If Griffin had that knowledge, he wouldn't still be hiding like he was. He would have taken Baker head-on long ago. Jonas was willing to bet that Griffin found a lucky slot, a one-time path at sliding under the defenses of the shield, accomplished in a moment of stress or exhaustion.

That was how Jonas did it the first time. It had taken a while to analyze *what* he'd done so he could repeat it consciously.

Once Jonas learned the trick of unraveling the knit of the net, any shield could be broken with enough time to work on it. Jonas taught the others that much, and he would offer to teach Griffin and as many renegades as he had to teach to get Sarah back. Even Evan could do it, since it was a passive class, though he was limited to eavesdropping on thoughts while he was there.

There was more that Jonas hadn't taught the others and had no intentions of teaching them.

Unraveling the net gave him a better understanding of the talents whose minds he entered. Jonas learned to weave webs of his own, creating shield-like pockets around a person to cut them off from outside influence, like a psi wave, without even touching the other mind.

It was impossible to hide anything in a link. Likewise, the type of control Jonas learned to exert allowed him special access. With minimal energy drain from a host mind, Jonas could use the other talent as a transmitter tower for his own talent.

So far, Sarah hadn't caught on to his subtle uses of her mind. She assumed the brushes of his lips on her forehead were simply psi-induced. It felt good to feel her skin under his lips, her hair brushing his cheek. Jonas smiled and kissed her again, then pulled back.

Evan raised an eyebrow. "What was that all about?" he demanded.

Jonas laughed. "It's a boy, Evan. I have a son."

A son who is not going to be raised without me.

* * * *

Jonas parked his car in the lot outside *Lynnhaven Mall*. He sighed. He hadn't done something this monumentally stupid since he went after Dillon alone in Lauderdale, but he was out of options. Jonas could play cat and mouse with Griffin until his son was in kindergarten, or he could put it all on the line and take this chance to make an ally out of his enemy.

He walked the mall, affecting the look of bored disinterest while he mentally issued the invitation to Griffin and his men. It had been damn near impossible to slip all three of his crew, but Jonas managed it. Now he had to get Griffin to grant him an audience.

"Tell Griffin that Paige wants to talk. No tricks. No traps. Just a private conversation. I want to make a deal with him."

Jonas repeated variations of that same mantra over and over, knowing the familiar sparks he'd felt from the mall all week meant Griffin had a few of his men hanging around either trying to lead Jonas in or sloppily trying at something he needed done. It was a sure bet that at least one of them could read what Jonas was doing.

Jonas actively scanned. He knew he'd made his catch when a group of three minor talents in E-series shields started following him through the mall.

"I'll assume you don't have telepathy. I'll wait at the carousel for your orders."

The carousel in *Lynnhaven's* center court had always been one of Jonas's favorite places. He remembered the days before they blocked the view from Lynnhaven Parkway with the squat two-story parking structure, when you could still see the twinkling lights of the carousel from across the wide road and the parking lot, bright against the shaded glass that made up the front of the mall. His parents had brought him there on Sundays, before he got shipped off to Clinton, before his father freaked about his mind-crushing son being a damper on his military career.

Sundays had always been Jonas's favorite day. Sundays meant a ride on the carousel, an ice cream and a few video games in the food court up the glass elevator in the solarium behind the carousel...and a haircut at *Cartoon Cuts* if he needed one. Jonas made himself a vow to bring his own son here someday. A day like that was worth passing on.

Jonas leaned against the metal railing that surrounded the carousel. He watched the children laughing on the horses, a couple of lovers spinning and screaming in the teacups and the interplay of lights and movements in the mirrors. He saw the short blonde approaching him in flashes of those mirrors. Two men stood further back, hands in the pockets of their jackets.

The woman's voice was low and tense at his back. "Go to Sandbridge. Park and sit on the beach."

Jonas pushed off the rail and headed out to his car without a backward glance. The shielded talents didn't follow him.

Tourist season over, Sandbridge was all but deserted. Jonas walked out onto the dark sand strip and sat, watching the waves roll in.

The shoring projects and wave breaks had saved the small island. The only danger to it now was the yearly hurricanes that took pieces of shoreline, but the city had gotten much better at staying ahead of that in the years since Jonas sat on this beach last. They were back up to three roads again, but they had been in danger of losing the island altogether, when he swam there last.

He felt the group of five coming long before the barrel of a gun prodded his shoulder. Jonas hooked his hands behind his neck slowly. "No tricks. I just want to see Griffin. Check me, if it makes you feel better. Paul can tell you I don't carry."

"Stand." It was the same female voice from the carousel.

Jonas pushed to his feet, unsteady in the cold sand for a moment. Hands patted him down, and he dutifully spread his legs and allowed the search.

"Hands."

Jonas sighed as he put his hands behind his hips for the cuffs. He hated handcuffs with a passion. Hands turned him until he faced the same short, blond woman.

She scowled at him. "Lucky for you Griffin wants to see you, Paige. Otherwise, we'd dump you in the tide."

He nodded, biting back a laugh at her belief that she would be doing anything he didn't want her to do. She waved him toward the panel van waiting to take him to Griffin.

* * * *

Jonas grimaced at the pull of the handcuffs on his wrists. Evan would be going nuts about now. He just hoped Griffin was what Jonas thought he was. If he wasn't, he might have a whole lot of practice breaking shields and pitting the renegades against each other.

He held his breath as he heard Griffin's voice ahead. It was definitely time to face the music. Of course, all Griffin's buddies had E-shields, but that could work to Jonas's favor. They thought they were safe. After all, Jonas hadn't broken through Evan in fifteen years.

Griffin kicked his feet up on the desk between them. "Sit down, Paige. Tell me what you want."

Jonas sat in the offered chair, his pose stiff thanks to the cuffs he kept on for show and to build trust between them. "I need your help."

The older man's smile spread. "The DoPT sends you after me on a dead or alive, and you ask me for a favor?"

"You know who your enemy is. Don't play games with me, Paul."

Griffin motioned to the woman standing behind Jonas. "Take those damn cuffs off him. With talent like his, it's a joke."

Jonas sighed as the cuffs came off, sitting quietly while another guard pressed a gun hard into his shoulder in warning. When both guards moved away, Jonas rubbed his arms to ease the pins and needles sensation he was left with.

He didn't look at Griffin. "I could have come in fighting in force. I'm sure you know who they partnered me with by now. I came alone like this on purpose. I need your help, and I can't get that fighting you."

Griffin slid a folded piece of paper across the desk. He nodded to it.

Jonas picked it up and flipped it open. It was a copy of Sarah's birth record. "How much do you know?"

A picture slid across next. Jonas took it, running his hand over the image of Sarah. By the date stamp, the picture was less than a week old. She was wearing one of his T-shirts over a pair of sweatpants. The bulge of their baby was already clearly visible, and her hand was placed along the underside, framing his son. She was looking out one of the bullet-proof windows in the rec room. Her expression was unreadable— not boredom, maybe sadness.

"I know that baby is yours," Griffin commented. "I know Baker set you up somehow."

Jonas rubbed at the phantom spot on his chest. He wanted to touch her and their baby. "Where did you get this?"

Griffin shook his head. "I have a man close to her. He's protecting her as much as that headstrong little lady will allow, and she doesn't allow much. She's quite tenacious, isn't she?"

Jonas nodded. That sounded like Sarah. She was an expert at ordering overbearing males out of her way. With Mac and the guys around, she had to be. "If you know all that, you know why I need your help."

"You have a timeline, and Baker isn't going to let her go easily." His smile turned cynical. "On the other hand, she has quite the little fan club going. That is an asset you don't want to ignore."

Jonas tried to dissect that statement, without success. "What are you talking about?"

"She's undermining a whole academy of kids. Baker's afraid to move her to another academy. This way, she can only interfere with one group."

"Undermining how?"

"She hasn't told you? I know she's in contact with you or her family."

"She's in contact with both, but obviously she hasn't told me this one."

"She's redefined the rules. They haven't had to use iso with any kid she takes an interest in for the last few months. She's teaching them to be their own keepers, and she's stood in the way of more than one being thrown in."

Jonas rubbed his forehead roughly. "Are you saying these kids will protect her?"

Griffin shrugged. "If push comes to shove? A few of them, at least. Flynn will. He's practically her second skin, has her back constantly when he's not in class. That one is impressive, a good man to have at your back in a fight, almost my level."

Jonas pushed his jealousy back. Just because Sarah hadn't mentioned this Flynn guy didn't mean anything. "What about your man?"

"He's a keeper. Not much he can do."

Jonas played at Griffin's shield, drawing information out as he went. Boyonton was his man next to Sarah. That was important to know.

"What's your plan, Paige? I know you didn't come here to ask me to turn myself in."

"How many talents can you lay your hands on?"

Griffin raised an eyebrow. "Why would you ask that?"

Jonas took a deep breath. It was time to find out if his bargaining chip was as valuable as he believed. "Can you really crush an E-shield, or is that bullshit Baker is slinging your way?"

Griffin blushed. "I...well..."

"You did it once, but you're not sure how."

He nodded. "I just can't find it again." Griffin scowled at the admission. "If you're counting on that, you're up shit crick, buddy."

Jonas chuckled. "Priceless." He slid in past his guards' E-shields and exerted class seven holds, ordering them to turn over their weapons to him. The guns dropped into his hands, rounds chambered for use. Jonas smiled.

Griffin launched to his feet with a sharp intake of breath, his hand moving to a 9mm behind him. He knew what Jonas did but not *how* he did it, just as Jonas intended.

Jonas placed both weapons on the desk between them, then pulled his hands back, palms up. "Just a demonstration, Paul," he assured the other man. "I don't want you dead any more than you want me dead."

Griffin sat, nodding his pale face in a jittery motion. "What the hell was that? I didn't see anything until you had control."

"You promise to go along with me— You get every talent you can lay your hands on, and I'll teach every one of them you trust to pull that trick. What is that worth to you, Paul? It's a passive class. Even your weakest can learn to bypass a shield."

"What do you suggest?"

"Walking into Clinton with a small army of captured renegades, of course."

"You're kidding. Baker will never fall for that."

"No. I'm not. I'll insist on holding the exchange there."

"There won't be an exchange. They won't give Sarah to you."

"No, but they will pretend like they will. That's all I need them to do."

Griffin grimaced. "You're using yourself as bait? If you demand this, they'll kill you to keep her."

Jonas motioned to the guns on the desk. "You mean they'll try to."

"Baker will paint you as a renegade."

"I care? Who's he going to send after me?"

Griffin laughed heartily. "You don't know the half of it yet, Jonas."

* * * *

September 2nd

Steven recoiled from Evan's reaction, as the keeper practically threw Jonas at the bed. "Christ, Evan! Watch it, will you?" Steven moved to the other bed, as Jonas settled unceremoniously on the one he'd vacated.

"Where the hell have you been?" Evan shouted. He rushed on without waiting for an answer. "Dammit, Paige! The last time you disappeared like that after renegades—"

Jonas started pulling off his jacket. "I got shot. You don't have to remind me, Evan. But *these* aren't renegades."

"They aren't fans of DoPT either."

"I'm not DoPT. I resigned, remember? We have a filing receipt."

Evan snagged him by the hand, as Jonas dropped his jacket to the bed. Steven winced at the bruises that ringed his wrists.

"I see Griffin welcomed you with open arms,"
Evan growled.

"That was the handiwork of his guards. I allowed it in good faith until I needed to make a point."

"Do you have any concept what this has been like? You go AWOL on me for ten hours, and I couldn't even call in backup, because then Baker would know you made contact. How the hell was I going to explain that one?"

"We don't have to explain anything."

"He's in?"

"Oh yeah. Paul wouldn't miss this one for the world. We figure all three of the big boys will be there."

"Gunning for you."

"That's the plan. We both knew that."

Evan groaned. "You have to be sure about this."

Jonas pulled a picture from his shirt pocket and stared at it sadly. "I'm sure."

Steven put his hand out, and Jonas placed the picture reluctantly in his hand. Steven knew that look. "She's sad. God, the baby is so big already. How did they get this?"

"They have a spy protecting her. A keeper."

Evan nodded. "Got a name to go with that?"

"I did a little snooping behind shields. Her guard—Boyonton. Can you check a Clinton student for me without raising flags?"

"Only general record. I can't get a comprehensive without someone noticing. What do you need?"

"Flynn. No first known. I need to know if I can trust him."

"A student? Why would you care?"

"Bear with me."

Evan pulled out his pocket PC and started punching buttons. Steven watched warily as Jonas started pacing.

"Okay. What do you need on this kid?" Evan asked.

"Start talking."

"Jeremy Aaron Flynn is sixteen. He's been at Clinton for a year. He's a runaway from Springfield, Massachusetts. Lived nine months on the streets, renegade to survive. Major red light on the home life. That's why he left. Daddy— Well, you can guess."

"What about his time at Clinton?"

Evan shrugged. "Remember your first three years?"

Jonas groaned. "Lovely. Useful skills?"

"He'd be handy enough if he can be trusted or controlled. That's strange."

Jonas stopped and turned back to him. "What is?"

Evan furrowed his brow, pointing at the small screen. "He went from juvie renegade to model citizen here. No iso or restraints in two months. I don't get it."

Jonas picked up a therapy ball off the dresser and started kneading it in his hand. "Why?"

Evan scowled. "I told you, I can't see that. No psych profiles or medical on the general form."

"What *can* you see?"

Steven sucked in his breath at the harsh undertones that crept into Jonas's voice. Jonas fisted his hand, his muscles bunched and his expression murderous.

Evan shook his head. "Let's look at the record of his last disciplinary call. Maybe he spent a long damn time in iso." His fingers flew over the keys. "Okay. Physical and renegade assault back in early July. He was stun-sprayed. No iso? Why no iso? They always use physical and neuro-restraint for any type of assault, and this was a double."

"Who did he attack? Student or staff?"

"Give me a minute. It's not in the descriptives. I need the statement of fact from the keeper on site."

Jonas crushed the therapy ball in his hand and watched Evan, every muscle taut.

Evan paled. His fingers froze over the keys. "Uh, Jonas. Is there something you know that we don't?"

Jonas pitched the ball against the wall, causing the crunch of cracked plaster. "He attacked Sarah, didn't he?"

"Yeah." Evan glanced at him out of the corner of his eye. "She wasn't hurt. In fact, she sent him to medical for assorted bumps and bruises. I don't know why they didn't put him in iso."

"She wouldn't allow it."

Steven tried to shake away the flat spin sensation. "Say what?"

"Sarah has made it her personal quest to keep the kids out of iso."

"Even when they attack her?" Sarah didn't like iso, but that was going a little far, even for his sister.

Jonas turned a furious look on him, and Steven backed off a step in confusion.

"Apparently. And now renegade junior is the head of her personal guard. So, I need to know whose back Flynn will stick the knife in if he gets the chance."

* * * *

Sarah gasped. She double-checked her shield, but it was firmly in place. Still, she felt the caress across the swell of her abdomen. She moved quickly, practically sprinting to her room and closing herself in.

She eased her shield down. *"Jonas?"*

His touch was everywhere. Sarah sank to the bed in surprise. This touch was different than his usual mental input that stimulated the feeling of his hands and lips on her. She could see the T-shirt smooth where his hand touched, feel his calluses when he touched her cheek.

"Jonas, please talk to me."

His hands traced their baby. *"So big,"* he whispered in her mind. *"Just let me touch you."*

Sarah groaned, as he massaged her, investigating their baby with his whole body—his fingers, the flat of his hands, his cheek and lips. It couldn't last long. She knew the energy outlay had to be incredible.

"I'm fine. Take off your shirt. Let me touch him, Sarah."

She smiled as she peeled the T-shirt off. *"I had to tell you it's a boy, didn't I?"* She sucked in her breath, as Jonas eased her sweat pants down over her hips.

At first, he brushed his lips over her, murmuring his enjoyment in her mind. When his hand closed on her breast, Sarah closed her eyes, envisioning Jonas over her in bed.

"That's right, Sarah. That's what I want."

Any questions Sarah had were answered when she felt his lips on her neck, his hands stripping her sweats and underwear from her legs. She kicked her shoes away then tipped her hips for him as her pants slipped to her knees, fisted in his hands.

His mouth closed on her breast as the sweats left her body. She felt his heat and softness as if he was really with her, his tongue making torturous trails over her body.

"Oh, Jonas."

His kisses were hot, drugging. His body pressed into her. *"I need you, Sarah. Please let me take you."*

She reached up to touch him, but Jonas captured her wrists, holding them above her head.

"Jonas, I need — "

Sarah sucked in her breath as Jonas spread her thighs and entered her in a single motion. His mouth covered hers, reminding her to stifle her reaction. Jonas wasn't gentle. Sarah felt the urgency as she had in the kitchen their first morning together. There was desperation in him.

His groan rumbled through her as Sarah sought out his mind, needing to touch him somehow. Her mind supplied fantasies, which he fulfilled for her. His motions became more fevered, driving into her while Jonas whispered loving words and encouragement in her mind. Sarah stifled her cry into a series of hitching breaths, biting her lip hard to maintain as much silence as she could as she shattered around him.

Jonas stilled inside her, his hands tightening around her wrists and hip. His voice was like a prayer in her mind. *"I'm coming for you, Sarah. Soon. I will be there very soon."*

Sarah sobbed, the enormity of how real she'd wanted him to be like a crushing blow. Jonas receded to a touch in her mind, his hands and body gone from hers. He'd kept her from touching the Jonas who wasn't there. Sarah curled to her side, feeling empty and alone. She'd never felt this alone, even in iso.

He cried with her, offering apologies. *"I shouldn't have — I need you, Sarah. I didn't mean to hurt you."* His weakness beat at her. Jonas had pushed too far, used too much to accomplish what he did.

"Jonas, you have to stop and eat now."

"I need you, Sarah."

"Jonas! It's time to recarb. You have to do it, now." She tried to hide her panic then let him see it clearly.

"Sarah — "

"Please, Jonas. You have to do this."

* * * *

Steven stumbled into the wall under the force of Sarah's connection. She was panicked, and she wasn't making sense. Her emotions were in a riot.

"Sarah, stop it. I don't understand."

"Help him, Steven. For the love of God, help him."

"Jonas?" Who was he kidding? Who else would have her so upset?

"Please, Steven."

"I'm going. Relax."

He pushed off the wall and grabbed a confused Evan by the shoulder, dragging him across the room.

"What is it?" Evan asked.

"Your boy."

Evan rushed past him, pushing into the room he shared with Jonas. They had left Jonas to rest after his night with Griffin and retreated to the room Steven shared with his mother. Steven wasn't through the door yet when curses from Evan brought him up short.

"Get Coke from the fridge," he shouted.

Steven snagged the six-pack of bottles and headed to the bed. He surveyed Jonas.

Jonas was tangled in the sheets. He was curled into a ball: crying, shaking and sweating at the same time. He murmured Sarah's name over and over. The unmistakable smell of arousal hung in the air, but beating off, even linked to Sarah, couldn't send Jonas into shock-state.

Evan cracked the first Coke and half-forced a mouthful down him. "Dammit, Paige! Back off and stop wasting the energy. She doesn't want this."

Jonas shook his head. "Not leaving her," he whispered.

Evan turned on Steven. "Make her break off. I can't reach him until she does."

Steven nodded and reached for Sarah. *"Block him out. Evan can't do anything as long as you're holding onto him. Let him go."*

"I can't abandon — "

"Now. This is serious. If he doesn't recarb..."

He felt her upset. *"All right. I will."* Her pain was like a living thing. Sarah pulled away, her shield coming up slowly, weaning both men out of her mind as gently as she could.

Steven looked to Jonas, as he fisted the sheet in his hand and let out a strangled cry.

Sarah's misery pulled at Steven through the opaque barrier of her shield. It hurt her to let Jonas go, but whether it hurt to lose his touch, or because she was allowing herself to share his anguish was a mystery to Steven.

Jonas sobbed. "Sarah." Her name was the barest whisper on his lips.

Evan cupped his head up and pushed the Coke at him again. "Drink it. You can't have her until you've recovered. We won't let you have her until you are."

Jonas glared at him, but he started drinking. Steven breathed a sigh of relief as Evan cracked the second Coke. Evan ordered up food, while Jonas downed the second bottle. Jonas was still shaking heavily, but his mental state was clearing.

Evan traded the second empty for a fresh bottle. "What did you think you were doing?" he demanded. "I knew you were up to something, but—"

Jonas glanced Steven's way then stared at his drink, the muscles in his bare arms bunching. "I needed to feel her in my arms, Evan. I needed to touch my baby."

Steven shook his head. "Can you really do that?"

Jonas blushed. "I wasn't sure I could, but it worked. I couldn't let go. I miss her too much to stop."

Evan rubbed the back of his neck and groaned. "Tell me you didn't."

Jonas didn't answer. He drained the Coke in his hand and threw the plastic bottle against the wall.

Evan passed him another Coke. "Out of curiosity, are you *insane*?"

Jonas looked physically ill. "If I'm not, I will be soon. I need her, Evan. I can't see pictures of her and hear about her life from other people and not touch her."

Steven furrowed his brow. "I don't understand. What's wrong here? What am I missing?"

Evan closed his eyes and pinched the bridge of his nose between his fingers. "How is she, Steven?"

He shook his head. "Worried. A little upset, but more worried about Jonas than anything."

"She's okay? Be sure."

Steven shot him a look of confusion. "I'm sure. She's fine. Why wouldn't she be?"

"I'd guess that she's never had sex that way before, and neither has he."

Steven spun and left the room, trying desperately to reconcile what Evan just said. What Jonas supposedly did wasn't possible, was it?

Sarah was unhurt. Steven made sure of that several times. Whatever Jonas did, he hadn't hurt her, despite their fears.

CHAPTER ELEVEN

September 8th

Steven squared his shoulders, straightening the Kevlar T-shirts under his DoPT jacket. "I'm burning this damn thing after today," he grumbled.

Evan chuckled. "Don't try it. The fumes would be toxic. Just trash it. Is your badge out?"

Steven patted the silver-tone badge that pronounced him Alpha-Two with a grimace. "Yeah. I'm as DoPT as I'm gonna get."

He glanced at Jonas. *The operative.* That was the face that surveyed the assembled talents on the transport truck. There was no humor, no feeling. Steven hoped Sarah was never forced to see this cold, detached version of the man she loved.

Steven nudged Evan and jerked his thumb at Jonas. "He okay?" he whispered.

Griffin grunted. "He's fine. It's the training coming out. It's too dangerous for him to go in feeling."

Jonas turned to Steven, tossing a DoPT cap at him. "Keep your face straight or down and your collar up. Don't look up. Snipers will have a more difficult time picking you off that way."

Steven shuddered as he pulled the cap on. "That's a cheery thought. What a wonderful world you people inhabit."

Jonas ignored his comment. "They'll go for me first. They have to." That idea didn't seem to bother him.

Griffin smoothed back his salt and pepper hair. "My boys will take out the guards. You have to focus on the big boys."

"Gladly. Just remember that it's my show in there. You take your cues from me. Not a move without me, or you've made a new enemy."

Griffin nodded, and Jonas turned from him.

Evan flipped his collar up then nodded to Steven to do the same. His expression was suddenly as blank as Jonas's was. Griffin followed suit. One by one, the talents around him became cold as marble.

Steven shuddered. *This is the life they lead?*

Jonas nodded. "Yes. It *was*, but not for much longer."

Steven's hands shook as he raised the collar on his jacket. The realization that people could live this way shook him enough. Jonas sliding past his shield to read his thoughts without warning was what frightened him most. Steven wondered if Jonas was simultaneously scanning everyone around him, then wished he hadn't considered it when the other man met his gaze and nodded silently in answer.

Jonas looked toward the front of the truck again. "They'll welcome us in to put us off guard. The attack will come either in the rec room or one of the lockdown wings. They know I expect a trick, but they'll be counting on me being distracted."

Steven felt his stomach lurch. "Distracted by what?"

Evan answered in the same lifeless tone. "Sarah. They'll use her against us. Don't fall for it or you'll end up dead."

"She'll be in the middle of this?" Steven hadn't counted on that. She was important to them. He'd thought they'd have her locked far away and under heavy guard.

Jonas nodded. "They'll act like she's worthless to them. She's not. Their guards will be ordered to lay down their lives for her."

"But given the choice—"

"They *will* kill her."

Steven fought for a decent breath.

Evan ignored his distress and turned on Griffin. "Your contacts are set?"

Griffin nodded. "As soon as they get word that we've won, every major media and talent-friendly government contact will have copies of my evidence in their hands. There will be nowhere the three of them can run."

Steven nodded. "And if we fail?"

Jonas stared at him. "We won't."

"But—"

Evan squeezed Steven's shoulder. "If we die, the evidence goes out anyway. As soon as the word of that goes out."

"They'll kill her."

"If we fail, that's her only hope. I added an incentive to keep her alive to the package. It's the best I can do for her. She has nothing to lose—"

Steven shook off Evan's hand. "We're not failing. I won't put her in that situation."

Jonas pulled on his cap. "You're right. We won't leave her in their hands."

"What are you planning?"

Jonas turned away. "I got her into this. I'll get her out. If anything does go wrong—"

"You're the bait."

Jonas glared at him. For an instant, fierce emotion burned in him, then he was the operative again. "Yes. I am. And you'll take care of them for me."

* * * *

Sarah paced the room, rubbing her hands in slow circles over her baby, promising him silently that Daddy and the rest of the family were coming to take them home.

They are coming, and I'm the bait. Sarah was always bait. Worse, she was in lockdown, while Baker set the trap for them.

The door opened, and Bill stepped in. He nodded to her. "Come on. They're asking for you. Apparently, they're close."

"I know." Sarah preceded him into the hall, willing herself not to shake. She kept her head high. The halls were empty. "Where are the children?"

"Locked in the two furthest wings."

"Out of the line of fire," she mused.

Bill nodded. "Yeah. No one is *that* stupid."

Sarah managed a nervous laugh. "The bad press would be political suicide."

"Yeah. It would."

They didn't speak for the rest of the trip. Sarah vaguely noted that they passed through a dormitory and the classrooms next to the rec room and caf before they entered the minimum-security lockdown wing. She held her breath as they passed the secondary bank of iso tanks, but Bill kept walking.

Sarah took a calming breath as Baker came into view. He smiled at her, but the two men with him reacted very differently.

A mousy-looking man with limp, dark hair and dark eyes looked at her in shock. "What the hell is this, Baker?"

The other man, a man with hair so gold it appeared white and cold, blue eyes, reacted in fury. "Shut it, Childress. It's obvious Baker had his sights set on a bonus he didn't let us in on."

Sarah backed into Bill's chest, as the angry man closed on her.

He grabbed her wrist and dragged her away from the guard. "Paige's brat makes a handy bargaining chip."

Baker darkened. "Don't get any ideas, Bryant. That baby is more than a bargaining chip. He won't be born with a silver spoon, but the keys to the oval office, in his mouth. Raised my way, he'll be the ultimate tool to get us where we need to be."

Bryant turned on her with a leer. "Don't worry. Even if something *does* go wrong, we could bank sperm from a dead Daddy and try again. As long as Mamma is intact, we can do it over and over. After all, Randalls are lethal at four or five, and we have more than a decade lead time."

Sarah tried to pull her arm away in shock. He wanted to make her a baby factory, carrying Jonas's test tube babies from his frozen sperm? "No. Let go of me."

Childress shook his head. "That's going too far."

Bryant smiled, a smile that seemed to make the hallway go ten degrees colder, and Sarah shrank from him.

He leaned toward her, brushing his nose against hers. "One more thing, Princess."

"W—what?" she stammered.

Bryant pulled his gun, his attention not leaving her. His hand tightened on her wrist as he waved the barrel before Sarah's face and brushed it over her cheek and throat.

Sarah swallowed hard and straightened her spine. He wanted her scared. She couldn't let him see it.

Baker growled his displeasure. "That's enough, Bryant," he ordered.

Bryant smiled as he dragged Sarah against his body and fired the gun behind her back, shielding her ear with his upper arm.

Sarah squeezed her jaw and eyes shut tight, refusing to scream. She turned, shaking. Bill lay crumpled in a pool of his own blood.

Bryant pulled her back to his body, his eyes glittering in amusement. "He was your last line of defense from me. You're alone now."

Before Sarah could form a response, he pushed her into the closest room and hit the lockdown panel. She made it to the bed on shaking legs and curled under the blankets, shivering.

* * * *

Steven sank to the floor of the truck, trying to still the thundering of his heart. Sarah's emotions were raw. Her shield weakened with the force of her fear, then shattered completely. She wasn't talking. It was more like a formless screaming and weeping in his mind. Nothing made sense.

"The academy is in sight," one of Griffin's men noted.

Evan squatted next to him. "What is it?" he asked.

Steven stared at him, struggling to form words.

Jonas nodded. "It's started. They're using her to get to us."

Steven groaned. "Oh, Christ. She's a mess. I can't even make out what they did to her."

Jonas turned away then back again, an aimless movement that announced his upset when his face lied. "She's not making much sense. They threatened her. They killed someone. I'm getting disjointed images. She's terrified."

"Terrified? She's beyond terrified. I don't think there's a word for her state of mind."

"Trauma." Jonas got a faraway look.

Sarah's mind eased. Her fear melted into a drowsy stupor.

"What are you doing?" Steven asked.

"Calming her. She needs help. She can't go into this in that state."

"They'll know you're doing it."

"They can't stop me. I won't let them do this to her."

Steven sighed. "She's on the edges of sleep."

Jonas nodded. "She'll be able to face what comes next."

Evan searched Jonas's face. "Talk to me."

"Bryant is off the deep end. He's the one we have to take out first. He's mine now. Katie can have Baker. Steven is slowest at breaking shields. I'll need Katie on Baker."

The truck stopped. Jonas and Evan exited first, pulling down talents in psi wave shackles. Katie appeared beside them, her face grim. They were close enough to Sarah that their mother felt her pain as well. Evan whispered the new orders to Katie, and she nodded her agreement.

Griffin clapped a hand on Steven's shoulder, then snapped the shackles on himself. The shackles weren't a problem. They were essentially modified E-shield-protected mechanisms. Every talent on hand was capable of disengaging them when the moment was right.

Steven helped the last of the eight talent 'prisoners' to the ground. At the sight of the academy, he fisted his hand. He wouldn't rub his ribs. Steven wouldn't give them the satisfaction of seeing that.

Evan cuffed him on the back of the head. "Down," he grumbled. "You're making yourself a target."

Steven nodded and adjusted his cap. "Let's move out."

Steven and Jonas took the lead, while Evan and Katie took the rear. The main doors swung open before them, and they crossed the foyer. Jonas rolled his eyes as the inner doors also swung open without anyone keying them in.

"Nice of them to roll out the welcome mat," Steven grumbled.

Jonas glanced left and right. "Maybe they'll give us a clue soon."

"Maybe they just intend to shoot us and save themselves the trouble."

Jonas shook his head. "No. Baker has a huge ego. He'll want to look me in the eye."

The overhead speakers crackled to life. "Good afternoon, Paige," Baker gloated. "I see you brought me my prey. If you'd be so kind, escort them to the minimum-security lockdown wing. I'm sure you can find it, though max-sec was your usual address."

Jonas's jaw tightened. He turned left and waved for Steven to follow him. Steven shivered. He'd never been to Clinton, but he'd been to Edison and Carver. The same lousy architect and builders had done all the academies. That much was clear. Steven didn't need Jonas to lead him to min-sec or any other lockdown wing. He'd seen them all in the few months he'd spent at the academies.

Jonas stopped ten yards from the assembled men. Steven identified them from Evan's descriptions. Unless the guards were hidden behind shields or psi waves somewhere, it seemed the men intended to face them alone. The only other person visible in the hallway was the dead man between the two groups.

Griffin groaned, then swore under his breath. "It's Boyonton."

Jonas searched out Baker. "I've completed my assignment."

Baker smiled. "I see that."

"You know that means my contract is void."

"So I've heard. Sure you won't reconsider? You could have full reinstatement."

Jonas didn't dignify that with an answer. "Where are your pit bulls?"

"Protecting the children."

"From us?"

"Clinton is under attack by a run of renegades. Haven't you heard? The military has been notified. It will take them over an hour to get here. Since there are so many powerful telekinetics, I told them not to use air support, so they are stuck with ground only, and we have to handle it until then." He raised an eyebrow. "You could rescind your end of contract or run now. The choice is yours."

"Or kill you for putting us through this," Jonas suggested. He wouldn't act yet. Childress and Bryant were norms, but Baker was talent. It had to be flawless. All three shields had to fall according to plan, when Jonas gave the signal.

"You don't want to do that," Baker decided.

"Why not?"

"Couple of reasons. First—" His eyes glittered. "The sound is out of commission on the security system. Nothing we say is being recorded."

Bryant laughed. "If you make a move against us, it will prove you a renegade on the video."

Jonas nodded. "And?"

Bryant shrugged. "There is Sarah. You wouldn't want to do anything to endanger her and your brat."

Jonas laughed at that, a harsh laugh that held no humor. "Neither would you."

Childress shuddered. "Don't tempt him. You don't—" He shuffled back several steps, as Bryant shot him a scathing look.

Bryant nodded. "I do what needs done."

Baker scowled at them. "Enough." He glanced back at Jonas. "What's your choice, renegade?"

Jonas leaned against the wall and crossed his arms over his chest. "Renegade? Now the thing is... You act like being called a renegade is a bad thing. Let's see. I have the choice of killing you or being your slave. I think I'd enjoy being a renegade, if you were dead in the bargain."

Steven laughed heartily, joining in on the game. "After all, who would he send after us?"

Baker looked uncertain. "What's your plan?"

Jonas tipped his hat further over his eyes. "If I stand here until the cavalry shows up, it's my word against yours. Everyone will be arrested—well, except maybe you three, but you won't exactly be shown the front door either. The problem so far has been that everyone has *run* from you. They never stuck around to defend themselves.

"If someone starts a fight here, it won't be me. As long as I'm defending myself, I can hardly be called a renegade. The clock is ticking, Baker. When will the military be here?"

Childress shook his head in disbelief. "They'll shoot first and ask questions later, Paige. They'll be shielded—all in E-series. Baker told them to do it that way."

Jonas smiled a cold smile that rivaled Bryant. "Oh, I think we can handle that."

Steven felt the air around him crackle with energy as all the talents lit at once, their psi wave shackles falling away in a thunderous wave. Steven took advantage of their confusion to take Childress. In a matter of seconds, the DoD desk jockey was completely under his control.

He sucked in his breath at the rush of power that gave him. No wonder Ty got addicted to this. No wonder his mother refused to do it except when it was necessary.

Katie and Jonas were lit and working. In a flash of understanding, Baker tore the E-shield emitter from behind his ear and threw the micro-miniature assembly against the wall. His personal shield was already up in its place. It would take Katie time to break his personal shield, time they might not have, depending on the weave of his net. They wanted Baker alive, but Steven realized that they might have to kill him.

Jonas screamed in frustration, as Bryant smiled and dodged toward a lock panel, his inoperative E-shield replaced with another shield.

Talent? Christ, Bryant is talent, but there was no file in the DoPT database that listed him as talent.

His calm shattered, Jonas lunged toward Bryant.

Griffin cursed wildly as Baker fired. Jonas crumpled to the wall, and Bryant launched into the room he'd unlocked.

Evan crouched to Jonas. "Kevlar worked. Let's—"

Sarah's scream shook Steven's resolve. It was two parts fear and one part pain. Bryant slid back into the hall, a feral sort of glee etched on his face and Sarah locked in his arms.

Jonas pushed to his feet slowly and painfully, gasping for breath and rubbing the heel of his hand over his ribs. Whether he was subconsciously revisiting old wounds or examining his bruised ribs was uncertain.

Sarah tried to push out of Bryant's grasp. He grabbed her braid in one fist and crushed her to his chest, holding his gun to her neck in mute warning to the assembled talents. For a moment, everyone stilled. Steven took in the ragged breathing of all the combatants. All eyes were on Bryant, both sides watching him warily.

Bryant spoke first. "I hold the cards, Paige. I'm not Baker. I won't think twice. Despite her impressive lineage, Sarah isn't much of a talent. I can arrange a whole army of Paige-model super babies with willing female talents who are much more powerful than she is. This one is expendable to me."

Katie's hand tightened on Steven's shoulder. "Sarah," she called.

"I'm —" She grunted as Bryant tightened his grip on her. "I'm here."

Bryant scanned his eyes over them. "Don't try it."

Baker shifted nervously. He couldn't do anything.

None of them could, while Bryant had Sarah in that hold. Even if they'd carried conventional weapons, they couldn't risk moving now.

Jonas's jaw tightened, and he managed a sharp nod. "You hold the cards," he conceded. "What's your plan?"

"I'm leaving."

"The country?"

"Possibly. There are places much friendlier to talent than the good ole U S of A."

"Be sure to leave Sarah at the border. If you don't, I will never stop tracking you, renegade."

Bryant laughed harshly. "You won't. Will you?"

Jonas shook his head, his expression fierce and determined.

Bryant pulled back on Sarah's braid, forcing her face up to his. "Can't have that," he mused.

Sarah tried to pull her head away from his grasp. "What—" She swallowed hard and shook her head, her breathing going ragged.

"You know." Bryant's hand came up, swinging the gun to Jonas without taking his eyes from hers.

Sarah brought both hands up into his chin with all the force she could muster. "Not this time," she promised.

Bryant staggered back under the force of her blow, his shot going wild and hitting the bulb over Steven's head. Bryant pushed Sarah into the wall with a furious curse and turned the gun on her.

Baker shook his head in disbelief. "No," he shouted, suddenly panicked. His gun, still trained on Jonas, swung toward Bryant.

Steven had already issued his own order. Childress heeded his command before Baker moved a muscle. The puppet Childress put a bullet in the shoulder of Bryant's gun arm. Sarah shrank back, watching as Bryant fell around her, between her and safety. Bryant reached for his gun with his opposite hand, and Baker took a head shot to stop him. Sarah backed further away, shaking.

Steven tried to touch her mind, but her shield was shut tight. Unlike Jonas, Steven had never tried to break her shield. He was paying for it now.

Steven snapped his head around as Baker lunged for Sarah. He ordered Childress into Baker's path, as Sarah watched the flurry of movement fearfully. Jonas vaulted toward them. Childress collided with Baker. Sarah took one look at Baker's fury and turned, running for the central corridor to the rec room and caf. Baker growled his displeasure, throwing Childress toward Jonas and ending his interference with a well-placed bullet.

Jonas crumpled under the force of Childress's motion; Steven crumpled in the backwash of the fatal injury to the man he was connected to. Steven shook off the sensation, pushing to his feet, as Baker disappeared into the main corridor. Jonas shoved Childress away from him and passed Steven as they hit a dead run.

Steven shuddered as Sarah screamed in a mixture of anger and frustration. Hundred-yard dash be damned! She was more than six months pregnant, and Baker was ticked off.

* * * *

Jonas rounded the corner and stopped short. Baker was using Sarah as his shield, one arm wrapped below her breasts, pinning her arms to her sides. His other hand cupped her face in a vice-like grip.

Jonas touched the net of Baker's shield, but Baker had at least a clue of what he was doing. He shifted his shield, constantly remodulating the signal net.

No wonder Katie didn't break through.

Baker forced her chin up until Sarah winced, reminding Jonas that he could kill her easily. "Stop right there, Paige."

Jonas put a hand on Steven's arm to restrain him. "It's over Baker. Let her go. You can't win this one."

Baker's attention shifted to the talent amassing behind them, then back to Jonas. "Can't I? You're renegades. You know what the military will do. You've been on the receiving end of that already. They'll let you die this time, because there won't be a keeper there to save you."

Sarah's throat bobbed in what was probably a swallowed sob.

Jonas slipped past her shield to touch her mind. He looked back to Baker. "What then? The deck is stacked against you. All we have to do is hold them off long enough to state our case."

"You won't turn me over. You don't dare."

"Why is that?"

Baker ran the hand under her chest to the swell of their baby. "I'd hate to lose Sarah and this baby, but if you leave me with no other choice, I will take them with me." Baker's smile spread as he caressed her again.

Sarah took the opening to elbow him in the ribs.

Baker pulled her chin around until she looked at him over her shoulder. "Be friendly, Sarah. After all, you have just as much to lose. Or to gain." He brushed his lips over her forehead.

Sarah shuddered, paling at his blatant insinuation. "You're insane."

Jonas sent her calming. "He won't get the chance. I promise that."

Baker turned on him, reading his active talent outlay and guessing the use. He tightened his grip on Sarah until she squawked in protest. "Don't try it, Paige. You're the one who's going to lose this round." He backed toward the door to an iso tank, releasing Sarah's face long enough to punch a series of buttons on the control panel. The door slid open, and Baker entered more commands.

Sarah looked at the door, panic settling on her face. She started kicking at him. "No. I'm *not* going in there."

Baker snagged her chin again, his expression murderous. "Don't try it, Sarah. An hour or two in iso, and we'll go back to life as usual."

Jonas nodded slowly. Baker was unbalanced enough to kill her if Sarah balked him. Sarah stared into the chamber and swallowed hard, settling in Baker's arms.

Baker released her jaw and started punching buttons again. "That's better. Here are the rules, Paige. I'll be locked in the iso chamber with Sarah. You can't reach us. Interfere with the controls or try to get inside, and she is at my mercy. You know she's no match for me physically or in psi talent. She'll be dead, long before you break my shield or shoot me down. You know she will." He backed into the iso tank and waved as the door closed between them.

Jonas stormed to the monitor and punched up the camera system inside the tank. The screen lit up, and the speakers cracked to life. Evan took over on the control panel as Jonas moved closer to the screen.

Inside, Baker set Sarah on her feet. She backed away from him, her arms crossed under her chest. He moved toward her, and she dodged him.

"He's overridden the security features and passworded with a three-time loser. We can't play with that," Evan reported.

Jonas nodded grimly.

Baker shoved his hands in his pockets and smiled. "Has life been so terrible the last few months?" he asked.

"Have I stopped asking to go home, Mr. Baker?"

His smile disappeared. "Drew," he barked at her. "You know I want you to call me Drew."

Sarah flicked a look at the camera, then closed her eyes. "I want to go home, Drew."

"Why?"

Evan growled in frustration. "He's engaged the mag-lock protection. We can't even force it open. He knew what he was doing here. I can't even explain how he took the stun-spray nozzles offline, and you know he's carrying a mask for himself somewhere under that coat. Even if I got them back online and sprayed him before he made it to his mask, five won't be enough to get in there."

She looked around nervously and edged behind the restraint table.

Baker turned with her, facing Sarah across the insubstantial barrier she'd put between them. "You still want Paige? I can't imagine why. The man slept with you, because he was *ordered* to."

Sarah shook her head, but she didn't say anything that would incite him.

Baker pulled himself up on the table, folding one leg under him while the other kicked lazily off the edge. "I've seen the tapes, Sarah."

Her eyes narrowed, but she didn't rise to the bait.

"You really believed him, didn't you? You didn't know he was playing you."

Sarah paled and straightened her spine. Katie groaned and muttered a curse.

Steven sighed. "Now he's done it. He just sealed his coffin. I know that look."

Sarah turned cold eyes on Baker. "You should have studied my file closer before you flushed it, *Drew*. Oh wait. That's right. Your hacks could never get past my shield to find out what I could do, could they? I can't read thoughts, but I can read emotions.

"In fact, I read Jonas the first time we made love — every time we made love. I knew he was talent before he got much past taking my shirt off. Don't think for a second that he was playing *me*. If anything, he was playing *you*. You really believed he didn't feel anything, didn't you?"

Jonas slid a look of disbelief at Steven. "Christ! She's good."

Steven bit back a smile. "So, that's why."

"Why what?"

"Why she made a habit of purposely dropping her shield for you after that first time when she lost it accidentally. She knew you were reading her, and she liked it. Damn, but she is one devious woman."

Jonas groaned. "You were linking?"

Steven laughed lightly. "We're always linked when the shield comes down enough. Six times in thirteen hours. You *do* have stamina, Jonas."

Katie snickered. "And I thought Keith was insatiable. I can see how Sarah would become endeared quickly."

Steven cast his mother a boyish smile. "And he's good, too. Sarah never — "

Jonas blushed, reading the rest of the statement before Steven could verbalize it. "Enough. I don't need to hear about those losers. Anyone who treated Sarah like that doesn't deserve my time, even to renegade on him. Now I have to figure out how to save her from one more loser."

"Maybe we can help with that."

Jonas turned to watch the procession of children heading through the parting crowd. The one in the lead was a tall, red-haired boy in his late teens, twirling a guard's pass card through his fingers.

Evan leaned close to his ear. "Flynn," he confirmed for Jonas.

CHAPTER TWELVE

Jonas eyed Flynn and his rag-tag group warily.

Flynn pushed his hair out of his eyes and slipped past Jonas to the wall a foot or so from the doorway. He started giving orders. "Tyler, go to work on those bolts. Just like we planned. Slow and easy so you don't trip the interlocks. Alice, have Cindy ready to fry the circuitry."

Jonas touched his shoulder, and Flynn shook him off with a hard look.

"I'm working here, pretty boy. Take a hike."

"What are you doing? Opening the mag locks or disengaging the psi wave, so we can reach them?" Jonas asked, needing to plan his next move.

Flynn scowled at him. "Are you brain dead? Do you honestly think the safeguards for those are out here? They're buried behind six inches of brick and two inches of steel and have their own wave inhibitor, to boot." He rolled his eyes, as if everyone knew that much about the system they were fighting.

Flynn glanced at the preteen boy, Tyler, started to look away, then swung back around, paling. "Slow down, bonehead. You trip that interlock, and we can't do a damn thing for her."

Tyler looked at him in a mixture of sadness and pain. "Sorry. I just—"

Flynn nodded and clasped a hand on his shoulder. "No rushing. Be your own keeper. Remember Sarah staring Boyonton down. Five minutes, and she didn't move a muscle. She did that for you. It's her butt on the line now. Don't give Sarah less than she gave you."

Tyler nodded and turned back to his work.

Flynn glanced at a blond boy no more than eight or nine years old. "Talk to me, Danny."

"Sweet, bro. No spikes. She's all green board."

"Good job. Call Tyler off, if she twitches. Alice, be ready to pull that panel away. We're halfway there."

The leggy brunette handed a preschool girl off to Flynn, wiped her hands on her jeans and moved closer. "I'm your girl."

Flynn sent her an appreciative look. "Why else would I get you involved in this?" he teased.

Alice elbowed past him with a look of annoyance. "Because I'm the best."

"In more ways than one."

"Tease." She smiled at the comment.

"Let me pay off, and I won't be a tease, now will I?"

"Shut up and watch Cindy."

Flynn shifted the child onto his hip, perfectly at ease with holding her. "Okay, Cindy. We showed you which two wires. Hit them together and leave nothing but smoking insulation. You can do that for Sarah, right?"

"I *am* the best" Cindy offered in a conspiratorial tone, winking for effect.

Flynn laughed. "Yep. Now prove it."

"Piece of cake."

"How's it going, Tyler?"

"Outer panel coming off now, Jeremy."

"Danny?"

"Green lights. All green, but that was the easy part."

Alice knelt and started firing up as Tyler pulled the panel away and backed off, guiding it telekinetically to the opposite wall.

"My turn," Alice breathed.

Jonas looked to Flynn again. "What does this hardware control?" he demanded. He had to plan for the next stage.

"Interior psi wave. She won't be hobbled anymore."

"That means Baker can attack her at the first sign of trouble," Jonas protested, horrified at Flynn's idea of an answer.

Flynn rolled his eyes. "If you think that idiot from DoPT has a snowball's chance in hell against her, you don't know Sarah very well."

Steven groaned. "It wasn't a fluke."

Jonas turned to him in surprise. "What wasn't?" *What else haven't they told me about Sarah's capabilities?*

Steven was pale and jittery. "She's been practicing on the kids," he decided miserably.

"What wasn't a fluke? What has she been practicing?" Jonas demanded.

"She's developed a new trick." He turned to Flynn. "Can she control it? Is this a sure thing?"

Flynn laughed heartily. "They want to know if Sarah can control it."

Alice snorted. Tyler grumbled something unintelligible. Cindy giggled.

Danny groaned. "Why don'tcha just ask if the sun knows how to shine? Is *that* a sure thing?"

Alice snorted again. "You're the one who was too stupid to back off. Just had to prove that she'd break first, didn't you? Well, we know the answer, don't we? Sarah is queen of the hill."

Danny darkened. "At least I wasn't stupid enough to try a frontal assault," he grumbled.

Flynn cleared his throat, shooting Jonas a nervous look. "Old news. Back to work."

"Freeze!"

Jonas looked at Danny. His shout, coming without warning, sent chills down his spine. If they trashed the system, there was no telling what would happen.

The boy was breathing hard. "Amber. Let it reset," he cautioned.

No one moved. The kids barely breathed while they waited for the all clear.

Jonas looked to Steven. "What is this new trick of hers?"

He shook his head. "I don't know. She got me once—long distance. It was like my binding, but there was something inherently different about the feel."

Flynn chuckled. "It's a mirror. The more you throw at her shield, the more powerful the reaction that bounces back from her."

"I wasn't throwing anything at her," Steven insisted. "We were psi linked."

"Doesn't matter. Energy is energy. Sarah can rebuff anything from telepathy and scans to telekinetic attack. You send energy her way, and she can direct it right back at you."

"Green," Danny reported, wiping his forehead with the back of his hand. "Take it easy. She's twitchy now."

Alice nodded. "Spice up my life. I love a challenge."

Jonas rubbed his temple and watched the monitor intently. Baker paced the room, checking his watch; Sarah sat, her feet curled beneath her, in the corner. Was she resting or planning? He wished he knew.

"How did you learn to disable the psi wave?" Jonas asked quietly.

Flynn cocked an eyebrow. "It was repaired about six months ago, and the repair man had a three-thousand-series shield. All I had to do was hang out in my room over there and pretend to read a book for an hour or so, and I knew everything I needed to know about the system."

Jonas nodded. Flynn lived on lockdown wing like he had. Jonas resisted the urge to see if it was one of the rooms that he'd had the few times that he made it out of max-sec.

Alice grimaced. "Shut up, Jeremy. I need to concentrate."

A handful of tiny screws landed lightly on the floor. The inner card shook.

"Amber! Dammit, Alice. It won't take much more of this. We're flirting with interlock."

"Shut up, Danny. This is hard enough."

Flynn sighed. "Quit arguing. Sarah taught you better than this." He cast a sidelong glance at Jonas and Steven. "She's seen worse."

"Green. Wait. Amber again. This isn't going to work."

Jonas tensed at that proclamation.

"Don't move. Come on. Give me a green board, baby. Wait. She's green. Go."

Alice nodded. "Take two."

The card eased free of its mounting pins and barely past the opening in the wall.

Flynn squeezed her shoulder. "Easy. Don't overextend the wires. Cindy needs play."

"She's steady. Get Cindy in there."

He carried Cindy to the floating panel, and Jonas held his breath, resisting the urge to demand to do this himself. He could do anything they needed, and it sounded like they needed an EM burst of some sort. Jonas fisted his hands and let them work. The kids needed this, needed to know they did this for Sarah. He wouldn't take that from them.

Flynn pointed to the wires. "The one behind the chip that's marked for you and the one behind the breaker," he instructed.

"I know," Cindy snapped, as she reached tiny fingers in to clamp on the wires. She fired up. "Count me down, Jermy."

He put a hand up to shield her face and closed his eyes. "Prep," he yelled.

Danny and Alice closed their eyes. Jonas shielded his.

"Three, two, one. Spike her."

The wires in her hands burned white-hot for an instant, and Cindy pulled back with a cry of pain. She curled to Flynn's chest.

"Is she all right?" Panic edged Alice's voice.

Flynn fumbled for the child's hands, but Cindy fought him, screaming in pain and fear.

"Cindy, I can't do this if you don't—"

Jonas slipped past her insubstantial shield, imposing a class two calming followed by a class seven hold, forcing nerve impulses to be ignored. He touched her cheek gently. "It's okay. Let me see," he crooned to her.

Cindy reached her hands to him and smiled as he took them in his own.

Jonas checked her over. "First and second degree. Get some ice gel and skin bands for the blisters, and Little Miss Cindy will be just fine in a few days."

Flynn nodded and threw the passkey at Tyler. "You heard the man. Move."

The boy sprinted away toward the infirmary.

Flynn's mouth worked but produced no sound, closed, then opened again. "Thank you."

Jonas smiled. "You don't say that often."

He blushed. "Only to Sarah and you."

"Well, Cindy put herself in danger for Sarah. I don't forget my friends, and friends of Sarah's are friends of mine."

Tyler pushed past to smooth the ice gel on her burned fingers, and Jonas wrapped the skin bands on her.

"I think you can release her," Flynn noted.

Jonas nodded. He sent a class seven command for several hours of pain-free sleep before releasing her. "Hand her to Tyler and send her to her room," he ordered.

"What did you do?" Flynn demanded.

"She needs sleep."

"We need her for one more burst. Wake her up."

"We'll do it. Show me what needs done."

Flynn shook his head. "I need a small EM—very localized."

Jonas nodded. "That's me. Precise burns are more Steven's style, but EM is my department."

Flynn handed Cindy off to Tyler. "This is delicate," he warned. "One screw up, and everything we've done is wasted. Cindy is—"

Steven started laughing, while Katie raised an eyebrow in disbelief. The assembled talents erupted in a variety of nervous giggles and whispered comments. Flynn looked at them in growing unease. Jonas waved Tyler away.

Evan spoke first. "Jeremy, there is no one better. If he knew the plan, Jonas could have done all of this without pissing around with moving panels and burning hands. Tell him what you need and stand back."

Flynn nodded as Alice rose and backed away, the panel carefully placed back on its pins.

"It's ready," she informed them.

Jonas looked to Flynn. "Tell me what needs done."

"Disable the chip to the right of the breaker. Just the chip. Nothing else."

Jonas squatted to the opening and used a localized EM on the chip's delicate inner workings, destroying the electronic balance. "Done."

"Danny?" Flynn breathed.

"Black. She's dead. We did it."

Flynn turned to the monitor. "Go, baby go. Show Mr. DoPT what you're made of."

Alice grabbed his hand, winding her fingers through his. "Sarah will. You know she will."

* * * *

Sarah watched Baker pacing. It figured. Jonas and her family were here, and she couldn't touch them physically or with talent.

Baker checked his watch as he did every minute or two.

The bastard is still cocky. He's still — She could *feel* him. Sarah searched. She didn't have anyone else, no one outside, but she had Baker in here. She nodded to the camera, letting Jonas know that she understood, then pushed to her feet, leaning against the wall.

Baker turned on her, confusion etched on his face. She felt his touch on her shield and pushed back. Baker stumbled back, shaking his head.

"What the hell was that?" he demanded.

Sarah shrugged. "What does your file say?"

Baker sent a spike, and Sarah sent it back. Working with the kids had given her plenty of practice. She shifted to the

side, placing the table between them as Baker landed
unceremoniously on his butt and clenched his temples
between his hands.

Sarah took a deep breath and moved from foot to foot,
evaluating her position and the emotions that leaked through
Baker's shield. "Get the door open, Jonas," she screamed.
"Force it, if you have to."

Baker looked up at her, his eyes burning in the fury that
built like a tsunami in him. "You want to play with the big
boys?" he growled. He pushed back to his feet, his shoulders
bunching. "*I'll* play with you."

His next attack was telekinetic. The force of the return
wave knocked him back, and his head cracked against the
wall behind him. His expression clearly announced that the
games were over.

Baker squinted his eyes and rubbed the back of his skull,
fisting his other hand as he stepped toward her. "I don't need
talent to take you out. What can you do about that, Sarah?"

Sarah's mouth went dry. "Afraid?" she bluffed, praying
the muffled sounds outside the doors meant Jonas was close.

Baker stopped. "What did you just say?"

"Mr. DoPT himself is afraid to take on a barely talented
woman? People you want to intimidate are watching, Drew.
How will you control *them* if you can't even take *me* on?" She
motioned to the camera and cocked her head in mute
question.

He glanced at the camera, safe behind its electric field
wires and psi wave. Sarah could feel his confusion. She had to
push him further. She didn't know if she could take Baker
with talent, but she'd last a lot longer than she would taking
him on hand- to-hand.

"I guess it doesn't matter how you kill me. I mean, Jonas will kill you either way, right? Unless your troops get to him before he gets to you, but then— You still have to lead those people, and you can't even fight me. I expected more from the head honcho. Bet they did, too."

Baker turned back to her, his emotions black and his fury rising. Sarah stifled a laugh. She had known his ego was his weak spot the first time she met him.

He nodded in challenge, his jaw tight as he fired up for an attack. "I would hate to disappoint you, Sarah."

Sarah buffered her shield, glad that she'd carbed up when she knew her family was coming, lots of complex carbs that were still circulating her system, waiting for her to tap them. Sarah wasn't sure she could beat Baker, but she didn't have to beat him. All she had to do was hold her own until they broke through.

The spike in her shield was tentative at first. Baker was trying Danny's strategy. She'd handle him the same way she'd handled Danny, but Sarah wouldn't back off like she had with Danny. This was full steam ahead.

Sarah let the spike build, let him get confident. When she sent it back, Baker was unprepared for the blow. Like Danny, his scream of pain and frustration was ear-splitting. Like Danny, Baker refused to back down, certain that he was powerful enough to crush her. Unlike Danny, Sarah wasn't sure Baker was *wrong* in that assumption.

Her mind burned as Baker stepped up his power. Concentrating became difficult, and sweat ran down her face and stained her shirt. Her muscles were taut. Baker kicked it up again, and Sarah stifled a cry of pain behind her clenched teeth.

Baker grinned, panting out a cocky response. "Still so sure of yourself? He won't break through in time."

"I haven't even started yet," she lied smoothly. Sarah mirrored the spike he sent and chuckled at his grunt of pain. "See what I mean, *Drew*?"

His jaw tightened. "I tried not to hurt you too badly, but you've left me no choice."

Sarah staggered back a step under his assault. Her vision blurred. She couldn't fight at this level for long. She concentrated on one ditch effort, on something that she'd played at when Danny attacked her. Instead of deflecting his spike outright, Sarah created a maelstrom, letting the power grow with each second Baker continued to unload his stores at her.

She glanced at Baker's belt. No pouch. That was good. He couldn't recarb in here.

Sarah needed every ounce of her strength to force the energy to circle. She had one shot. If her return fire didn't incapacitate him mentally and physically, she was cooked. She released the crushing wave on him, and Baker collapsed to the floor. Still, he was funneling energy at her. Sarah grumbled a curse as she leaned on the table, sweat pasting her hair to her head.

She amplified the power flowing back at him. Desperate to end Baker— Desperate to choke the life out of him, if that was what it took to stop him, she clutched the edge of the table to find her balance.

Baker's eyes widened, and he started to push back to his feet. Sarah sucked in her breath and increased her amplification. She had to stop him. He'd kill her if he got his hands on her. Baker tried one last spike, one designed to incapacitate her and end her attack.

Sarah screamed in rage as she sent it back. Baker's head rolled back, blood flowing from his nose and his eyes glassy. He crumpled to his back with one leg folded under him, his gaze locked on the ceiling.

She watched him for several long moments before Sarah realized she was holding her breath. She had intended to match her breathing to his, to count his breaths, to gauge his condition without touching him. Baker wasn't breathing.

Sarah ran a shaking hand over her forehead. She took two steps, lurching toward the door, then sank to her knees. Sarah sobbed, wrapping her arms around her baby and curling to the cool linoleum.

I killed him. I actually killed a man.

Breathing became difficult, as the shaking increased.

CHAPTER THIRTEEN

Jonas punched the wall beside the monitor in frustration. "She's shock-state. We have to get this open."

Evan threw down the pry bar. "How? We can't get to the power source or the circuitry for the mag locks. Breaking his code could take us all day. How the hell can we get in there?"

Steven put a hand up. "I've almost got it."

Jonas worked at that, but he admitted defeat quickly. "Got what?"

"Dammit. I need your help, Jonas. Link with me and help me break this."

"Break what?"

"The psi wave is basically a shield. We can break it. I've almost got it, but it keeps slipping away."

Jonas linked to him hastily and reviewed the manipulations in Steven's mind before snagging a strand of the complex net. *"Katie! Evan! Get the hell in here."*

They both turned to the doors and linked in. "What are we doing?" Evan asked aloud.

"It's four intertwined strands, each with its own modulation and coding. We'll each take a strand, and I'll take out the power source when we've broken them."

Each individual strand was easily broken, and Jonas spiked the power sources for the overall psi wave and the mag locks. He stepped forward, concentrating a solid burst of telekinesis at the doors as Evan reached for the pry bar again. Flynn and his troops scattered as the doors jerked halfway open.

Jonas slid between them. He had Sarah gathered into his arms and his cane out, before the others reached their sides.

She was pale and in a cold sweat, her shaking severe. Jonas popped the first of the cubes into her mouth and touched her cheek, murmuring encouragement to her.

Evan snagged her hand without Jonas asking and checked her level. His groan was answer enough for Jonas. "Flynn," Evan shouted. "Use that passkey to get a glucose IV down here."

"No," Jonas corrected him. "Not here. Alice, show us where her room is. We'll do it there."

Jonas popped a second cube in Sarah's mouth, noting the faint sucking motions that announced her body's attempts to cooperate. He stood, lifting her easily and following Alice through the hallways in the direction they came. Evan reached around his shoulder to administer another cane cube, when her sucking stopped.

Flynn beat them to her room.

Jonas locked his jaw. *Max-sec lockdown wing. After all this time, she's still in max-sec, and of all places, in the room that was most often my room while I was at Clinton.*

"You should have known he'd pull that one on you," Evan growled.

Jonas nodded and settled Sarah on the bed. He took over on the cubes, while Evan handled the IV. At the first sign of her stirring, Jonas sighed. "Flynn, we need a Coke."

Flynn scowled and reached into a small fridge in the corner. He tossed over a sixteen-ounce bottle of juice. "Danny, take a few of our new friends and convince Fuller's chef to make one of those chocolate shakes she likes so much."

Danny's smile spread. "Gladly." He grabbed two of Griffin's finest by the arms and pulled them along to the hall with him.

The adults looked at Griffin in confusion but left with the boy, when their boss nodded his agreement.

Jonas raised an eyebrow as he cupped Sarah's head up and brought the juice to her lips. "I take it this means something?" he asked pointedly.

Flynn shrugged, pulled out a plate of bananas and plums, then added a Ziploc of cheese cubes for the protein stabilizer. "We know her favorites. She doesn't do much caffeine. The baby."

Jonas nodded stiffly. It was another rude reminder of how much he'd missed. "She's done this before?" he asked.

"No. She's needed recarb, but never shock-state." Flynn smiled weakly, setting the food on the bedside table. "We're easy pickings for her. She called us untrained kids. Not even Danny was stupid enough to push her that far, not that he could have lasted half as long as half-baked did."

By the time the juice was gone, Danny was back with a forty-ounce cup with a spoon standing straight up in it. "Extra chocolate, extra thick," he announced.

Jonas nodded his thanks as he accepted it and started feeding spoonfuls to Sarah. He felt the spike of calming from Steven and Katie. "Thanks, guys. She needs that."

Katie smiled and waved a hand at him. "She's halfway there."

Steven nodded. "She's confused and scared, but the link is helping."

Alice paled. "You're inside her *mind*?"

Steven furrowed a brow at her in confusion. "Of course."

"Who *are* you people?"

Evan cracked a smile. "Sarah never told you what was really going on here?"

Danny snorted. "Course not. You'd think our lives depended on not knowing."

"It might have." Evan's voice lost all humor. "What *did* she tell you?"

Flynn laughed. "That she didn't want to be here anymore than we did...and her name."

Steven scowled. "And that didn't tell you anything?"

"Why should it? I'd never heard of Sarah Paige before. No idea why, though. Power like that and balls of steel— She should be a legend."

Jonas brushed his knuckles over her cheek. "Thank you, Flynn. Thank you for that."

"Jeremy. Sarah believes in calling a person by name. Why don't you fill us in before the bad guys get here? We have a few minutes."

Jonas fished out his ID folder and tossed it to Jeremy. He fed Sarah another spoonful, noting that her shivering had all but stopped. Jonas leaned to brush his lips over her forehead, then fed her another bite.

Jeremy cursed fluently. "What is this? Some sort of civil war? I know you. You *are* a legend. But why is the Alpha-One trying to take down the DoPT?"

"*Former* Alpha-One. I quit."

"Is that why Sarah was here? To blackmail you?"

Jonas nodded, his jaw tight. "And her family." He waved to Steven and Katie. "You've heard of the Randalls, I'm sure."

Jeremy gaped at them, and Alice choked. It seemed neither of them was capable of managing another question.

Evan sighed. "We have to meet the incoming troops in a few minutes. We'll discuss this later. Everyone who's handing themselves over to fight their way out of this legal mess better head for the doors. Those who aren't sticking around...well, go where you're going, but make it quick."

Several took the hint. Others stayed.

One of Griffin's guys managed a weak smile. "I'll let *them* explain it and just meet them on my knees with my hands behind my neck, thanks."

Jonas couldn't argue that. It might be safest that way.

Evan looked around at the remaining group. "Jeremy, you and yours should go back to your rooms. It stands to reason they'll be coming in with nervous trigger fingers, and Sarah would not want you in the line of fire."

"Fair point," Jeremy replied. He tossed Jonas's ID on the edge of the mattress, then disappeared with a tip of his head, his pint-sized army in his wake.

Sarah pushed at the spoon and tried to roll away from Jonas. He pulled her back to his chest, pressing the spoon to her mouth. "Eat. The IV isn't enough," he pleaded with her.

Jonas noted the flurry of telepathy between Steven and Sarah.

Steven groaned. "You're going to have to force this on her, Jonas."

He nodded and slipped past her shield to place a class seven hold on her and force her compliance. The milkshake was gone, and Sarah had eaten a banana and some cheese before he felt her fighting his hold. Jonas sucked in his breath. He'd seen it on the monitors, but he never would have believed how strong she was until he felt that push for himself. He released her, feathering a touch on her mind as he pulled back.

Sarah darkened and averted her gaze. "What happens now?" she whispered.

Jonas looked to Katie and Steven in confusion. "We go home." He turned back, stroking a stray hair from her cheek. "We go home," he repeated with more confidence.

Sarah squeezed her eyes shut. "I killed him. They won't be letting me go anywhere."

Evan groaned. "Baker was the renegade. You used allowable defense. Between the security disc, everyone's testimony and Baker's brief file—"

Jonas startled. "The scrubber will have destroyed that."

Evan laughed heartily. "I disabled it after I saw the message. They haven't erased anything from my recorder. A modified version is being distributed with Griffin's evidence. There's also a link to the Pittsburgh Police database. Guess who is on Mac's wanted poster?"

Jonas shook his head, at a loss to guess this one.

"Mac got a great shot of Pendle coming out of Sarah's apartment."

Jonas cracked a smile and nodded his thanks. "You see?" he asked Sarah. "Everything is fine now."

She shook her head. "Nothing is fine. I killed him."

* * * *

Jonas carried Sarah to the iso chamber with Evan at his heels and the shielded soldiers surrounding them. He ground his teeth as the psi wave closed behind them. To calm himself, Jonas played at one of the internal strands.

I can do this. Sarah needs me to do this.

Evan settled in one of the chairs set up around a conference table, and Jonas sank into the one next to him, pulling Sarah further into his lap.

The Colonel in charge of the military unit sent out raised an eyebrow at the move but didn't comment. He was afraid to. Jonas had been keeping tabs on what the soldiers were thinking. They thought Jonas had gone mental on them, despite his calm demeanor.

It had started when the first squad made it to them. Jonas had calmly informed them that he didn't care where they locked him as long as Sarah was with him. Because she was still being fed the glucose solution, he had been allowed to stay there, locked down with E-shielded guards outside the door and full visual and audio surveillance.

It only got worse when he and Evan were summoned before the debrief committee. They hadn't questioned Jonas when he calmly stood with Sarah in his arms and started walking. The grunts decided to let the big boys make the waves. No one wanted to take Jonas on, unless it became necessary. As long as his demands and actions weren't dangerous, it was deemed unnecessary.

The colonel cleared his throat. "I'm Colonel Carter Pruitt. These are my council aides, Majors Allen Timmons, Derrick Williams and Robert Lewis. You face some very serious charges, but by DoPT directives, I am forced to debrief you before I make my report and recommend charges in your case."

Sarah shuddered.

Jonas nodded and rubbed her back. "After they see our evidence, it will be okay," he assured her.

Pruitt scowled. "Baker reported you as renegades this morning. Baker, Childress and Bryant are all dead now. The video we have shows them killing each other and Baker running after Ms. Adams. We have no audio to go on. The wiring was cut. Were Childress or Baker under control of your group?"

Jonas sighed. He had to play the whole thing straight. "Only Childress."

"Who ordered Childress to kill Bryant?"

"No one. Steven ordered him to incapacitate Bryant to keep Bryant from shooting Sarah. I'm sure you saw that he intended that on the video. The shot was a shoulder hit."

Pruitt cast a sidelong glance at Lewis, who was busy taking notes and running the recorders. "Steven Randall?" he asked for clarification.

"Yes. It was done in defense of Sarah, so it was justified force."

"What connection does Steven Randall have to Sarah Adams?"

Sarah stiffened. "Sarah *Paige*," she insisted.

Evan sighed. "Sarah Angelique Randall." He slid a copy of her birth record across the table to Pruitt.

Pruitt glanced at it and passed it to Timmons to add to the mounting file in front of him. Pruitt took a moment longer to consider Sarah. "Why are you using the name Paige?"

She didn't look at him. "I would *be* Paige already if it weren't for Baker."

Jonas nodded. "She's my fiancée."

Williams snorted. "A Randall married to a DoPT operative? That's rich."

"Former operative. Baker broke trust when he kidnapped Sarah to force me to continue my contract."

Pruitt tapped on the table. "And just how does a DoPT operative get close to a Randall?"

Jonas darkened. "He's ordered to do it by Baker, Bryant and Childress. And he's good enough to pull it off."

Timmons looked at the swell of their baby pointedly. "I'm sure they didn't order you to get that close," he noted dryly.

Evan leaned forward. "You're wrong. Paige resigned rather than use doctored condoms with her. But that's what they handed us, and that's what they ordered him to do."

Williams shook his head. "If he refused— How did this happen?"

Jonas ran his hand over Sarah's arm. "They set me up. They substituted doctored condoms without my knowledge. By the time I resigned, it was too late...and they knew it."

Lewis rubbed his neck. "Why would they want this?"

"The psych guys said it would make Sarah, the Randalls and me easier to handle. Personally, I'd like to levy charges on them for even making predictions like that for Baker. It does imply a certain knowledge of and conspiracy in the plot," he grumbled.

Sarah shook her head. "It's not just that. Baker wanted a Randall-Paige baby to turn into his personal weapon."

Pruitt sat back, eyeing them warily. "Do you have proof of any of this, or am I actually supposed to believe it?"

Evan pulled out his PC and recorder and hooked them into the screen set up on the table. "Where do you want me to start?"

"Prove who she is first. We have a damned convincing file on her."

"Baker's specialty," Evan grumbled. He punched in keys, pulling up Sarah's file from his database. Timmons hooked his own PC into another port on the dummy, and Evan motioned to the file on the screen. "Start here. This is Sarah's real file."

"Punch up Katie Randall's file," Jonas suggested. "You can clearly see how it was changed to create the fake you have. Katie's has been changed in the DoPT database, too. They had to wipe Sarah out of it."

"It's clean in my memory files," Evan added. "After that, hook to Pittsburgh Police missing persons open files. Sarah is a missing."

There was quiet discussion between the four men for several minutes. Pruitt looked up at them. "Baker did this?"

Jonas nodded.

"Why?"

Evan sighed and produced a micro-disc. He placed it in the slot in his PC and punched up the files. "This was delivered by Griffin to the media and government officials an hour ago."

Timmons didn't look up from his PC. "What is this?"

"Baker's secret files. Deleted files like Sarah's, changed files, plans. You name it, he had a file on it. This is what Griffin had on Baker, and this is why Baker wanted Griffin dead."

Timmons looked up in surprise. "This says Bryant was a talent."

Jonas nodded. "He was. Baker suppressed the file back in twenty-ten. I wish Paul had mentioned it. I almost got Sarah killed, because I didn't know he was."

Pruitt shot them a speculative look. "What was his plan?"

Evan took a long, slow breath. "Get elected to the oval office. Place closet talent like Bryant in key positions. Stir up trouble to get civilian talent to stand with him."

Williams blanched. "Against who?"

"Norms. An unbreakable talent hierarchy. A class system with him at the top. Personal freedoms would cease to exist."

Pruitt glanced at Sarah. "Why the baby with that army behind him?"

Evan grinned as he pulled up a new file. "Two reasons. Look at the deleted portions of Paige's file and multiply that by Randall genes. What does it look like to you?"

Timmons paled. "No shit!" He flicked a sheepish look at Pruitt, then bent back to his work.

Pruitt folded his hands on the table. "And?" he prodded.

Evan's smile disappeared. "Give me a child until he's seven..."

Lewis whistled. "He's mine for life."

Sarah shivered in Jonas's arms, and he kissed her forehead. She was withdrawing further into herself with every comment.

Pruitt nodded. "You're saying Baker was a renegade."

Jonas nodded. "Baker, Bryant and about two dozen others listed in those secret files. The rest are norm conspirators like Childress."

"Why would they go along with this? The norms? What was in it for them?"

Evan shook his head. "Ask them. I doubt Baker told them the whole truth. They probably had a patriotic vision of a strong America, guarded by talent like Jonas. Baker wasn't even straight with Bryant about his whole plan. Why would he be straight with the norms?"

Timmons spoke up. "These changed files... Some of these names are talents we have in other iso tanks, waiting transfer."

"Yes, they are. They want their names cleared. They're willing to take this chance and turn themselves in to get that. There's also a list of wrongfully imprisoned and executed talents Baker set up for the slaughter. They should be out-processed and compensated as soon as possible."

Pruitt sighed. "Every imprisoned talent is going to demand a new trial."

"I know, but I'd start with the ones in those files. I'd assume most of the others are there rightfully, especially if they have adequate witness against them."

"What about Griffin?"

Jonas furrowed his brow. "What about him?"

"He and two of his buddies slipped away before we got here."

"He probably figured that he was safer hidden...for the time being. I'm sure he'd be happy to be freed."

Pruitt steepled his hands. "But?"

Evan sighed. "On the run from Baker, he's had to actually renegade to stay alive. A dead or alive is a serious matter."

"He's not sure he'd be freed?"

"Exactly. In fact, he was probably afraid you'd shoot him on sight."

Pruitt nodded then looked to Sarah. "Baker kidnapped you?"

She nodded. "I've been kept here as a prisoner for the last four months."

He glanced to Evan. "Do I need to ask?"

Evan pulled up the brief file he had saved. He paused it as the montage of images started, frozen on Jonas kissing Sarah the first time. "I'd like to skip the next few minutes," he requested.

"Why?" Williams asked.

Jonas's cheeks burned at the reminder. "Baker recorded us illegally. We weren't aware of it, and neither of us wants that portion of the tape shown publicly."

"It's..." His eyes widened.

"Yes. Very explicit stuff."

Pruitt nodded. "Skip it." He paused, shooting a nervous glance at Sarah. "I think we have proof enough of the relationship involved."

Evan punched a few more buttons, asking for the exact time stamp he needed. The image switched to Jonas telling Sarah he loved her. They watched Sarah's discovery that she was pregnant, her kidnapping, and Baker's gloating. The military men were silent for several moments.

Finally, Pruitt cleared his throat. "Why didn't you renegade?"

Jonas closed his eyes. "They held all the cards. As much as I would have loved to skin Baker alive, until I had Griffin as a bargaining chip, I had no way to Sarah, Baker or anyone else."

"Did you kill Baker?"

Jonas gaped at him, at a loss to understand the question, let alone answer it. "The recorder in the iso tank— The camera was working. The monitor was working. I know it was."

"The recorder was disabled by Baker, along with the other major system interlocks."

Jonas nodded, considering his options. He could tell them he killed Baker to save Sarah this interrogation. Evan would back him, but there were eleven other people in iso tanks who could tell the truth before he could reach them.

As if reading his mind, Sarah groaned. "Don't do it, Jonas. *I* killed him."

Timmons shook his head. "That was a psi kill, and you have no offensive talent."

Evan cut in. "It's a *defensive* talent called mirroring." He used Flynn's term for it, giving it an official sound.

Pruitt's brow furrowed. "I've never heard of it."

"No one had until Sarah displayed it, but Randalls are like that, aren't they? She can't be attacked by talent if she's carbed up enough to handle the assault. She mirrors back energy thrown at her."

"What kind of energy?"

Jonas barked a laugh. "Any kind. You name it, and she can rebuff it. We've seen her do it with telepathic, telekinetic — "

Pruitt raised an eyebrow in surprise. "So, she's the ultimate defensive weapon? She can't attack, but she can't *be* attacked?"

Jonas nodded.

"That would mean Baker attacked her," he mused.

Sarah's grip on his shirt tightened. "Yes. Baker tried to kill me. I just..." She faltered.

Jonas pulled her closer to his chest. "It was Sarah and my son or Baker. It was allowable force. Ask the others. They all saw it on the monitors."

Pruitt nodded. "Well, Baker illegally drafted Steven and Katheryn Randall, so his charges of impersonating a DoPT operative are a moot point. You have some damned convincing evidence to support your position. Who killed the guard?" He glanced at a sheet Timmons handed him. "Boyonton?"

Sarah groaned. "Bryant. Bill would have protected me."

Evan shook his head. "Boyonton *was* protecting her. He was working for Griffin, keeping her safe."

"Okay. We'll review these files and question the other prisoners. I trust we can move you out to lockdown rooms? There won't be any...handling problems?"

Jonas nodded. "Together, if you don't mind. Sarah needs the rest, but we should keep an eye on her. She's never been pushed this far before."

* * * *

Six hours later, the five of them were released. Jonas cradled Sarah out to the van the military set up to drive them to the airstrip and the personnel transport plane that would carry them home.

Sarah buried her face in Jonas's chest, her blue eyes glittering with unshed tears and wide in shock. All around them, cameras flashed and reporters pressed in only to be gently rebuffed by the soldiers who formed their protective shell. Questions were screamed at them, questions that went unanswered.

The airstrip was secure. It was on Westover AFB. That gave them a reprieve from the insanity, though the excitement and mistrust the soldiers were throwing off was surely torture for Sarah. She fell asleep somewhere over lower NY.

The fervor started all over again on the other end, but Sarah was blissfully unaware between her deep sleep and the shell of her shield. At Greater Pittsburgh International Airport, Mac and his crew rebuffed the reporters, much as they had been rebuffed by the soldiers at Clinton.

The door to the Randall house closed behind them, and Mac dragged Katie to his chest before sending her off to Keith and Alex. He paused at the sight of Jonas. "Alpha-One, huh?"

Jonas sighed. "Not anymore, Mac." He hadn't been formally out-processed, but it was official. Jonas had been assured that there would be no more tricks to keep him. After all, *that* was against the law.

"Yeah." Mac touched Sarah's shoulder, but she was oblivious to his presence. "Is she okay?"

Jonas shook his head. "She's disconnected herself."

"Ah, Christ! Not that again."

Katie sighed. "It will take time. She's been through a lot."

Mac's expression hardened. "Like? You saying someone has been through a lot doesn't sit well with me, Katie."

Katie shook her head. "She killed Baker, Mac. With talent."

Jonas winced at the shock on Mac's face. "In self-defense," he qualified. "She didn't have a choice, Mac."

"What do we do now?" he asked quietly.

Jonas sighed. "All we can do is give her space and time. We'll be there for her when she's ready and hope she comes out of this soon."

CHAPTER FOURTEEN

September 16th

Sarah slipped out the basement door into the darkness of the backyard, pulling the ballcap that covered the mass of her hair down over her eyes. She used the shadows to hide her from the few reporters that still haunted her parents' house, stalking her every movement. They were impossible to get rid of, despite her blue-shirt uncles and prepared statements given to them by Mac.

The reporters had already gathered by the time the doors at Clinton opened for them. Sarah's memories of that day were hazy, but she remembered the mob of people: their hope, anger, disgust, frustration and outright hate making her head spin. The reporters' feelings hadn't been much different than the feelings of the soldiers, when she caught glimmers from them.

Sarah didn't remember much about the interrogation a week earlier. She knew Jonas and Evan went into the iso tank with her. Sarah knew she had been held to Jonas's chest in the mind-numbing psi wave. She knew she answered questions, though she forgot most of what they asked immediately after answering. She told them she killed Baker, but they let her go. Sarah still wasn't sure why they let her go.

She slipped across the deserted expanse of Sterling Street and through the woods to the flats. On Carson Street, she hid in the shadow of Stutz' Pharmacy. Sarah checked her watch. It was 3:30. The first 54C bus to Oakland would be there in less than ten minutes, if it was running on time.

Sarah rubbed her forehead. She should have talked to Jonas. She still could. She could turn around and go back. He would be in Steven's old bed, where he had slept every night since their return to Pittsburgh.

She ran her hand over the baby growing inside her and stifled a sob. He would be hunted, sought after by any nut with an agenda. Sarah was no match for what would come for him. Though she had the power to kill, she didn't have the heart to. She couldn't condemn her baby to that life.

Sarah ran from the shelter of the storefront and got onto the bus, dropping her money in the tower and retreating to the seats behind the rear doors where she had a clear view. This early, there were only two other people on the bus, aside from the rather bored-looking driver. The security guard half-asleep near the front ignored her, but the silver-haired woman a few rows away peered at her.

"You okay, honey?" she asked.

Sarah managed a weak smile and nodded.

"Bad breakup?"

She bit back a sob and nodded again. It was over, but Jonas didn't know it yet. He'd never forgive her. He'd never understand. She'd lose him over this.

The woman nodded. "I can always tell." She handed Sarah a Kleenex from the pack in her coat pocket and settled back in her seat. "You're better off without him, honey. If you're that miserable, that's a given."

Sarah dropped her chin to her chest and mopped at her eyes. She wouldn't be better without Jonas, but Sarah wouldn't curse her child with a mother that half the world considered a renegade and a lineage that would ensure torture.

Halket Street came up all too fast. Sarah considered staying on and following the loop all the way back to Oakland a second time, but the people entering on the other side of the bridge were making her distinctly nervous. There was too great a possibility of someone recognizing her in the brightly-lit bus.

She meandered up and down the strip between Halket and Craft, window shopping for things she didn't remember looking at two windows later. She bought a donut at *Mr. Donut* that she trashed after a single bite and avoided the eyes of the other people on the street. Even at four in the morning, Oakland was never devoid of foot traffic. There were always college students heading to and from *Kinko's*, campus security and police getting a cup of coffee at *McDonalds* or *Crossroads*...and the nameless rabble that Sarah intended to blend in with if she could.

Sarah wasted an hour that way before she couldn't find the drive to keep hiding in plain sight. The clinic wouldn't open until 8:30, but the hospital lobby was open twenty-four hours a day. Sarah slipped in the doors and found a seat in a corner, out of sight of the desk.

For more than an hour, her ploy worked. No one noticed her, until a security guard passed the waiting area. He stopped and backed up to look again, taking in her oversized jacket and Pirates' cap with distaste that rang clear even without the grimace that pulled at his lips.

Sarah smoothed the jacket and fought a grimace of her own. There was something irreverent about wearing a man's clothes while you planned to abort his baby, but Sarah's own clothes didn't fit. She shook her head to dislodge that idea. Sarah had argued this with herself at least a dozen times.

Using the talent allowance for a late-term termination, she would simply have to swear that she didn't know Jonas was talent when she got pregnant. She would be lying, but not by much. Sarah certainly didn't know what *kind* of talent Jonas was, and she hadn't had the opportunity for an early termination she should have had.

She had considered terminating when she found herself pregnant, though only as an alternative to having Jonas share the experience with her. Sarah wouldn't have to press charges on him as a renegade, because they had been using condoms. Technically, her plan was foolproof—except that she would lose Jonas in the bargain.

The guard started for her, and Sarah groaned, dropping her gaze and hoping that he hadn't seen her face. Her hiding time was over, if he had. If he recognized her, Sarah would never make it until the clinic opened. If he didn't call the press, someone he told would, and they would be all over her.

"You can't sleep here," he told her in a crisp voice.

Sarah cleared her throat and forced her voice to calm. "I'm not sleeping. Just got off work and waiting for the clinic to open."

"That's more than two hours away. You'll have to leave."

"And go where?"

"Home."

"Too far," she lied. Sarah could make it back and forth three times with favorable busses and six times in a car, but the guard couldn't know that.

"Go get some breakfast at Mickey D's."

"Fasting procedure." She wasn't sure if it was or not, but the thought of food made her feel sick anyway.

The guard nodded. "Okay."

Sarah sighed as he moved away without a backward glance. For the remaining two hours, she sat with the cap pulled low over her eyes, scanning the doorway, hall and minds for any signs of pursuit.

She didn't wait for the guard to tell her that the clinic was opening. The last thing Sarah wanted was to give someone a second look at her. She hesitated with her hand on the doorknob. She had to do this.

Sarah resisted the urge to run her hand over her baby. "No choice. I can't let you live this way," she whispered. She pushed the door open and walked to the desk, determined to follow her course to the end.

"Can I help you?" the nurse asked without looking up.

Sarah stilled. Emotions assaulted her despite the stronger shield she had erected.

Fear at first...then that was gone. *Comfort, safety* —

"W — what — " she stammered.

"Can I help you?"

Sarah closed her eyes, searching for the mind touching hers. It wasn't Jonas or Evan, and wasn't any of her family.

Warmth, holding, safe —

She tried again to touch the mind, but the emotions were muddled sensations, muted, without form. Touching her baby had become a habit. Sarah did it as she considered what this connection meant.

"Are you all right, Miss?" the nurse asked.

A touch of warmth, happiness, safety, trust —

"No," Sarah breathed. "Julian?"

"Do you need a doctor?"

Sarah snapped her eyes open, horrified at what she was doing. "No. Restroom. I don't — I don't feel well."

"If you're sure — "

"I am. Please." She took a step back from the desk.

"You don't look well."

Discomfort.

"The restroom?" she gasped.

"Down that hall."

Sarah turned and pushed through the door, walking to the restroom on shaking legs. She couldn't do this to a baby she could feel like this. Sarah couldn't pretend that it meant nothing when it was a child she was communicating with.

Still, Julian will never be safe. I can't do anything about that.

He trusts me to keep him safe. I'm his mother. I have to find a way.

There was nothing in her stomach to lose, but Sarah hunched next to the toilet in the handicapped stall, shaking and crying. When had everything gotten so complicated? Why was there never an easy answer?

She didn't know how long she sat there before she heard the outer door open. Sarah looked at the stall door in disbelief as the lock snapped open, pushing into the corner and preparing to defend herself. The lock wasn't opened with a coin or the edge of a key. Someone used a telekinetic push to do it, and no one would do that unless they knew who she was.

It's started already.

The door swung in, and Jonas loomed in the doorway. Sarah sucked in her breath as his emotions assaulted her, a complicated mix of relief, pain and fury. Then they were gone, hidden carefully behind his simulated E-shield.

He didn't speak. Jonas scooped her into his arms and started walking. He wasn't rough with her despite his fury. His hold was gentle, though Sarah had no doubt that it wouldn't be if she fought him.

"You're right about that," he growled against her hair.

Sarah nodded and burrowed her damp cheek into his chest. If he was reading her, he knew. "I'm sorry, Jonas."

"We'll discuss that later."

She grimaced at the cold edge to his voice and pulled her shield as tight as she could.

* * * *

Jonas kept up a minimal shield. Most of his energy was poured into scanning for potential problems and keeping his anger in check.

He ground his teeth as Sarah put up that damned super-shield she'd constructed after fighting Baker. That was the cause of all of this, her hiding. It couldn't continue. He couldn't let it.

The way out of the hospital was uneventful. Jonas was thankful for that. His hold on himself was strained enough as it was. If someone had challenged him, Jonas was sure he would have renegaded without thinking twice. If Sarah had fought him, he wasn't sure what he would have done.

Jonas breathed a sigh of relief as he unlocked his SUV by remote. He swung the door open and set Sarah in the seat. She didn't shrink from him, but she didn't speak to him or look at him either. Jonas stifled a harsh curse and placed her seatbelt in her hand.

Sarah nodded and fastened it carefully, placing the straps so they wouldn't hurt the baby in a crash. Jonas watched her in amazement. This was the same woman who'd snuck out, intent on having an abortion? He shook his head, then slammed the door. He'd never understand women, Sarah least of all.

He slid into the driver's side seat and put the key in, but Sarah placed her hand over his before he could start the engine. Jonas looked at her in irritation.

She blanched and turned her face away, pulling her hand back to her lap. "Seatbelt," she reminded him in a whisper.

Jonas stared at her, trying desperately to make sense of her actions. He tried to untangle the web of her shield, but she had wound her strands tight, a knit that not even he would be able to unravel, the shield she had shut herself behind for the last week. He wondered if she'd dropped it to aid her in her plan. That was likely.

"Please, Jonas. I know you hate me, but humor me. I don't—" She shook her head and leaned back in her seat, her face pale and tear-streaked.

He pulled his seatbelt on, wondering at her statement. Sarah thought he hated her? Jonas certainly wasn't feeling overwhelming love for her. He was angry, but he didn't hate her, did he?

He stifled the urge to ask Sarah if she'd read that in him or just assumed it. He decided that he didn't want to know the answer to that, didn't want to delve into the possibility that she had read something like that in his riotous emotions.

Jonas pulled out into traffic and headed for the parkway. He waited until he was out of the city proper before he pulled out his cell phone, not willing to chance Mac and his boys interfering with this before it was settled. He called Evan first.

"Got her?" Evan asked without any pleasantries. He had taken the news of Sarah's disappearance almost as seriously as Jonas had himself.

"Yeah. Just as we thought." After her complete disconnect with the world, Jonas had Evan check into any place Sarah could invoke the talent allowance and abort quickly and quietly. There was only one place she would go.

This move didn't surprise Jonas. He'd seen it coming, but he wouldn't let her do it this way. If Sarah ultimately decided not to have the baby, he would find a way to let it go. Jonas kept promising himself that he wouldn't force this on her, but he wouldn't let Sarah do it while she was in this condition, when she hadn't made a rational decision, when she might regret it in a clearer frame of mind. If Sarah decided to do this, she'd have to prove to Jonas that she was reasoning and not reacting out of desperation. If Jonas could, he'd convince her not to do it at all.

Evan sighed in relief. "Good."

"Which house?"

"The far side of the lake. I have a cover for the SUV, and no one is going to come looking. I liberated the keys. Since we're still technically on the rolls..." Evan didn't need to be more specific than that. This had been carefully planned days ago.

"Good. I'll see you in an hour."

Jonas met Sarah's startled gaze head-on as he disconnected. She looked out the window, searching for familiar landscape, as if the idea that they weren't headed to her parents' house was news to her. Was Sarah so lost in her own mind that the fact hadn't registered with her, until he mentioned it to Evan?

She didn't ask where they were headed or argue it in any way. Sarah seemed resigned to whatever he intended to do.

That worried Jonas. She couldn't keep hiding from the world. She had to connect to someone...somehow. Even Katie had her rock when she disconnected, one solid relationship that she'd held tight to.

He watched her as he drove. Sarah stared at the passing miles without locking her gaze on any particular thing. Her eyes drifted shut. She was exhausted. It was a miracle that she'd managed to pull this off at all.

Jonas flipped the phone out again. He took a deep breath to calm his nerves. Now came the hard part.

"Randall home," he ordered the auto-dialer.

He expected to hear Katie or Keith on the other end, but Steven picked up on the first ring.

"Where the hell are you?" he demanded, obviously using the caller ID next to the phone to make the determination.

"We're going away for a few days to work this out." Jonas secretly wondered how long it took Steven to make it to his parents' house after Jonas bolted out that morning.

Katie hadn't questioned his flight. She'd simply cleared the way toward the door and invited him to go. Sometimes, Katie did things that convinced Jonas she knew a lot more than she let on about what went on in her family's lives.

"You can't do this," Steven thundered.

"Sarah needs a break. No more reporters. No pressure. Just time to heal and regroup."

"No pressure from anyone but you, you mean."

Jonas sighed. "No, that's not what I mean. We are going to discuss this but not until she's ready."

"I want to talk to her."

"She's asleep."

The seconds ticked away with no reply from Steven.

"She's asleep, Steven. No stun-spray. No drugs. I didn't put her in a sleeper hold or the Vulcan neck pinch. I haven't forced anything on her. Asleep. We'll see you in a few days."

"She'll contact me. You can't stop that."

"I can, but I won't. You have my word on that. Until Sarah regroups, she won't contact anyone willingly. You know that. Hell, I'd be happy if she contacted you. It would mean she was acknowledging that someone else inhabited the Earth with her. I won't interfere with her contacting you or anyone else."

"I don't like this, Jonas."

"I'm not giving you a choice. Let me try to salvage this. It's all I have left. It's all I've lived for...the whole time she was gone. I can't walk away until I know this is what she really wants. Let me have that."

"Three days. After that — "

Jonas managed a strained smile. "You'll be tracking me as a renegade. I know. Goodbye, Steven."

He hung up and stared at the phone for a moment before destroying its internal circuitry. There'd be no tracing him that easily. Jonas tossed the useless phone on the rear seat next to the gym bag.

Sarah slept through, as Jonas pulled into the treeline next to the cabin and passed the gym bag off to Evan to stash inside for him. He settled Sarah in bed and stripped her down to his T-shirt and her underwear. Evan put his hand out for the keys to the SUV and left without a word.

Jonas settled in the bed with her, knowing Evan would cover the SUV and check it carefully for tags before he left. In a real emergency, Jonas could hot-wire the vehicle. Other than that, they were stranded here until he called for Evan. They'd arranged plans for every eventuality.

Sarah lay curled in on herself, tense even in sleep, her shield as impenetrable as steel beneath bare hands. No wonder she was so exhausted. She never relaxed, not even when she should be recharging. Jonas sighed, wishing Sarah would migrate to him in her sleep as she had before she was taken, sprawled against him with the silk of her hair draped over his chest.

* * * *

Sarah curled further under the blankets, reveling in the silence. There were no unguarded reporters' emotions tumbling over each other until her mind felt like a pinball in a confusing maze of bumpers and lights.

She stretched, then stilled as she encountered something hard and smooth. Her eyes snapped open, and Sarah followed the expanse of cotton-covered chest up to Jonas's face. His expression was unreadable, though she could feel his muscles tense under her hand.

Jonas — Sarah groaned and closed her eyes. He'd taken her from the hospital. He knew what she'd intended to do. He must hate her for it. For one mad moment, Sarah considered opening a crack in her shield and trying to read Jonas, then decided that she couldn't survive it if she found what she feared most in him.

"Are you hungry?" His voice was as emotionless as his face.

Sarah moved further away, unwilling to look him in the eye and see what he thought printed there—or worse, the same cold disinterest she'd seen in the car.

"I'm going to cook lunch. There's a bathroom through the far door. Come out to the kitchen when you're ready."

She nodded, waiting for Jonas to close the door behind him before she moved from the bed. Sarah considered crawling back in after she washed up, but her stomach protested that idea. She headed out to the table, resigned to facing Jonas.

He didn't face her. Sarah stared at his back, straining against the T-shirt as he cooked, and the muscles of his thighs under his worn jeans. She lowered her face and stared at her hands, folded in her lap. Remembering what his body felt like was torture. He'd never want to touch her again.

Jonas lowered a bowl of beef stew in front of her. "Eat," he ordered.

Sarah nodded and forced down the first spoonful. A glass of milk slid in next to her, followed by a croissant. "Thanks," she managed.

She cringed inwardly as she forced down another bite. Of course Jonas was feeding her well. He'd do that much for the baby. If anything, he probably expected Sarah to starve herself.

They ate in silence. Sarah choked down most of her meal, determined to prove that she wanted this.

Her mind was a damper on her appetite. Why would Jonas believe she'd had a change of heart? He had no reason to. Her meager hunger appeased, Sarah tried to escape to the bedroom.

Jonas locked his hand on her wrist. "Sit with me." His voice brooked no argument.

Sarah sank to the chair. "I won't—"

"I know. Just sit with me. Is that so terrible?"

"No." She hazarded a look at his eyes. They were emotionless. That was almost worse than seeing his anger or hate. At least, she'd know he felt something. Sarah looked away, swallowing a sob.

He released her wrist. "Why can't you look at me?" he asked.

"You know why."

"No. I don't. Tell me."

"You know what I almost did." She glanced at Jonas, then away as the fury in his eyes made her stomach rebel. *Okay, that's not better.* "That's why."

"Why didn't you?"

Sarah took a shuddering breath then shrugged. "I couldn't. He trusts me. I can't..." She buried her head in her hands, at a loss to explain how feeling their son changed everything.

There was a moment of silence. "You want to."

"No." It was the last thing she wanted, but there weren't many options presenting themselves.

"Why?"

"Julian trusts me," she whispered.

"Why *did* you want to?"

"I didn't want him to live this way." Sarah glanced at his shocked expression, then closed her eyes again.

"What way?"

"Hunted, scared. I can't— I don't want to kill, to...have to kill again. I can't protect him from physical attack. He'll never be safe."

Jonas pulled her to his chest. Sarah hadn't heard him move. He was just there, around her, with her silently.

"You think I'd allow that?" he asked gruffly.

"You can't always be there."

"Yes, I can." He carried her back to the bed, crawling in beside her again.

Sarah started to pull away, but Jonas locked her to his chest.

"No more hiding. You have three days to work this out with me. You're not leaving my side. You stay with me, or I will cuff you. It's your choice."

She shuddered. "No cuffs."

"Good. I'd rather see you catch up on your sleep comfortably."

Sarah closed her eyes. As Jonas's scent teased her senses, she wondered whether or not the cuffs would be kinder.

CHAPTER FIFTEEN

September 19th

Jonas pushed up on his elbow, watching Sarah as she slept. The food and sleep were helping her physical state. Her eyes had lost the dark, haunted circles she'd had three days earlier. Her appetite was good, though Jonas was sure that a healthy portion of what she ate was feeding the shield that she still maintained, even in sleep.

Her mental state was another issue altogether. They talked, but only when he initiated conversations. The only words Sarah volunteered were thanks when they were appropriate.

Jonas had let her set the pace for two days. He was running out of time. He had to know if there was any chance before the end of the day. If the sun rose on the next day, and he hadn't returned her to Steven, Jonas would officially be reported for kidnapping or renegade, whatever Steven felt in the mood to throw at him.

Sarah snuggled to him in her sleep. She had reverted to that the first night, firing his hope that sheer proximity might snap her out of her cocoon, but it hadn't worked that way. Jonas wondered if Sarah would open to him if she were unguarded.

Could it be any worse?

Probably, but I have to chance it.

Jonas ran a hand up her leg, cupping Sarah to him and nuzzling her jawline. Sarah groaned and turned further into him, her lips seeking his in the semi-darkness. She was passionate, and Jonas hardened in light of her reaction. He pulled her against the ridge forming in his jeans, his mouth urgent on hers, nibbling and possessing alternately.

Sarah wound her hands in his hair, pulling Jonas over her as her tongue sparred with his. Jonas held himself up on his arms, meeting her hungrily mouth to mouth while he allowed the barest contact of his abdomen to hers, cautious of the weight he could place on their son.

"Sarah?" he breathed, needing to know that she was making a conscious choice to accept him.

She shook her head. "Please don't. Don't talk now."

Jonas stilled, bringing his head up to look at her. "Why?"

Sarah searched his face, then dropped her gaze, curling her hands back to her chest.

"Sarah?"

"Why do you want this?" she whispered.

"What?" Sarah wasn't making sense. Why wouldn't he want this? He loved her. He'd spent the last four and a half months doing nothing but dreaming of this and plotting to get her back.

"What do you want from me, Jonas? I'll do it. I swear. I know you have no reason to believe me—"

"Is *that* what this is?" he asked in disbelief. "You're just going to have sex with me because you think that's what I want?"

She shook her head, seemingly lost and confused.

"Why did you kiss me, Sarah?" he asked more gently.

Sarah wiped away a tear. "I—" She searched his face, then took a ragged breath and looked away.

"Do you want me or not?"

"You know I do."

"No. I don't. *How* would I know? You won't look at me. You don't touch me. You don't tell me. You won't let down that damn shield even a crack."

"You could—"

"No. I won't force you to open up to me. You have to want to." Jonas didn't add that he couldn't force her, if she were unwilling. Sarah could stop him and often did, whether she realized it or not.

Number one in the world? No. Sarah has me beat in this department. That was a depressing thought, when it was working against him so effectively. "Do you want to?"

Sarah stared at him, seemingly lost. As if in realization, she sucked in her breath and touched his cheek with a shaking hand. "Why are you here, Jonas?" Her voice barely registered as a whisper.

"Don't you know?"

She shook her head, blinking back tears.

Her words in the hospital parking lot taunted him. *"I know you hate me..."*

Had he done anything to dispel that statement? Jonas hadn't even argued the point. What had that move said to her?

Jonas kissed her trembling lips, a gentle brushing of his body against hers. "Let me show you." He didn't wait for her agreement. Jonas stripped his shirt from her and pulled her hands to his jeans. "Do you want me, Sarah?"

Sarah's fingers fumbled at the buttons, and she made no verbal response, but she stripped Jonas and settled back to run her hands over his chest.

He leaned forward, skating his tongue around one darkened nipple. Jonas caught the hardened peak in his mouth and silently cheered the soft cry that escaped her lips.

Her hands stilled, and Jonas peered up at her as he trailed his lips to the other nipple, puckered and waiting for him. Sarah stared at him in wide-eyed wonder, as he sucked in the beaded nipple and flicked the tip of his tongue over it.

Jonas pulled back slightly. "Did you miss me?" he asked. He circled the nipple with the tip of his tongue while he waited for her response.

Sarah managed a jittery nod.

"I dreamed of you every time I closed my eyes," he assured her. "And sometimes even when they were open."

Her eyes closed, as he started to trace the opposite nipple. He teased his fingers inside the crotch of her panties, playing at the heat and moisture he'd stirred in her. She stifled a cry, as his fingers slid inside her, and her eyes opened wider than before.

Jonas stared at the swell of their son in longing. He passed by the tempting mound, knowing Sarah would misinterpret the move in her state of mind. Instead, he settled his mouth between her thighs, administering a single lick across her clit that broke her silence.

Her scream of longing stole his breath. Jonas dragged her panties off, noting that Sarah looked shattered by a mere touch. Jonas settled on his back and lifted her until Sarah straddled him, the length of his erection twitching against the heat of her spread over it.

"Do you want me?" he asked again.

Sarah moved against him restlessly. "Yes, Jonas."

He ground his teeth, trying to control his need. "Forever?"

She stilled, her breath coming in gasps. "You still—" A blush spread from her face down her neck and chest.

"Drop your shield, Sarah."

She tried to pull away, her expression one of stark terror. "I can't."

Jonas locked her to him. "What are you afraid of?"

Sarah shook her head, fighting back tears again.

"Are you afraid I'm angry at what you tried to do? That I'll hate you for it?"

She slumped, her chin dropping to her chest. "I don't want to feel that," she admitted.

Jonas pulled her to his chest, wrapping his arms around her shoulders. "I don't and I won't. You said you don't want that, that you've changed your mind."

"Why would you trust me? You have no reason to."

"You could solve that."

"How?"

Jonas brushed his hands through her hair, noting her shaking. "Drop your shield."

"No. I—"

"Remember who I am, Sarah. If I can read you, I'll know for sure."

Sarah shook her head. "I can't."

"I trust you. Trust me. Drop your shield for me. I want you to know how I feel."

She swallowed hard.

"You're still afraid?"

She nodded.

Jonas eased Sarah to the bed. She started to turn away, but he stopped her, shaking his head.

"No. If I have to do this the hard way, I will."

"The hard way?" Sarah intensified her already rigid shield.

He kissed her. "Not that way, Sarah. I said I wouldn't force you, and I won't."

"Then what?"

Jonas smiled. He ran his fingers in delicious little circles up her inner thigh, forcing a gasp of surprise from her lips.

"Give me this much. The rest will come in time."

Sarah groaned, tipping her hips for him in silent appeal.

Jonas obliged her, inching his hand up her thigh as he kissed her, firing her into a fierce arousal. It was sweet torture for them both, the barest touch of skin to skin after a long fast. Sarah wound her hands around his neck and pulled him closer, her fingers curling, as Jonas eased his fingers into her again.

"That's right," he breathed. "Just feel." *Remember what being alive is like.*

She furrowed her brow in confusion as Jonas pulled her hands from his shoulders.

"I want to taste you. That is something I could never do while you were gone. That is one thing no psi talent I have could have given me."

Sarah nodded, rocking her head back as he feathered his thumb over her clit.

"You are so beautiful." *I have to make you mine again. I can't live without you.*

Jonas slid down to replace his fingers with his mouth. Sarah was hot and ready for anything he wanted, but he wanted her to give herself to him, fully and freely. Her taste was wilder than Jonas remembered, heavier in musk. It teased his mind, playing at the last of his sanity.

She grasped at his hair, her breathing coming in ragged gasps. "Jonas, please—" Her shield flickered for a moment before Sarah fortified it.

Damn! So close. Jonas changed his rhythm, groaning into her body as a fresh wave of her musk washed over his tongue.

Sarah's fingers tangled in his hair, flexing and gripping, her desperation clear in every movement.

"Tell me, Sarah." He licked a slow path through her labia, then circled her clit.

She screamed and bowed up beneath him.

Jonas raised his head, staring at her, waiting for some verbal response. "What do you want? Tell me."

"I want—" Sarah swallowed hard, looking tortured.

"Trust me." He buried his tongue in her, drinking in her reaction as she writhed against him.

"I want you to make love to me," she pleaded.

Jonas raised his head to gauge her mood, smiling at her frightened expression. "I thought you'd never ask."

It was the only right answer. If she'd have said 'have sex' instead of 'make love,' Jonas wouldn't have touched her.

He slid up Sarah's body, pulling her to her side and drawing her leg over his hip. They'd been here dozens of times, and still it felt new. Perhaps it was because it was the first time there were no secrets between them.

No secrets and no condoms. He feathered his lips against hers, greedily breathing in the puff of air escaping her lips at the move.

"I'm making love to you, Sarah," he breathed. *I've always made love to you.*

She nodded, wrapping her arms around him. The anticipation was too much; he didn't question that they both needed more. Jonas shuddered and stilled as his cock adjusted to her heat encasing him, his breathing degrading into gasps of precious Sarah-scented air.

Sarah's fingers brushed his chest. "What's wrong?"

He groaned, pulling her hips to him to slide to the hilt. "They lied."

"Who?"

"Those idiots at Trojan who claim it feels like not wearing anything." He moved slowly, adjusting to the new sensations. "My God, this is good."

"Yes. Please don't stop."

Jonas smiled as he speeded his pace, matching her breathless cries as Sarah urged him on. He lost track of his plan in his need to come in her, to feel her body react to the warm explosion building in him.

Sarah's shield folded, her internal muscles gripping him as she screamed out his name and tightened her leg around his hip. As always, her wants and needs assaulted him, and Jonas let them wash over him. The shattered images of sexual fantasies merged with images of a wedding, their son and other babies they'd have together.

Jonas groaned, his pace furious. "Yes, Sarah. All of that and more. I promise."

He furrowed his brow. Sarah was using telepathy of some sort, but Jonas couldn't seem to identify her contact. He linked with her and sucked in his breath at the sensations coursing through her.

The physical sensations captured the least of his attention. He zeroed in on the emotions that held her captive, not his own emotions, which were shunted to the back of her mind.

Warmth, comfort, safety, trust —

Trust?

What had Sarah said the first day in the kitchen? "*He trusts me. I can't — Julian trusts me.*"

Her words made sense, with the addition of this new information.

Jonas ran his hand over their son, reveling in the baby's enjoyment. "Oh, God," he breathed. "You hear him."

Sarah sobbed. "You see? I could never—"

"Shhh. Never." Jonas captured her mouth, connected to Sarah in every intimate manner at once. He tensed, his release rolling through all of them in the physical and in the link.

Sarah's nails bit his shoulders hard as his heat flooded her. Jonas felt her scream mingle with his own as he surged into her again and again. Sarah's pleasure mixed with their baby's contentment and Jonas's continuing spasms of release, a potent drug that made his senses swim.

He held her to him as he stilled. Jonas threw his head back and roared the loss of their connection as the last of his control slipped away. He kissed her throat, forcing his hands to ease their grip.

Jonas pulled his head back and met her tear-misted eyes. "I didn't hurt you, did I?" He hadn't planned to be so rough with her.

Sarah shook her head. "No. I'm fine."

He raised an eyebrow. "Fine? I think my ego took a shot."

She blushed. "Better than fine."

Jonas laughed, his hands roaming over their son. "Yes. You are better than fine. I may have to use the cuffs, after all."

Sarah's smile disappeared. "Why?"

Jonas reached over her body and pulled them from the nightstand drawer.

* * * *

Sarah shook her head in confusion. What had she said or done wrong? She stiffened as she heard the cuffs shift against each other.

Jonas held them suspended over her, and Sarah stared at them in the dim light, her fear melting into stunned disbelief. She started laughing hysterically, tears rolling down her cheeks as she smacked his arm. They were her cuffs, the ones from her stash of sex toys.

Her laughter choked off as Jonas rubbed the fur lining over one hard nipple, then the other. The throbbing for him started again. Sarah brushed her cheek over the rough stubble on Jonas's chin, tightening her leg around him and urging him closer.

"Christ, Sarah! Give it a rest. It's only five thirty. Some of us have to go to work and be productive today."

She laughed harder. *"Go away, Steven. Put your shield up. Just because I'm here doesn't mean you have to listen in."*

Jonas was suddenly in her mind. *"Go to sleep, Steven. I'll block for you."*

Sarah stared at him, shocked at that pronouncement. "You can do that?" She sucked in her breath as Steven disappeared from her mind. She reached out to him, but there was a dead area around her. Sarah pushed at Jonas, needing to escape, feeling the stifling psi wave closing in on her.

Jonas smoothed his hands down her arms. "Shhh. I'm here. If it bothers you that badly, I'll stop."

She calmed, the touch on her mind reassuring. "What are you doing?"

"I'm just keeping the peace with Steven. Does it bother you?"

She shook her head. "You'll stop when I ask?"

"Always. Is it okay?"

Sarah nodded. It wasn't really like the psi wave. That kept her from reading even people right next to her. She had Jonas and Julian. She could do this. It could even come in handy someday.

Jonas's smile widened as he resumed his torture of her with the faux fur. "What's the matter?" he teased as she tensed.

Sarah fought to think clearly. "The cuffs."

"You're afraid of being tied up and at my mercy? I seem to recall that you used to enjoy it quite a bit." Jonas pushed visions of her tied to her bed that first night into her mind, teasing Sarah with what he wanted to repeat.

"I do. It's just—"

"You thought I'd put plain steel cuffs on you? To keep you here?"

She bit her lower lip and nodded.

"Never." He ran his hand up her neck to cup her face. "I would never have hurt you."

"Even—"

"Even then." Jonas kissed her. "I knew you'd try. I thought I'd have to stop you. I didn't expect you to stop yourself. I'm glad you did."

"What do we do now?"

"Do you want to marry me?"

Sarah blushed. "You know I do. You saw."

"Then what's the problem?"

"He'll never be safe. Fantasy is one thing, but this is reality I have to deal with."

"What if I could guarantee his safety?" Jonas offered.

"How? Neither of us is rich. I know what DoPT operatives earn."

Jonas silenced her with a kiss. "What if we had a job together?"

Sarah backed away, shaking her head. "You're not recruiting me. We had a *deal*. You were getting out." She tried to roll off the bed, determined to get as far away from him as she could.

Jonas gathered her back to his chest. "I have no desire to be a DoPT field operative, and I would never allow you to take that chance."

"*Allow?* How dare you—"

His mouth came down on hers, hard and urgent. Sarah's body played traitor to her outrage, leaving her in a confused haze as Jonas rolled her beneath him. He eased her hands from his neck and pressed them into the pillow beside her head, his mouth moving to the spot behind her earlobe and nipping at her gently. Sarah shifted her head, giving him better access as he—locked the cuffs on her wrists.

Sarah's mind cleared, and she pulled at the cuffs, finding them threaded through two of the spindles in the headboard. Gritting her teeth, she shook the cuffs and glared at Jonas. "Get these off me," she demanded.

Jonas raised an eyebrow. "We will discuss this."

"I'll—"

"No. You won't. I've taken care of that, remember? Even if you did contact Steven, how can he help you? Do you know where we are? All you'll do is worry him."

Sarah groaned. "You're not winning points here, Jonas."

"Promise to settle down and talk to me, and I'll take them off."

"I'm naked, Jonas. Where am I going?"

"The last time you promised to hear me out, you attacked me and ran from me with no coat, despite fair warning that you were in deep trouble."

"You shouldn't have brought that up," she grumbled.

"Sarah?"

"Look where it got me last time. I'll talk to you. Otherwise, I may spend the next four months cuffed to this bed."

"You'll hear me out?"

"Yes."

"Okay. We've been offered a job—the two of us together."

"Jonas? The cuffs?" she reminded him.

"In a minute."

"You promised."

He darkened. "I want to make sure you don't hit me and run when I tell you what the job is."

"Oh, hell. You want me to work for the DoPT."

"Indirectly," he admitted.

Sarah closed her eyes. "We *agreed*—"

"They want us to head a new halfway house. It'd be a cross between a foster home and a boarding school."

She looked at him in confusion. "An academy?"

"Not quite. The psych guys and social workers like what you did at Clinton. The kids are controlled, happy and have self-respect. Much like the children in your family tend to grow up, I might add."

"And?"

"They like it enough that they want to segway kids into the population in smaller group homes that can give the kids that one-on-one interaction. They want to entice talents to train young talents to be their own keepers, like your family has done for each other."

"I don't understand."

"They want us to take on a test group, the worst of the worst the academies have to offer."

Sarah hesitated. It was a good idea, but the timing was wrong. "I'm pregnant, Jonas. I don't know if I can—"

"That's why we'd do this together. Let me tell you about the test group."

"Okay."

"We'd have a group of a dozen, mixed ages, family group. The youngest is six. The oldest is seventeen. We'd have help."

"Help? Not guards."

"No. Our keeper on staff is Evan, if you agree to this. Our original dozen will include some old friends. The idea is that the ones who are trained already will help police the new arrivals."

Sarah fought for a decent breath. "Jeremy and Alice?"

Jonas nodded, biting back laughter. "And Danny, Tyler and Cindy. The other seven will be our tough guys. Aaron and Ella are from Trenton. Carlos is from Carver. Paul is from Andrews. Stephanie is from Edison. Parker and his little sister Sam are from Paine. I refused to take Parker, unless we kept the family together."

Sarah fought back tears. "Oh, Jonas."

"We'll have stun-spray, but we'll only use it if we have to. We can send a child back for disciplinary at the academy, for specified periods of lockdown—"

"No," she protested, horrified at the thought of inflicting that.

"Sarah—"

"*No.* I won't send a child into iso."

Jonas smiled. "Neither will I, but the kids don't need to know that."

"Are you suggesting that we play good cop, bad cop?"

"Well, we have the cuffs," he noted.

Sarah ran her foot up Jonas's leg. "Yes. We do."

Jonas shot her a hungry look. "No changing the subject. Now, are you willing to see the site we're considering?"

"It's in Pittsburgh?"

"Not far outside. It's a rambling old farmhouse in Somerset."

"Close enough."

He sighed in relief. "You'll consider it?"

"If we set the rules, and it gets Jeremy and the others out of Clinton, I'll do it."

"It's a long-term commitment. We'd be taking these kids on for years."

"Are you trying to talk me into this or out of it?"

"They'd protect you like Jeremy protected you. They'd be big brothers and sisters to Julian." He ran his hands over their baby.

"You'll have to marry me. Even foster kids need a stable family."

"Funny. Your mother told me about the nicest little chapel, just before we left."

"Uh huh."

His hands moved to cup Sarah to his body, his cock hard against her hip. "I have a ring in that drawer."

"Is that a yes?" she prodded him.

"I could keep the cuffs on you until you agree to marry me."

"No."

"Why not?"

"Because I intend to agree right now."

"And?" Jonas asked, his eyes glittering.

Sarah leaned forward and brushed her lips over his. "I have another use for the cuffs. Understood, operative?"

"Keep in mind who is Alpha-One around here," he replied gruffly.

"In your dreams."

"The first to break loses?" Jonas offered.

"It's a deal. Hope you enjoy being Alpha-Two, Paige."

THE END

MAX-SEC

A RENEGADE SHORT STORY

DEDICATED TO...

Sean and Lisa, for always asking, "What next?" Now, I have the knack and can't let go.

Tamer, for helping me banish demons from my past.

PROLOGUE

February 10th, 2015

"Welcome to Carver, Katheryn," the headmaster greeted her. "Steven."

He extended his hand to them, but neither of them took it. Steven curled his lip in disgust.

Katie fought back her anger. They'd never be free if they didn't prove themselves trustworthy, but they were being provoked almost beyond reason, at this point. She hadn't been able to reach Alex telepathically in two days, and that was maddening. "Mrs. Randall will be fine, Mr. Raines. Now...Where is my son?"

He darkened. "That's a bit..."

"Mr. Raines, the fact that I can't feel him at all limits your options for a believable answer. I'd make the explanation a good one if I were you."

"Are you threatening me?" he demanded.

One of the academy guards tensed behind him. Katie met his gaze with practiced boredom, then turned back to Raines.

"If you've read my file, you know I won't harm you physically, but if my son is not returned to me in five minutes, my lawyers will have a new injunction on you within an hour."

"Phone use..."

She chuckled. "Mr. Raines, I don't *need* a phone."

He looked from Katie to Steven, his shield fluctuating in frustration. He pasted on a smile and turned toward max-sec.

Steven shuddered, one hand creeping to his chest and then retreating again, his spine stiffening in defiant pride.

Katie squeezed his shoulder in comfort. "*There are no bands, Steven,*" she soothed him. "*You won't be alone here.*"

"Why is my son in iso?" she asked calmly.

"He broke out of his room one evening. Actually, he broke a lot of rules that night. He also physically assaulted the guard who found him...with talent, of course."

Katie faltered, coming to a halt as the image assaulted her. It wasn't from Alex but rather from someone *over* Alex.

The focus turned toward the door as the guard rushed through, his baton raised and a look promising death on his face. A girl screamed in terror.

"*No,*" *Alex shouted. His hand appeared in her field of vision.*

As the baton came down, the guard flew back.

He hit the wall hard and slumped to the floor.

The girl sobbed, and the scene blurred, most likely in her tears. She looked at Alex again. "*What do we do now?*"

His face was pale, his wild gaze locked on his shaking hand. "*Oh, God,*" *he whispered.* "*What have I done? They'll kill me for this.*"

"*No, this was my...*"

"*Don't say it,*" *he warned, pulling his hand back slowly.* "*Don't interfere. Promise me.*"

"*You were only protecting —* "

More guards came through the door. Alex closed his eyes, grimacing as they dragged the sobbing girl away from him. The stun-spray came next. She screamed, reaching for him as the slack look settled over him.

"*He was only protecting me,*" *she wailed.*

"Katheryn?" Raines asked.

She shook off his hand in disgust. "Your guard would have killed them, Mr. Raines."

"There is no evidence that..."

"He swung his baton at them."

Raines turned toward an open doorway, glaring at a preteen girl with blond braids and sad green eyes peeking at them around the doorframe. She startled and ducked back into the room.

Katie rounded him and followed her. The girl sat, curled on her bed with her knees to her chest, looking terrified.

"It's okay honey," she crooned. "It was you that night, wasn't it?"

She nodded. "I've seen you," she whispered.

Katie grimaced. "On TV?"

"No. We're not allowed to watch it. Alex..." She looked past Katie and dropped her gaze, shivering.

She ignored Raines, making a mental note to tell the Supreme Court how frightened the children were of him, at a later date. "What's your name?"

"Ginny. Ginny Reynolds."

She nodded. "We'll talk again, Ginny. Right now, I have to get Alex out of iso."

The child sighed in relief. "I knew you would."

"Now just a darned minute," Raines protested.

Katie turned on him, forcing back the urge to instruct him in what a real talent could do when provoked. "Even if my son was guilty...which he's *not*, Randalls and Thompsons are their own keepers, Mr. Raines!"

"Your son certainly didn't act like it," he countered hotly.

"My son was attacked, and he's a child. Until he matures, I am his keeper...and *Kyle* is his keeper. You won't have any more problems from Alex."

"I had better not, Mrs. Randall. If I do, and you stand in my way, you and your son will find yourselves in neighboring iso tanks. Don't doubt it."

"You don't intimidate me, Mr. Raines. I've fought a talented murderer a hundred times more powerful than you are...almost more powerful than I am. Nothing you can do to me could be worse."

Legally. That is what the whole Supreme Court case hinges on, after all. What is legal *treatment for talents? Are we afforded the same rights as* normal *people, or does carrying a lethal arsenal in our heads make us less than human?*

He stared at her, as if he wasn't sure if she was serious. Katie could easily learn what he was thinking; his shield was weak enough not to be much of a barrier against her, but with the freedom of every talent stolen from their homes and incarcerated in these damned academies riding on it, it wasn't a chance she could take.

"My son, Mr. Raines," she reminded him.

"Of course, Mrs. Randall."

He led her to iso tank number three and ordered the doors opened. Steven took an involuntary step back, and she sent him a reassuring smile.

Katie entered the room alone, forcing herself not to grind her teeth as the psi wave isolated her. It was disconcerting to be in the same room with one of her children and not be able to touch his mind, but Alex depended on her to get him out of here.

She crossed the room and knelt next to the air mattress placed on the floor, curling her nose at the smell of sweat. He hadn't bathed in the two days he'd been isolated, of course. She'd expected that, but it seemed he hadn't bothered with the most basic hygiene he was allowed, which was a surprise.

Or he wasn't free to do it. She shuddered at that thought. If they'd kept him bound for longer than a few hours, God only knew what his mental state would be.

"Alex," she called.

He didn't respond.

She touched his arm gingerly, well aware that his responses might be volatile. "Alex?"

His eyes opened slowly, and his muscles tensed in preparation to run or fight.

"Alex, it's Mom. Give me a sign."

He turned, looking up at her in confusion. Then tears welled in his eyes, and he threw himself at her, hugging her tightly while he sobbed. "I'll be good," he whispered. "I promise. Please, don't leave me in here."

Katie struggled to her feet, dragging his shivering form up and guiding him to the doors. "Let's get you out of here," she soothed him.

She glared at Raines, then followed him down the hall, Alex stumbling along, still holding her in a death grip.

Ginny stood in her doorway, tears in her eyes. Alex looked at her and then away, his shaking more pronounced. The girl turned away with a sob and disappeared behind the door to her room.

Katie resolved to talk to her once Alex was settled in his "room." This wasn't her fault, and Ginny couldn't be allowed to think that it was, but Alex's situation was more dire.

She steered him into the room Raines indicated and onto the lower bunk, pulling his arms away with the intention of getting a washcloth to bathe his face. He grasped at her hand, shaking his head wildly.

"I won't leave you," she promised.

He sighed, closing his eyes, though his grip didn't lessen.

Katie made a mental note of everything he needed: a shower, food, sleep, and constant interaction with others, starting with the class two calming touch she started to administer. There was no way to do that and contact Sarah at the same time.

"Steven, I need your sister to contact Marcus. Can you..."

"I already have," he grumbled. "Every second of it."

She nodded her thanks, scanning the room and scowling at the red light indicating the cameras were turned on.

This was the best Marcus could do for them until the Supreme Court made their decision...three rooms on max-sec corridor. Steven and Alex would share a room; she and Kyle would have their own. Like it or not, they were stuck here, praying for the justice system to set them free.

CHAPTER ONE

March 20th, 2029

Alex Randall read the card in his hand again, shaking his head in disbelief. "Ginny Reynolds," he breathed. How long had it been since he'd seen her? Fourteen years? "A lifetime ago."

More than a lifetime ago, when he still felt alive, when he wasn't constantly looking over his shoulder and jumping at anyone in Navy blue and beige. It hardly seemed possible that there was a time he didn't waste his energy scanning for attack constantly. Then again, if he'd been scanning that night, maybe he wouldn't have sent a man to the hospital for nearly a week and himself to hell for the last decade and a half.

Ginny Reynolds had been his partner in crime. Two years older and no happier at being torn from her family than he'd been, she'd been his willing counterpart in any number of schemes that Raines suspected them of but could never really prove. She'd been his family in a place that had robbed him of family, the straight man to his comedy act, his first crush and the one touch of humanity that had kept him going...for as long as it lasted.

Are you going to stand here all day? he berated himself. Already, he'd stood there in front of the posh building on Granby Street for five minutes, earning him suspicious looks from the guard behind the desk.

What are you afraid of? This is Ginny.

A Ginny that's fourteen years older and shows up out of the blue with an invitation up to her place to talk about old times?

Ah, isn't paranoia a wonderful *life skill.* He'd wanted to thank some politician properly for more than half of his life for that gift.

I didn't come all this way to turn back now. After all the memories and all the dreams, he couldn't walk away until he saw her. He couldn't live with the image of her sad, pitying eyes. He had to see that she came out of the academies okay...and act like *he* had, or she might blame herself forever.

He pushed through the door and ambled to the desk, praying this wasn't some sort of prank...or that someone hadn't used his former friendship to lure him into something unsavory.

Paranoia talking again, bud!

"I'm here to see Ms. Reynolds," he began, feigning nonchalance while he scanned his surroundings constantly.

The guard smiled. "Identification, if you please, Mr. Randall."

He handed over his driver's license, furrowing his brow at the petite brunette. He automatically searched out the cameras around him and suppressed a shudder of unease. He took his license back, sliding it into his wallet.

"Up that elevator to the penthouse," she instructed. "I'll release it from here."

Alex nodded his thanks and headed up to Ginny's home. He glanced at the camera in the elevator and then away. Cameras made him nervous. Surely, Ginny remembered that. In fact, he couldn't understand how *she* could live in a place that had so many in the common areas.

The elevator doors opened, and he hurried to the inner door. Alex winced at the sight of another camera. What was it with Ginny and all these cameras? He knocked, eyeing the closest lens in growing unease.

The door swung open, and he turned back to it, his heartbeat skipping at the sight of her. Ginny had been beautiful at twelve. At twenty-six, she was stunning. Her deep gold hair was pulled back in a ponytail behind her head, and her pine green eyes glittered in amusement.

"Alex?" she asked. "Are you all right?"

"Yeah. Sure. Just..." He swallowed a hot lump in his throat as she shifted, her silk bodysuit outlining the bare breasts beneath. "Fine," he finished breathlessly.

Ginny chuckled. "Good. Then come in." She moved aside to let him pass, closing the door behind them.

Alex raised an eyebrow at the living room décor. Everything was done in shades of beige and Navy. The furniture was from the finest companies: a Pierre Original sofa set here, a Jacobian table collection there, Azultia figurines on the shelves.

"What do you think of it?" she asked.

It looks like max-sec hell! "You have good taste in designers," he offered diplomatically, wincing at the bars over the windows. What would a tenth-floor apartment overlooking a cliff need bars for? A chill ran down his spine at the sight of them.

Just like old times. Wahoo. Aren't memories great?

"And you don't lie very well," she noted in amusement.

Alex grinned. "No. I guess I don't. I hate it, if you want to know the truth. It gives me the willies."

Ginny breezed past him to a bar...beige stained wood with a Navy-veined marble top. "That's better. Would you care for one?"

"Sure. Make it a double." *Maybe I can forget my surroundings if I have a few.* "Rum. Thanks."

"Will do." She poured the drink, then a matching one for herself, offering him one of the glasses. "Aren't you going to ask?"

He swallowed a mouthful of the alcohol, thankful for the burn that helped fight off the chill of his memories. "Do I have to?"

"Ahhh... I see. It still bothers you that much."

He grimaced, taking another mouthful down. "Is there any reason it *shouldn't*?" A defensive note crept into his voice at that. The academies were hell on earth, a hell he'd fought very hard to ensure no more innocents had to endure.

"Is there any reason it has to run your life?" she countered.

Alex stared at her in disbelief. "Seems to me that it runs yours just fine."

He expected her to be angry at the observation, but she laughed heartily.

"Do you have any beige or Navy in your home, Alex? Any at all?"

He tried to refute that, wracked his brain to come up with something that was, to no avail.

"You don't," she stated with confidence. "If someone buys you something that is, you exchange it, don't you? *Buuut* people know not to buy you things that are beige and Navy."

Alex drained the rest of his glass. It wasn't helping; the bars over the windows seemed too close, the feeling of people watching him too real. "So, I went to one extreme, and you went to the other," he dismissed her.

"Actually, this isn't where I live...not on a regular basis."

"Then why did you bring me here?" he demanded, his temper rising.

Ginny's hand covered his, the warmth strangely disconcerting. "You saved my life once. I've never forgotten that."

"This is a hell of a way to repay it!"

"Alex..."

"What's your game, Ginny? Why did you bring me to this..." He waved his hand uncertainly.

"Mock-up. My father had it built for me. It took him two years to break me of my fears, and this mock-up was the first step in that rehabilitation process." She hesitated, her expression abruptly uncertain. "His approach was a bit different, of course. He was dealing with a child and..."

Alex's heart pounded double time. "Is that what this is? You want to...cure me?"

She bit her lower lip, stroking his hand.

He set the glass down a little more forcefully than he intended, willing his breathing to even in light of the concept of spending any length of time in this room. "I appreciate the offer, but my Dad had the best..."

"Were they there?" she interrupted him, her voice a whisper.

"What?"

"Did they live on max-sec, Alex? Even on min—sec?"

He shook his head. "Of course not."

"I did. Let me try."

Alex looked around at the room again, not quite holding back a shudder. He hated that response; he hated that they still had a hold on him. If there was any way out, could he ignore the possibility?

"What do you have in mind?" he asked.

"It's simple, really. Put yourself in my hands."

"And you do what, precisely?"

Ginny pulled his hand to her lips, tracing the knuckles slowly. He watched the motion, unable to tear his attention from her, his cock abruptly painfully erect.

"There's no better way to banish a bad memory than with a good one."

* * * *

Ginny didn't need her talents to know that Alex wanted her. He'd needed her companionship when they were ten and twelve. He needed more than that now that they were adults and able to pursue more.

And she wanted him. They'd shared one kiss...one heart-stopping kiss...and she'd never forgotten it.

"Will you stay?" she asked.

He nodded, seemingly stunned by the offer.

"Good. We'll build on an already happy memory."

Alex snorted in disbelief. "Of the academies? There isn't one."

Ginny swallowed a lump of pain at that. "None?" she inquired.

His twisted grimace disappeared in what she assumed was a flash of understanding. He stood, cupping his hand around her neck and drawing her mouth to his.

The kiss was tentative at first, much as it had been at the academy. That approach never lasted long between them. In less than a minute, Alex's hunger won out. By the time he pulled back, they were both panting in arousal.

He pressed his forehead to hers. "God, that gets better every time."

She smiled. "It can get even better than that," she offered.

Alex looked to the couch. His voice was rough when he spoke again. "Are you offering..."

"Yes. I am."

His gaze stayed locked on the Navy Pierre Original stretch. "Why?"

"Have you thought about that kiss, Alex? Have you thought about me?"

"Yes. I have."

"So have I." *Maybe, if I do this, I won't obsess over it anymore.*

He nodded, stripping off his suit coat and tie and laying them over the bar. "I have protection."

"We don't have to..."

He shot her a wary look, and she nodded. He didn't trust her to handle it. All things considered, that was to be expected.

Alex took her hand and led her to the couch. For a moment, he stared into her eyes as he had that night. He didn't speak; he didn't touch her. He simply leaned forward and touched his lips to hers.

She sighed, her eyes fluttering shut. *Yes.* This was the moment she remembered, that perfect instant when he'd kissed her. Ginny pulled back, reminding herself to play her part exactly as she had before.

"The cameras," she whispered.

He paused, swallowing hard. Ginny could almost hear his rationalization that there were no guards, though his thoughts were shielded from her.

Finally, he managed to say it. "No one knows we're gone. They won't be watching."

His hands circled her waist, and he pleaded silently for her agreement. He needed human contact; he needed to feel alive.

She wound her hands around his neck and kissed him. Alex eased to the couch, drawing her down with him. His erection was thick and heavy, ready for her. Their kiss became fevered and desperate.

She could mark the moment when the guard burst in, and so could he. His groan rumbled into her mouth, and his hand closed on her breast. They hadn't made it this far last time; they likely wouldn't have, considering their ages and situation. But, they were adults now...and they were free.

Ginny eased the buttons on his shirt open, shifting her weight to accomplish it. Her movement allowed Alex to start undoing the hooks down the front of her coveralls. All the time, his mouth was busy at hers: manic, hungry, seeking fulfillment.

He pushed the silk down her arms, baring her to the waist. His mouth left hers, and he ranged his gaze down her body. Ginny placed her hands on the arm of the couch and raised herself until her breasts were even with his mouth, offering herself to him.

He sampled them, slowly at first and then vigorously. Alex pulled open the last few hooks and pushed the silk down her thighs, his hands stroking over the smooth skin beneath. Ginny went still as one hand circled to the front of her body and his fingers slid inside her. God, the man knew exactly how to touch her. She sat back over his thighs, the silk around her ankles spreading her body over his as if designed to position her for sex.

She opened his pants and eased them down his hips. Ginny smiled at the sight of him, his chest bare between the open sides of his dress shirt, his cock bared but little more... This is almost what he would look like with his coverall undone, and they wouldn't have undressed completely that night. An image of Alex in the coveralls assaulted her. Yes. She'd like to peel him out of them slowly.

Alex fumbled in his pocket, coming out with a condom. She took it from him, stroking his length and considering...

"No," he pleaded in a whisper. "No time."

Ginny met his eyes, sucking in her breath in surprise. It wasn't so much that Alex was immersed in the illusion that shocked her, but that he was reading her mind through her shield. She'd known he was powerful, but...

"Ginny," he grumbled. "Now. Please."

She ripped open the condom and rolled it down his length.

"Stole it from the infirmary," he whispered conspiratorially.

Her body pulsed at that. Only Alex would have dared steal at the academy. Not that he ever had...

"That you know of," he finished for her, a sly smile curving his lips. His hands closed on her hips, guiding Ginny toward his cock. "Now, I'm going to break a few more rules," he promised.

She held him by the base, aiding him in seating himself inside her. She moved her hand to his abdomen a split-second before he thrust into her.

Alex didn't give her a chance to catch her breath. She closed her eyes as he slid deep inside her again and again, his muscles rippling beneath her hands. Her head spun. The image of them in the rec room was so vivid that Ginny found herself stifling her cries into whimpers and gasps.

"Quiet," he whispered, reinforcing the illusion.

He tested that by thrusting deeper, chuckling as she ground her teeth. She threw her head back, moving in counterpoint to the rolling motions of his hips, feeling her body tighten around his length. She was close...so close.

"It'll be Raines's office next," he promised. "On the bastard's desk."

Ginny opened her eyes, too stunned to stop her scream of release. It was there in her mind...the two of them on the headmaster's desk, his files pushed to the floor, papers strewn from the potted lemon tree to the door onto min-sec corridor.

"You," she gasped. *That was not my imagination.*

Alex had implanted the image. She wished the cameras could catch that.

Alex roared, tensing as he climaxed. His hands tightened on her hips, making Ginny yelp in response. His eyes darted around, locking on the camera recessed in the far wall. Too late, she remembered that he was in her mind.

His jaw tightened, and he jerked his hands away. "Off," he ordered.

"Alex, let me—"

"Off!"

An uncomfortable bubble of energy set her senses on alert. It was a warning not to balk him, a tangible barrier between them. She scrambled off the couch in response, unwilling to court a more powerful reaction from him, and kicked her coveralls away.

She didn't hesitate. Alex was dragging his clothes back on; she didn't have time to waste. By the time she returned with the DVD in hand, he was busy stuffing his tie in the pocket of his jacket. He scowled at her, a deadly glare in his eyes, the bubble fluctuating in warning.

Ginny offered the case to him, willing her hands to be still.

He looked at it in confusion. "What is that?" he asked warily.

"It's just us, Alex. No guards. No iso tank. No batons and stun-spray. Just us. I only want to help. If you decide to forgive me, you know where to find me. Any time, day or night, I'll be here for you."

He looked from the disc to her face, his uncertainty melting into fury. Alex snatched the DVD and stormed out the door, slamming it behind him with an amazing burst of telekinesis.

Ginny sank to the couch, fighting back tears. "I just want to help."

CHAPTER TWO

March 26th, 2029

Alex punched his pillow, cursing himself for even considering going back to her. He'd stared at the DVD he'd thrown on his desk, where it had lain for three days before he'd broken down and watched it. He'd spent the next three days watching it endlessly, until he felt sure it would cease to function from pure overuse.

The fact that he was aroused by what he saw was disconcerting at first, annoying after the first day and addictive for the last twenty-four hours. But stroking himself to the damned video couldn't hold a candle to the reality he'd had.

For fourteen years, he'd dreamed of what Ginny would be like in bed. Now he knew, and he wanted more.

Can I trust her? He had agreed to put himself in her hands. Was it really necessary for her to tell him what she intended?

That was a sticky subject. Part of him argued that she should have. After all, she knew how he felt about cameras, but he'd never asked how this was supposed to work. Was she hoping to desensitize him to the things he disliked? If so, she was off to a good start.

Already, he nearly salivated at the thought of her in that blue bodysuit. How was it that he'd never equated it with a coverall until he watched the DVD?

Because it's made of silk?

Maybe. Coveralls certainly weren't, but like everything in her arsenal, it was, yet was not, what he remembered.

The furnishings were a designer chic version of academy décor. Though he wouldn't have thought it possible when he walked in, he certainly hadn't had any problem getting it up in that atmosphere. The thought of having sex with Ginny had overpowered his misgivings about his surroundings without breaking a sweat.

As if that wasn't troubling enough, Alex found himself rationalizing the decision to go back, analyzing every expression and movement the camera recorded until he felt he might go crazy. Had he really played a game of life in the academy and enjoyed it? As much as he'd like to deny it, he must have.

Alex stared at the computer, needing to be sure.

Maybe if I watch it again...

* * * *

Ginny grumbled a curse at the chimes rousing her from sleep, grasping the phone in uncoordinated fingers. "Yes?" she asked in a thick voice.

"Ms. Reynolds? You have a visitor."

Her eyes opened wide, and she fought for a decent breath. "Alex Randall?" she asked hopefully.

"Yes, Miss. If you'd like me to—"

She threw the quilts back, pushing to her feet. "No. Let him up...in a moment."

"Yes. Of course."

Ginny dropped the phone back on its cradle and bolted through the door into the mock-up. She pulled a Navy blue satin robe from the closet, belted it sloppily, and rushed to the mirror to fluff her hair.

An impatient knock came at the door. She calmed herself, then walked across the room and opened it.

Alex stood with his arm braced against the doorframe, his expression unreadable. For a long moment, he simply stared at her. "Aren't you going to invite me in?" he asked, dark amusement in his tone.

She took a calming breath and nodded, moving back to let him pass. Maybe this was a bad idea. Post-academy sufferers weren't the most stable of people, and Alex was the most powerful talent she'd ever met.

He ambled past her with a bark of laughter. "Not true. You've met Steven," he reminded her.

"Stop that," she snapped at him.

A smile curved his mouth. "I seem to recall that you enjoyed my talents a week ago."

Ginny felt her face heat at that. Her body followed suit, her womb throbbing and weeping hot lubricant, her nipples coming to aching points.

She looked to Alex's smug smile in realization. "You... W-what are you doing?" she stammered, fighting to normalize her breathing.

"Do you want me to stop?" he taunted.

She swallowed, shaking her head slowly. As if in reward, her body exploded in waves of pleasure. Alex wrapped his arms around her, turning her so that she could use the back of the couch for balance.

"Why?" she whispered.

He dragged his sweater off and dropped it to the floor, looking past her. "Are your cameras turned on?" he inquired, a cold edge to his voice.

Ginny turned her head, staring into the lens. "Yes. They always are."

He reached for his jeans. "Good."

* * * *

She looked back at him, her green eyes wide. They panned down his nude chest to the length of him that he'd freed from his jeans. He'd like to pretend that the sight of her did this to him, but he'd been hard and aching for half the drive over here, unable to get back to sleep until he saw her again.

"I put myself in your hands last time. Are you willing to do the same?" he challenged her.

Ginny ran a shaking hand through her sleep-mussed hair. It simply wasn't fair that she could look this good when he'd dragged her out of bed at three in the morning.

"Yes." Her voice wavered a bit, but her eyes were bright with interest.

He nodded, bringing his mouth down on hers, cradling her head with one hand until her balance was sure. He pulled the condom from his pocket and rolled it on, starving for another taste of her.

Alex unknotted the robe and dragged it off of her. He tossed it away and turned her so that she leaned over the couch and faced the camera fully. He forced her feet wider, smiling at the thoughts rushing through her mind. Oh, yes. He fully intended to rock her world.

"Watch the camera, Ginny." He slid to the hilt in her, closing his eyes in pleasure. How had he forgotten how good this felt? All those memories were a joke in comparison. Of course, if he remembered this, he would have been back here two days earlier.

She stifled a cry of surprise, and he forced his eyes open, smiling at the lens. She'd promised to place herself in his hands. He was going to make her glad she had, but Ginny would have no more clue what was coming than he had.

Alex was in her mind already, past the net of her shield, just as Steven and Jonas had taught him to. Grasping control from that vantage point was a simple task. The rush of power nearly sent him over, and he found himself focusing on her pleasure simply to keep his own from swamping him.

Ginny pleaded with him, panting out his name.

It was time. The illusion he wove in her mind was intricate...down to the soft warmth of the leather at her wrists and ankles. She looked down and squawked, her muscles tensing, then locking at the length of the imaginary bonds he'd placed on her.

Alex thrust deeper into her, groaning aloud. "Not to your liking?" he taunted, though he knew very well what she thought of his surprise, knew very well how everything he did affected her.

Her body pulsed around him, the first whispers of climax already beating at her consciousness. "You know it is."

The rest of her thought filtered into his mind, sobering him. "Only with me," he breathed.

"Alex," she pleaded.

For a moment, he considered changing the illusion. He rejected that. Ginny did enjoy it, and Alex certainly enjoyed being the one in charge of the restraints.

Maybe it's therapeutic in its own way.

Fuck therapy! Alex started thrusting hard and fast, lost in the cascade of thought and sensation coursing from Ginny to him. He pushed away the irreverent thought that this whole thing was "fucking therapy." Instead, he concentrated on the illusion he planted for them, closing his eyes so that he could visualize himself in the dream world with her.

It was as far from an academy as someone could get and still have restraints involved. Ginny was bent over a padded counter covered in red velvet, her wrists and ankles strapped to large metal rings at the tops and bottoms of the legs, keeping her spread wide and up for him.

The room itself was dark wood and stone, rustic but warm and comfortable. The light was a flickering yellow firelight, mellow and soothing.

There was nothing soothing in the sex. It was hot and hard, all consuming, all of the pent-up need from the last six days poured into his possession of her. Or maybe it was more than that. The role-playing with her had been fun, but this screamed of the release of fourteen years of wanting her.

Ginny begged for more, begged for release, then screamed harshly when her explosive climax forced him over after her. The illusion shattered, and Alex opened his eyes to the camera lens, smirking at what he was about to do.

He eased out of her body and lifted her limp form to the couch, looking away from her parted lips when the urge to kiss her into another round almost overpowered his common sense.

"Enjoy?" he inquired.

She groaned, her nipples tightening.

"Good." He pulled his jeans up and tucked himself back inside, avoiding her eyes. "When you recover, you'll be making two copies of the disc." He peeked at her while he did the button, waiting for her response.

Her brow furrowed. "Two?"

Alex chuckled, retrieving his sweater from the floor. "This round is by my rules. Remember?"

She nodded. "Of course."

He dragged the sweater over his head and slid his arms back in, using it to hide the fact that seeing her sprawled out on the couch had him hard for more.

"One will go with me," he informed her. *Oh, what a torture watching this one will be!*

"And the other?"

"You'll be watching that one." He raised a hand to silence her questions. "I'll leave the frequency up to you, but I want you to see what submitting to me feels like. You did enjoy being restrained with me, and that's not something you typically enjoy. Is it?"

Her eyes glittered. "An excellent first step," she congratulated him. "You're taking control of your dislikes."

"We'll see. If you're as willing to place yourself in my hands as I was the first day... If we can truly trust each other, there may be more steps."

The light left her eyes, and she winced. "Will you come back, Alex?"

"Of course. How else will I know? But..." He trailed a fingertip up her inner thigh lazily, shivering as her breathing went ragged. He couldn't take her again tonight. That wasn't the plan. "This is a trade off. I trust you only as far as you trust me."

"Agreed." She sighed as he pulled his hand back. "When will I see you again?"

He smiled. "Soon."

CHAPTER THREE

March 31st, 2029

Ginny hit the play button again, then hit replay, cursing herself for it. She hadn't watched the first recording as Alex obviously had. Now she knew what watching had been like for him. It was addictive, memories of his thought plants warring with the stark reality of the mock-up. Still, there was no question that they had each been completely engrossed in the experience...and in each other.

"He has to come back," she moaned.

She considered the situation miserably. She hadn't set out to fall in love with Alex; she'd only wanted to help him over his post-academy syndrome. Why wasn't it that simple?

Because this is Alex! How many dreams had she had over the years? How many lonely nights had she longed for the simple human touch he'd offered her at the academy? Not just that kiss but the jokes and looks behind Raines's back, the telekinetic play and minor rule breaking? How many daydreams had she had in which Alex wanted more from her? She'd been setting herself up for this for the last decade and a half, in one form or another.

On the disc, they reached their climax again. Ginny moaned as it restarted, praying Alex would come back soon. He hadn't contacted her in the last five days; and if he didn't soon, she felt certain she'd go insane in wanting him.

The chime of the phone jangled her nerves, and she launched toward it, scooping it to her ear. "Yes?" she asked urgently.

"You have a guest, Ms. Reynolds."

She tried unsuccessfully to hold in a peal of laughter. "Send Alex up," she requested.

"Immediately." The phone disconnected.

Ginny dropped it back to the base and ambled to the door, considering how best to greet him. She unknotted the robe with a smile and dropped it to the floor. Then she opened the door and waited for the elevator.

The doors slid open, and his attention swung from the camera beside him to her. He scanned her body from head to foot, striding toward her with a manic look on his face. He hoisted her up in one arm, tossed a backpack into the room, and slammed the door behind them.

"Oh, yeah," he growled, following her down onto the couch, his hands and mouth already busy driving her crazy.

She nodded, pulling up his "Jörg for President" T-shirt. "What's in the bag?" she asked, secretly hoping it held sex toys.

He laughed heartily, dragging the T-shirt off for her. "That too." He yanked his sweatpants down, looking at the television and smiling.

Ginny screamed as he filled her, grasping desperately for clear, concise thoughts. "Too?" she asked.

"Mmmm... A change of clothes, but with this reception, I don't envision needing them anytime soon." He guided her face to the side, so the screen filled her field of vision, his hips sliding back and forth. "Do you like watching?" he whispered.

She licked her lips, watching the Alex on the DVD thrust into her, his eyes closed, sweat shimmering on his pale skin.

"Ginny..."

"Yes. I love it...but not as much as I love this."

"Watching while we..."

"Yes."

He groaned precisely in time with the recording, making her wonder how many times he'd watched it.

"Endlessly," he answered her unasked question.

Alex turned her face back, sealing his mouth to hers. His kiss was slow and deep, and his lovemaking followed suit.

In moments, she'd almost forgotten the DVD was playing. It was impossible to tell which moans and pleas were the current encounter and which were *Memorex*.

"Is this better?" he asked.

Ginny nodded, incapable of imagining anything better than making love with Alex. She wanted to spend the rest of her life... She cut off that thought, abruptly aware that he was probably listening in.

Alex sighed, cupping her breast in his hand and stroking his thumb across the nipple. "The rest of your life?" he asked.

Her cheeks heated at that. What was she going to do when he walked away? "I..."

"Ask me to stay." His blue eyes were serious.

She didn't stop to consider what she'd do if it was a joke of some sort. "Don't leave."

"Oh, God," he groaned.

She gasped, arching up as he climaxed, his heat gushing into her. Ginny clutched at his hips, parting her lips for him and groaning into his mouth as she followed him over.

He pulled back, his smile pleased and lazy. "Nude... You don't really want to wear those coveralls, do you?"

"No," she admitted. Silk or not, they weren't her favorite form of dress. They served a purpose, and she wore them for the effect of creating a scene.

His cock pulsed inside her. "Then we won't wear them."

Today. She bit her lip at his sigh. "You're not leaving, are you?"

Alex chuckled. "I trust you, even if you do want me to wear a coverall."

"How long will you stay?"

He leaned on his elbow, seemingly considering something of importance. "That depends."

"On?"

"Whether or not you change your mind about the rest of your life when you see me before my first two cups of coffee." His smile disappeared. "But for now, we have work to do." He eased off of her and sat on the edge of the couch.

"Work?" He was confusing her with all this jumping from subject to subject.

"We're going to break me out of my fears once and for all, and..." He looked at the backpack, a faint smile pulling his lips up again.

"And?" she prompted him.

"We're going to indulge your love of bondage."

CHAPTER FOUR

April 8th, 2029

Alex shifted uncomfortably on the table, glad that there wasn't a psi wave pulsing in the walls. "You're not going to strap me down, are you?" he asked nervously, reminding himself that he trusted her.

Though Ginny had asked him not to read her mind today, he knew she had only his best interests at heart. So far, only her first attempt at lockdown in the small iso-style room had gone sour, and that was only a matter of an anxiety attack. Overall, she was an expert at making him forget or disregard the memories that normally submarined him.

She smiled. "Not this time." Ginny reached behind him and raised the head of the table to a fifty or fifty-five degree angle.

"Iso tables don't do this," he noted, more comfortable with the difference than with how perfectly the table was recreated otherwise.

"Max-sec doesn't have Pierre Original furniture, and academy coveralls aren't made of silk, either."

He chuckled at the memory of their romp in the silk suits. As usual, she'd proven that he could find an odious academy reminder arousing in the right circumstances. Ginny on her knees, the silk cupping his sac while she sucked him, had been about as arousing as you could get, arousing enough that he'd made love to her over the marble bar top and again as they watched the recording in the control room.

"All very true," he conceded.

She raised the padded blocks on either side of his head, and he grasped her wrist. Images of the head straps crossing over him while he lay immobilized by stun-spray assaulted him. Alex forced himself to calm, loosening his grip on her arm. He nodded, letting her know that he was under control, that they wouldn't have to abort whatever she'd planned for the iso room again.

"No restraints," he reminded her. He doubted that he would ever find that arousing, from the standpoint of being the one tied down, though tying Ginny up was proving to be a *most* enjoyable venture.

Ginny leaned across him, her pert breasts pressed to his bare chest. She nipped at his lips, enticing him to raise his head for a heated kiss.

Visions of tying her to the table and licking her to orgasm taunted him. Alex resisted the urge to plant them in her mind. He'd promised not to slip past her shield today, and he wouldn't, no matter how tempting it was.

"We'll be using this table for another reason tomorrow," he vowed.

Her breathing hitched, and she shot him a hungry look.

His cock hardened painfully. "Climb on top," he growled. "I don't care that it's an iso table. That's what you want."

"After," she promised.

Alex dropped his head back between the blocks, biting back a vicious curse.

Ginny pulled a small remote from under the table, aimed it at the wall across from him, and pressed a button. One of the two foot by two foot white tiles lit up, and an image of them took shape.

"We've done this," he commented in confusion. Cameras were so much a part of their play that he'd almost ceased to notice them. This was a step back, wasn't it?

"Not quite."

"Tell me the rules." There were always some sort of rules involved. He steeled himself for what was sure to sound unreasonable.

"Watch the screen and don't move."

"Don't move. While you do what?" So far, it sounded like a simple sex game, but these excursions were never the three-hour tour, when it came down to it.

"Anything I want to." Her eyes issued the challenge.

"And if I move? Is there some sort of penalty involved? This is an iso mock-up."

She chuckled. "You won't." She waited for a moment and then pointed to the screen, indicating that he should watch it as instructed.

Alex sighed, forcing his shoulders to relax and concentrating on the image of them on the screen. The sooner he complied, the sooner they could get down to something more enjoyable.

"Hmm," she purred. "You're not as aroused now. I need to take care of that."

He snorted in laughter. Well, this part was sure to be enjoyable. "Take care of..."

He shook his head in disbelief at the white can that appeared in her hand, his muscles tensing at the threat. "No," he protested. *She wouldn't! She can't. Where would she get stun-spray? It's impossible.*

The icy blast hit him full in the face; though he knew he should force his breath out, he was shocked into the

334

inhalation. In the blink of an eye, he was under its spell. His psi talents useless, Alex couldn't defend himself as his muscles went lax and his touch-based nerves ceased to function. He was essentially a thinking mind trapped in a useless shell, his eyes locked on the screen.

Ginny stroked his renewed erection. She used the remote to zoom the camera in on it.

"You see, Alex," she managed in a breathless voice. "You wouldn't be excited by being tied up. I know that about you, but I've learned that stun-spray has this effect on men. You might not even have realized it. Since you can't feel or see it...unless someone arranges this..."

He *had* known about it but only because he'd overheard guards joking about the reaction. No one knew why it happened. No one had bothered to find out why it did.

Her lips closed around the head, and Alex wished he could vent his frustration. Ginny closed her eyes, taking his length in and out, seemingly savoring the sensations he couldn't feel.

Arousal lit in him, not the tightening of his balls and physical ache but the hunger for her, raw and insistent. Alex wanted her on top of him. He wanted to see his length sliding in and out of her, though he couldn't feel it. It was maddening. He couldn't touch her or hold her, couldn't beg her to make love to him, or grasp her and pull her over him.

Some corner of his mind argued that he should be angry with her for doing this to him. Then she pulled back and laid a lick across the head, and all he wanted was more...more that he could feel.

The five minutes felt endless. The certainty that he'd climax the moment feeling returned made him crazy.

Then it happened. The first whispers of sensation were so fleeting, Alex was certain he was imagining them. Ginny circled her tongue along the veins, working her way up his length, and he felt it.

He tested his abilities and found they hadn't caught up. He couldn't touch her, either physically or with talent. He was powerless, stuck in the moment, feeling everything but held more effectively than even the restraints in iso could accomplish.

She teased him with her tongue again, and he groaned. Alex wished he had a clock to count down the time. It had to be close to the magic mark when everything came back. If they ever tried this again, he'd ask for a clock on the readout. He groaned again at the thought of it.

"Gin," he rasped, forcing his voice out. "Plea...ease."

Ginny groaned around his length, making a concerted effort to push him over.

"N...no." He ground his teeth, staving off his release. "On...top."

She released him, looking up in confusion. "Feel you," he managed.

Ginny rose as if in a daze and climbed over him. She met his eyes, then ducked her head to the side, kissing his shoulder and giving him an unobstructed view of the screen as she guided him in. She stroked back and forth along his length.

Alex gasped. "So good."

She sat up and settled in his lap, studying his face as she started moving again. "You do feel it. Tell me."

"All...sensa...shun. All...need. Need you."

She threw her head back, licking her lips as she rode him toward release. "Don't leave me," she whispered.

"Never." He wasn't lying. If she'd have him, he'd never leave.

Sensation crept back into his muscles, a warmth pushing back the icy chill of the stun-spray. Alex tested his abilities again, grasping the back of Ginny's neck and dragging her mouth down to his.

Her wide, panicked eyes fluttered shut as he sealed her mouth to his, his tongue caressing hers. Alex pushed the headrests away with a telekinetic shove, then angled her head to deepen the kiss.

Free to move, he took her in hard, sure strokes, pulling his head back as she came just to hear her scream for him, a scream he echoed only moments later.

Ginny bowed her head, laying a lick that captured a sweat bead rolling down his chest. He shivered in response.

"Where did you get stun-spray?" he mused.

She darkened. "I spent a lot of money. It's the only can I've ever managed to find...probably the only can I'll ever be able to get. If this had failed, I couldn't have tried again."

He chuckled. "Guess the next can is on me, then."

Her eyes widened. "Next can?"

Alex bucked his hips, aroused again by the thought of it. "Baby, you have no concept what I'm going to do next time you try this...actually, what you'll do for me."

Her breathing came in ragged gasps, and she shifted over his renewed erection. "What will I do?"

"Whatever I want."

"What do you want?" She moved restlessly over his length, driving both of them toward another climax.

Now or never. Alex sent the image of them in the chapel Sarah and Jonas were married in.

"Oh, God!" She shattered again, pushing down hard on his hips.

"Yes?" he asked.

"Can't you tell?"

"I promised not to look," he reminded her.

"Yes." Ginny sought out his mouth, her kiss nearly frantic. "Yes. God, yes."

EPILOGUE

May 25th, 2029

Alex sighed as Ginny draped herself across his lap, kissing him passionately.

"Get a room," Steven complained.

Ginny blushed.

"Not the one upstairs," the eldest Randall continued.

"Picky, picky," Alex drawled.

Steven scowled at his beige slacks and Navy on eggshell pin-stripe shirt.

Alex met his eyes in challenge. "If you let the past control you, you never grow past it."

His brother rolled his eyes at that.

Katie ambled out onto the deck, smiling at the sight of her younger son and his wife. She sighed. "It's so good to see you happy."

Stephen made hairball noises, stopping only when their mother shot him a look of warning.

She sat, sipping her iced tea. "The strangest thing happened," she continued as if the interruption had never occurred.

"Really?" Alex answered, raising Ginny's hand to kiss her knuckles.

"Two cans of stun-spray have gone missing from the cabinet at Alpha House."

"Two?" Ginny asked urgently, her eyes wide.

"Yes. The inventory showed it. You know Sarah and Jonas never resort to using it, but they check their stores every few months. The children seem honest in not knowing how it happened, so they are asking anyone who's been in the house in the last month if they have—"

"Taken stun-spray?" Steven barked. "Who the hell has a use for it? Not even Sarah and Jonas have ever..." He stopped and shot a suspicious look at Alex and Ginny. *"You didn't!"*

Alex kissed his wife's hand again, pasting an innocent look on his face. "Sorry, Mom. I have no idea what happened to the cans."

"Oh, God! You did do it. Why on earth would you do this?" Steven's link was laced with sick disbelief.

"Big brother, if you knew what I do about stun-spray..."

"T.M.I. Please, for the love of God, do not go there." But, he buried a streak of envy a little too late.

Katie looked from one son to the other, calculating something. She couldn't tell when they talked telepathically like Sarah and Jonas could, so both men knew their conversation was safe. They offered her smiles, Alex's in amusement and Steven's slightly strained.

"All right," she decided. "Keep your secrets. I'll just let Sarah know the cans are safe...and that it *won't* happen again."

Ginny bit her lip as Alex hardened against her. "I'm sure it won't," she offered in a voice that spoke her doubts that it would be the last time Alpha House came up short.

Alex swallowed a chuckle, and Steven groaned.

THE END

ABOUT THE AUTHOR

Brenna Lyons wears many hats, sometimes all on the same day: former president of EPIC, author of more than 100 published works, owner of Fireborn Publishing, columnist, special needs teacher, wife, mother...and member in good standing of more than 60 writing advocacy groups.

In her first ten years published in novel−length, she's won 3 EPIC e−Book Awards (out of 15 finalists) and finaled for 3 PEARLS (including one Honorable Mention, second to NY Times Bestseller Angela Knight), 2 CAPAS, and a Dream Realm Award. She's also taken Spinetingler's Book of the Year for 2007.

Brenna writes in 26 established worlds plus stand−alones, poetry, articles and essays. She's a bestseller in indie/e fantasy and horror, straight genre and cross−genres thereof. Brenna has been termed "one of the most deviant erotic minds in the publishing world...not for the weak." (Rachelle for Fallen Angels Reviews) Milieu−heavy dark work is practically Brenna's calling card, with or without the erotic content.

She teaches classes in everything from POV studies to advanced editing, networking to marketing. Brenna enjoys hearing from people who read her work and can be reached by e−mail.

Website: http://www.brennalyons.com/

Facebook: http://www.facebook.com/brenna.lyons

Email: brennalyons4168@live.com

ALSO BY THIS AUTHOR

Available from *Fireborn Publishing*

KEIF'S DEN AND PACK
Keif's Pack
Mother of the Keif
Keif's Den (Coming Soon)

PROPHECY
Prophecy: Revelations
Prophecy: Rapture
The Prophet's Mate
Prophecy: Rampage – Meet Gavin
Prophecy: Rampage (Coming Soon)

THE FANTASY CLUB
The Consort

WEREWOLF U
Werewolf U
Second Daughter

RENEGADES SERIES
TYGERS
Renegade's Run
Alpha House (Coming Soon)

URBAN GRIMM
Catch Me, If You Can
Three Wishes
Temptation of Eve
Put on Your Dancing Shoes (Coming Soon)

With Great Power
Undead Underway
Beyond the Veil

Fairy Wishes (Coming Soon)
Mine for the Night
Once in a Blue Moon
Overtime Pay
Stay With Me
The Fire God's Woman
The Punishment of Phoebus Apollo

Available from **Fireborn Publishing** in PRINT ONLY

NIGHT WARRIORS
Night Warriors
Will of the Stone
Bearing Armen
Hunter's Moon
Veriel's Tales I: Crossbearer Turned
Veriel's Tales II: Losing Regana
The Blutjagdfrau Chronicles

Bride Ball
Fire and Ice
Lovers' Kiss anthology
Monsters and Mayhem anthology
Paranormal Paramours anthology

Available from **Phaze Books**

ANGEL—WING SAGA
Sons of Heaven: Beldon
Daughters of Man: Prize Match
Sons of Heaven: Unexpected Mates
Daughters of Man: Claiming a Princess

BRIDE BALL
Bride Ball
Poison, Lies, and No—Win Choices

COLOR OF LOVE

The Color of Love

FIRE AND ICE
Magmon's Hunger
Magmon's Lover

INSTINCT SERIES
Animal Instincts

KEGIN SERIES
Conquest
The Last of Fion's Daughters
Last Chance for Love
Rites of Mating
In Her Ladyship's Service
Matchmaker's Misery

KIELAN SERIES
The Lady's Lowborn Lover
Time Currents
Cubed

NIGHT WARRIORS
Night Warriors
Will of the Stone
Bearing Armen
Hunter's Moon
Maher Men
Choosing a Mate/Starting a War
Raised to Be His Own
Veriel's Tales I: Crossbearer Turned
Veriel's Tales II: Losing Regana
Blutjagdfrau Lost
The Warrior's Man
Damsel in Distress

STAR MAGES
The Master's Lover

XXAN WAR
Daahan Rising
Crossbred Son
Raashh Decisions

Enslaved
All I Want for Christmas is You
Fates Magic
All's Fair...
Black Sail
Mama's Tales
Dream Walk
Unexpected Daddy
Phaze in Verse
We Shall Live Again
May the Best Man Win
Nevermore
Marked
And It Was Good

Available from **Mundania Press**

STAR MAGES
Written in the Stars

Fairy Dreams
Monsters of Myth Anthology

Available from **Under the Moon**

Evil Overlords Union Issue #1 Anthology
Undead Embrace
"Playing Games" in *Forbidden Love: Bad Boys*
"Marked" in *Forbidden Love: Wicked Women*
"The Master's Lover" in *Forbidden Love: Sacred Bands*

Available from *Logical Lust*

"*Mine for the Night*" in *The Cougar Book* Anthology

Available from ***Coming Together Charity Anthologies***

INSTINCT SERIES
"*Foundling*" in *Coming Together: Into the Light* Anthology

"*Claim Mate*" (available separately and as part of the *Coming Together: Against the Odds* Anthology)
"*The Fire God's Woman*" in *Coming Together: Under Fire* Anthology

Available *self — published*

KEGIN SERIES
Earth — Born Lord
Graham: Training the Earth — Born Lord

NIGHT WARRIORS
Claiming a Lady
Stone Lord
Mother's Son

COLOR OF LOVE
A Safe Heart

Snapshots from a Poet's Life

AWARD—WINNING BOOKS

EPPIE/EPIC eBOOK AWARDS WINNERS
Coming Together: Against the Odds – 2010
Time Currents – 2010
Coming Together: Into the Light – 2011

EPPIE/EPIC eBOOK AWARDS FINALISTS
Fion's Daughter – 2004
Collected Poems: Book One – 2005 (now titled *Snapshots of a Poet's Life*)
Renegade's Run – 2005
Rites of Mating – 2006
All I Want for Christmas – 2006
Phaze in Verse – 2008
"The Fire God's Woman" in *Coming Together: Under Fire* – 2009
Three Wishes – 2010
Matchmaker's Misery – 2010
The Cougar Book – 2011
The Master's Lover – 2011
Bride Ball – 2011

DREAM REALM AWARDS FINALIST
Last Chance for Love – 2003

PEARL HONORABLE MENTION
Night Warriors – 2004

PEARL FINALISTS
Schente Night – 2003 (now included in *The Last of Fion's Daughters*)
König Cursebreakers – 2004 (now titled *Will of the Stone*)

JOYFULLY REVIEWED BEST BOOKS OF 2010
Written in the Stars – 2010

SPINETINGLER'S BOOK OF THE YEAR 2007

NOBODY: An Anthology of Dark Fiction – 2007 (Brenna's pieces of the anthology can be found in *Beyond the Veil*)

TRS's CAPA FINALISTS
Ultimate Warriors – 2004 (Brenna's portion is now available as *With Great Power*)
Written in the Stars

LOVE ROMANCE AND MORE CAFÉ BOOK OF THE YEAR RUNNER UP
Last Chance for Love – 2008

ROAD TO ROMANCE REVIEWERS' CHOICE AWARD
Prophecy: Revelations – 2004

LOVE ROMANCES REVIEWERS' CHOICE AWARD
Black Sail – 2003

ROMANCE JUNKIES BOOK CLUB STAFF PICK
TYGERS – 2003

FALLEN ANGELS ROMANCE RECOMMENDED READ
Devon's Price – 2005 (now available in *Bearing Armen*)

JOYFULLY RECOMMENDED READ
Fairy Dreams – 2008
The Last of Fion's Daughters – 2009

TREBLE HEART FINALIST
Prophecy: Revelations – 2003

www.ingramcontent.com/pod-product-compliance
Lightning Source LLC
Chambersburg PA
CBHW050915250626
47155CB00001B/247